The Lamplighter's Bookshop

Sophie Austin was born in Kent and she earned her Bachelor's degree in Philosophy from King's College London in 2013. After spending five years working in marketing, Sophie moved to Sweden to focus on her novel writing and gain her Master's in Transnational Creative Writing at Stockholm University. Now, Sophie works as a Creative Writer for Minecraft, the best-selling video game of all time. When she's not writing YouTube scripts for millions of viewers, she retreats to the turn of the century to write historical novels about a time where old Victorian values and turn-of-the-century inventions collide – a perfect, conflict-rich backdrop for her debut romance novel, *The Lamplighter's Bookshop*. Sophie is hard at work on her next historical romance.

Find her on social media:
- @saustinauthor
- @sophieaustinauthor

The Lamplighter's Bookshop

SOPHIE AUSTIN

HarperCollins*Publishers*

HarperCollins*Publishers* Ltd
1 London Bridge Street,
London SE1 9GF

www.harpercollins.co.uk

HarperCollins*Publishers*
Macken House, 39/40 Mayor Street Upper
Dublin 1, D01 C9W8

First published by HarperCollins*Publishers* Ltd 2025
1

A catalogue record for this book is available from the British Library

ISBN: 978-0-00-866412-1 (PB)
ISBN: 978-0-00-866409-1 (TPB)

Typeset in Meridien by HarperCollins*Publishers* India

Printed and bound in the UK using 100%
Renewable Electricity at CPI Group (UK) Ltd

MIX
Paper | Supporting
responsible forestry
FSC™ C007454
FSC
www.fsc.org

This book is produced from independently certified FSC™ paper to ensure
responsible forest management.

For more information visit: www.harpercollins.co.uk/green

This is for all my family and friends who told me I could, even when it felt like I couldn't. Thank you all.

Chapter One

Evelyn Seaton watched her breath mist against the window and said, with a calmness that belied her thudding heart: 'There are a lot of strange men coming towards the house, Bessie.'

Six black carriages rattled through the gates, twisting with the bends of the mansion's immaculately pruned driveway. The dust kicked up from beneath their wheels made it look as though a great snake was slithering towards the house in the morning sun, coming to swallow them whole.

Bessie moved beside her and sucked in a quick breath. 'Those look like police wagons, miss.'

'A whole battalion of them,' Evelyn said, watching the horses trot closer. They were great, shaggy shires built for hauling heavy loads, and she wondered why they had brought so many men – and such large wagons.

The men were stepping out now, forming a cluster on the gravelled pathway. They could not be local police, for surely all of Yorkshire did not have so many men as this? And now they were looking up at the windows, no doubt experiencing the same thing all did when they first set eyes on Riccall Hall: wonder. For this grand old house, this wisteria-covered, sandstone leviathan was large enough to keep a whole regiment in private rooms, and yet now it housed only Evelyn, her mother and the handful of staff they could still afford. But these men might not know that. They might ask for the man of the house.

And her mother's melancholy would start all over again.

Evelyn took a deep breath and wrenched her gaze from the window. 'Bessie, whatever this is, I believe I should greet them. You know how Mama rises late at present, and besides, she is still too . . .' She closed her lips over the word. *Fragile* was such a poor word to describe her mother, usually such a vibrant, energetic creature but heavy now with a sadness she wore like a shroud.

Evelyn had done everything she could think of to cheer her, and when that hadn't worked, she'd tried to provoke her instead, walking into the breakfast room in a parade of increasingly ridiculous outfits: wide cycling bloomers, a gentleman's top hat, even pearls – for surely if anything could rouse her mother from her stupor it would be pearls before six – but all her efforts had been met with a cursory glance, a sigh and a sinking feeling that tugged so painfully at Evelyn's stomach she imagined she had swallowed her mother's own sadness. She thought they'd turned a corner before Christmas, but then spring had come, and her mother had grown languid again. The contrast of it had been odd, her mother retreating to her chambers just as the frost thawed and the breeze took on a sweet edge.

'Greet them, miss?' Bessie's wide, wrinkled face crumpled. 'With all due respect, I am not sure that is the best idea.'

'Oh, come now. I can be charming when I want to be. Now, I think a suit should do it. The tweed?'

Bessie's grimace said otherwise. 'What do you think they want?'

'They must be lost,' Evelyn said, with a confidence she did not feel.

'But you can't get lost in Riccall.' Bessie snorted. 'You're out of Riccall before you even realize you've reached it. And I do think it would be better to await your lady mother.'

The doorbell jingled then, three sharp pulls of the bell, as though the person on the other side was short of time or patience or both.

Evelyn shook her head. 'I would rather not have Mama vexed if we can avoid it. I can handle one set of guests by myself, surely. I am twenty-four, after all.'

'Yes, but you can also be rather blunt, miss. Which the likes of me don't mind, but the likes of them men downstairs might.'

Evelyn rolled her eyes. 'I am not blunt – merely honest.'

'Precisely,' Bessie said, though she went to the wardrobe, opening the great creaking doors with vigour. 'People dislike honesty.'

'Untrue,' Evelyn said. 'I believe the people who say they dislike honesty actually dislike themselves. That is why they are so offended when I tell them the truth. After all, if they do not say it to themselves, then why should they suffer the likes of me saying it to them?'

Bessie's mouth became a firm line. 'And that's why your mother should deal with these official-looking gentlemen. You do have rather a tendency to say odd things.'

Evelyn huffed as Bessie wrapped the corset around her waist, holding it in place so that she could secure the ribbon through the eyelets at the back. Downstairs, the doorbell rang again. Four blasts this time, even more forceful than the last, and Evelyn's heartbeat quickened.

'One comment at the debutante ball and suddenly I have the reputation of being *the one who says odd things*.'

'You did tell Lady Violet that she was a bully.'

'Which she rightly is.'

'And you also told her that she was spiteful to others because, secretly, she was spiteful to herself.'

'Which I also believe.'

'But don't you see, miss? One shouldn't say that to others! *Especially* not at one's presentation to society.'

Her corset laced, Evelyn turned to pull her blouse over her head, knocking some dark curls loose of their pins. 'Do you know,' she said, her voice muffled beneath the sheer cream silk. 'I rather believe life would be simpler if people said what they thought more often. Wouldn't that be a breath of fresh air?'

'No, miss,' Bessie said. 'I do not believe it would. I believe everyone would be rather upset.'

'Well, I wouldn't,' Evelyn said, buttoning the tweed skirt closed at the waist. The final effect was just the sort of severe schoolmistress look she had been hoping for, though in truth the outfit was for cycling and not for confronting hordes of uniformed men. But it was the turn of the century, and fashion should be versatile.

Bessie twitched the last button on Evelyn's jacket and said in a quiet voice: 'Perhaps they bring news of your father? After all, we've heard nothing of him since all those articles in the paper—'

Evelyn flinched. 'We shall not speak of those articles. Not now, not ever. And especially not in front of Mama.'

'O'course, miss,' Bessie said, a flush rising on her cheeks. 'I would never.'

'I know,' Evelyn replied, meeting her eye in the mirror and giving her a hesitant smile. 'Now, will you go and ask Mr Deeley to let the poor men in so they can stop ringing the doorbell? If Mother was not awake before, there is a high chance she will awaken on the third ring.'

Bessie stepped away, but Evelyn didn't immediately

follow her. Instead, she lifted her chin to meet her reflection
in the mirror, trying to mask her trepidation in the set of
her shoulders, the downwards tilt of her head, the faux-
steady look in her dark eyes. She knew that even if what lay
downstairs was not a simple mistake, she had the courage
to confront it – she simply wished she didn't need it. She
had had to use so much of her bravery to do the simplest of
things these last two years, and she was growing tired of it.

'But if it will protect Mama, then it is worth it.' She lifted
trembling fingers to her jacket buttons and fastened them.
And then she turned, making for the stairs and the men who
lay beyond them.

In the empty breakfast room, the table was set for two,
with boiled eggs and cold roast ham, freshly baked bread
and homemade marmalade. Sunlight ribboned through the
windows in patterns drawn by the blooming wisteria outside,
caressing the oil paintings that hung from the walls and
illuminating the air in glittering slices. Usually the unsteady
light flashing in her eyes bothered Evelyn, but today she
was grateful for the house's snaking vines, for it gave her
a modicum of privacy, a barrier between her and the men
clustered like beetles on the lawn.

'Percival?'

The footman poked his head around the door in a manner
that suggested he had been padding back and forth for a
while and she had caught him by surprise.

'You may send him in now – whoever is leading the
calvary at our doors.'

Percival squirmed. 'Mr Deeley said to wait for the lady of
the house to awaken before letting anyone inside.'

'No, I will tend to this,' Evelyn said. 'Right away.'

Percival's face flickered, though he said: 'Right you are,
miss,' and turned on his heel.

Evelyn sat at the table, in her usual spot facing the window, and wiped her clammy hands down the soft material of her skirts. Perhaps it was a training procedure, or an army exercise. Perhaps these men were not policemen but army men? She wondered if she should sit on the other side, so that the sun was not in her eyes, and then wondered if she should be sitting at all. Would the gentleman assume she was ready to eat, rather than ready to receive a guest? Perhaps she should have told Percival to bring him through to the parlour instead, though it was too late for that now. She settled on pacing quietly back and forth instead, her footsteps in time to the gentle tick of the grandfather clock in the corner, its gold pendulum casting the sun's glow into her dark brown eyes.

Percival stepped inside briskly. 'The chief of the London constabulary to see you, miss.'

'The London constabulary?' The buzzing feeling in Evelyn's stomach grew. 'Send him in.'

She listened to him come, his boots heavy on the hardwood floors, though the man who stepped into the room was surprisingly lithe. He took off his hat hurriedly, showing her an almost perfect circle of bare scalp where his grey-white hair had started to thin. 'Lady Seaton. I was beginning to think no one was home.'

She could see the impatience written into the stiffness in his neck, the tremor that seemed to lace his limbs. 'Lady Seaton is my mother,' Evelyn said, proffering her hand. 'I am Miss Evelyn Seaton.'

The man's affable smile wobbled. 'Chief Constable Watts. Is your mother . . . away?'

'She is asleep,' Evelyn said. 'And I should not like to wake her.'

The man cleared his throat. He could not quite meet her eye, though this was not unusual. Evelyn had been told more than once that she could be rather *over-earnest*, although she thought that was an unfair judgement. She simply gave the person she was speaking to her full, unwavering attention, which was surely more polite than doing what the policeman was doing – staring at the strident painting of her great-grandfather, the first Baron Seaton, who wore the curled white wigs of the previous century.

'With all due respect, I would suggest you wake her. I came personally, as was promised, and given the . . . *sensitivity* of the matter, I imagine she'd rather like to hear what I have to say.'

'With equal amounts of respect, Chief Constable Watts, I shall not.' Evelyn gave him her most charming smile. 'So, now that the formalities are over, why don't you tell me the reason you have brought a battalion of men to breakfast?'

The man pressed his lips together, casting an exasperated glance at the doorway.

'And if you are about to ask if the man of the house is here, the answer is no. So, you *do* need to deal with me directly.'

'I know he's not here, Miss Seaton,' the man said, a thread of pity running through his voice now. 'He's in London, in a sponging-house. That's why we've come.'

The light in the room stilled, and Evelyn's breath stilled with it. 'A sponging-house?' She had heard of them, but she could not think why.

'It's where men with great debts go while they endeavour to raise money and satisfy what they owe. And your father owes a great deal.'

The words crept down her spine like a chill. She should not have been surprised, for her father always seemed to find *inventive* new ways to shame her and her mother.

But debt?

That was new.

'How ever could he be in debt?' Evelyn asked, her voice trembling a little now. 'And to whom?'

'There's not just one claimant, Miss Seaton.' Chief Constable Watts blew a breath through yellowed teeth. 'And the amount is high – too high. That's why we're here. I am afraid we must seize your father's goods and chattels, plus any growing crops or profits from the land.' He cast a limp hand around the room. 'It will then be sold at auction.'

So that was why they had brought the wagons, the draught horses. Evelyn's mouth was dry, and when she spoke there was a tremor to her voice. 'But my father owns everything in this house – every cushion, every spoon. You cannot . . . you would not take it all, surely?' She turned to look at the picture of her great-grandfather. It was a ridiculous painting, all pomp and grandeur. 'Who in their right mind would wish to bid on my great-grandfather George! You surely cannot take it all?'

'Yes, my dear. I'm afraid they can.'

It was her mother who spoke then, and Evelyn turned to see Lady Cecilia Seaton standing on the threshold, her brown-blonde hair pinned neatly back, her sombre grey dress making her look older than she was, more pallid.

'With the crop of livestock from the lands, plus the money these gentlemen will get at auction for our belongings, the hope is that your father's debt will be made back.'

Evelyn felt something twist in her chest. 'You *knew*?'

'Your father wrote to me,' Cecilia said, stepping into the room, 'at the beginning of the spring.'

So that was why her mother had sunk back into her gloom. Because he'd told her – warned her.

Cecilia turned her gaze back to the policeman, her usually warm brown eyes clear and cold. 'Though John promised me that the sale of the property would not be necessary.'

'That will be at the discretion of the court-appointed trustee, Lady Seaton,' the policeman said, his eyes downcast.

'*Sale of the property*?' Evelyn repeated. There was a chill fear in her now, freezing her hands, making her breath catch in her throat. 'Where are we to live if not in this house? And what of the staff? Those who stayed with us after Father left? And Bessie! What are they to do?'

'The same as us.' Her mother sighed quietly. 'They must leave.'

Evelyn heard a gasp from behind the door, and the patter of footsteps retreating down the hall.

The policeman shifted uncomfortably from one foot to the other. 'You are permitted to take some clothes and personal belongings with you, but nothing gifted from the baron. Nothing that can be claimed under the writ.'

Evelyn's mouth twitched downwards. 'What a preposterous thing to say. All we own was paid for by my father. Do you wish to seize the dresses from our backs? The shoes from our feet?' It came out with a little more heat than she'd intended, and her mother gave her a sharp look.

'Evelyn, please. It is not this man's fault, and your hysteria will not help matters.'

'My *hysteria*?' Evelyn turned her incredulous gaze to her mother. 'I think I am rather entitled to some opinions on this matter, don't you?'

'Not here, and not now.' Her mother's voice was like a whip-crack in the quiet room. 'You are a baron's daughter. I pray you act like one.'

Evelyn felt the blood rise to her cheeks, and Chief Constable Watts gave her the same look one might give a mewling kitten.

'I am sure I would not need to check a suitcase or two. If you load a wagon, however, I will need to go through and ensure you are not taking anything covered by the writ of *fieri facias*.'

'A suitcase or two?' Evelyn swallowed, the bluster of her anger petering now, leaving a hollow feeling in its place. 'You wish for us to pack our lives into *a suitcase or two*?'

'Bessie will help you,' her mother said, reaching to grip her hand and squeezing it so hard it hurt.

'But where are we to go? To live?'

'We will go to my Aunt Clara's, in York,' her mother said, though her voice was less steady now, less sure. 'We shall ask her for room and board.'

Evelyn's eyes bulged. 'But Great-Aunt Clara never even invites us for tea! Do you really think she will allow us to live with her?'

'Honestly, Evelyn' – her mother looked at her then, and Evelyn saw that she was wearing her own cloak of false resolution and that beneath it, she was crumbling, too – 'I do not know. But I cannot think where else we might try.'

'Then I shall go and pack,' Evelyn said stiffly, turning so that the impatient, balding man could not see her cry as she hurried from the room.

Chapter Two

Evelyn gripped the banister, wiping roughly at her cheeks. She could not picture a life where she did not walk down this staircase each morning, trailing her hand against the paintings' carved wooden frames, watching her fingers speck with gold as minuscule slivers flaked away – a life where she didn't creep past the suit of armour in the corner for fear of knocking it, or where her grandfather's plates upon the wall didn't clatter if you stomped by too fast.

She wondered what this entryway would look like when it was empty and stripped of all its chintz, of the velvet-backed chairs and her grandfather's trinkets and the gramophone in the corner.

She drew a sharp breath then and pinched the back of her hand. *I must pack.* For she could feel herself teetering, could feel the drop that awaited her on the other side of that ledge, and she could not tumble down it yet. Not when there was work to do, practical things to set her mind to. She would simply have to box it up and save it for later. *Along with everything else.*

* * *

Two suitcases seemed frightfully inadequate, and in the end, Evelyn packed and repacked four, though she could still take only five pairs of shoes, one morning dress, one wrapper, four day dresses, a travelling cape, her riding outfit and a single emerald-green evening gown. She still needed separate boxes for her hats, and when she and Bessie had finished battling the overfull suitcases and had finally buckled them all and laid them on the bed, Evelyn wondered whether the pitying London policeman would wish to check she had not stashed the silverware inside.

By the time they were ready to leave, it was midday, and Evelyn clutched Bessie tightly, trying very hard not to cry into the woman's lace collar.

'I shall be fine, miss,' Bessie said, patting her back. 'There are always advertisements for experienced lady's maids. It's you I worry about. How will you survive with no income, with no prospects? What will you and your mother do?'

Evelyn felt the box within her creak open then, felt a thought slither from it. *She is right. You will not simply be homeless but destitute, too.*

'Don't you worry for us,' Evelyn said quickly, drawing back. 'Mama and I will manage. We have managed thus far.'

'You have spirit, my girl,' Bessie said, pinching Evelyn's chin affectionately. 'Remember that.'

It was only once the carriage door had closed, once Evelyn and her mother were alone inside that rattling compartment, the breeze wafting the smell of wildflowers and damp grass through the window, that the fear washed over her in a wave so huge she thought she might drown.

'I hate him,' she said, closing her eyes and sitting back against the jolting leather seat. 'I hate that he has done this to us.'

'If I had thought it would come to this, I would have told you sooner,' her mother said, leaning to rest a consolatory hand upon her knee. 'But your father promised me – *he promised me* we would not lose the house.'

'And you believed him?' She cast her mother an incredulous look, but Cecilia's gaze was fixed firmly out of the window. She was the picture of tranquillity, her small bag in her lap, her hat pinned neatly to her hair. Even her dress looked as though they were bound for a morning of social visits, for she had changed into a dusty blue day gown with a smart black trim. 'How are you so calm? Have you really *nothing* to say about it?'

Her mother drew in a deep breath, and Evelyn watched the sunlight pick out the high curve of her cheekbones, watched it flicker into her mother's eyes, turning them a deep gold. Cecilia had a luxuriant kind of beauty, the type one found in decadent oil paintings.

'I have had two months to come to terms with it,' she said at last, her voice quiet. 'I have spent two months hoping this day would not come, fearing it, wondering whether to tell you and prepare you or to believe him and protect you, and now it has happened, and everything has fallen in upon us, I just feel . . .' She gave a long, low sigh. ' . . . relieved. It was the waiting that was killing me.'

'But his mistakes have cost us everything this time! Was it not bad enough that he took three quarters of the household with him to London and left us with an empty house? Even before then, he all but ruined my presentation? *And* the subsequent summer seasons in London?'

'You cannot blame your poor seasons upon your father,' said Cecilia. 'You spent every evening standing in the corner of whatever ballroom we were in.'

'Because Father's reputation had preceded us, and every man who danced with me did so because they wanted news on the American investments Papa had brokered. It was *excruciating*.'

Her mother's gaze flicked to her then, hovering somewhere between compassion and pity. 'Darling, it is outside of our control. You cannot bend your father to your will, just as you cannot command the sun to shine. It is better to sit back and allow yourself to be carried by the current.'

Evelyn detested that idea. She felt the anger in the coiling sensation in her stomach, in the twitching in her chest. 'I do not want to be at the mercy of another's folly, Mother,' she said. 'I do not want to place my belief in someone and then be forced to watch as they lead me over a cliff edge. It does not do well to give others so much power over you, even if you love them. *Especially* if you love them.'

Her mother watched her for a moment, her expression unreadable. 'Evelyn, my dear, if you believe that, then you will never trust anyone.'

'Well, perhaps that is better,' Evelyn said, turning to watch fields that were no longer theirs pass them by, the corn stalks already growing tall. 'Perhaps, in fact, that is best.'

Chapter Three

The journey to York was a long one compared to the usual jaunts they took in the carriage, and Evelyn found the boredom suffocating. It was also quite warm, the weather having broken into a humid sort of heat after two o'clock, and by the time the road beneath them turned from a dirt track to the clattering cobbles of the city, Evelyn could feel the sweat rolling in beads down her back.

Porthaven House, where Great-Aunt Clara lived, was a crooked little townhouse squashed in a street to the east of the city. The roof seemed to overhang the entire building, casting a shadow on the draughty glass windows, of which there were only three visible from the front. It was an odd place, taller than it was wide and deeper than it was tall. The first time Evelyn had stepped inside, she'd imagined the whole house was built of a single room upon each floor. The reality was there were three rooms on the ground floor, two on the middle and a single, sprawling attic at the top, which had seemed rather a novelty for Evelyn at the time. Looking at it now, it seemed as though the house had shrunk further, the windows smaller and boxier than she'd remembered, the ceilings not quite as lofty as she'd thought.

Aunt Clara, however, had not changed at all. Toweringly

tall for a woman of seventy-three, she was soberly dressed in a black silk gown with a white trim. She still wore the old fashion: wide, hooped skirts that made it nigh impossible to sit comfortably, or, apparently, step through the doorframe. She settled on standing just within the threshold, calling to them in her scratchy, warbling voice: 'You know, my dear, only milkmen turn up unannounced.'

Evelyn's mother turned a pinched face to her daughter. 'She's going to say, "I told you so," and I am going to have to admit that she was right.'

'She might be kinder than that,' Evelyn said, trying to muster some courage of her own as she stepped down from the carriage behind her mother.

'Really now.' Aunt Clara seemed quite distressed to find them walking towards the door, for her hands had begun to wave about. 'What is all this? I am rather too busy today for tea, Cecilia. You should have sent me a note before coming all this way.'

Evelyn glanced up to the empty windows of the other houses, the high afternoon sun turning them into a wall of blinding light. She had no doubt that there were people behind those windows, shadows watching their shame.

She heard the *slither-thud* of the driver unloading their suitcases from the back of the carriage then, and Aunt Clara's eyes widened in fear.

'Cecilia!'

'We have lost the house, Aunt Clara.'

Evelyn's mother held her chin up, kept her gaze steady, but Evelyn could see how violently her hands were trembling behind her back.

'And I had rather hoped you would let us stay with you, for otherwise we have nowhere else to go.'

'Goodness.' Aunt Clara blew a haughty breath through her lips. 'You know I prefer vexing news *after* my afternoon tea.

One should not swallow shock on an empty stomach.' She was still blocking the doorway, her gaze flitting between them, the coach and the empty street. 'And really, you know my temperament is not one improved by company. Surely there must be someone else – his brothers, perhaps?'

Cecilia kept her head high, though Evelyn could feel what it was costing her now. 'There is nowhere, Aunt Clara. Truly. His family will not help us, and you are the only relation I have left.'

She hesitated, and Evelyn's mind flashed an image of what would happen if she refused them: the pair of them sent to the same dank workhouses they'd once raised funds for, sat at those long, cramped benches to eat watered stew, the fatigue written in their slumped shoulders. A quiet horror coiled in her stomach, and she turned her beseeching gaze upon her aunt.

'Please, Aunt Clara. Otherwise we shall be cast to the streets.'

'Oh, for goodness' sake.' Aunt Clara tutted, stepping back from the doorway. 'Get inside, the pair of you, and we shall speak of it over tea.'

Inside, it was dark, the curtains still drawn despite the time of day, and Evelyn bumped into the wall as she tried to follow the silhouettes before her into the morning room at the front of the house.

'Should we open some curtains?' her mother said, clearing her throat as the door yawned open into even more gloom. 'It's quite dim in here, Aunt Clara.'

Evelyn heard her great-aunt's displeasure in her short huff as she strode past. 'If you weren't in such a state of shock, I might take that as a criticism.'

Aunt Clara snapped a set of drapes back so that the light could seep in. It came in thick, dust-filled slices, illuminating the jumbled room and turning the walls from a greyish blue to swathes of pastel pinks.

In the centre, on a thinning Persian rug, stood the settee, worn red velvet and mahogany, flanked by grandmother chairs in the same upholstery. The fire was unlit, and the mantelpiece was stuffed with trinkets: stout brass candleholders, a delicately engraved clock that wrongly suggested the time was a quarter past five, and little white porcelain figurines: a girl at one end with a shepherd's hook and her sheep at the other, grazing on a layer of dust.

'Now, stay here.' Aunt Clara used the same tone one might use to placate an overexuberant dog. 'I shall fetch the tea.'

Cecilia paused, halfway to lowering herself onto the settee. 'I thought you had a maid? The last time I was here—'

'I always hire a couple of girls when you come,' Aunt Clara said. 'Another reason why it is polite to send notice ahead – so that when your prim and proper niece visits, you can at least feign a semblance of *richesse*. Thank goodness I lit the oven this morning, that's all I can say.'

Evelyn and her mother sat together in silence, listening to Aunt Clara's shoes clacking against the hallway tiles and then getting lost amongst a far greater clatter at the back of the house, where the kitchens were. Her mother let out a deep sigh and reached to knead at her carefully plucked eyebrows.

'No servants. What are we to do without servants?'

Evelyn gave her mother a look. 'Did you not hear what she said? No wonder dear Aunt Clara is always so averse to us popping by. And there was me thinking she was simply antisocial.'

'She *is* antisocial,' her mother corrected.

'Well, then we shall be a perfect match, the three of us, for society will soon be anti-us.' Evelyn looked up at the walls, studying a set of lazy country landscapes, all yellow grass and clouded skies. 'They loathed to love us before, when we had money and land. Now they'll simply love to loathe us.'

'If you are thinking we shall spend the next few weeks sat in this morning room, then you are quite mistaken,' her mother said. 'We shall not admit defeat so easily. Many a family has lost their fortune before us, and they did not retreat to nothingness.'

'I am sure *some* of them did.'

'Well, not us.' Her mother's expression was like that of a pawing bull, horns low and eyes up. 'The debt is embarrassing; there is no shirking from that.'

'Society has always called us upstarts,' Evelyn said. 'I suspect that even if our family held Riccall Hall for the next hundred years, they'd not forget that Great-Grandfather George's title wasn't inherited, and was instead granted on the merit of his being married to one of Queen Anne's favourites.'

'It was more than *that*,' Cecilia said sharply. 'It was his business sense, too. His politics.'

'My point is that it shall never be good enough,' Evelyn replied. 'So perhaps it is simply time we embraced it.'

The pale shock on her mother's face said otherwise. 'I will not have someone else tell me who I deserve to be,' she spat. 'I do not care if a baron is a low title amongst nobles. I do not care if I was born far beneath it. I do not care what they whisper of me at balls and parties. I am a titled lady, and even penniless I shall stay a titled lady. The Lord knows I have fought too hard to get here to give it all up now.'

Evelyn looked away. Perhaps there had been a lick of sense in Bessie's words. Not everyone always wished to hear the truth. 'So, what do you recommend, Mama? That we pretend nothing has happened? Or that we own up to it?'

Her mother tilted her head to one side. 'We needn't announce it, but we cannot lie either. Word will get around eventually, I'm sure, but in the meantime, I believe our next step is to follow the rules of etiquette to *the letter* and to show the world that we are still impeccable women of society.'

'I am not sure they ever believed that,' mumbled Evelyn.

'Nonsense,' said Cecilia. 'We must secure some letters of introduction, for that is surely the best way to ingratiate ourselves into society here in York – not to mention the proper thing to do.'

Aunt Clara came in then with a tray of delicate china cups and a pot of tea. 'The proper thing to do would be to go find that dastardly husband of yours, clasp him by the ear and drag him back to Riccall. I *knew* that man was trouble the moment I laid eyes upon him – and your mother, Ethel – *your* grandmother' – she looked at Evelyn – 'knew it, too. For all his money and charm, she *knew it.*'

Cecilia sighed. 'I know well enough that my mama disliked John. We need not dredge up ancient history.'

'No indeed, for now it has dug itself up, and you must stand and face it.' Aunt Clara raised two thin eyebrows. 'I am merely telling you what your mother *would* say, were she still with us: that she was right all along.'

Cecilia's already wire-thin voice became wearier: 'Aunt Clara, sometimes one's opinions are kinder when kept to oneself.'

'Nonsense,' Aunt Clara said dismissively. 'I am seventy-three years old. I have more than earned the right to say all my opinions out loud.'

Cecilia turned eyes full of warning back to her daughter. 'You see? You see what becomes of you when you let your mouth run like a steam engine in the face of decorum?'

'Returning to the topic of introductions,' Evelyn said flatly, 'surely we have no one to ask?'

'Of course we do.' Her mother sat stiffly while Aunt Clara poured the steaming liquid into her cup. It had steeped so long that it was a rich, reddish-brown colour. 'Lady Violet is nearly always here in the summer. You will go to the club's chambers and see if she still keeps her rooms there. Whomever there is to know in York, she will surely know them, or at least her father will. And she will be able to make the right introductions.'

Evelyn had been halfway to plucking her own full cup from its saucer, but now she froze. 'You wish for me to beg Lady Violet to write our letters of introduction? Are you mad?'

'Not mad,' said her mother. 'Slightly desperate, perhaps, but certainly not mad.'

'I am not sure she would help, even if I begged.'

'Well, you will have to try.' Her mother sipped her tea. 'Whatever she says will set the tone for how this news is received amongst our friends.'

'I believe true friends should stand by your side through trials as well as joys,' Evelyn replied. 'If they don't, then they've proven not to be true friends at all.' Which was why, she supposed, she considered herself to be friendless – a lonely thought if one focused too intently upon it, and so one Evelyn tended to ignore.

Aunt Clara's eyebrows shot up. 'What a thing to say! Cecilia, does she always talk like this?'

Cecilia turned back to Evelyn. 'Society doesn't work like that. The peerage are like fish: one scent of blood in the water and they flee, lest the sharks snatch them up, too. Lady Violet is the daughter of the Duke of Pembury – she's our best chance to smooth this news away.'

'Honestly, this new generation,' Aunt Clara said haughtily. 'One would think the coming century to be a quagmire of sin and opinions. I can only hope I will die before it gets too much.'

'*Besides*,' Evelyn's mother said, trying to wrangle the conversation back, 'you and Lady Violet debuted together, and if there is one thing a debutante must do, it is aid her peers.'

'I am quite sure Lady Violet did not agree to that,' Evelyn replied. 'She would have refused to be presented if those had been the terms.'

'You will go.' Her mother gave her a look that was half ferocious and half imploring. 'Or else we are doomed.'

'My goodness,' said Aunt Clara. 'You could be on the stage, my dear, with that flair for the dramatic.'

Evelyn placed a hand upon her mother's wrist. 'I just don't see why we must trust someone outside of the family to help us. Surely it is best if we keep this amongst ourselves?'

'We have no one else to turn to, Evelyn.'

Aunt Clara set down her cup. 'Charming.'

'Oh, come now.' Her mother's mouth drew into a bemused line. 'My side of the family only serves as further scandal when it comes to *society*. John's brothers are in America and will no doubt ignore any requests for money and blame the great, sprawling ocean between us.' She sighed. 'We must tackle this ourselves. And quickly, before the gossip mill begins to churn. Will you go to see Lady Violet, Evelyn? For my sake.'

'And for my sanity,' Aunt Clara chimed in, 'so that I need not listen to this rubbish a moment more.'

Evelyn looked at her mother. How many times had it been just the two of them, facing down her father's mistakes? Her love for her mother always triumphed over her dislike for the task – even when it was as great as this. 'If it will cheer you,' said Evelyn, 'I will go this very instant.'

'It would cheer me greatly.'

Evelyn set her teacup down and stood. 'Aunt Clara, will you call the carriage?'

Aunt Clara snorted into her tea. 'My dear, where do you suppose it lives – in the attic?'

Evelyn fumbled, for she had no idea how to get to the club chambers without a carriage. She had no idea how to get *anywhere* without one. 'So, you wish me to walk halfway across the city?'

'Surely not,' her mother said, shocked.

Aunt Clara rolled her eyes. 'Mrs Billingham has a governess cart,' she said. 'She lives in the house on the end. You can go and knock tomorrow afternoon and ask if she is headed to town for the market, as she usually is on a Saturday.'

Evelyn disliked that idea intensely. It would be bad enough to ask Lady Violet for help – now she must demand it of a stranger, too?

But her mother nodded and said: 'A marvellous plan,' and that was that.

Chapter Four

The following day, Evelyn was in luck, for Mrs Billingham did indeed need to go into York, and now they were both rattling about in her low governess cart, the donkey that pulled them hawing occasionally as they passed sleek-coated carriage horses and scrawny cab-nags.

Evelyn sat quietly, watching the city fold in around them. York felt narrow and cramped compared to Riccall. Even the houses seemed intent on blocking out the sky above them, growing thicker as they grew higher and tipping inwards on the narrow roads. There was a charm to it, though – a city with crumbling castle walls and ancient gateways, oak-beamed Tudor houses and the magnificent, gothic cathedral. They trotted alongside the river, sluggish and glimmering in the late afternoon sunshine, and she could see women walking in pairs with their parasols, children skipping hoops down the pavements and small dogs yapping at their heels.

Mrs Billingham turned a wary eye to Evelyn. 'First time in York, is it?'

'Not quite,' Evelyn replied.

There had been a time when she'd come into York often – before her father had left. He used to spend the day ensconced in the Yorkshire Club while she and Bessie would fritter away their time amongst the sweet-smelling flowers at the Museum Gardens, buying slices of sponge cake at the small tea-room there. More often than not, her father stayed on in the city, leaving her and Bessie to spend the carriage ride home giggling or dozing, depending on the quantity of cake consumed. The thought of it sent a pang into the pit of her stomach. For Bessie. For all the hours they had spent together, the *years*, in fact – and now her father had taken that away, like he had taken so much else.

'Talkative one, aren't yer?' said Mrs Billingham, drawing the donkey to a halt. 'Here you go. Museum Street.'

Evelyn glanced up at the familiar red-brick of the club chambers and felt her heartbeat thrum.

'I won't be long at the market,' said Mrs Billingham. 'If you're not done by the time I come past, you can hail a carriage of your own back to your aunt's.'

'I am sure this will be quick,' Evelyn said, half in hope, stepping down from the carriage and crossing to the liveried men standing before the entrance. 'The Honourable Miss Seaton, daughter of Baron Seaton, to see Lady Violet, daughter of the Duke of Pembury.'

The men glanced at one another and then reached as one to swing the great oak doors open.

Chapter Five

The club chambers was a decidedly unique place for two reasons. The first and most intriguing was it was one of the only aristocratic clubs in England to allow women to lodge there. Of course, most ladies sojourning in York preferred The Royal, the palatial hotel that sat beside the railway station, or Harker's in St. Helen's Square – but then again, most ladies did not have the Duke of Pembury for a father, for he'd single-handedly financed the building's entire renovation.

And so to the second reason: for despite this seemingly great leap forwards in equality, only one woman had ever taken a golden key from behind the club chambers' reception desk and kept it.

Lady Violet.

Though Evelyn supposed that only Lady Violet could feel utterly at home in a building where everyone else was merely passing through, where ladies were very visibly in the minority, and where every minute spent waiting seemed to stretch. Evelyn crossed her ankles one way and then the other, watching the footmen hurry back and forth, and the maids crisscross the great entryway. There were flowers everywhere, sprouting from blue-and-white marbled vases, cut into delicate stems for the low coffee tables or arranged into dazzling bouquets. The morning's newspapers were spread on the table before her, but she didn't wish to powder her fingers in ink, so she only cast a glance at the headlines, the largest of which revolved around Queen Victoria's eightieth birthday and the celebrations to be held in London the first week of June. Then came the resurgence of bubonic plague in Egypt and the sale of a new drug called Aspirin. Once she'd read them twice, one of the footmen approached, a tight grimace stitched upon his face.

'Lady Violet is aware of your arrival.'

'Wonderful,' Evelyn said, though she didn't believe Lady Violet would send for her quickly. This waiting – keeping her in the lobby like a commoner, staring at the white rose of York and the red rose of Lancaster intertwined on the entryway's tiles – was clearly an intended snub.

A raised newspaper snapped back then, revealing a young, blond man with flushed cheeks.

'If she's not come straight down then I suspect she won't see you at all, you know.'

Evelyn quirked an eyebrow. He had hair like summer corn and bright blue eyes. His nose was crooked – his smile, too – but the effect was rather charming, for it made him look like the kind of man who had a secret to tell, or perhaps one to keep. But the most interesting thing about him was his accent: the smooth, honeyed drawl of an American.

'That would work in my favour actually,' Evelyn said, with a fleeting smile. Then she would not have to face Lady Violet's stinging words.

His polite expression flickered. 'I . . . what?'

'I would be quite content to sit here a little while longer and then leave – that way, I can at least say I tried. How about you?'

The man looked quite befuddled. 'How about me?'

'Who are you waiting for?'

His gaze slid away. 'Lady Violet as well. But I've been here for two days already, and she's not called me up.' In an Englishman's mouth, it might have been a sour comment, but he said it all quite jovially.

'You've sat here for *two days*?'

'Not consistently,' he retorted quickly. 'I have called upon her both afternoons, and twice I have been rejected.'

'Rejected? Or ignored?'

He gave her a twitching smile. 'Both.'

Evelyn tilted her head to one side. 'Because you're American?'

'Because I have riled her.' He pushed a strand of blond hair back from his face. 'What should my being American have anything to do with it?'

'Objectively, nothing at all,' Evelyn said. 'But for the likes of Lady Violet, being American is . . . oh, worse than being in *trade*.' She narrowed her eyes, looking at the slump in his shoulders, the lines of fatigue written beneath his eyes. 'Let me guess,' she said, sliding closer so she didn't have to raise her voice. 'You're the son of a wealthy New Yorker, come to woo Lady Violet, only to find she has locked herself away, lest she cause a scandal by taking luncheon with an American.'

She watched the bemusement flicker across his face. 'In fact,' he said, clearing his throat, 'I am the son of a wealthy Massachusettsan, sent on behalf of Lord Pembury to try to coax Lady Violet up to Scotland for the summer. I studied at Oxford with her brother.'

Evelyn scrunched her nose. 'That's far less exciting than a grand, romantic gesture. Are you quite sure you're not madly in love with her?'

The American folded his newspaper quickly, placing it on the empty seat beside him. 'Why are *you* here?'

'Oh, you know.' Evelyn flapped a hand dismissively. 'Women's follies.'

'I most certainly don't know.' He gave her a languid smile. 'Why don't you tell me?'

'Yes, Miss Seaton. Why don't you?'

They turned as one at her voice: for Lady Violet had appeared like a spectre from behind a wide display of dusk-blue hydrangeas. She looked like a wildflower herself in her violet day dress, her white-blonde hair curled and pinned neatly beneath a velvet-rimmed hat. When her green eyes were trained on you, it felt like being blinded, and when coupled with her brittle beauty and her jewels, it could cause a room to hush. She certainly had that effect on the American, who had still not stood to greet her and now, in his rush to do so, knocked the low coffee table with his shins.

'Finally.' He took off his cap, flourishing a bow. 'I thought you would leave me here another day.'

'Nathaniel, for the hundredth time, you must tell Papa I am not going to Scotland.' She gave him a prim look, before turning to Evelyn. 'I came to see what on earth *you* might want, Miss Seaton. The footman said it looked as though you'd walked all the way here, though I said: "Surely not from Riccall?" And then he told me something *very* interesting.'

It was as though the gentle clatter of footsteps on the tiles, of bells ringing behind the main desk had all hushed, leaving only Lady Violet's voice, loud as a clock's chime.

'He told me that a number of wagons passed through York on their way to Riccall earlier this week. Police wagons. They stopped at the Royal Station Hotel for directions.' She turned to the American then and said: 'Riccall is so tiny you're more likely to drive through it than discover it.'

'I see,' said the American.

'And I thought to myself: how curious that Kemper should see a clatter of wagons on their way to Riccall, and then you, Miss Seaton, should show up a few days later on my doorstep!' She cast her gaze over Evelyn's shoulder again. 'Miss Seaton lives at Riccall Hall.'

'I had gathered,' the American replied.

'So then, Miss Seaton.' Lady Violet turned her bright, curious gaze back to Evelyn. 'Why have you come to see me?'

Evelyn wished ardently that she could turn and walk away from that grand lobby and pretend she had never come. She wished her mother had not sent her, that her father had not ruined everything, but most of all she wished Lady Violet would stop looking at her. For it seemed with every second she looked that she would discover the truth of it all.

'We are taking your lead, Lady Violet,' Evelyn said, though it came out stiff and stilted. 'We are summering in York.'

'Odd, when most avoid it when the heat rolls around.' To the American, she added: 'whereas I am content anywhere Papa and Mama are not, and they do so hate York when it's warm. They say it stirs up miasmas from the river.' She took the seat beside the American, so that she could keep her razor gaze on Evelyn's face. 'However, that does not explain why all those wagons rattled up there.'

Evelyn swallowed. She detested lying, and she could feel the weight of it already in her stomach. But the alternative was to tell the truth to a woman who could turn a charitable donation into the scandal of the century, and Evelyn would not have her mother's life ruined twice in one week. 'They were lost,' she said stiffly. 'That is all.'

'I'm sure.' Lady Violet's lip twitched at the edge. 'So, you arrived in York and came to announce your presence to me directly?'

'I came to ask for letters of introduction,' Evelyn replied. 'Mama sent me.'

'And how is your dear mother? I do hope she is improving after what your wretched father did.' To the American, she added: 'Up and left them – went to London for "business" and never came back. The papers showed him doing all sorts – and not very much of it business. Unless your father invests in ballerinas?'

Evelyn felt her cheeks flush scarlet.

'Oh, and I am sure his leaving was very hard on a woman like your mother. All alone in that big house? And having come from such *humble* beginnings, she must have truly been lost. My mother said it was a wonder the place didn't crumble, and I was inclined to believe her. But now look! Two years later, and here you are, unstarved and standing before me.'

The American, at least, had the grace to look bashful. 'That sounds truly dreadful.'

Evelyn felt her skin become clammy. This was why she hated dealing with Lady Violet. She was like a dog at the hunt, persistent and dangerous, whereas Evelyn could do nothing more than retreat deeper and deeper into her burrow and hope her reaching claws would not catch flesh.

'Either you will write the letters for us, or you won't,' Evelyn said carefully, focusing on each word. 'I needn't sit here and listen to gossip.'

'Come now.' Lady Violet's voice grew louder. 'I was merely bringing my friend here up to speed!'

Evelyn did not look at the American but kept her gaze most firmly on Lady Violet. 'Will you write the letters, or won't you?'

Lady Violet pouted. 'Where are you staying while here in York?'

'With a relative.'

'Which relative?'

Evelyn saw the claw reach out again, swatting into darkness. 'Why, so you can update the American on them, too?'

'My name is Nathaniel Morris, ma'am,' he said quietly. 'And I needn't know—'

'Really, Miss Seaton!' Lady Violet gave her an affronted look. 'I ask so that I know which address to give my acquaintances, of course! Lest they want to reach out and call on your mother?' To Mr Morris, she said: 'Though I do not see why they would. Lady Seaton was raised in a workhouse and naturally has as much in common with a lady as a horse does with the mouse beneath its hooves.'

There it was. The moment those reaching claws met flesh. Evelyn felt her cheeks burn scarlet, though not with embarrassment. She was not ashamed of her mother, nor of her beginnings. She was proud. But in this moment, she felt small – powerless. She wished she could find the words more readily, wished she could land a scratch herself. But she couldn't. It was all she could do to retreat into the quiet darkness of her own mind.

'By Jove,' Mr Morris said, in a feeble attempt to defuse the crackling tension. 'Women's follies are rather akin to men's fights. Do you ladies always speak to one another thus?'

'Oh, of course not.' Lady Violet placed a gloved hand on the man's forearm. 'Miss Seaton and I have a rather special friendship – don't we, Evelyn?'

'Thank you for agreeing to write the letters,' Evelyn said, standing abruptly. 'You can send any correspondence to Porthaven House, in the east of the city.'

And with that, she left quickly, looking at neither Lady Violet nor at Mr Morris, only at the doors.

Chapter Six

Outside, Evelyn turned left, circling the building until she could stand in the cool shade of an alleyway. She pressed her forehead to the red brick, trying to quell the sharp, painful thumping of her own heart. She did not know whether to be angry at herself, or pity herself, or both. She was twenty-four years old, and up until a few days ago her life had followed a predictable, if somewhat tiresome pattern. Now she felt unmoored, untethered.

She slumped down the wall and buried her head into the soft pillow of her arms with a groan. She didn't care if her mother would faint from shock to see her daughter crouched on the street. All she wanted was for the world to swallow her up, for the shade above her to expand and darken and hide her in its gentle gloom. It felt as though she'd missed a step in the dance, and now she was moving to one beat and the rest of the world to another, such that she was jolted every second step. And once she added to that the humiliation of having her family's history paraded in front of a stranger . . .

'Are you unwell, ma'am?'

Evelyn glanced up. There was a young Black woman standing before her, carrying a basket of laundry, looking down upon her with kind, brown eyes.

'Not unwell,' Evelyn said.

The woman gave her a gentle look and shifted the laundry from one hip to the other. 'Are you lost?'

'Quite lost, yes.' To Evelyn's horror, she felt her throat begin to close, as though she would cry.

'Where do you need to get to?'

Back to how it was before. She needed the clock hands to run backwards, to take her back to when everything had made sense and she had known who she was and what she was doing in life. Because now? Now . . . she was sitting on the floor, embarrassing some poor woman who was just trying to go about her day.

'Porthaven House,' she said, wiping at her cheeks and standing. She was nearly of a height with the woman in front of her, perhaps an inch taller, which was unusual, for Evelyn's family were like willows. The woman was striking, too: her eyes framed with impossibly thick eyelashes, high cheekbones, and a full, smiling mouth.

'It's on Long Close Lane in the east of the city. I am supposed to have a carriage coming for me, though we didn't exactly arrange a time—' And Mrs Billingham hadn't exactly offered one. Perhaps she had already finished at the market and gone home? Evelyn supposed she had been quite a while at the club chambers, and now, when she looked up, she saw that dusk was beginning to settle in the clouds above them.

The woman watched her, as though calculating something. 'I live in the east of the city, too,' she said. 'How about I wait with you a short while? That way we can walk there together if your carriage doesn't show up.'

'Oh, no. I couldn't make such demands on your time.' Evelyn shook her head. 'I am sure I could find my way if I needed to.'

The woman's half-smile said otherwise. 'I am a little early with this,' she said, nodding towards the laundry. 'And I

can't give Mr Kaye a reason to think I'll always rush his
orders – my mother and I would go out of business if word
got out. But if we're going to wait, let's do it in the sunshine.'
She began to walk from the alley, turning to Evelyn when
she didn't follow. 'Come on, now. Only rats and drunkards
dally in side streets.'

They sat upon one of the benches outside of the club
chambers, where the women with parasols had been but a
few hours before, giving their children crumbs for the ducks
bobbing past on the river. The sun was still warm, though
now it was beginning to set in great, honeyed brushstrokes,
turning the slow-moving water into a dazzling gold mirror.
The woman had placed the laundry between them, and
Evelyn could see it was sheets, all starched and stiff and
neatly folded, scented with lavender.

'Who's Mr Kaye?' Evelyn asked.

'He works at the Black Swan Inn.' A smile had begun to
curl the edge of the woman's lips. 'He's the night porter there
for now, but he wants a job at the big hotel. You know, the
one at the station.'

Evelyn did know it. It was the finest hotel in York. 'An
ambitious man, then.'

'I think so,' the woman said happily. 'It's nice to meet a
man with dreams, you know? Too many are happy to potter
along, never wanting more.' She placed her hands in her lap.
'But you don't want to hear about all of that.'

'On the contrary,' Evelyn said. 'I could do with a slice
of someone else's life for the moment.' Anything to distract
her from the shattered rubble of her own. 'What about you?
What are your ambitions?'

The woman gave her a sideways glance. 'Well, for one, Mr
Kaye could grow a little courage and ask me out to tea. Still,
I've no control of that myself, and as my mother always says:
"Only be driven mad by your own doing, not anyone else's.

You must focus on what you can reach out and touch in this life, or else you'll never be happy."'

'That's good advice,' Evelyn said quietly, looking down at her own, empty palms. 'So then why don't you ask this Mr Kaye to tea? Instead of waiting on him.'

'You know, that's what I was just wondering myself. Hark at me, giving out advice and yet ignoring it completely.' She laughed, an infectious kind of giggle, and Evelyn chuckled a little alongside her.

When the gentle lapping of the river once more became the loudest sound, the woman cleared her throat and said: 'I have this dream, you see. There's a little house on Regent Street. I couldn't afford it alone and couldn't buy it neither, but Jack – I mean, Mr Kaye – and I could manage it together perhaps. I'd love to sit in my own living room, drink a cup of tea, and—' She stopped, her cheeks flushing. 'Look at me. We're not even stepping out together, and I'm already putting a house on the table! You must think me pushy, miss.'

'It's not what I was thinking at all,' Evelyn said, giving her a reassuring smile. 'And please, call me Evelyn, not "miss".'

'Then you must call me Naomi,' the woman replied. 'You know, when I saw you in that alley, I thought you'd be some grand old toff, half drunk. Mr Kaye has a writer friend who would've loved that.'

Evelyn bristled. 'He's a journalist?'

'A novelist, I think,' Naomi said. She looked from the laundry to Evelyn and back again. 'Now then, what do you reckon on your carriage? Is it coming, or should we walk?'

Evelyn looked at the streets, bathed in the low sunshine, at the pools of scarlet reflecting the blushing sky.

'It is a fine night for a walk,' she said, with a courageous smile. 'If you don't mind.'

'O'course not,' Naomi said, hefting the laundry back onto

her hip. 'So long as you don't mind a stop at the Black Swan on our way so I can leave this on the back doorstep.'

'Will I get to meet this mysterious Mr Kaye?'

Naomi laughed. 'He doesn't start until much later, but I like your gumption. Now come on – we've a fair way to go.'

On the walk home, they discovered that they were both only children. Naomi spent the length of Walmgate recounting how her father, the son of a diplomat, had come from Madagascar to study at the Quaker school in Bootham and met her mother. Evelyn hoped there would be a romantic end to the story, but Naomi only laughed.

'He couldn't handle the wet, Yorkshire winters,' she said. 'Went back to Madagascar before he knew Mam was pregnant.'

Once they had parted and Evelyn was back once more at Porthaven House, she thought over their conversation, her mind snagging over and again on how hard Naomi was working to build something for herself. It should have inspired her, should have pushed her to try to clasp her hands around something of her own, but all it did was encourage her to line up the blocks of her own life.

Her mother still ascribed to the view that a woman's life only truly took wing after marriage, and Evelyn – though in disagreement – had been content to stagnate in uncertainty since her father had abandoned Riccall, and them, for England's capital. They had stopped summering in London after that, and whenever they did send out calling cards, they were rarely returned. But while Evelyn had been waiting for something to happen, Naomi had been working to *make* something happen. She had been building something for herself. Couldn't Evelyn do that, too? After all, what did she have to show for her twenty-four years, other than four suitcases, three hatboxes and the woeful number of books she'd thought to grab from her bedside table? A sorry account of a life, indeed.

She tried to explain as much to her mother and great-aunt come Friday evening, when Aunt Clara called her a 'sour grape' at dinner, and her mother put her fork down with a clatter and said: 'Really, Evelyn, I quite agree. What on earth is wrong?'

When Evelyn explained, Aunt Clara laughed. 'Are you forgetting your education, child? Your governess? You can play instruments, sew, sing in harmony. And you speak far too many languages for any of them to be *useful*.'

'Plenty of people can sew,' Evelyn replied. 'I am saying I wish I had something more to show for my life. But I have nothing.'

Her mother pushed her chair back, and for a moment Evelyn thought she might walk from the room. Instead, she threw her napkin down and said: 'As soon as the letters from Lady Violet arrive, I shall be able to form a plan.'

Evelyn rolled her eyes. 'Every day you say that, Mother. And every day I shall say this: I do not believe she will send anything.'

'Well, I believe she will,' her mother said primly. 'So we shall see who is right.'

It was her mother, in the end, who was right. For three days later, a letter arrived.

Chapter Seven

22nd May 1899
Porthaven House, York

Evelyn was sitting in the morning room, slumped into one of the grandmother chairs, her sleek teal day dress bright against the faded velvet. Aunt Clara sat opposite her, tutting as she stirred the milk into her tea. Evelyn had cracked the windows ajar, much to Aunt Clara's disdain, and now a cool breeze made the room smell a little more of pollen and a little less of dust. It might have made for a cosy tableau if it wasn't for her mother's frantic pacing.

'Lady Violet is hosting a ball,' Cecilia read. 'This Friday, at the Royal Station Hotel, and here is the invitation! Isn't that marvellous, Evelyn? I cannot remember the last time you were invited to anything at the behest of one of the Pembury family!'

'You don't think that's quite a late invitation?' Evelyn said, taking the proffered cup of tea from Aunt Clara. 'If the ball is this week then surely it has been planned for months. She could have invited me in person at the club chambers, but she did nothing of the sort.'

'Perhaps she forgot.' Her mother paused. 'Do sit up, Evelyn. We may be penniless, but we are not rag dolls.'

Evelyn straightened, crossing her ankles neatly beneath her. 'I am sure there is a reason we have never attended their balls before, and a reason we are invited now. And unlike you, I do not believe those reasons are good.'

'The difference was that you'd offended Lady Violet at her presentation,' her mother said. 'Now she is being kind, and *you* of all people wish to snub her?'

Evelyn sipped her tea and grimaced. The milk had been poured too liberally, and now the liquid was grey and bland. She looked at Aunt Clara, who gazed pointedly to the window and then back to Evelyn, a challenge in her eyes.

'I do not wish to *snub her*,' Evelyn said. 'That would suggest I could embarrass her with my lack of attendance. If anything, I am trying to avoid *her* embarrassing *me*.'

Her mother sat down. 'Only you could see an invitation to a ball as a disaster waiting to happen.'

'Because it is! Don't you see? Word from London will travel up eventually, if it hasn't already, and then what? We'll only spend the evening having to account for Father's idiocy, for his shame – *our shame* – in person. It will be just like the summers in London, except this time Father hasn't made a trivial mistake nor an erroneous comment – this debt is a disaster, and we shall be expected to answer for it. Forgive me if that doesn't sound like a *thrilling* way for us to spend an evening.'

'Not us – *you*.' Her mother gave her a tight little smile. 'I am not invited.'

Evelyn threw her hands up. 'All the more reason to refuse!'

'No, all the more reason why you must go. You will hold our position in society. Your attendance will show them that we cannot be shamed into hiding.'

Evelyn sighed. 'What happened to being impeccable society ladies? Surely my unchaperoned attendance will encourage *more* questions, not fewer?'

'Yes, well,' said Cecilia. 'Sometimes one must bend the rules to suit one's needs.'

Aunt Clara slurped her tea. 'Good to see you haven't forgotten your own motto, Cecilia. For you broke every rule in the book when you met John—'

Cecilia flushed. 'Aunt Clara, now is not the time—'

'How else could a lady's maid, brought up in the work-house, with a bricklayer for a father and a seamstress for a mother, marry the first-born son of a baron?'

'Really!' Cecilia huffed.

'Because they fell in love,' said Evelyn. For that was the story she had always been told: they fell in love, and everything else was merely logistics.

'No. *Because rules are meant to be broken,*' Aunt Clara said, her eyes sparkling behind her teacup. 'This sort of nonsense is *exactly* how she courted your father.'

'And see how well that turned out,' Evelyn murmured. She felt as though the already-small room was getting smaller somehow. Even the shepherdess on the mantelpiece seemed to be watching her. *Leering.* 'I don't want to go – not to hold our place in society, and certainly not to be paraded like a village heifer before the sons of dukes and viscounts and country squires. Do you think they're blind to that sort of thing?'

'I don't suggest you *parade* yourself, dear,' her mother said sternly. 'You will dance with them and make light conversation.'

Evelyn felt something coil in her stomach. 'You know how bad I am at light conversation.'

Aunt Clara snorted. 'In my day you could almost get married without exchanging a word. That would suit you well, child. Better than well, in fact.'

'Aunt, please.' Cecilia gave her a sharp look. 'She's not so bad as that. She just needs to . . .' She broke off, licking her lips, and glanced at Evelyn. 'You must simply refrain from asking so many reaching questions.'

'Do you know what she asked me yesterday?' Aunt Clara said with a sour tone. '"What is the biggest regret of your life?" As though Englishwomen speak of such things! I find that this new generation bandies their emotions around like rice on a wedding day. No one ever asked me how I felt when I was a young woman, for no one cared, and nor did it matter. Well, I've the answer to your question now, girl – I regret letting the pair of you through my doorway!'

'Aunt Clara, *please*.' Evelyn's mother pressed her fingertips to her forehead, as she did when she felt one of her migraines coming on. 'Enough, the pair of you. Evelyn, you will go to the ball. You will dance, and goodness knows, you may actually enjoy yourself.'

'I suspect I won't,' Evelyn said, keeping her gaze out of the murky windows.

'And you' – Cecilia turned to Aunt Clara – 'could learn to put a modicum of kindness into your words.'

Aunt Clara brought a hand to her breast. 'Me? Unkind? What rubbish.'

'I don't even have a dress to wear,' Evelyn said. 'My emerald gown isn't truly a ball gown – it is more of a dinner dress.'

'Well, it will have to do,' her mother said, giving her a wide smile. 'I am sure you will look wonderful.'

Standing in front of the smeared mirror later that evening, watching her reflection stare warily back at her, Evelyn did not *feel* wonderful. She felt as though she were walking through tall grass and any moment she would hear the metallic *snap* of the hunter's trap clamp its teeth around her.

She had been right about the dress. Although it was pretty – sparkling green with a scooped neck and darker, crushed velvet sleeves – it was not elaborate enough for a ball. The detail was minimalistic – a little black and gold lacing across the low neckline, a little on the outside edge of her sleeves – but it was not *showy*. And balls required *showy* dresses, something that shouted: *Look at me! See how much money we have!* All this would shout was: *I miscalculated the splendour of the evening*, which would make her feel even more out of place than she already would.

She huffed, turning from her reflection, and sat down in a pool of silk upon her bed.

God above, even when she'd worn all the right things in London, she'd felt like a donkey amongst a herd of sleek-coated horses. The parade of balls and dinners, teas and afternoons in London had been torment – mostly thanks to Lady Violet. She had been the top hen in their little pluck of ladies: everyone turned to listen when she spoke; everyone sought her approval on their gowns, their jewels – all except Evelyn.

It wasn't that she didn't care how she looked or what people thought; she did care, but she had been made to feel the odd one out for so long that she had stopped trying to be a part of the group – ever since she'd been sent home from boarding school with a firmly worded recommendation that her parents continue her education privately.

And in return for being different, for not seeking her approval, for appearing to not care, Lady Violet had made sure Evelyn felt the sting of her beak each time they were together.

This felt like more of the same. Except this time, she had wrapped it up in kindness, and Evelyn could not feel the sting of it yet. But she was sure she would, as soon as she stepped into that ballroom on Friday.

She was certain of it.

Chapter Eight

26th May 1899
The Royal Station Hotel

The Royal Station Hotel was a palatial sandstone structure. It had been built as railway travel became popular and was made lastingly famous when Queen Victoria had stopped in for luncheon. Evelyn could see why the Queen might have felt comfortable here: from the gold-plated banisters that swept up the grand staircase to the great chandelier that hung above them and the silver-threaded rug beneath her feet, everything felt luxurious, and the ballroom most of all.

It looked as though summer had bloomed within it. The high ceiling had been netted, and a blanket of wildflowers hung from it, their perfumed scent making the room smell dizzyingly of violets and honeysuckle. Where the garden doors were open and the breeze rolled in, it looked as though the flowers were waves tossed upon a sweet-smelling sea, the petals burnished gold where the light beneath them flickered. There were candles everywhere, arranged in great, shining bouquets, and between them were even more flowers: dripping down pedestals in curving teardrops, wrapping around the wide fireplace like vines.

It was a dazzling display, and Evelyn hesitated on the threshold. It looked as though she were not simply entering a room but another world – one in which she was devastatingly underdressed. She was a weed amongst the roses, a struggling daisy in comparison to the women sauntering past her in their bejewelled dresses, and she had half made up her mind to leave when she heard a voice say: 'May I escort you inside, ma'am?'

She turned to find the American standing behind her, looking far more turned out than the last she'd seen of him. He was in white tie, his shirt starched and crisp, his hair slicked back with Macassar Oil. Unlike the other men walking past them in a blur of black and white, Mr Morris wore a red and blue handkerchief tucked into his lapel pocket. He smiled when he saw her notice it and said conspiratorially: 'I thought it best to advertise the fact of my being American, lest I cause any more scandal. Though I don't suppose my attendance at Oxford and my careful adherence to British language and customs counts in my favour?'

'Not with the people inside that room, Mr Morris,' she said, giving him a slightly strained smile. The tide of people around them was building, and they were thoroughly in the way.

'Please, call me Nathaniel – Mr Morris is my father.' He smiled at her expectantly. 'So, what do you say, shall I escort you in, Miss Seaton? Or do you plan to hover here the whole night?'

Evelyn grimaced. 'I had rather intended on sneaking past the master of ceremonies so that he didn't have the chance to shout my name to the ceiling. In fact, that was rather the point of arriving so late.'

Nathaniel frowned. 'You don't want to be announced?'

'It is a private ball,' Evelyn said. 'I don't see why there is a Master of Ceremonies in the first place.'

Nathaniel shrugged. 'Lady Violet always appoints one. She says it's because she likes to know who arrives when.'

'Which is why it's far better if I slip in unseen, and ensconce myself in a corner until the night is over.' She imagined her mother's face then, her twitching displeasure if she'd overheard her. *You never know, Evelyn. You could meet your future at that ball.*

He laughed then, a rich, warm sound that carried. 'You are an odd one, aren't you?'

'So I've heard,' Evelyn said flatly.

'Come now.' Nathaniel walked forwards, holding her arm fast in the crook of his elbow. 'It won't be so bad if we are together.'

'No, really.' She turned to look past the crowds, back to the open doors and the cool, summer night that lay beyond them. 'I had concocted a whole plan – I can just walk through the garden and step inside through the veranda.'

'Don't be preposterous.' Nathaniel swept them both towards the footman, his grip tightening upon her arm. A moment later, the master of ceremonies announced them both in a strident tenor – 'Mr Morris and The Honourable Miss Seaton' – and though the entire room did not turn to look at them, Lady Violet did.

'See?' Nathaniel said, walking them over to where the crowd was thickest. 'That wasn't so bad, was it?'

But Evelyn was not listening. She was watching Lady Violet glide towards them, clusters of people parting and then closing up behind her, like shoals of fish. If it wasn't for her scarlet dress – bright as blood – Evelyn might have lost her. Instead, she watched her approach in glimmers of red: the long feather in her headdress, the high neck of her collar, the flash from the bottom of her skirts, until she was standing before them both, one neatly gloved hand clutched tightly around a glass of champagne.

'I thought you wouldn't come,' she said, and though her gaze was on Evelyn, she tilted towards Nathaniel, her skin even paler against the crimson silk. 'I had rather lost hope.'

'I found Miss Seaton hovering by the door,' Nathaniel said, giving her a wide, easy smile, 'and thought to bring her inside.'

'Why, yes.' Lady Violet looked Evelyn up and down quite carefully. 'Otherwise, how would you have been able to see all your old friends?'

Evelyn kept the placid look stitched carefully onto her face, though her heart had started to thump a little harder. 'Old friends?'

'I've invited some of our fellow debutantes from London.' Lady Violet waved a hand to the eastern wall, and Evelyn saw that she wasn't lying. She recognized nearly all of them. 'I thought we could make quite a reunion of it. And before you ask, Nathaniel, of course we'll introduce you to them all before the dancing begins.' Lady Violet took his arm languidly and pushed Evelyn to one side.

'Which reminds me.' Nathaniel cleared his throat. 'I had wished to ask you for the first dance, Lady Violet, if I may.'

Nathaniel had taken on the same twitching edge that thrummed through Evelyn's own veins, though he hadn't seemed nervous before, neither at the prospect of the announcement nor at stepping into such a busy room. Evelyn's gaze slid south then, to the coloured handkerchief tucked into his pocket. The blue was hidden now, and only the red showed as if he'd intended it to match Lady Violet's ball gown.

Lady Violet batted her white-blonde eyelashes. 'Poor

thing. I have given my first dance to the Duke of Wrexham. But I am sure Miss Seaton's dance card is empty, isn't it, Evelyn?' She gave Nathaniel a generous smile. 'She suffered from the same ailment in London, if I remember correctly.'

'I have only just arrived,' Evelyn said, reaching for a passing glass of champagne and feeling the stem of it slide through her white lace gloves. 'It would be quite impressive if my dance card was already full.'

Lady Violet leaned ever further into Nathaniel and said: '*Some* of us have been taking dance requests for weeks. But we cannot all be so lucky, I suppose.'

Nathaniel's smile didn't waver, though now he turned it upon Evelyn. 'I would be honoured to have the first dance with you, Miss Seaton, if you'll have me.'

'Of course she will,' Lady Violet said, taking a dance card from a passing footman and giving it to him. 'From what I've heard, she's hardly in a position to refuse.'

Evelyn heard the barb amongst her words immediately. 'What does that mean?'

'Come now,' Lady Violet said, waiting for Nathaniel to scribble his name and give the card back, before sliding her hand through the crook of his elbow and leading him away. 'Let Evelyn and I introduce you to our friends.'

Evelyn had forgotten what it was like being around them all again: Miss Mary, Miss Margaret, Lady Rosalind, Lady Jane. But she remembered repeating the same: 'Are you well? Very well,' over and over.

It felt like that summer her father had taken them all to Saltburn-on-the-sea, with its stretching pier, the neat little changing rooms mounted on wide, wagon wheels so they could be hitched to horses and rolled away when the tide came in. The waves had seemed endless that day, the sea choppy, and she'd ignored Bessie's warning and her father's placid agreement not to venture too far from the shallows. She hadn't expected the sand beneath her toes to drop away like it did, hadn't expected to go under until she could taste salt, until she opened her eyes to the murky water and flailed. She remembered the noise of it, a great, roaring sound in her ears as though the ocean itself bellowed at her, as the waves washed over her, relentless, her nose and throat stinging from the salt until Bessie had grabbed her by her hair and yanked her out.

'I thought it best we all be here,' Lady Violet said, now that they all stood in a loose horseshoe, Nathaniel having been sent to fetch drinks, 'to offer our joint condolences.'

For a moment, Evelyn assumed Lady Violet was talking to someone else. Only belatedly did she realize that all eyes were trained on her. 'Your . . . condolences?'

'For your father.' Lady Violet's eyebrows were slanted in mock sympathy. 'For his imprisonment.'

Evelyn could hear it again, the rush of blood in her ears. 'He is not in prison.'

'Oh, but sponging-houses aren't much different,' said Lady Jane.

'What did you expect?' Lady Violet's voice again. 'If Lady Seaton learned to run a household by reading a book, is it any wonder they've run out of money?'

Evelyn felt her cheeks flush. 'My mother has nothing to do with this.'

'It's quite ironic really.' Miss Margaret's voice. 'A barony won with money, and now it'll be lost with it, too.'

'Or the lack of it,' said Lady Rosalind.

'I don't think that's ironic,' said Miss Mary. 'I would say it's poetic.'

'Not quite so poetic when she is penniless.'

'Are you penniless now, Miss Seaton? Why, you must be to wear a dinner dress to a ball.'

Evelyn could feel her heart racing, could feel the cold sweat upon her spine, and though her mouth was open, she could not think of a single word to say. All she wanted to do was disappear, for the wave of flowers above them to fall and drown her in that blanket of petals.

'You're a wretch for inviting her here, Lady Violet. You've put a fox amongst the chickens, letting her loose around all these rich young men.'

Lady Violet gave Evelyn a slow smile that was all teeth. 'Are you a fox, Miss Seaton? Is that why your mother sent you here, to snare yourself a husband, just as she snared one herself all those years ago?'

'A lady's maid marrying the son of a baron – such obscenity. My mother always said it was a marriage built upon trickery.'

'Mine thought charms. Did your mother buy a love charm, Miss Seaton? Did she magic your father under her sway?'

'And now she's parading her daughter amongst us. As though you fit in here,' Lady Rosalind scoffed.

'As though she ever did,' Miss Mary added.

Lady Violet lifted her chin, fixing Evelyn with a determined glare. 'Well, she certainly doesn't now.'

The cluster of women were closing around her, and her mother's words echoed back to her: *you know what they are like when they smell blood. They are fish.* But these women were not fish. No, these women were sharks, each biting a chunk from her and then spitting it out to come back for more.

At that moment, Nathaniel appeared from behind Lady Violet's shoulder, a footman in tow carrying a full tray.

'Now then, ladies,' Nathaniel said, putting a flute into the nearest empty hand, which was Lady Jane's. 'What have I missed?'

It was as though his voice reached below the water and

pulled her up, allowing her to finally gasp for air. Only now, blinking, did she feel the tears that had begun to roll down her cheeks. 'I'm sorry, Nathaniel,' Evelyn said, picking up her skirts, 'but I cannot dance with you.'

And with that, she turned and walked from the room, from the laughter bubbling up behind her like sea foam.

Chapter Nine

While Evelyn fled for the cool summer night outside the hotel's doors, a young, dishevelled man stepped out of York Station. His tangled black hair grew like thorns, and beneath his deep brown eyes were the dark smudges of fatigue. He hadn't left the station with the rest of the passengers from the London train but had followed twenty minutes later, as though he'd perhaps been asleep in his chair or hidden in the wash closet, so that the conductor couldn't check his ticket.

He stopped for a moment, dropping the suitcases he held in each hand, and threw his head up to the night's sky. It had been a long time since William was last in York, a long time since he'd breathed the city air or seen the stars stitched above him. He spotted one at first, and then another, until they became a whole blanket of distant light. He'd missed them dearly in London and had found only one spot, high up on Primrose Hill, where he could get a good view of them without the new electric streetlights bathing the city in an orange haze. His mind made shapes of them, wide scullery pots and tall archers, prowling bears and cascading waves. It made his heart ache, not because it was beautiful, nor because he was homesick, but because, if he was honest with himself, truly honest, he hadn't thought he would see them again. He hadn't thought he would come back to York.

He turned his head then, catching the squeal of a violin on the night's breeze. Someone was having a fête at the grand hotel; he could hear the beginnings of a waltz, and he wondered what it must feel like to be in there. To be dancing and drunk. To be carefree. To be anyone, *anyone* other than him.

He sucked a deep breath through his nose.

What would he tell his uncle? What would he tell his friends? The thought of it was like a punch to his stomach, a nauseating reminder that the hard part was not yet done, and William grimaced. He would deal with that in the morning. First, he needed to wash, to sleep. And though life had been cruel of late, today, it was kind. There, dozing outside the station, was one single cab, as though God himself had put it there for William to ease his weary bones into.

As he reached down to pluck his suitcases from the pavement, he paused. There was a note trapped beneath, a crumple of paper he'd caught with the weight of them, and he read the looping handwriting:

Help wanted at Morton's Emporium. Enquire within.

William scooped it up, tutting, and stuffed it into his pocket, before striding towards the cab.

Evelyn gulped in the night air like a drowning woman. She wished she felt more anger, anything but this heavy hopelessness that had congealed in the pit of her stomach. After all, she almost agreed with them: she didn't belong there anymore, didn't have a place amongst them. If she was honest with herself, perhaps she'd never belonged, but the difference was that it had been her choice then. And now . . .

She blew a breath through her teeth, trying to steady herself. She wanted to go home, to curl into her bed, pull the curtains around herself and sleep for an eternity. Too late, she realized she was picturing her old bedroom – with the wide sash windows and yellow satin curtains – and that she would have to go back to Aunt Clara's, to her new truckle bed in the attic, the faint light filtering through the small, high window, the greyish, flaking walls. Her throat grew sore anew, as though she might cry again, but she scrunched her eyes closed and focused on the sharp rise and fall of her chest until it dissipated.

There was a cab on the other side of the road, the horse dozing quietly, its head tucked into a hay bag. The driver looked like he was resting, too, his cap pulled down over his face, and she walked quickly towards him. Her mother had slipped two shillings into her hand before she'd left and said: *provided Lady Violet doesn't offer her carriage first*. Her mother would no doubt be disappointed when the shillings didn't return and vexed to find that there was only one name on her dance card, and an American at that, but Evelyn would worry about that later. She greeted the slumped driver, stepped around to the door, and hesitated.

Stuck upon it was a piece of paper. It was crumpled, held in place by the force of the wind alone, and she plucked it from the carriage's side.

Help wanted at Morton's Emporium. Enquire within.

As she held the paper between her fingertips, a shadow of a thought came to her. She folded it neatly into her purse and wrenched the carriage door open.

On the other side, at exactly the same moment, a young man did the same. And there they both stood, silhouetted against the carriage's flickering lanterns, one at each side, a face in the doorway.

'Excuse me,' said the young man. 'I believe this is my cab.'

He had the loveliest face she'd ever seen: high, elegant cheekbones and eyes as dark as the sky above them. His hair grew in a wild tangle, giving him the look of some fae creature, though the curse that now slipped between his lips was spoken with a brackish Yorkshire accent.

'Your cab?' She didn't let go of the handle. 'It looked to me as though we arrived at the same time.'

'I was here first. Fractionally, I'll admit, but first, nonetheless.' He thrust one suitcase inside, then a second, the leather on both so battered and beaten she was half surprised they didn't split apart. 'I am usually more chivalrous, but I hope you can believe me when I tell you I have had a day from hell – a *year* from hell actually – and that I need this carriage more than you do.'

He was climbing into it, and Evelyn had but a split second to decide. The station was dark, the last train having left some time ago, and there would be no more cabs until the ball was over. If she didn't clamber into this one, she could be waiting here for hours – or worse, be at the mercy of Lady Violet's private carriage. She imagined having to walk back into that room, having to swallow the cloying scent of flowers and ask for such a favour, and it made her grip the handle all the tighter.

'It cannot be any worse than my evening has been,' she said, stepping inside, 'so I am afraid we shall have to share.'

The cab was small and cramped, and had his case not been placed between them, pressing Evelyn to the edge of the low seat, they would have been sat thigh to thigh. 'Let me guess,' he said, a lilt to his voice now. 'You went to that fancy party they're having at the hotel. But your golden carriage didn't arrive, and now you must flee from it in a common Hackney?' He looked down at her feet, as though he could see well enough in the quiet gloom around them.

'I certainly don't see any glass slippers. So, if you're not a pauper transformed into a princess, you must have another reason for leaving so early.'

She pursed her lips. 'How do you know there's a party?'

'Because I have ears,' he said, raising his dark eyebrows. 'But seeing as it's not late, and the party is in full swing, and you are the only person out here . . . I can only conclude that something must have happened.'

Evelyn met his eye. 'Perhaps I just hate parties.'

'No one hates parties.'

'Perhaps I do.'

He shunted a half-laugh through his lips. 'Maybe that's because you always leave them immediately? Here, let me do you a favour. You stay, enjoy the party, and I'll take this cab to my inn.'

'Here's another idea,' Evelyn said with a smile. 'How about *you* stay, and I'll take the cab home?'

'Well now, that wouldn't work. You're dressed for it, like a dazzling peacock. Whereas I' – he gestured down at his plain brown suit – 'am not.'

'I won't go back there.' She found she couldn't hold his gaze in the way she could with other people. It was like grasping a hot poker from the fire, and it sent a flutter to her stomach. She turned to stare down at her white lace gloves instead. 'You will have to come around to this idea of sharing.'

'And what if we are not going in the same direction?' He pressed.

'Then the driver shall have to take a convoluted route,' Evelyn retorted, as said driver's snore began to waft through the window.

A smile still curled at his lips, though there was an air of exasperation about him now. 'You cannot expect me to believe a lady such as yourself, dressed as you are—'

'Like a peacock?' she supplanted.

'I said a *dazzling* peacock – it was a compliment – that a lady such as yourself has only one way of getting home? Don't all you people have private carriages?'

Evelyn quirked an eyebrow. 'All us people?'

He waved a vague hand towards her. 'Ladies and lords. The folk with money.'

'I am not one of them,' she replied. 'I have nothing. I *am* nothing.'

'Hah!' His voice was suddenly louder. 'Now, I know *that* to be a lie.'

'I don't lie,' Evelyn said simply. She held out her gloved hand. 'My name is Miss Seaton, and I can most ardently promise you I am not one of "the folk with money".'

'Well, I am William,' he said, not taking her hand.

'Just "William"?' It was highly improper not to offer a last name, though the curling grin upon his face seemed to suggest that this had been entirely the point.

'*Everybody* lies, Miss Seaton. You can't get through this life without it.'

'I don't,' she said firmly.

William opened his mouth and closed it again. 'So, do you mean to tell me that if someone asks you how well they look in a dress that makes them seem like a trussed-up sausage, you would look them in the eye and tell them so?'

Evelyn tilted her head to one side. 'There are kinder ways to put it, but yes, I would be honest with them.'

William laughed, a rich, warm sound that filled the small space. 'Then you're a better friend than I. Or a worse one, depending on who is doing the asking. Most people do not take criticism well.'

'Is it a criticism if I say that other dresses suit them better?'

'I will let you debate that with your lot,' he said, leaning towards her, so close that his hair brushed her cheek. He smelled like dust and sage, and for a mad moment she wondered if he was going to kiss her. Then he reached for the handle and swung it outwards. 'Off you go. Ask them. I would say you can report their answer back to me, but that *would* be a lie, for I have every intention of leaving the instant you step out.'

Evelyn gave him a flat look, before reaching to slam the carriage door. The sound seemed to finally wake the driver, who gave a startled: '*Where-to-then?*'

'I wasn't lying,' she said through gritted teeth. 'I have no other way home. So, tell me where we can drop you and your bags, and I shall take you on my way.'

William narrowed his eyes. 'There is a story there. I can sense it. Not Cinderella, perhaps, no pumpkins or mice . . . but something. I am a writer, you know. I have a nose for these things.'

'Good for you,' she said. 'I am sure whatever story you make up will be far more exciting than what actually happened.'

'Aha!' He gave her a bright smile. 'So something *did* happen? Come now, you must tell me. I survive on stories. Without them, I would surely perish.'

Evelyn gave him the sweetest smile she could muster. 'Then tell me *where* you will wither away so that I can drop you there.'

He gave her a look of mock-injury. 'You don't care a jot, do you?'

'No, because you are merely exaggerating. Which I suppose is another writerly trait?'

He looked at her then, and she felt her stomach flutter anew, though instead of another witticism, he said: 'Coney Street. The inn there.'

'Coney Street?' She recognized the name, but she could not think why. 'Aren't you from here? I had thought from your accent that you were.'

'I'm from here.' Now he sounded genuinely affronted. 'Do I *look* like a tourist?'

Evelyn shook her head. 'I'd just assumed you'd have a house to go to.'

'I do.' He cleared his throat. 'I just . . .' He shook his head. 'The inn will be fine, thank you.'

She narrowed her eyes. 'There's a story *there*,' she said. 'I'm no writer, but even I can sense it.'

'No, there is not,' he said curtly. 'And I am tired, and I've had a long journey. So if we really must share a cab, then perhaps we can do so quietly?'

'Interesting that when the glass shoe is on the other foot, you've suddenly nothing to say,' she muttered, before casting her voice out of the window. 'Long Close Lane by way of Coney Street, please.'

And the carriage rattled forwards into the night.

Chapter Ten

Evelyn had been lucky enough to avoid her mother when she arrived home – Cecilia had gone to bed early – but she could not avoid her at breakfast, no matter how long she'd dawdled in her room, brushing out her curling brown hair, fiddling with the buttons on her high-necked morning dress.

Last night, she'd dreamed of the man from the carriage, except in her dream he'd not sat in sullen silence the entire ride home. Instead, he'd told her stories, fantastical ones of carriages and mice, and his words had hung in the air like sparks, leaving behind a shadow of smoke where they'd been. She'd awoken to a rocking sensation, as though she were sat in the carriage still, and it had taken her a moment to realize she was in her truckle bed, and that the rocking was merely the springs digging into her spine each time she moved.

Now, they sat together in the kitchen, a bowl of boiled eggs and a rack of toast in front of them. The grate was cooling, the windows open to allow the morning breeze and the smell of cut grass into the room.

'Well, come on then.' Cecilia's face was bright. 'Tell me *everything*! Who was there?'

Evelyn reached for a piece of cold toast, casting a sideways glance at Aunt Clara, who was pretending not to listen from behind a battered issue of *Home Notes* magazine.

'A few of the ladies we met in London. They were as barbed as ever.'

Her mother gave her a flat look. 'I hope you didn't cause another argument.'

'I was polite,' Evelyn said truthfully, 'but I cannot say the same for them.'

Her mother rolled her eyes. 'I don't understand why you rub against people so! Is it really that difficult to be friendly?'

'I *am* friendly.'

'Clearly not, if they all treat you so harshly. Those ladies have never been anything but delightful towards me.'

'To your face, Mother. What they say behind your back is another matter entirely.'

Aunt Clara snorted behind her magazine, and then turned the page loudly to try to cover it.

'You see! This is what I mean. You are so distrustful of people. Who is to say they speak cruelly behind our backs at all? Just because you assume the worst of people doesn't mean that we all do – nor that we should.'

Evelyn took a bite of her toast, chewing and chewing as though it would save her from ever having to speak again. She could not tell her mother what they had said – that Lady Violet and the others had laughed at her, at her beginnings, that they'd accused her mother of being the reason they'd lost the house in Riccall.

It would break her heart.

Cecilia sighed. 'Very well. If you're going to go into one of your silent stupors, tell me instead who you danced with? Did you bring your dance card home, as I asked?'

'I did,' Evelyn said, taking another bite.

'Well then? Let me see.'

She hesitated before sliding it across the table.

Cecilia stared at it for what seemed like eternity. 'Is this a jest?'

'No.' Evelyn reached for another piece of toast, keeping her focus on carefully spreading the warm butter onto cold bread.

'You danced with *one man*?'

'Not exactly.'

'Oh.' Cecilia's tone brightened. 'So, there were more men? You just didn't use your card?'

Evelyn reached for the jam. 'I didn't dance with anyone, Mother.'

Aunt Clara sucked in a breath from behind her magazine, and for a moment, the room was quiet.

'What did you say?'

Evelyn looked at her mother. 'You heard me, Mama. But it was not out of insolence, I promise you. I just . . . I couldn't.'

'You *couldn't*? But you had all those dance lessons! Before your debut! Don't tell me you were too scared?'

'I wasn't scared to dance,' Evelyn said carefully.

'Well, then what? Did you hide yourself in a corner again? Oh, Evelyn, *tell me you didn't*.'

'There is more to life than balls, Mother. And more to do than simply wait around for a proposal! It is not 1850 any longer—'

'More's the pity,' muttered Aunt Clara.

'—why, I have read of women becoming doctors, and more and more women these days are choosing to have careers of their own. Perhaps having husbands will go out of fashion entirely—'

'Evelyn,' said Cecilia, her voice dangerously quiet, 'tell me you did not hide away in the corner all night?'

'I didn't hide anywhere, Mother. I just . . .' *I left.* 'I don't think anyone but Nathaniel would have asked me anyway.'

'*Nathaniel?* You're on first name terms with this Mr Morris already?' Her mother's eyes were sharp upon her, her fingers tapping a jittering melody into the wood.

Aunt Clara's magazine folded down. 'Do you know, Cecilia, dear, I think we need more bread.'

'He's American,' Evelyn explained. 'They don't stand much on etiquette over there. He asked me to call him Nathaniel.'

'Well, unless you have engaged yourself to him, you must call him Mr Morris.'

Aunt Clara cleared her throat. 'But of course, I cannot walk all the way to the market. Not with my creaking bones.'

Evelyn rolled her eyes. 'Very well. Mr Morris invited me to dance, though how much he wished to do so and how much he was forced to is a debatable matter.'

'Forced to? By whom?'

'Lady Violet all but pushed him towards me.'

'Lady Violet was *clearly* trying to help! You forget that I've seen you at these events, my darling. I know how you hide. Like a spider spinning its web! I should have asked to come with you, but I do so hate asking after an invitation that is not given. It feels debasing.'

Evelyn knew why Lady Violet had not invited her mother – so that she could spend the evening disparaging her. But she didn't say that. Instead, she said: 'I am sorry that it didn't go well.'

'Not as sorry as I am,' her mother said, turning her gaze to the table, to the untouched egg in its white porcelain cup.

Beside her, Aunt Clara cleared her throat. 'Is no one going to volunteer to go to the market for bread? Are we to starve to death in this cold, cold kitchen?'

'It is the end of May, Aunt Clara. It is hardly cold,' Cecilia snapped.

'I will go,' Evelyn said, standing quickly. Anything to be

free of her mother's disappointment. 'If you make me a list, I can fetch everything we need.'

'At least *someone* listens to me,' Aunt Clara said, unfolding a scrap of paper from her pocket and sliding it across the table. 'I've written some directions on it, too. Walk straight until you hit the bridge, then keep going. If you reach the Minster, you've gone too far. And dress soberly, my dear – none of this coloured silk business. Markets are no place for a lady of means, but an ordinary woman will fare just fine.'

'What a preposterous idea!' Her mother's face was turning red. 'Evelyn is not an ordinary woman. Aunt Clara, you will ensure she goes with Mrs Billingham in her cart.'

'But, Mama' – Evelyn met her gaze – 'Aunt Clara is right. I'm not a lady anymore – not one of means, anyhow.'

'Of course you are a lady! You were presented before Queen Victoria! How many common women do you imagine have curtseyed before the Queen?'

'Be that as it may, Mrs Billingham can't be at your beck and call,' said Aunt Clara.

Evelyn's mother rose from the table then, pushing a sharp breath between her teeth. 'You think this is play-acting? You think it a novelty to walk to the market, to buy your own bread and cheese? You will not think it a novelty when you are counting the coins in your pocket and wondering how to make them stretch another week. You have *no idea* what I endured to give you the life you lead, Evelyn. If you did, you would not make me suffer so.' She gave her daughter a sharp, trembling look. 'Now, if you will both excuse me, I fear you have given me a migraine.'

She swept from the room, and Evelyn turned to her great-aunt with wide eyes. 'I did not imagine she'd react so strongly to the idea of me going to the market.'

Aunt Clara shook her head. 'Your mother became a lady

by acting like one. I imagine she believes she may stop being one in much the same way.'

'Perhaps,' Evelyn said with a sigh. 'But we must face the truth eventually.'

Evelyn's route to the market stretched the full way down Walmgate, the road that connected the clustered, cobbled city centre with the factories, the squashed terraced houses and timberyards to the east. She hadn't taken herself into the city yet, and when Naomi had walked with her home, it had been dark and quiet. Now, she noticed the metallic *thunk* of the ironworks bouncing off the brick walls, the sharp hiss of steam that whistled from the milliner's. Some of the houses had hung their laundry between their upper windows and as the sweet scent of soap drifted down Evelyn thought again of Naomi, and the lavender that had been pressed between her bundle of sheets.

It hit her then. *Coney Street*. Of course! The road that the odd, handsome man from the train station had asked to go was the very same road she and Naomi had walked down to reach the Black Swan Inn. Was that where he was staying? The same inn where Naomi had taken a fancy to one of the night porters?

It seemed quite a coincidence in a place so large as York. Riccall had certainly been small enough for the world to rotate on a much tighter axis, but here in the city, it felt different – as though being surrounded by people somehow made you less noticeable. Another person might have hated that idea, but not Evelyn. She relished blending with the dark brick, with the sober outfits of the women that walked past her. You would have to look closely to notice how fine the fabric on her tweed suit was or that the cuffs were threaded with silver, and no one on Walmgate was walking slowly enough to look closely. Even the carriages that passed were going at quite the pace – horses hauling cages of live chickens, crates of vegetables and sacks of flour, all come from the farmland outside the city walls, all heading, as she was, to the market.

As she neared the city centre, some of the grey clouds above began to dissipate, revealing patches of blue sky and sunshine that spilled like honey over the rooftops. She could see the river sparkling in the distance, and for a moment it was beautiful enough to lift some of the weight that had settled on her chest: the look on her mother's face, the disappointment that had sat behind her eyes. Evelyn knew her mother didn't want to hear that their social stars had fallen. Her mother wished for them to go back: back to Riccall, back to their grand old house, back to being the sorts of women who were waited upon, women of means, of status. But if last night had taught Evelyn anything, it was that they didn't belong in that world anymore. The balls and dinners, the afternoons spent making calls and the days spent at the hunt. If it had ever belonged to them, it didn't anymore.

Her father had made sure of that, not to mention Lady Violet.

What Evelyn didn't know was what that meant. If they could not go back, then where could they go? How could they rebuild their life?

As she was passing over Foss Bridge, she stopped abruptly. On her last journey into the city with Mrs Billingham, her neighbour had pointed out the crooked structure on the bridge as the Lamplighter's Bookshop, but the faded sign most definitely read *Morton's Emporium* – the bookshop from the leaflet she'd seen last night.

It grew up from the street like a wizened old tree, each of the three floors an overgrown branch dangling precariously over the one beneath it. Built of the same medieval black oak beams that peppered the inner city, it teetered above its neighbours and cast a long, crooked shadow onto the cobblestone bridge. Smoke puffed from the steep roof, despite the warmth of the day, and Evelyn imagined she could smell the sweet scent of a wood fire.

Perhaps it was soot that had stained the building's walls, turning them from a creamy white to a flecked grey that was fading and flaking, just like the windows: a patchwork of square-cut glass in a sliding scale of yellow, the oldest being so sun-stained and opaque it was a wonder anyone could see through. You certainly couldn't see much of the bookshop within, just a handful of books on display at the front: a beautifully bound book of hours that looked ancient, a complete set of encyclopaedias and a copy of Bram Stoker's *Dracula* with the word *NEW* on a small sign beside it, though Evelyn was sure she had read it through the subscription library a full year ago.

The interior looked dark, and she wondered whether it was closed.

It was only then she noticed the mismatched gargoyles that flanked the door: one with its stone muzzle drawn up over its teeth, the other rather more placid, with its tongue hanging from its jaw. On one of them hung an *exceedingly* small sign – declaring that the shop was, in fact, *open*, and suggesting that visitors come in and *shout*, for the bell wasn't working.

The oak door sighed on its hinges as Evelyn stepped inside.

Chapter Eleven

'Come in!' an unseen voice called from the depths of the shop. 'I'll be right with you.'

It took her eyes a moment to adjust to the gloom. From the outside, she'd thought it would feel small and cramped, but when she looked up, she saw that the bookshelves to her left and right extended all the way to the top of the second floor, each with a dizzyingly tall ladder pressed against them. In the far corners were two matched, curling staircases, leading up to a shared mezzanine from which she imagined you could look down and see everything: including how to walk through the labyrinthine maze of shelves before her. They were arranged haphazardly, so that you needed to zigzag between them, and there was a layer of dust coating everything that made it seem as though a snowstorm had recently blown through.

'Good day, madam.' The voice came from behind her, and Evelyn started. She had assumed the shopkeeper was upstairs, but as she turned, she realized the man had come from an archway in the wall that was cloaked in shadow. 'In need of a book?'

Though he was broad shouldered, he had the hunch of a man who'd spent his life trying to appear smaller than he was.

If she were to guess from the laughter lines at the edges of his eyes and the straight creases upon his forehead, he was roughly of an age with her mother. His dark hair was thrown into a messy knot at the nape of his neck, and his beard clearly had not been trimmed in a long while. His eyes, though, were kind – and brightly fixed upon her through his circular spectacles.

'Are you looking for something particular?'

Evelyn shook her head and pulled the crumpled piece of paper from her purse. 'I saw your advertisement,' she said. 'About needing help.' Looking around, she understood it, too. It was a mess in here: a dust-encased mess.

'My advertisement?' The man blinked rapidly. 'What advertisement?'

She pushed the paper into his hands, damp from where it had been clutched in her palm.

He unfolded it, the frown-line between his eyebrows deepening. 'Where did you get this?'

'The station,' she said, 'though I think it must have blown away from somewhere. It wasn't pinned.'

'Curious,' said the man, narrowing his eyes at her. 'I wrote this, of course – you can see my signature here.' He pointed to an illegible scribble. 'But I stopped short of sending them out. Perhaps the bookshop sent them.'

Evelyn hesitated. 'The bookshop?'

'Yes,' he said, quite serious. 'I believe it does that sometimes. My father never believed, but I do.' He reached to stroke the nearest wall with the same care and attention with which one might pet a cat.

'It . . . sends out leaflets?'

'They were on my desk. No doubt a sensible man would say a gust came in through the window and carried them all the way to the station. After all, that's more logical, isn't it? But I know better.' He wiggled his eyebrows at her, and she wondered for a moment whether she'd met this man before.

'May I ask why you decided not to send them out? The leaflets?'

'Ah, yes.' He gave her a brief smile. 'I decided I didn't need help.'

Evelyn glanced at the unwashed windows. 'I'd beg to differ, Mr—'

'Morton,' the man replied, pushing his glasses up his nose, which had a sheen of oil upon it. 'My family has owned this bookshop for generations.'

'I see,' she said, turning her gaze away from a layer of dust so thick it looked like sheep's wool. 'So then, why did you change the name?'

The man blinked. 'I'm sorry?'

'The name of the bookshop. I have heard it called the Lamplighter's Bookshop, but the sign outside reads *Morton's Emporium*. When did you change it?'

Mr Morton rubbed at the back of his neck. 'Ah, well, you see, when my great-grandfather opened it, people called it that as a bit of a . . . well, a bit of a snub, I suppose. They didn't imagine a lamplighter had any business running a bookshop, a sentiment that perhaps my great-grandfather feared was right. He named the place Morton's Emporium, in the hope that people would forget that a lamplighter had ever owned it.' He shrugged. 'You can't control which nicknames stick, I suppose.'

'And you've always run it on your own?'

He shook his head and began to walk away, beckoning Evelyn to follow. The hardwood floor beneath their feet was occasionally peppered with the odd fraying rug, though there seemed to be no consistency in the colour or the style, and they walked from red to blue to orange to a horribly faded brown in the space of a few, winding shelves.

'My nephew used to help.' Mr Morton's gaze was distant, but his smile brightened like the sunlight pressing against the windows. 'Now he's an author – got a publishing deal from a big press down in London, you see. I'll need an entire shelf just for him soon.'

Evelyn sidestepped a pile of books that had been left upon the floor. 'So, you've been alone since he left for London?'

Mr Morton looked back at her over the top of his brass-rimmed glasses. 'Have experience as a shop assistant, do you?'

'None,' Evelyn said cheerily, 'but I'm willing to learn.' She picked up one of the books from where it had fallen, leaves-first, upon a shag rug. It was only when she tried to squeeze it back onto the shelf that she realized why it had fallen in the first place. The books were packed as tightly as wet sand, the row straining in the middle. She laid it gently on top instead. 'Do you know,' she continued, 'I have never stepped foot in this bookshop before. What does that tell you?'

Mr Morton raised two bushy eyebrows. 'That you would not be the best choice of assistant if I were to hire one.'

'No,' Evelyn said, though she realized belatedly that she could have phrased it more elegantly. 'That the outside of your shop isn't very inviting.'

The man looked affronted. 'I have a sign.'

'A very small sign.'

'An averagely sized sign.'

She raised her eyebrows and stepped past him to the nearest shelf. The books were all piled one atop the other, such that she couldn't even read the spines. 'Have you ever been to a subscription library?'

The man gave her an interested look. 'Why should *I* join a *subscription library*?'

'They have a marvellous way of ordering all their books.

Firstly by type and then by author name. How do you organize the books here?'

Mr Morton tapped his temple. 'You tell me which book you are looking for, and I shall find it for you.'

She narrowed her eyes. 'I'm sorry?'

'Go on.' He crossed his thick arms over his chest, and she realized how broad he was – bear-like, almost, though he held himself like a dormouse. 'Try me.'

She scrunched up her nose. 'What have you by Emma Brooke?'

He was silent for a moment, and then: '*A Fair Country Maid* is on the top floor, fifth shelf, third in. *Superfluous Woman* is somewhat more racy, and so it's on a lower shelf – I don't like to hide the outrageous books like other shops do; I rather think it sets me apart if I display them more prominently – so that would be the fourth shelf, just below eye level, and if you start by looking at the middle of the shelf, it'll be somewhere to your right.'

'I see,' Evelyn said with a small smile. 'And what if I had walked in with no idea of which book I would like to buy?'

He blinked at her. 'If you don't know which book you would like, then why walk into a bookshop?'

'To browse?'

His eyebrows furrowed. 'I suppose one *could*.'

'And say I *was* browsing, how would I happen upon Miss Brooke's work? And how should I know that another of her novels is on a higher shelf?'

'I would tell you,' he said with a shunted breath.

'And if you were busy?'

'Why should I be busy?'

'With another customer, perhaps?'

He frowned once more. 'It's unlikely I'd have two people in this shop at once.'

Evelyn reckoned from the sheer size of the bookshop that

there should be a sea of people in here, one down every shelf-created alleyway. But it was empty.

'I imagine, Mr Morton, that if you made a few, simple changes, such as keeping the door open and dusting and cleaning the windows and reordering the shelves, then you'd find you had a great many more people in here.'

He pursed his lips. 'I am not a two-penny bookshop, Miss—'

'Seaton.'

'Miss Seaton. I am a connoisseur of novels. I buy only the *best* narratives, and I collect rare works of art. Did you see the book of hours in the window?'

'The gold-leaf prayer book?'

He nodded. 'Some say it was owned by Anne Boleyn herself – clutched in her very hands the night before she was sent to her death. That book is one of a kind. Those pages hold a story that none other can attest to. *Those* are the books I sell here, Miss Seaton. And if the shop is empty, then perhaps it is because the people I am trying to attract are not the sort one finds on Foss Bridge every hour of the day.'

She realized that he had walked her all the way back to the front door, which he now held open, the noise from the street wafting into the cool, dripping silence of the shop. 'The answer is no, Miss Seaton. I thank you for your concern, but I do not need help. I can manage just fine on my own.'

Somewhere in the depths of the bookshop, she heard the *slither-thunk* of a stack of books losing their battle with gravity and sliding to the floor.

'I disagree, Mr Morton. I believe I could be a great help here.'

'How very charitable of you,' he said, flourishing a hand towards the busy street.

'Not charitable at all. You would be helping me, too, you see. A job would be . . .' The words caught in her throat.

'I need a job most urgently, Mr Morton. Almost as urgently as you need my help.'

'Good day to you, Miss Seaton.' His smile was kind, but his tone was firm, and she saw in the flickering muscle of his jaw that it would do no good to simply stand here and toss this same ball back and forth. He did not seem the type of man who responded well to that kind of thing.

'Very well,' she said, though there was no defeat in her voice. As she cast a final glance into the gloom behind the door, she felt a prickle at the back of her neck, as though something looked back at her. Which was preposterous, because Mr Morton was standing beside her in the warming sunshine, and she knew, logically, that there was nothing through the door but stories and paper. 'But I promise you this: you *will* see me again.'

Mr Morton sighed. 'I imagine I will.'

Chapter Twelve

In the days after meeting Mr Morton, a plan began to form in Evelyn's mind, and it solidified on Monday evening as they sat in the morning room, Aunt Clara clucking at Cecilia because she was running out of candles at a rate of knots, and they were, of course, to blame.

'How long do you plan to stay here?' Aunt Clara chided. 'How long until that husband of yours settles his debts? How many candles, how many loaves of bread do you expect me to keep paying for?'

'I am sure it won't be for much longer, Aunt Clara,' Cecilia said wearily. 'I am sure John has it all in hand.'

'Oh, yes. I am sure he does. From his *sponging-house*.'

'I could get a job,' Evelyn said, putting down her book. 'Then we would at least have some money.'

'What an excellent idea,' Aunt Clara said.

'Absolutely not.' Her mother's voice took on a sharp edge. 'Ladies do not get *jobs*. They do not *work*. That is what lower class women do.'

'Yes but, Mother, we're not ladies anymore.'

Her mother's gaze turned dark. 'You must stop saying that, Evelyn, lest you begin believing it. We *are* ladies. Your father is still a baron. We are still respectable – despite your best efforts.' She huffed a breath through her teeth. 'It is bad enough that we have been disgraced – you needn't make our temporary stumble more shameful by *succumbing* to it.'

'Only today I was reading about the Marshal of France, who lost his fortune because of his obsession with black magic,' said Aunt Clara.

Cecilia wrinkled her nose. 'Not that nonsense with Ouija boards?'

'It was in the fifteenth century, my dear, so I doubt they had anything so advanced to commune with spirits.'

Evelyn cleared her throat. 'I could work in a shop,' she said, determined not to let Aunt Clara divert the conversation. 'As some kind of assistant.'

'In a *shop*?' Cecilia said it as though Evelyn had suggested drowning a sack of kittens.

'You said we could bend the rules to suit our needs? Well then!' Evelyn gave her mother what she hoped was a confident smile. 'Let us bend them.'

'*Ladies do not work*,' replied Cecilia. 'And that is one rule you *cannot* bend, for as soon as you do, you are no longer a lady!'

Aunt Clara stuck out her bottom lip. 'If you worked in the grocer's, would we get cheaper butter?'

'She cannot work in a *grocer's*!'

'Your grandfather worked in a grocer's,' said Aunt Clara.

'And his granddaughter married a baron, so that *her* children wouldn't need to,' countered Cecilia.

'Then what do you suggest?' Evelyn said. 'Clearly we cannot stay here and eat Aunt Clara out of house and home.'

'No, you cannot,' said Aunt Clara with a huff.

'You can find a way to occupy your time while your father gets his affairs in order,' Cecilia said. 'He *will* fix this. And we will get our house back, and Aunt Clara will be repaid, and all will be well again.'

Evelyn looked at her mother. 'Do you truly believe that?'

'Yes,' Cecilia said resolutely. 'I truly believe it. And in the meantime, if you're feeling restless—'

'I am not *restless*. I am *frustrated*.'

'In the meantime,' Cecilia repeated, 'why don't you go into town and see if Lady Violet has something for you to do? She volunteers on three charity boards, so I imagine she'll welcome the offer of help.' Cecilia gave her an encouraging smile. 'Hmm?'

Aunt Clara huffed. 'What use is a charity to us? Unless there's one specifically for wives whose husbands have pissed their fortune against the wall—'

'Aunt Clara!' Cecilia exclaimed.

'What? All I shall say is that a grocer's assistant would have been more useful.'

'I shall take your advice, Mother,' Evelyn said, for it struck her then that her mother had given her a reason to go into the city – and given her an excuse to be there regularly, too. Of course it would be a lie, but it would a lie by omission. That wasn't quite the same thing, was it? Especially when it was necessary. 'I shall go tomorrow, in fact.'

And so Evelyn went into town every day that week, but she did not see Lady Violet. Instead, she visited the other bookshops: Chapman's on Coney Street, which sold mostly fiction, alongside stationery and typewriters; Pickering's on High Ousegate, which was smaller but meticulously organized; Sampson's, which had its main shop also on Coney Street and had a small kiosk at the train station as well, selling newspapers, serials, and books to travellers.

If she was to get more people into Mr Morton's Emporium, she would have to get them out of Sampson's, and *how* she would do that she was not quite sure.

But she knew a good place to start would be convincing Mr Morton to hire her.

The following Monday morning, Evelyn walked alongside the milkman's carts and the paper boys down the stretching road of Walmgate, heading towards the bookshop. She hadn't known that the brickworks blew their whistle to call the workers to their shifts, but she could hear it now, a piercing blast that blared over the rooftops. She hadn't realized that the greengrocer's and fruiterer's got their deliveries in the same cart, but now she watched it rattle along and unload wooden crates outside each of their doors, the great shire horses snorting. She heard the jingle of a bell beside her and returned a bright 'good morning' to the basket weaver who had come to stack her wares outside the door to better entice people inside. She could feel it, the fizz of a city awakening – could feel the excitement of it running in her own veins. It felt like she was standing on the cusp of something new. Something different. Something *hers*.

By the time she reached the bookshop, most of the merchants on Foss Bridge were open, save the perfumer, which opened at ten, the Red Lion, which opened at eleven, and the Emporium itself. There was a newsstand opposite that sold incredibly weak tea, and she bought a cup for a halfpenny and stood, watching the sun climb ever higher over the river, watching the water sparkle.

She waited.

And waited.

She watched the perfumer open at ten, wafting the sweet smell of lilacs into the street. She returned her empty cup to the man at the newsstand, who looked at her pityingly and asked if she'd like another. Then the Red Lion opened at eleven, the smell of old smoke and in-trodden ale creeping from the doors and windows. She watched as the barman brought a rug outside and hung it over the bridge's edge, not to beat the dust from it as she'd first assumed, but so it could dry in the sunshine.

And still she waited.

By the time she heard the broken clang of the Emporium's bell, she'd counted six people peering in its windows, two of whom had even tried the door, though both had walked towards the handle as though it were more likely to bite them than open.

By the time Mr Morton appeared at the doorway, Evelyn had long returned the little china cup from her second drink of tea, and her feet were beginning to feel sore from standing so still for so long.

'Ah,' Mr Morton said, rubbing at the back of his neck as he spotted her. 'I had rather hoped you would leave.'

He was wearing an untidy brown suit, and his hair was loose over his shoulders. It was longer than she'd imagined and frizzier, too. Evelyn crossed the street, a bubble of frustration in her stomach.

'You knew I was out here?'

'Why, yes,' he said. 'I live above the shop, you see.' He pointed up, past the faded sign and the broken lamps that flanked it. 'I have a little window that looks down upon the bridge.'

She bristled. 'So you *deliberately* kept the shop closed?'

'No, no,' he said sincerely. 'I open it once I've had my breakfast and seen to my chores.'

She raised an eyebrow. 'It is practically midday.'

'I am aware,' he said good-naturedly. 'I had a lot of chores.'

Evelyn folded her arms over her chest. 'Do you know how many people have walked past and stopped to look in your window, even tried to come inside, this morning?'

Mr Morton pushed his glasses up his nose. 'I suspect you're about to tell me.'

'Six,' she said. 'Seven if you count the paperboy, who spent a full five minutes with his nose pressed to the glass looking at the encyclopaedias.'

'I don't believe Gregory can read,' said Mr Morton. 'He was probably admiring the binding. I do it myself, you know.'

Evelyn narrowed her eyes. 'How much does an average book cost?'

'In my shop there is no such thing as an *average book*.'

'Very well,' Evelyn said. 'But I imagine that's a least a few pounds you've lost in one morning.'

'Assuming they would have bought something and not merely touched everything before walking out,' Mr Morton replied. 'If they truly want a book, they'll come back. Everyone knows I have no set opening time.'

'Sampson's on Coney Street opens before nine. And he has a bookstand that opens even earlier, in time for the first train in.'

'Sampson is a glorified newsagent,' Mr Morton huffed. 'True readers come to me.'

'They would if you were open,' Evelyn said. 'But how many will remember to come back once they've been past the butcher's and into the market? You could *double* your business by opening earlier.'

Mr Morton studied her, his gaze flicking over her plain black skirt and white linen blouse, then coming to rest upon the raven feather hat pinned into her hair. She had dressed as she imagined a bookseller's assistant might, although perhaps the hat had been too much.

'You really think I need help?'

'I think you'll do much more with it than without it,' Evelyn said, following his retreating back into the shop. 'Hire me, and I'll open the shop at nine for you every day. I'll sweep the dust from the shelves and make recommendations and think up ways we can attract more people inside. I'll even help you organize the books.'

'They *are* organized,' he huffed, disappearing behind a shelf. '*This* is why I decided not to hire anyone. I don't like people *meddling*.'

'Meddling suggests that things are perfect the way they are, Mr Morton. And, if I may be so bold, I do not believe that is true.' They were of a height, and she looked straight into his kind, brown eyes. 'Hire me,' she said. 'Give me a trial for six months or so – say, until Christmas. If I am right, you will make my wages twice over.'

'And if you're wrong?' Mr Morton said.

'Then you may undo all I've done, and we shall part ways amicably,' she said. 'But I shan't be wrong. You'll see.'

He took his glasses off, pinching the bridge of his nose. 'You have spirit, Miss Seaton. Has anyone ever told you that?'

'Once or twice,' Evelyn said.

He kept his gaze upon her. 'It'll be hard work, you know. Have you ever stood so long on your feet that it felt like there were needles pressing into the soles of them? Ever woken up with your body as tired as it was when you fell into bed the night before? *That* is what hard work feels like, Miss Seaton. It hurts. It's tiring. It's a commitment, and one that you must step to even on the days when you want to crawl back into bed. So, before I hold out my hand, before we shake on this, I want you to be quite sure.'

She raised her chin. 'I know what you think you see in me,' she said firmly. 'You think you see a lady of means, one that has done naught but lift a sewing needle all her life. Well, I'm not that, Mr Morton. Not anymore. I am willing to work. I am willing to commit. If you'll just give me the chance, I'll show you all I can do.'

He looked away, untucking the edge of his shirt to clean

his glasses. 'Do you know,' he said quietly, 'I find I believe you.' He replaced his spectacles and held out his hand. 'I'll pay you the same as I paid my nephew: a pound and two a week, so long as you can do the same job as him from Monday to Friday, and sell the same number of books as he did. And as you suggest, we'll revisit it at Christmas.'

'What about weekends?'

'Only I come in on the weekends,' said Mr Morton. 'Saturday we're quiet, and Sunday we're meant to be closed. Monday to Friday will be quite enough, don't you think?'

Evelyn nodded. One pound and two shillings a week. Which meant she would earn around fifty-seven pounds in a year. Surely that would be enough to rent somewhere? Even if it was minuscule! Even if it only had two bedrooms, and a kitchen. And possibly a garden big enough for herbs?

She grinned at Mr Morton, a wide, childish beam. 'Thank you,' she said, gripping his calloused fingers. 'You won't regret it.'

'Ah, but you might,' he said. There was a curling smile to his lips now, gathering the wrinkles to the corners of his eyes. 'Now, follow me, and we shall get started.'

Chapter Thirteen

While Evelyn explored the bookshop, William Morton awoke to a thud on his door. He sat up groggily, pushing his dark hair from his face, and marked with a distant kind of disgust that he needed to wash. He'd spent too many days in this small room, with its thorn-spring bed and its guttering tallow candle – too many days circling the same ten steps between the tight walls.

The thud came again.

'Will? Are you up?'

It was Jack's voice at the door, and William turned a bleary eye to the window, where the bright, midday sunshine creeped through the panes.

'What are you doing awake?' Will croaked. 'Weren't you working all night?'

'Mr Hillock needs the room back tomorrow, so he says tonight's your last night.' The door opened a crack. 'Sorry.'

'Get in here,' Will said, sitting up. 'No need to advertise my eviction to the rest of the hallway.'

Jack sidled into the room. He'd been scrawny as a boy, but now they were both in their twenties, he'd filled out and grown into his ears a little, too. His nose was still crooked from their schoolyard scrap with Larry Davies, and his hair – lighter than William's, a reddish-brown – still curled a little where it fell down over his forehead.

He fixed William a familiar, lopsided smile. 'Misfortune my foot. Yer might've had a reputation for poor luck before, what with every newspaper in York refusing you as a writer—'

William groaned.

'And then that failed poetry venture?' Jack made a face. 'But now look! No man who's come back from London with as much gold in his pocket and as much promise in his future can say he's still a victim of *poor luck*. I'm happy for you, Will. I'm sure it's the Bible that says a wise man makes more opportunities than he finds, and yer carved this one out all by yourself.'

Will smiled, though a prickly feeling had begun to poke at his stomach. 'I think that was Francis Bacon, actually.'

Jack shrugged. 'All the same. You should be proud. I know I am. And you know who else will be?'

Will's smile stretched painfully. 'Don't say Uncle Howie,' he said, and crossed to the window, easing it open. He could taste something sweet in the air. The confectioners nearby perhaps, boiling sugar for candied peel.

'O'course Uncle Howie. I still can't believe you've not seen him yet.'

'You know why.' William turned his gaze back to the window. He had a lovely view of bricks, for the buildings had been constructed too closely together. He was almost tempted to reach out and try to touch the wall opposite, but he didn't. 'If I go back there, Uncle Howard will have me stacking shelves, when I should be finishing my novel. I only have a few chapters completed, and my publishers aren't giving me money for nothing, you know.'

'Right now they are,' Jack said, picking up a shirt from where Will had slung it on the floor and hanging it on the back of the lone chair. 'Mad that they'll pay you on the promise of what you'll write. What if this book of yours is crap?'

Will snorted. 'Such confidence in me, Jack. I appreciate it.'

'Hear me out!' Jack sat on the chair, which creaked worryingly. 'Don't you think it's mad that they've read your work and gone: "Well, he's got some talent, that lad," and then they've agreed to pay you, in advance, to write the rest of it? And you've just, what, promised 'em you will? Nodded yer head and said, "Yes, o'course, sirs, and it'll be great, sirs," and now yer back up here?'

'You make it sound easy,' Will said, not looking at him. 'You don't know what it's like, to take your work to place after place, to wait outside countless offices, talking to faceless men over and over again only to hear the same rejection, the same criticism.'

'Ah, but you got there in the end.' Jack gave him a bright smile. 'As the good Lord says, experience is just the name we give our mistakes.'

'That was Oscar Wilde,' William said. 'My point was just that it's hard. And besides, I still have to *write* the novel. They've seen a few pages, sure, but I have to complete it.'

'And how's that going?'

'Wonderfully,' said William brightly.

'Really?' Jack raised two thick eyebrows. ''Cos I've not seen a single scrap of paper on that table since you arrived.'

'How do you know I don't hide them when you come in?'

'Oh, right.' There was a mischievous glint in Jack's eye. 'So, if I check these drawers, I'll find fistfuls of new pages, will I?'

Jack hovered a finger over the handle, and William sighed.

'Very well! You are right – I've done nothing since I came back to York.'

'I knew it.' Jack said in a self-satisfied way. 'Here's me, sticking my neck out for yer, and you're sat in this room – day in, day out, from the smell of it – doing naught but drinking downstairs when you know I'm there to disappear the tab.'

'That's not true,' Will said, with mock offence. 'I drink in the bar even when you're not there.'

'Well then. For all the good turns I've done you, perhaps you can give me a hand with something tonight.'

It was Will's turn to grimace. 'Not with that drunkard again?'

'What? No, no.' Jack rolled his eyes. 'I'm finally going out with that Miss Clark, and she said she would bring a chaperone.'

'A chaperone?' Will's eyebrows shot up. 'How very proper.'

'She *is* very proper,' Jack said, with a hint of steel in his voice. 'She is a very sweet lady.'

'A sweet lady who asked *you* to dinner?'

Jack folded his arms over his chest. 'That's not what happened.'

'Oh, no, you're right,' William said. 'She started the sentence, and you finished it, so technically *you* asked *her* to dinner.'

'We asked each other at the same time.'

He waggled his eyebrows at his friend. 'Sure you did.'

'Shush,' Jack said, standing and brushing the dust from his trousers. 'Meet me downstairs at a quarter past six tonight. And wash, will yer? And wear something clean?'

William moved to the wash bowl and plucked a snowflake of dust from it. 'I know how to behave around women.'

'Sure you do,' Jack said, turning. 'Quarter past six!'

'Quarter past six,' Will repeated, dabbing water on his face as Jack closed the door. It was lukewarm where it had been sat in the bowl too long, though still cold enough that when he splashed it under his arms and around the base of his neck it made his skin prickle with gooseflesh.

That was it then. His time at the Black Swan Inn was up. He'd half hoped he would be able to hide in this corner room for a lot longer, not least because it was free. Now, he would need to pay for board somewhere else. Which meant he needed money. Which meant . . .

He sighed, staring at himself in the mirror.

Perhaps it was time to see Uncle Howie, and answer all the questions he'd been avoiding.

Just as soon as he was ready.

Chapter Fourteen

Mr Morton showed Evelyn how to open the shop with its stiff lock and gnarled, rusted key. He showed her how to leave the heavy door ajar with an oversized paperweight if the weather was fine and how to attach the ringer back onto the bell if the weather was not.

'I thought the bell was broken,' she said. 'That's what the sign says.'

'It is broken,' Mr Morton said with a smile. 'But you'll hear it clank if someone comes in.'

'Why don't you just replace it?' she asked. 'The lamps above the sign are broken, too.'

'I'll replace them all,' he said. 'Eventually.'

Next, they swept the floor – or rather, Evelyn swept it while Mr Morton gave languid instructions from behind the morning paper, which he occasionally narrated to her: 'Did you hear the prisoners at York are complaining of the air quality? Too smoky, they argue. How very modern.'

Only after he was satisfied that she knew how to ready the shop for opening did he turn to the books, pointing out the individual sections. There was everything: from astrology to history, zoology to spiritualism. There was an entire corner dedicated to the medicinal powers of plants, as well as an entire wall for religious works. The only thing that didn't have a defined place was fiction; instead, the books were arranged based on the closest subject matter, which is how she found *The Jungle Book* squashed amongst the travel tomes.

'Surely that means you must read them all then, to know where to put them?'

'I read as many as I can.' He nodded. 'I bind a good many myself still, and that takes time, so I have the book open while I stitch the leather. Although it means I often don't read the endings.'

Evelyn furrowed her brows. 'Doesn't that drive you mad? Never knowing how it ends?'

'I quite like the not knowing,' he said with a little, inward smile. 'That way I can imagine a happy ending.'

'Even if the true ending is bad?'

'*Especially* if the true ending is bad.' He plucked a book at random from the shelf beside him – *The War of the Worlds* by H.G. Wells, which, she realized, was nestled amongst the military history books. 'Now, you should know that not all the prices are written in the covers.' He opened the hardback, which creaked. 'See? Nothing.'

'So then how will I know how much it costs?'

'You ask me.'

'And if you're not here?'

Mr Morton twitched his nose. 'Let me see – if it's in three separate hardback volumes, start negotiating at three pounds and six. If it's a volume that's been condensed, then it's lower, perhaps as low as six shillings but best to start at nine. If it's a yellowback, then I'll take no less than two shillings for it.'

Evelyn nodded, trying to commit it to memory. *Three pounds, nine shillings, two shillings.* 'I'll remember,' she said, with more confidence than she felt.

'If it's rare, then start the bidding higher.'

'How will I know it's rare?'

'Because I keep them here or in the window,' he said, walking her over to a thick shelf beside the desk.

There must have been twenty tomes upon it, a mixture of all sorts, all beautifully bound. It reminded her of her great-grandfather's library at Riccall Hall, a whole *room* of books from floor to ceiling, each with a spine of gold. Those books would have all been sold now. They would all be gone.

'Now, there is one final thing,' he said. 'There are two rules that you must swear to keep if you are to work here. They are simple rules, and if you follow them, we shall do very well together.'

'Of course,' Evelyn said.

'Rule one: you must always bring me the post the moment it arrives. *The moment.* Even if I am upstairs. Even if I am asleep, you may wake me for the post. If I am out, then tell me the moment I return, although I am very rarely out. I plan my day around the post.'

Evelyn thought that curious but didn't show it. She nodded. 'Of course.'

'And the second rule, and this is very important.' He leaned in closer. 'You must *never* leave the shop unattended. Always lock the door first, for this' – he spread his arms wide – 'this is not just my life's work but my father's and his father's before him. This is all I have, and it is very precious to me. And now I am entrusting its care to you, too.'

'Always bring you the post, never leave the shop unattended,' she repeated, ticking them off on her fingers. 'I understand, Mr Morton.'

'Very good,' he said. 'Now, you may dust. Might I suggest you start with the philosophy section on the mezzanine? I doubt anyone's been up there for years.'

* * *

By the end of the day, her back hurt, her legs were stiff, and her voice felt scratched from breathing in so much dust. She had not made a single sale, because when a customer had finally stepped through the door at a quarter past three, she'd not known what to do, whether she should hover near them or stand back. As it was, she had done a little of both – shouting from across the shop to the customer, a woman who'd jolted at Evelyn's call as though she'd been electrified and then put the book down at once.

At six o'clock, Mr Morton flipped the sign to *closed*, the bell clanking against the door.

'You'll get the hang of it soon enough.' He handed her a key. 'Set up before nine, as I've shown you, and I'll be down at ten. If you need anything desperately, I'm just upstairs.' He pointed at the door tucked into the mezzanine. She'd tried the handle of it earlier, while dusting, but it had been locked. And now she knew why. 'Best to just shout up. As I said, you shouldn't leave the shop unattended.'

'Of course, Mr Morton,' she said. 'I'll remember.'

He held his hand out, his palm scratchy against hers. 'Good work today, Miss Seaton. Good work indeed.'

Chapter Fifteen

Evelyn was in such a daze as she left the bookshop that she did not hear her name being called. She was too busy feeling the ache in her bones, the sleep pulling at her eyelids, but more than all of that put together: pride. For while it wasn't quite as impressive as being amongst the first female doctors, for her it felt just as monumental. She had taken a step today. She had *worked* – and done a good job, to boot.

'Evelyn!'

She turned to find Naomi dressed head to toe in the most beautiful pastel pink, her hair falling in shining tresses down to her shoulders.

'Naomi!' Evelyn said, smiling as she crossed the gap between them. 'What are you doing here?'

'I could ask you the very same.' Naomi smoothed down her skirts, hefting a great, relieved breath from her lungs. 'It's as if the angels heard my prayers!'

Evelyn was momentarily confused. 'You prayed for Mr Morton to give me the job?'

'What? No—' Some of the tautness dropped from Naomi's expression. 'Mr Morton gave you a job?'

'He did,' Evelyn said, feeling a little pride blossom in her chest. 'Five days a week.'

'That's a surprise.' Naomi blew a breath through her teeth. 'I always thought of him as a miser, but Mr Kaye speaks kindly of him, so perhaps I should be more generous in the future. My mother always says: assume less, learn more.'

Evelyn gave Naomi a small smile. 'And how is Mr Kaye, if I may be so bold as to enquire?'

'Well, that's just the thing,' Naomi huffed. 'We're finally going to see each other tonight. He asked – or rather I did. *We both asked*, I suppose would be the sum of it. I started to invite him for tea as in a *cup* of tea, and then he thought I meant tea as in the evening meal and jumped in and invited me to the Blue Bell—'

'That's wonderful!' Evelyn said.

Naomi nodded. '*Except* he misunderstood me. You see, he was talking all polite and saying things like whether *I'd be so kind* as to *care* to *consider* to join him for a bite to eat, and all that nice kind of talk, and so I made a joke about him being such a gentleman that I'd need a chaperone. It was just a compliment! And I thought he understood that I was commenting on how proper he was being. I was trying to encourage him.' She was fidgeting a little now, trailing a short line back and forth in front of Evelyn.

'A fine encouragement,' Evelyn agreed.

'Except he clearly thought I was speaking literally, for *he's* brought a chaperone! They're sitting at the Blue Bell together right now, and if I show up alone, it'll be ungainly and awkward – and what's worse, I'll look improper compared to him!' Naomi gave an exasperated laugh. 'My mother told me, she said: "Nomi, the good Lord rewards plain talking and plentiful prayers," and I agree with her, but I was trying to show off to him, wasn't I? Trying to show him how witty I am, and now look. All I've done is wrap myself into a real web!'

Evelyn reached to place her hands on Naomi's shoulders,

stilling her. 'Then I shall come with you,' she said. Her mother thought she was assisting Lady Violet anyway, so it would not be a massive leap to assume she'd dined with Lady Violet, too. 'And Mr Kaye will never know that you weren't serious, and you will have your long-awaited dinner without feeling improper or ungainly or awkward. I can even do my best to entertain whatever friend he has brought.'

Naomi closed her eyes. 'Thank you,' she said. 'Thank you, thank you, thank you.'

'Nonsense,' said Evelyn, linking her arm into Naomi's. 'You found a lost woman on the roadside, and you walked her home. The least I can do is accompany you for dinner. I just hope I am not dressed too sombrely for an evening meal.'

Naomi laughed: a rich, warm sound. 'You're kidding, surely? You look like you're ready to step into the opera house in that outfit.'

Evelyn looked down at her relatively unembellished skirts, at the delicate lace cuffs of her blouse. But this was her plainest outfit, her most boring hat.

'We're both a little overdressed, if truth be told,' Naomi said. 'But we shall have to celebrate this new job of yours! After all, life will always feel like it has more downs than ups if you forget to honour the good times and only remember the bad.'

'That is also sound advice,' Evelyn said. It felt like her life had consisted of nothing but downs of late, and the thought that she now had something worth clinking a glass to was a buoyant one. 'And secretly, we shall also cheers to your Mr Kaye summoning his courage.'

'Secretly,' Naomi agreed. 'Now come on, the Blue Bell is just around the corner.'

* * *

Evelyn had never been in a place like the Blue Bell before. Her mother ascribed to the old view that eating out too regularly was improper, which was why she'd wrangled them invitations to any number of private dinners during the London seasons. Thus Evelyn could count the number of times she'd eaten out on one hand. Today would be the sixth.

The Blue Bell wasn't a restaurant, as Evelyn had assumed, but a narrow little pub, with a dark mahogany bar that took up one corner. Great sprigs of dried hops hung from the ceiling beams, filling the room with a stale kind of sweetness that half hid the damp smell of the beer-soaked rugs underfoot. Evelyn had assumed the inn was named for the flower, but now she saw the enormous cerulean bell behind the bar and realized she'd been wrong.

'There they are! In the corner.'

The men were getting to their feet now, one black-haired and the other brown – but it was only as they reached the table and the candlelight flickered between the four of them that Evelyn realized she recognized the darker-haired man. From the curious expression on his face, it was clear he recognized her, too.

'*You*,' he said.

'Miss Clark,' said Mr Kaye, taking off his hat and clutching it, his fingers shaking slightly. 'That there's William. And I am Mr Kaye, but you may call me Jack.' He looked at Naomi as he said it. 'The both of you.'

Naomi's voice took on a silken edge. 'This is my friend, Miss Seaton.'

'You must call me Evelyn, please, if everyone else is on first name terms.'

'Evelyn?' William repeated it in a low voice. 'Well, we are in the presence of a lady now, Jack. Best be polite.'

Jack had already looked blindsided, but now he looked like a rabbit facing down a fox.

Evelyn cleared her throat hurriedly: 'I'm Naomi's friend,' she assured him. 'You needn't stand on ceremony with me.'

'And yet,' said William, 'I'd wager a silver penny that you've stood in the same room as the Queen.'

Evelyn lifted her chin. 'Well of course I've stood in the same room as the Queen. One cannot be presented to society *without* curtseying before the Queen.'

'See, Jack?' William's dark eyebrows slanted. 'Any bad behaviour on your part, and I'm sure she'll be reporting it. To *royalty*, no doubt.'

Naomi gave William an indulgent look. 'Jack told me you were tricky, William. I am happy to see he's an honest man.'

'And I'll be on my best behaviour,' said Jack, helping Naomi with her jacket, and stumbling over a jumbled torrent of compliments about how pretty her gown was, and how pink.

William didn't move.

'So how do you two know one another?' Naomi asked, taking the seat opposite William.

'It's a long story,' said William.

'It's not,' said Evelyn. 'We had the misfortune to share a cab once.'

'In London?' asked Jack brightly. 'Will's just got back from London, y'see. Tell them about your publishing deal, Will.' William opened his mouth, but Jack continued: 'He took his first chapters round hundreds of houses he did – *thousands of 'em* in fact – and then he took it to one publisher, and they loved it. Loved it so much they've asked for a whole novel.' He slapped his friend heartily on the back, his chair creaking as he sat back down. 'Can you imagine! Little William here, a published author. Like the good Lord says, endurance always conquers bad fortune!'

'That wasn't the Bible – that was Virgil,' said William.

'Goodness.' Despite herself, Evelyn was a little impressed. 'And here was I thinking writers subsisted in the various suburbs of Paris and London, with ink-blackened hands and growling bellies.'

'And would you have pitied me if I *was* that kind of writer?'

'Pitied you?'

'Mmm. To pity: to feel sympathy at someone else's misfortune,' William said, holding her gaze. His eyes were beautiful, the colour of dawn sunshine on autumn leaves, and Evelyn felt something flutter deep in the pit of her stomach.

'Not at all,' Evelyn said. 'I was merely saying—'

'Because they've given William a huge advance,' said Jack, rubbing a nervous sheen of sweat from his upper lip. 'He's going to rent the top floor of one of the fancy houses across from the park – you know the sandstone buildings? – and write with a view of the whole city. Can you imagine! My little William, in a house like that.'

'I do wish you would stop calling me *little*,' William said, picking up the glass of ale in front of him and taking a long sip. 'But yes. I can't stay at the Black Swan forever.'

'Not with your good fortune,' said Naomi. 'You must be very proud of your friend, Jack.'

Evelyn watched as Naomi reached to place a hand upon Jack's jittering fist, which was resting halfway across the table. Jack jolted as though she had passed an electric current through him, but his hand stilled for the first time since they'd sat down.

Naomi continued: 'What is your book about, William?'

'Oh, this and that,' he said dismissively. 'Adventuring. Fighting.'

'That sounds exciting,' Naomi said encouragingly.

'Will it be like *The Heart of Princess Osra*?' Evelyn asked.

'God no,' said William. 'There's not a shred of romance in mine, and certainly no men driven insane for their love of a vapid woman.'

Evelyn rolled her eyes. 'I always think it interesting how *she* is the only one described as vapid, when all the men fall in love with her based on her looks alone.'

'I completely agree.' William's gaze snagged upon Evelyn. 'Far better to dislike someone despite their beauty, I say.'

A silence settled over the group then, and Jack's hand began to twitch once more.

'Shall I ask what the specials are?' he said, standing up so quickly that his chair fell backwards and landed on the floor with an almighty *crack*.

'Let's,' said William, and then Evelyn was sure she heard beneath his breath: 'Let's not drag this out too long.'

Jack picked up the chair, and it squealed as he pushed it back beneath the table. 'Sorry,' he said, slicking a strand of hair back into place. 'I'm a bit all over the place today.'

'I'll come with you,' Naomi said, standing gracefully.

'Oh, no, you don't have to—'

'I insist,' Naomi said, giving Jack a wide, beautiful smile.

Evelyn watched them walk away. He was a tall man, Jack, a head or so taller than Naomi, and a comely one, too. He had kind eyes, and Evelyn could see that he'd made an effort with his clothes and his hair, though he'd used too much Macassar Oil, leaving his red-brown tresses thickly coated. They stood at the bar together, and she watched Naomi laugh, watched some of the tension release from Jack's shoulders.

'So, how do you know Naomi?' William asked, breaking the quiet between them. 'Did you hop into her carriage, too?'

Evelyn turned back to him. 'She walked me home a few

weeks ago,' she said. 'Just after I'd first arrived in the city. I was lost.'

'You seem to get stranded often,' William said, raising his eyebrows. 'There are easier ways of meeting people if you are new to town, you know. You needn't wander the streets, claiming you are lost.'

'I *was* lost,' Evelyn said indignantly.

'Mmm. Just like that carriage was the *only* carriage you could have taken home.'

'It was!'

William waggled his eyebrows at her. 'I still want to hear that story, you know. Perhaps I'll write it into my book.'

'Well, now I'm definitely not telling you.' Evelyn's firm tone was somewhat undermined by the smile tugging at her lips. 'Though I am curious about one thing.'

'Only one thing?' said William. 'And here was me thinking I gave off an *exceptionally* mysterious aura.'

'Mr Kaye – I mean Jack – said you arrived back in York in a blaze of glory. But you told me that evening you had had a day from hell. A *year* from hell, in fact. That does not sound very glorious to me.'

William bristled. 'Is a man not permitted to have an off day?'

'Of course,' Evelyn replied. 'But why would you call a year in which you received what sounds like a very good publishing deal *a year from hell*?'

William rubbed at his eyebrow. 'I am sure you are mis-remembering.'

'I am sure I am not.'

'*You are*,' he said, his tone suddenly sharper. 'Now, let's change the subject.'

They were saved from an uncomfortable silence by Jack, who returned at that moment with four glasses of sherry and a small, black chalkboard with the day's menu scrawled upon it.

'We're celebrating,' Naomi explained, for William was eyeing the drink as though it were poison. 'Evelyn got a job today.'

'A job?' William snorted. 'Aren't people like you allergic to that sort of thing?'

'Congratulations,' Jack said, ignoring William entirely, and giving her a wide grin. 'What'll you be doing?'

'Working at a bookshop,' Evelyn said, taking the glass from Naomi.

'The Lamplighter's Bookshop,' said Naomi.

'It's not called that—' said Evelyn and William in unison, before William's expression slackened.

'I'm sorry, what did you say?' said William, at the same time as Evelyn said: 'It's called Morton's Emporium. Mr Morton took me on today.'

Jack's expression froze, but it was William who spoke, his voice like a whip-crack. '*What?*'

'You know it?' asked Evelyn.

'Know it?' William's hand tightened around his drink. 'That's my uncle's shop. Howard Morton.'

'Yes! That's the very fellow who hired me today.'

William drank his sherry all in one go.

Belatedly, Jack said: 'Cheers!'

'That's *my* job,' William said stiffly.

'Now, now,' said Jack, putting a hand on his friend's shoulder. 'I thought you said the whole reason you weren't staying with your uncle was so he wouldn't try to put you to work? So, this is perfect really, isn't it?'

'No, it's not bloody *perfect*.' William tapped a finger against his glass, making it chitter. 'I can't just sit here for a year and spend all the money they've given me. I was going to go there tomorrow and see if he'd take me on a few days a week – to cover expenses, and the like. Otherwise I'll have burned through my advance before Christmas.'

'Wait, sorry—' Evelyn shook her head. 'Did you say Mr Morton is your uncle?'

'He's more than an uncle, really,' Jack said. 'He practically raised him, he did. Will got sent here from Liverpool after—'

'Enough.' William smacked a hand against the table, causing the glasses to jump. 'Thank you, Jack, but I can divulge my own life story if and when I want to.'

Jack gave him a sheepish smile. 'Sorry. You know what I'm like when I'm nervous.' He opened and closed his hand in a talking motion.

'Don't be nervous,' Naomi said. 'I'm not nervous in the slightest.' She lowered her voice slightly. 'I think it's wonderful for us to finally see each other outside of work. It feels like I've been delivering laundry to the Black Swan for a very long time.'

'Two years,' Jack said, nodding. 'Two years, three weeks and four days, if you want to be precise.'

Evelyn turned her attention back to him. 'How do you know that?'

'Because I wrote it in me diary, y'see. I wrote that I'd seen the most beautiful woman in the world and that I hoped she'd come again tomorrow, and then she did, and then—' Jack stopped, and a flush began to creep up his neck. 'I've done it again. I've let me mouth get away with me. Please don't be embarrassed, Miss Clark, I didn't mean—'

Next to him, Naomi beamed. 'I think that's the most romantic thing I've ever heard,' she said.

William stood. 'If you'll excuse me,' he said. 'I must go and speak with my uncle.'

'Come now,' Jack said. 'He won't give Evelyn the sack just because you said so. Now sit and have some dinner.'

'Won't he?' William sat down reluctantly, giving Evelyn a look that was full of challenge and something else she couldn't decipher. 'We shall see about that.'

Chapter Sixteen

'William Morton is like a holly bush,' Evelyn said, as she and Naomi walked home together afterwards. 'Admirable from a distance but spiky and uncomfortable up close. Do you think he meant what he said – that he would try and have me fired? I've barely even started!'

Naomi twisted her mouth at the edge. 'I shall give you the same advice my mother gave me when I started working,' she said. 'Which is: "it's better to walk towards a fight, and get smacked in the face, than to walk away and get shot in the back."'

Evelyn's eyes widened. 'I didn't realize laundries were quite so cut-throat.'

'My mother's advice tends to be rather catch-all,' Naomi replied with a shrug. 'But she's right about one thing: if you want something, you need to be prepared to fight for it.'

'Fight *William* for it, you mean.'

It was a thought that followed her all the way home, until she opened the door to find her great-aunt standing in near darkness. She had her ear pressed to the closed morning room door, her nightgown pooled around her feet.

'Do not go in,' Aunt Clara said gravely. 'Your mother is crying.'

Evelyn unpinned her hat as quickly as she could. 'Why? What happened?'

'Well, her daughter disappeared all day, to begin with,' Aunt Clara replied, with a pursed mouth of disapproval. 'You were not even home for dinner, and I suppose she has been worried about you. Or perhaps she is crying simply because she hadn't imagined she'd be sitting in my morning room so many hours of the day.'

Evelyn gave her great-aunt a flat look. 'You mean to say you haven't gone in and *asked* why she is upset?'

'Heavens no,' said Aunt Clara. 'Then she would tell me and I would have to listen, and that would be the whole evening gone. I have a routine, you know. At nine o'clock I have my evening tipple, and by ten o'clock I am abed.'

'Aha,' Evelyn said. 'Is that why you are hovering at the door? Because your sherry is inside?'

Aunt Clara tried to mask the flash of guilt that passed over her face with indignation, but Evelyn saw it. 'I always have *my* moments of despair in my *own room*,' Aunt Clara said, 'as is only *polite*. That way I do not disturb anyone.'

'I shall tell mother to plan her emotions a little better next time,' Evelyn said, rolling her eyes as she opened the door.

Inside, it was dark; the curtains were drawn, and not a single candle was lit. She could barely see the silhouette of her mother upon the sofa, and if it wasn't for her sporadic sniffling, she might have thought the room empty.

'Mama?' Evelyn said softly. 'Why on earth are you crying in the dark?'

'Because I shan't waste your poor aunt's candles for no good reason,' Cecilia replied, clearing her throat. 'I do not need light to cry.'

'But it is light enough outside,' Evelyn said, twitching back one of the curtains and allowing a thin slice of blue twilight through, enough to bathe the room in gentle hues of grey.

Behind her, she saw the flicker of Aunt Clara's candle as she stepped inside. Next, she heard the glass decanter open with a pop.

'Don't mind me,' Aunt Clara said. 'I'm not here.'

Evelyn sat down beside her mother, taking up her hands and squeezing them. 'What is wrong, Mama? Please tell me.'

Cecilia didn't look at her. 'All of my calling cards have been returned to me,' she said, pressing her handkerchief to her eyes once more. 'Can you believe that? Not a single one of my luncheon ladies wishes to meet with me. Not even the women I thought to be my friends.' Her mother squeezed her hands so tightly that Evelyn felt it burn. 'Do you know how hard I have worked over the years to be accepted by them, Evelyn? And now it is all lost, and I am . . . I am alone once more.'.

'You are not alone.' Evelyn pulled her mother into a hug. 'You have me. And we shall not live here forever.'

'We shall.' Cecilia sobbed into her shoulder. 'We shall live here forever, and I shall become just like Aunt Clara and start drinking before the sun has even set.'

Evelyn heard Aunt Clara snort, and her voice came clear from the hallway: 'You make it sound like a bad thing.'

'Would you like to know what I think?' Evelyn said gently. 'I think we have been given a chance to start over.'

'I do not *wish* to start over!' Her mother's voice was a gentle rumble against Evelyn's shoulder. 'I picture all the women I thought of as friends laughing at me, at my return to nothingness. *I want our old life back.*'

A week ago, Evelyn would have agreed. But now?

Now, Evelyn felt as though she had spent her entire life in the same room, staring at the same four walls, and a door had finally been cracked open.

'I believe we must find our own place in this world. Our own standing,' Evelyn said, holding her all the tighter. 'Don't you think?'

Cecilia sat up, rubbing the wetness from beneath her eyes. 'I have already done that once, Evelyn. I have neither the energy nor the pride left in me to do it again.'

'Then I shall do it,' said Evelyn quietly, determinedly. 'For the both of us.'

Her mother squeezed her hand. 'As long as you stick with Lady Violet, I believe we shall land on our feet. Did she have something good for you? Some charity or other to focus your attention? You dined with her, I suppose?'

Evelyn wouldn't lie to her mother directly. She couldn't. And so instead she said: 'I have certainly found something worthwhile.'

'Good,' said Cecilia, sucking a deep breath into her lungs. 'That comforts me greatly.'

'Do you know what else is a great comfort in trying times?' Aunt Clara's voice bounced down the stairs. '*Sherry.*'

William stood on Oxford Close and looked from the scrap of paper in his hand to the house in front of him then back again. It was certainly the right place, though the advertisement in the *Yorkshire Herald* hadn't mentioned that the house looked as though one strong gust might see it topple.

He put his suitcases down on the bottom step and clambered up to ring the bell. From within he heard a woman shout and then a man bellow back. Heavy footsteps clumped closer, and he counted them unconsciously until the door swung open, revealing a ruddy-faced man with a boar-like physique: all bristle and fat.

He crossed his arms over his chest, so that his belly stuck out beneath them. 'You know, most people don't answer adverts by sending a letter. They just show up at the door.'

William gave the man an apologetic smile. 'I thought it best to write ahead, in case you let the room before I had a chance to come past.' If he was going to keep up the pretence of being a successful author, he couldn't very well move back into his cramped little room at Uncle Howard's – especially not when the whole point of going to London had been to strike out on his own.

The man merely shrugged. 'I'll show you the basement room first,' he said, looking William up and down. 'It's the cheapest.'

William smelled the mildew the moment he stepped inside. Somehow, the room was freezing, despite the warm weather, and the window was so soot-blackened that only the smallest amount of light trickled through. There was a bed pushed into the corner and a chest beside it for one's belongings. Next to that was a small, cracked bowl for washing one's face, with a half-broken jug inside. And that was all. Four things, in a room that smelled like mould and felt like a winter's pantry. William had thought his tiny room at the boarding house in Soho was bad, but at least that had possessed a chest of drawers. This place looked as though someone was trying to recreate the aesthetic from York's prison.

'It's functional,' Mr Lache said loudly. 'A bit cold in the winter, but that's what blankets are for, eh?'

William cleared his throat. 'And the more expensive room?'

'Is upstairs,' Mr Lache replied. 'Follow me.'

They trudged up the two flights together, and William realized the staircase snaked all the way up. Somewhere above him, a baby was screaming.

'This is the other room,' Mr Lache said, swinging the door open.

This one was much larger and brighter, thank goodness.

The bed stood in the centre, flanked by two worn side tables. In one corner was the wardrobe, one door hanging slightly lower than the other, and across from it was a chest of drawers. There wasn't anywhere to write, but William could go to the bookshop for that.

'This one's seven shillings a week, first week payable in advance. The basement room is two shillings a week, but unless you've webbed feet, I'd recommend you take this one. The basement has been known to leak in the winter.'

William placed his suitcases down and reached into his pocket for his wallet. Seven shillings was a larger chunk of his remaining wealth than he would like to spend, but he could not very well live on the streets. 'Here,' he said, plopping the coins into the man's red palm. 'I shall take this room right away.'

'I do like a man who makes a quick decision,' said Mr Lache, pocketing the money. 'The privy is outside – go downstairs and follow the corridor out – and it's a shilling a month for the waste removal.'

William grimaced. 'Right,' he said, adding that to his mental calculations.

'Any questions, I live on the second floor.' Mr Lache leaned closer. 'But I prefer tenants who don't have questions, if you catch my meaning.'

'Understood,' said William, who was now itching for the man to leave so that he could take stock of the room on his own. 'I shall try not to bother you.'

'There's a good man,' said Mr Lache, the door stuttering shut behind him.

William stood there for a long moment, looking around. Then he closed his eyes.

He tried to imagine what it would be like inside one of those new, whitewashed buildings on St. Leonard's Place, the ones you could see from the Museum Gardens. He imagined the shushing sound of his shoes on the steps, the way it would echo as he walked through the entryway, craning his neck to look at the grand paintings: hunting scenes and fruit in elegant bowls. Would he follow a footman upstairs? Most likely. And then the room itself – how enormous it would be, how airy. He tried to imagine whether the bed would have a thick down blanket upon it, perhaps stitched in velvet or silk, so that it was soft to the touch.

He imagined the kind of man who would stroll into that room, the kind of luggage he would have with him, the kind of stride he would walk with, the easy smile upon his face.

It wasn't him.

Whoever the man in his mind was, it wasn't him.

He bit down on his lip, hard enough to split the skin. He'd been lying. To his friends. To this landlord. To the newspaper boy at the stand on Gillygate, to the woman who'd barely asked in the bakery that morning. He'd told them all the same thing. *I am successful,* he'd said. When really what he'd been saying, what he wanted to say was: *I'm not a failure. Don't you see? Not anymore.*

Even that was a lie.

He scrunched his eyelids shut all the tighter, trying to hang onto the gilded picture in his mind, a room the colour of warm sand, with sash windows draped in cream silk, and a writing desk carved from an ancient oak tree. But it was already slipping, disappearing.

Leaving only William, with his tangled black hair and his battered suitcases and his emptying pockets, sat alone in this small room between flaking walls.

Chapter Seventeen

7th June 1899

As Evelyn neared the bookshop on Wednesday, she saw that William Morton was waiting for her upon the edge of the bridge, his back to the water – a mirror of pale blue in the early morning light.

She had thought it brisk enough to take her cape with her this morning, but he held his jacket in his hands, his dark hair falling across his face, his sleeves rolled up, revealing forearms browned by the sunshine.

He looked up then, and she saw him notice her, a shadow of a smile tugging at his lips before it was wrestled quite comprehensively into a frown.

When there had been no sign of him yesterday, and no mention from Mr Morton of any nephew coming to take her job, Evelyn had hoped he'd rather forgotten. But he here was after all.

'You're early,' he said, jumping down gracefully to meet her. 'Got a key?'

'Good morning to you, too.' She kept walking, though now with William following her. 'And I am actually on time. The shop is opening at nine today.'

'*Nine?*' She couldn't see the frown on his face, but she could hear it. 'The Emporium never opens at nine.'

'It does now,' she said, stepping up to the door and sliding the rusted key into the lock. It was stiff, and though she thudded her shoulder against it like Mr Morton had showed her, it wouldn't budge.

'Here,' said William. 'Step aside and I shall help.'

'No, thank you,' said Evelyn, giving it another *thwack* with her shoulder and feeling the black feathers in her hat crumple against the wood. 'Because I have a sneaking suspicion if I step away, you'll flit inside, and I'll end up locked out on the street.'

William quirked an eyebrow at her, though the half-grin tugging at his lips suggested that her suspicions weren't *entirely* unfounded.

'Very well,' he said. 'Have it your way.' And he stepped behind her, one hand closing around her gloved fingers where they held the key, his shoulder pressing against the door. 'We shall try together.'

'Really!' huffed Evelyn, feeling a flush bloom across her cheeks. He was close enough that she could smell the soap-and-woodfire scent of his skin. 'I can manage.'

'Christ,' said William, grunting as the door shuddered again. 'It's not usually *this* stuck.'

'Perhaps the bookshop doesn't wish to let you in,' said Evelyn.

William made an exasperated noise behind her. 'Oh good. Howie has already told you his nonsense theories? Come on, let's try pushing together,' said William. 'Upon my count. One, two—'

The door swung open on *three*, and Evelyn staggered, feeling equal measures of horror and relief when William's arm caught her around the waist to steady her. Inside, the bookshop smelled of trapped sunlight and dust, the drawn curtains casting a dull gloom over everything.

'Careful,' William said, his gaze sliding from hers to focus intently upon the top of her head. 'You wouldn't want to ruin your . . . nest?'

Evelyn fixed him with the best scowl she could muster, despite her heart thrumming unrhythmically in her throat. 'It is a *hat*. And you may wait outside. Mr Morton didn't give me permission to let people into the shop.'

'I'm not people,' William said, stepping past her with a confident smile. 'I'm his beloved nephew, who is going to see you out of a job today.'

'I thought if you were serious then you would have done that already.'

'Ah, but I've been busy.'

Evelyn followed at pace; he was making for the set of stairs that led up to the mezzanine, and she needed to get there first. She all but ran, spreading her arms across both banisters to block his path.

'Really?' William said, quirking an eyebrow at her. 'This is childish.'

'I am merely mirroring you,' Evelyn said. 'You saw someone else playing with a discarded toy and realized that you did, in fact, want it.'

'That's not what has happened here.'

'No?' said Evelyn. 'Then what has happened?'

'An unfortunate miscommunication.'

Evelyn snorted. 'In which you have misunderstood that my new job is up for debate, you mean?'

'Oh, for goodness' sake.' His voice was sharper now. 'It's *my* family shop! It is run by *my* uncle.'

Evelyn shrugged. 'I am not stopping you from seeing him.'

'You are not welcoming me, either,' he said. 'You expect me to squeeze past?'

'I expect you to try.'

'Very well,' he said with a huff. 'Have it your way.' He

jammed his body against the banister, his chest pressing against her elbow. 'You know, if you wanted to be close to me again, you could have just said so, rather than forcing me into circus-like contortions.'

Evelyn crossed her arms at once. 'I do *not* want to be close to you.'

William stepped past her with a chuckle. 'Somehow, I believe it when you say it like that. Now if you'll excuse me . . .'

Evelyn watched him hop up the stairs two at a time, and the sloshing feeling in her stomach became full waves. But Naomi was right. If she was going to prove she should keep the job, then the best way to do that was by *working*. And right now, that meant getting a still half-dust-filled shop ready to open in forty-five minutes.

Nine o'clock came, and Evelyn propped the door open with the paperweight Mr Morton kept on the register's desk. She moved the *open* sign so that it was hung on the door itself, and not on the gargoyles outside, and then she stood in the quiet gloom of the shop and waited.

And waited.

At a quarter past ten, someone came to peer in the window at the gold-leafed book of hours. Evelyn caught the woman's eye through the glass and gave her an encouraging smile.

The woman immediately turned and walked away.

At half past eleven, a man stepped inside so briskly and confidently that Evelyn was sure of a sale. *This* was the kind of customer Mr Morton had been talking about: the kind who knew precisely what book they wanted and where to buy it!

Of course he then handed Evelyn the post, and she realized her mistake.

Two of the letters were advertisements, one for a paper merchant in Ripon that promised to undercut whatever rate Mr Morton was currently receiving and the other for a miracle tonic that promised to regrow balding hair, no matter how bald one was.

The third was thick, the envelope battered, with a stamp that read: *Calcutta*. Who did Mr Morton know all the way in Calcutta, she wondered? On the back there was no return address, just two simple letters: *G.N.*

'Is that the post?'

Evelyn whirled, stuffing the letter beneath the advertisements. 'Just arrived, Mr Morton. I was about to lock the door and bring it up to you.'

'No need, no need – I'm here now,' he said. holding out a hand expectantly. He didn't look at the post, simply stuffed it into the pocket of his jacket. 'How is your little experiment going? Any sales this morning?'

'Not yet,' Evelyn said, trying to keep the confidence in her voice. 'But it will take people a week or so to get used to our earlier opening hours.'

'Or a week or so for us to realize that there is no point opening before eleven.' William stepped out from behind his uncle, giving Evelyn a glittering smile.

'Now, William here has told me of his predicament,' Mr Morton said. 'I assume he has told you the same, Miss Seaton?'

She nodded, her heart thumping loudly in her chest.

'Good, then at least we are all on the same page. Now, of course I did not plan on hiring any help whatsoever, so this is a rather sticky situation.'

'Not sticky,' William said. 'You've already agreed to take on one person. Simply swap that person out.'

'William—'

'Please don't, Mr Morton,' Evelyn said, taking a step towards him. 'I am a hard worker, and I have plenty of ideas for the shop. Just this morning I was wondering if perhaps we could put one of those boards outside, you know, like the butcher does? We could use it to advertise new releases, or perhaps just to tell people to come inside. So many people seem to walk past the shop – I am beginning to wonder whether we need something else to catch their attention.'

'Do you hear that, Uncle Howie?' William caught Evelyn's eye. 'She wants to take advertisement advice from the butcher.'

'*William.*' Mr Morton's tone was a warning. 'I am not going to fire you, Evelyn,' he said gently. 'But nor can I afford to hire the pair of you *ad infinitum*. So I believe the best thing to do would be to amend the terms of our little experiment.'

'You mentioned nothing about an experiment,' William said, perturbed.

Mr Morton pushed his glasses up his nose. 'Between now and Christmas, I shall have you both working here. Whoever sells the most and brings the most money into the business can keep their job.'

'Uncle!' William's face had paled. 'You cannot be serious!'

'Of course I'm serious,' Mr Morton replied. 'And I shall also reinstate a prize for whomever sells the most each month.' He turned to Evelyn. 'William and I had a dram of whisky as the prize when we worked here together, but it seemed like a rather drab thing to do by oneself.'

'As if a *lady* like Evelyn would drink whisky,' William said, rolling his eyes.

'I've drunk whisky,' she said indignantly. She'd once sneaked some from her father's carafe in the study. It had stung her throat.

'This is preposterous,' William said. 'You cannot expect me to compete with her. I'm your nephew. She's just . . .

she's just some random woman who wandered in here on a whim and decided she'd get a job for the novelty of it!'

'I am *not*.' Evelyn gave him a withering look. 'And I would thank you to stop making assumptions about me.'

'Indeed, she did her research,' said Mr Morton. 'She even brought me a full report, so we'll have a lot of new ideas to try this summer, which will hopefully mean more sales. That brings me to my next point: I obviously cannot afford to pay you both a pound and two a week on the income this place currently makes. So you'll have to see to it that our sales go up, or else your pay will go down.'

'You've never minded about sales before,' William said indignantly. 'You said that people who want books will come and buy books.'

'Yes, well,' his uncle replied, pushing his glasses up his nose from where they'd already slipped back down. 'It seems that mindset is a little outdated when we have competitors doing a roaring trade and this marvellous emporium sitting here quite empty. It is time, I think, for a change.'

William huffed and stalked up the stairs, where she heard him knock into a pile of books on the mezzanine and curse loudly.

Evelyn turned back to Mr Morton. 'I do not think he is enamoured with the idea of us working together.'

Mr Morton chuckled. 'I do not think William is enamoured with the idea of *working*, my dear. He is a good lad but a lazy one. It's nice to see someone light a fire beneath him for once.'

'And you mean what you say – whoever sells the most will keep their job?'

'I am completely serious, Miss Seaton,' he said, patting her shoulder. 'Though I should remind you that William has a decade of experience up his sleeve, and you do not, so if I were you, I would work on my sales technique. Now, if

you'll excuse me, I have some very serious post to consider.'
He began walking back to the mezzanine, muttering things
like: 'Oh good, another tonic to stop me balding – I daresay
I'd rather they made a tonic that unknotted knotted hair.'

Once she was alone, Evelyn took a breath for the first
time in what felt like hours and smoothed down her skirts.
She would not lose her job. All she had to do was sell the
most, charm the customers.

How hard could that be?

Chapter Eighteen

The answer, it seemed, was quite hard, for by the end of the week, Evelyn had still not made a single sale – 'Not even to the regulars!' laughed William – and by the time she stepped through the doorway of Porthaven House on Friday evening, she was feeling rather defeated.

Until she saw the look upon her mother's face, the unreadable look in her eyes. For a moment, Evelyn thought she would be scolded for leaving the house so early or returning home so late every day, but her mother's pallid complexion, the tell-tale tremor in her fingers suggested she was back to her old habit of awakening in the late afternoon and then drinking copious amounts of tea to compensate for her sluggishness.

'I need to tell you something,' said Cecilia, helping Evelyn off with her coat. 'But before I do, know that I have done it with your best intentions in mind.'

Evelyn stopped unclipping her cape, her mouth suddenly dry. '*Mama*—'

'I believe you will thank me,' Cecilia said quickly. 'I reached out to that kind gentleman from your dance card.'

It took Evelyn a moment to realize what on earth she was talking about. And then: 'Mr Morris? Nathaniel?'

'Yes! Mr Morris, the American. You know, he seems quite charming from his penmanship alone.'

Evelyn hung her cape upon the coatstand. 'Mama, why were you writing to Nathaniel? *How* did you write to him? He doesn't have a residence here in York.'

'No, indeed, his family hail from a place called Massachusetts apparently. Did you know they publish books? Anyway, of course I couldn't send a letter there, so I wrote to Lady Violet. After all, she was the only one who replied to my letters, because she is a sweet, sweet soul. I enquired after him, and she enclosed a letter of mine to Mr Morris, and then he wrote one back the very same way!' Her mother frowned then. 'She didn't mention this to you?'

'No,' said Evelyn, cautiously. She had forgotten her mother was corresponding with Lady Violet. That was . . . *dangerous*. Though she supposed if Lady Violet had said anything to break her ruse, she would have known it by now. 'But, Mother, *why* are you writing to Nathaniel?'

'Because you'd never lift a finger, darling, and sometimes one must take the first step. And it worked! He wishes to meet us both for dinner when he is next in York.'

Evelyn reached to pinch at the bridge of her nose. 'Did you think to wonder whether *I* would like to go for dinner with *him*?'

'Oh, of course you do,' Cecilia said, flapping her hands in front of her face. 'You are a young woman, he a young man. That is what you are meant to do! Stare at one another over the candlelight—'

'Always romantic when chaperoned by your mother,' muttered Evelyn.

'And one never knows, you may even take a fancy to one another.'

Evelyn's expression grew taut. 'You think because the man agreed to a pity dance that he'll wish to marry me?'

'I said nothing of the sort.' Cecilia turned and walked down the long corridor, not into the morning room as Evelyn had expected, but into the kitchen. There were enough carrots to feed a herd of ravenous donkeys strewn across the table, all in varying states of unpeeled and chopped. 'Let us just go for dinner with the man. That's all.'

Evelyn crossed her arms over her chest. 'Really? That is *all*?'

'For now, yes.' Cecilia gave her a small smile. 'Later, if it so happens that you fall in love with him and that at your marvellously grand wedding all the friends who refused to write to me now see us in our splendour and begin to call upon us again—'

Evelyn sighed. '*Mama.*'

'—then that would simply be an added bonus! Now go and wash before dinner. Aunt Clara refuses to hire a cook, so I am fixing dinner instead.'

Evelyn rubbed at the tension that was forming behind her eyebrows. There was so much wrong with her mother's logic that she didn't know where to start. Instead, she said: 'What on earth are you making that requires so many carrots?'

'Soup, I think,' her mother said. 'I plan to simply boil them down until they're soft enough to swallow.'

Evelyn made a face. 'I thought this meal was meant to be comforting?'

'Comforting because then Aunt Clara will reconsider the notion of hiring a cook,' her mother said cheerfully. 'Now go and wash.'

In the quiet of her room, Evelyn splashed water on her face, dragging her fingers down her cheeks. She didn't want to go for dinner with Nathaniel. No doubt Lady Violet had forwarded her mother's letter only for an excuse to read it and then tell her cackling little flock of followers that she was right, that Evelyn's mother *was* on the prowl – and that Evelyn was, too.

She could still see their contorted faces, cast yellow in the candlelight, could still smell the cloying scent of the flowers hanging from the ceiling.

Are you penniless now, Miss Seaton? Why, you must be! A fox amongst the chickens. Is that why your mother sent you here?

She closed her eyes, waiting for the echo of their barbed laughter to dissolve. Then she took off her day dress and laid it carefully on the chair beside her bed. Well, they were wrong. She would not marry her way out of this. She would not rely on anyone but herself to get them out of this mess.

Downstairs, she heard Aunt Clara shriek: 'My God, woman! How many carrots have you peeled? We'll be eating them for days!'

Chapter Nineteen

Monday at the bookshop was marginally better. Two men came in at five past ten, looking for the latest periodicals – Mr Hutton, whose glasses made his eyes enormous, and Mr Barnes, who spoke little and smiled even less. Then a woman popped in at a quarter to twelve and asked whether they sold stationery. They didn't, but the very fact she'd thought to step inside and ask was an encouragement. Although she did scrunch up her nose and say: 'My, it's a bit gloomy in here.'

Evelyn followed her gaze up to the spiderwebs that collected at the edge of the old ceiling beams and the grit that had built up on the windows, and she found she agreed with her.

And so she made a list.

For the rest of June – to William's great horror and Mr Morton's enthusiastic encouragement – she put them both to work.

While she swept and mopped the floors the first week, William half-heartedly washed all the windows, even the tiny ones on the mezzanine, opening them up to let air into the shop. The following week, they began to catalogue the books, which sparked an unexpectedly heated argument as to how the philosophy section should be sorted ('Evelyn! I am telling you. All the philosophers worth reading go by first name alone!')

In the end, Evelyn agreed that William could categorize the books on the mezzanine however he liked, as long as he left the main shop floor to her. It was only later that she realized William had tricked her into doing the lion's share of the work, for when she was only a third through the ground floor, he was spending his spare time hanging from the shop's door and calling things like: 'Sir! You look like a man who needs a bit of Dickens in his life!' and: 'I have just the kind of wind-swept romance for you, ma'am!' into the street.

Evelyn was quite sure he would have earned himself more than one clip around the ear if his smile wasn't so charming, but as it was, he made a total of seven sales that week alone, and she made none.

The upside, however, was the bookshop itself. Previously gloomy corners became neat little nooks again, and shelves with rows of indistinguishable brown books became glittering displays of multicoloured spines. In an odd way, it felt as though the bookshop was finally taking a breath, the windows all pushing open at once and then, later, slamming shut in harmony. If Evelyn didn't know better, she'd even say there was a bit more jingle in that broken bell than there had been before.

One quiet Thursday afternoon at the start of July, Evelyn was sitting cross-legged on the floor behind a set of shelves, trying to organize a discarded pile of books. The shop was empty, a woman and her young boy having left just after lunch with a newly imported copy of *Dot and the Kangaroo*, a tale Evelyn was quite sure was too advanced for a boy of three, though William, who had elbowed his way into the sale and then taken the coin for it, had vehemently disagreed.

'What's this?' William called to her, still stood at the register. She heard the rustle of paper.

Evelyn scrunched her mouth into a line. 'You know I cannot see you.'

'Oh my,' said William. '"Idea number one: set up a stand at the train station. Could William do this? Pros: he would be out of my hair. Cons: He would be able to take credit for the sales."'

Evelyn's eyes widened, and she stood hurriedly. 'Put that back!'

'"Idea number two: change the shop's name? Everyone calls it the Lamplighter's Bookshop, so perhaps if we swapped the name to match, more people would come in? Can't be an insult after a hundred years, surely?"' He tutted at her. 'By that reasoning, you should change your name to *Incredibly Frustrating*, as that is my favourite nickname for you. "Idea number three . . ."' He gave a chuckle. 'Oh, this is a good one. '"Would new signs in the shop help? I should like to be able to remember which section is which without consulting my map."'

She was marching towards him now, and William looked up.

'You've made a map of the bookshop?' He flipped the paper then and saw it. 'Oh my! You have! And what a neat little map this is—'

'Return it to me,' Evelyn said, holding her hand out to him. 'Those are *my* ideas.'

'Which you so kindly shared with me by leaving them tucked into the gap between the register and the wall.' He gave her a wide, bright smile, and Evelyn reached to snatch at the paper. She expected William to relinquish it, but he didn't.

Instead, they stood there, her hand clasped over his, and the longer they stood there, the more her heart seemed to drum against her ribcage.

'That train station idea is a good one,' he said, his voice

low. 'There's a boy down the way who sells the papers once the newsstand packs up at midday – perhaps he'd like something that pays a little better?'

'Perhaps I shall ask him,' she said, when William released the paper and she could finally step back. Her face inexplicably felt warm.

'Oh, I know young Gregory. I can ask.'

'Absolutely not,' said Evelyn. 'Because then you'll ask for a share of the profits.'

'Not a share,' said William, his lips curling a little now. 'If I arrange the boy *and* the stand *and* which books should be taken, then I should get all the sales.'

Evelyn huffed a breath through her teeth. 'Do you really need the money so badly that you'll sink to stealing my ideas?'

'It's one thing to think something up, Evelyn, and another thing to do it.' His eyes tracked behind her for a moment. 'I tell you what, if you sell to the next person who walks through that door, I shall arrange the stand *and* speak to Gregory *and* let you keep all of the profits. How about that?'

Evelyn narrowed her eyes. 'This feels like a trick.'

'No trick,' William said, showing her his palms. 'Just a simple gentleman's agreement.'

'And if I don't sell to the next customer?'

'Then we split it. Fifty-fifty.'

'Even though it was my idea,' she said pointedly.

'Which you didn't act upon,' William replied, raising two dark eyebrows in challenge.

Evelyn huffed, but he was right. She'd done nothing but let the idea languish beside the register. And though she'd not made a single sale yet, she removed her glove and held out her hand like a man might. 'Fine. You have a deal.'

William hesitated and then took her hand. His dark eyes met hers, and for a moment they stood like that, hands clasped, his palm soft against hers, sending a flicker of warmth to her cheeks.

The door clanged open then, and she drew her hand back sharply.

'As we agreed,' William said pleasantly, gesturing towards the front of the shop. 'And good luck.'

Evelyn turned and saw the postman standing there, rifling through his post-bag, and realized it *had* been a trick.

And then Naomi stepped out from behind him.

'Which of you came in first?' Evelyn asked quickly.

'Me,' said Naomi, her wide smile faltering a little. 'Why?'

Evelyn turned to William, her tone brittle. 'But you saw the postman walking up the road, didn't you?'

'Absolutely not,' William said, though the lopsided smile on his face said otherwise. 'Why would I place a bet on you selling books to someone who no doubt doesn't even carry money while doing their rounds?'

'Well, indeed,' Evelyn said, her eyebrows raised.

'Lunch?' Naomi asked, pointing to the basket she was carrying. Evelyn spotted a half-loaf of bread poking out from it.

'Yes, please,' she said. 'Just do me a favour first, would you?'

Naomi watched quizzically as Evelyn ducked into the box of two-shilling yellowbacks and pulled a Mary Elizabeth Braddon novel from the pile.

'Can you buy this?'

'No, don't buy it,' William said quickly. 'You'll hate it.'

'What is it about?' asked Naomi.

'Murder,' Evelyn said.

'See?' William made a face. 'Awful.'

'Nonsense,' said Naomi, taking out her purse. 'I love a good detective novel.'

'And this was one of the first,' said Evelyn.

'The first is never the best,' said William. 'Might I suggest you have a think about it, and come back tomorrow?'

'I'd never get anything done with that mindset,' said Naomi, sliding two shillings onto the table. 'I shall take it with me today.'

'Ha!' Evelyn turned back to William. 'Now, tell the boy to set up the stand with mainly fiction. And because I am fair, you can take a twenty per cent cut for helping set everything up.'

'Fifty-fifty would be kinder,' he said.

'If we're to base this on kindness alone, then I'd give you nothing, considering you attempted to steal my idea and then trick me.' Evelyn gave him a glittering smile.

'Very well,' he said, with a look on his face like he'd eaten lemon rind. 'But you can't hope that friends will walk inside each time you need a sale. You will have to sell to an actual customer at some point, Evelyn.'

Evelyn took the two shillings and rang them into the till. Then she handed Naomi the book. 'I will repay you for it,' she whispered.

'Bring lunch next week, and we'll call it even,' Naomi said, hooking her arm into Evelyn's. 'Now come along. I've only a half-hour.'

'You two seem to be getting along like kindling and flame,' Naomi said, leading her past the bridge and down the steps that would take them to the water. There wasn't a walkway down there exactly, but there was space enough for the pair of them to sit with their legs dangling over the ledge, the basket of bread and cheese and ripe red apples between them.

'He is the most maddening, the most quarrellous . . . the most—' Evelyn clamped her mouth around the word *handsome*, which had slipped into her mind unnoticed.

She took a chunk of bread and rolled it between her fingers instead. 'The most *infuriating* man I have ever met.'

'Like and dislike walk a fine line.' Naomi nodded, taking a slice from her apple and eating it with a crumbling chunk of cheese. 'That's what my mother has always said.'

'I've never believed that,' said Evelyn. 'It's very clear to me that I like you. And it's also very clear that I *don't* feel the same sentiment towards William.'

Naomi grimaced. 'So, you wouldn't be convinced to chaperone a little picnic I am having?'

Evelyn hesitated mid-chew.

'Jack's just started a new job at the Royal Station Hotel, and I want to do something for him to celebrate. Mother suggested I invite him for tea, though then she would leap down the man's neck, and I don't think he's ready for that.'

'Your mother and my mother have that in common, I think,' Evelyn replied.

'That's why I thought we could have a picnic instead. He said his first day off from the new job is a week on Sunday, and perhaps you could come and hold William's attention again so that I can try and ease more than three words from Jack.'

Evelyn pushed her lower lip out. 'He spoke a fair amount when we were last together.'

'To the group,' Naomi agreed. 'Not to *me*. Around me, he still seems so nervous.'

'Because he likes you, of course,' Evelyn said, ripping off another chunk of bread. 'Yet another reason why I couldn't possibly like William. I was nervous only for the day I thought he would take my job.'

Naomi gave her a pleading look. 'I was going to make a quiche. It's this French sort of egg pie, with cream and bacon. My mother learned how to make it when she was a governess in Normandy. Is that enough for you to bear a little more of William's company? Bacon quiche?'

'I don't need a quiche,' Evelyn said. 'If you need me there, I can put up with him for another day.'

In truth, something fizzed inside her when she thought of seeing William outside of the shop, though she pushed the thought away as swiftly as it had come.

'I'll do something nice for you in return,' Naomi promised, handing her a slice of apple. 'You help me avoid my mother's madness, and I'll help you avoid yours. What has she done?'

Evelyn looked out over the shining water. When the sun was as high as this, it made the river look like a stream of light, so beautiful it was almost blinding. 'Made plans for me to dine at the Royal with a gentleman of her choosing. It's not that the man in question is awful, I just . . .'

'Don't want to go?' Naomi suggested.

'Precisely,' said Evelyn. 'Or rather, I don't want to encourage what my attendance means. Which for my mother is no doubt a favourable marriage.'

'And for the man?'

Evelyn looked down at the slice of apple in her hands. It was browning at the edge, and she sank her fingernail into it. 'I imagine there's something in it for him, but what that something is I don't know.'

'Well,' said Naomi, 'if you're having dinner at the Royal, Jack will be working. Perhaps he can interrupt? Say there is some kind of book emergency?'

Evelyn gave a half-laugh. 'What, like "William has gone on a rampage and is re-sorting the entire shop by binding colour, rather than surname"?'

Then her mother would be scandalized for three reasons: that Evelyn was working, that a man worked with her, and that she and said man were on a first-name basis. None of this she mentioned to Naomi, of course, for then she would have to explain why she had lied to her mother. Why she was *still* lying. And the thought of that was too prickly for even Evelyn to grip.

'Jack could think of something,' Naomi said, leaning back on her hands. 'You know how he talks when he's nervous.'

'Any excuse to leave would work marvellously,' Evelyn laughed, breathing in a lungful of the river air. You could almost ignore the steam coming from the east of the city when you sat this close to the water, for the wind funnelled through, hopping from sluggish wave to sluggish wave. 'Now, what should I bring for the picnic?' Evelyn asked. 'Preferably something that doesn't require cooking or baking, unless you have a penchant for carrot-based dishes.'

Naomi laughed. 'I am not all that interested in the food, if I may be honest.'

'Just Jack,' Evelyn said, with a sparkle in her eye.

'Just *the conversation*,' Naomi corrected, laughing as she hauled herself to her feet and then held out a hand to help Evelyn do the same. 'Now come on. I need to be getting back.'

Chapter Twenty

With Evelyn gone, William found a scrap of paper and a fountain pen with some ink left in it and began scribbling. Mr Morton – Uncle Howie, to him – had told him that, while he had paid both William and Evelyn in full so far, they needed to sell at least thirty books a week if he were to continue doing so. Which was a stretch, as the shop's record was twenty-three. That was the year before he'd left for London – the year William Morris died and there was an unexpected rush for *The Wood at the Edge of the World*, of which Morton's Emporium stocked the most copies in the whole of York. It was one of the only times Uncle Howie's literary gambles had worked in their favour – William was quite sure that if he went downstairs, there would still be boxes of *Love or Lucre* by Robert Black, not to mention dozens of volumes of comically incorrect Portuguese-to-English phrasebooks, which William had spent a much younger summer learning by rote. It had become a secret language between Howie and him, a bond between a gangling youngster and an overwhelmed man, back when the bell still jingled and the shelves were less dusty, back when his uncle spent all his time downstairs, rather than locked in his room.

William smiled a little at the memory, dropping a blot of ink amidst his sums. They'd achieved half of what they needed to sell so far this week. If Uncle Howard paid him only half . . . well, that would barely cover his lodgings, and Mr Lache didn't seem the kind of man who'd be generous when it came to missing money. He seemed like the kind of man who would more readily kick William out on his arse – or worse, confine him to that awful, dank basement room.

He grimaced, his fingers catching at a knot in his messy black hair, just as Evelyn stepped through the doorway and called: 'It's getting hotter and hotter out there!' into the shop.

The warmth had flushed her cheeks, and as she unpinned her hat and set it upon the stand, he saw that the wind had pulled tendrils of her curling hair from the tight knot at her neck.

She turned then, catching his gaze and giving him a dazzling smile. 'You should step outside, too,' she said. 'Get some fresh air.'

He shook his head. 'You know you've not sold a single thing since you started, Evelyn?'

'That's not true,' she said, coming to stand beside him. 'I just sold a yellowback to Naomi.'

'Very well. *One sale*. Out of how many weeks? My uncle won't keep paying you the full amount if you've not earned it. And nor will he pay me if we've not sold enough.'

She blushed now, her sun-warmed skin turning a violent shade of red. 'I know I am no good at this at the moment, but I will get better. I just . . . I need more time to practise.'

William turned his attention back to the page before him. 'If you believe that then you'll believe anything.'

'You could always help me, you know.'

His lip quirked at the edge. It took a certain kind of arrogance to admit her failure and then ask for his help, and his instinct was to say no. But somehow, when he looked at her, all the spiked words he had readied on his tongue seemed to dissolve.

'I'm sure there's a trick or two you could teach me?'

'No,' he said, his heart racing as he balled the paper up and stuffed it into his pocket. 'Fail on your own, just like everyone else.'

Her expression changed. 'I don't think it's failing if you're learning,' she said.

'We are rivals, Evelyn. You think I am going to help you beat me?' His tone was sharper than it needed to be – he could hear it – but his face felt hot, and he wanted her to go back to where she had been standing by the door. All he could smell were the lilacs pressed into her clothes.

'I'd hoped you'd at least see to it that it was a fair fight,' she said.

'You were the one who wanted us to go against each other,' he said, lifting his dark gaze to meet hers. 'I never promised to fight fair.'

'Then don't do it for me,' she said. 'Do it for your uncle. It'll help his business.'

'So will you quitting.'

He expected her to snap back at him, to give him one of her quick retorts, but this time she was quiet, and when he looked at her, it was like she wasn't there, like she'd retreated, disappeared somewhere far away, and he felt the regret like a knot in his stomach.

'Next week will be better,' she said softly, her eyes on the oak table, on the knot of wood in the centre of it. 'Once we've got the stand at the train station.'

'Once *I've* arranged that, you mean.'

She looked at him then. 'I will do it if you don't wish to. Jerry from the newsstand can help me if you won't.'

William squeezed the paper in his pocket. 'I'll handle it,' he said. 'I said I would.'

'Good,' she said. 'Then I'm going to take the books that need rebinding downstairs.'

William sighed, pinching the skin at the bridge of his nose as she disappeared behind the shelves. Uncle Howard had always said he had a flaring temper, and William agreed, but once he'd started, it was like watching a wagon wheel roll faster and faster down the road. All those seconds he wasted watching was time he'd spend later trying to catch it, and the remorse that came afterwards was always swift and crushing.

He should apologize to her. After all, it wasn't just her fault. And the bookshop *did* look so much nicer thanks to her idea of dusting and mopping and his window-washing. It looked closer now to the way it had when he'd first seen it, some seventeen years ago. Brighter. *Happier.*

She strode past him, a stack of books in her arms, and William said: 'Evelyn, wait.'

She turned. There were so many that she had them balanced beneath her chin, all of them with their hardbacks falling off or crumbling. Uncle Howie would need to rebind them when he had the time.

'What?' Her tone was terse. Tense.

'I shouldn't have spoken to you like that. I'm just . . .' *Just what?* Scared. Of the basement room. Of falling even further than he'd already fallen.

But he couldn't tell her that – couldn't tell anyone that. They all thought he was living in that beautiful sandstone building opposite the park. They all thought he was successful. They all believed the lie.

'I'm sorry,' he said.

He watched her pause, one shoulder pressed against the

cellar door. 'Me too,' she said, giving him a small smile. 'Next week will be better.'

'Next week will be better,' he agreed, and watched her slip behind the rust-red curtain, into the basement.

The cellar was dark. It took all of her concentration not to lose her footing down the steep staircase, sending the books – and her precariously balanced candle – toppling into the gloom. When she finally reached the bottom and could slide them onto Mr Morton's binding table, she paused.

Beside the stack of receipts, organized in no real fashion whatsoever, was something else. It wasn't a book but a series of papers, held together with a string at one corner. For a moment, she wondered whether these were the inventory slips Mr Morton had been looking for, but when she brought the stack closer to the light, she saw they were handwritten pages. There was a title: *Felix's Unlucky Adventures in London*, and then beneath it was the name: *William Albert Morton*.

Evelyn stared at it for a moment, her mouth suddenly dry. This was his manuscript! It didn't look like the whole of it – a handful of chapters, perhaps? But what on earth was it doing in the cellar? She knew she should put it back, that she shouldn't look at it, but she was already turning the page, reading the first lines: *Felix had not known how large London would be, nor how foul-smelling, nor how foggy, nor how grey. Yet when he stepped from the train, he saw his future: laid out before him as steadily as the train tracks he had ridden to get here.*

She flipped to the last page then and saw that the ink had changed colour, from blue to deep black – the same as the ink they used upstairs.

Felix wished he could travel back in time, to when men wore armour so thick that no one could see what lay beneath. For when she looked at him, it was as though she saw past his skin to his very soul, as though she could strip him bare and see all that he was.

And what he was? It wasn't enough.

It would never be enough.

'Evelyn?'

William's voice was loud at the top of the stairs, and she started, almost tipping the candle towards the pages.

'The post has arrived – can you come up so I can take it to Howie?'

'Yes,' she squeaked, taking some of the receipts and scattering them over the manuscript's pages, so that William would not know that she had seen them. It felt oddly intimate to read his writing, as though she had found a secret window into his mind, and now she could peek through it.

'Evelyn?'

'Coming!' she called, hurrying back up the stairs.

Chapter Twenty-One

At a quarter past six, Evelyn closed the heavy bookshop door behind her, rubbing the nearest gargoyle's snout affectionately.

It was sticky and warm, the sun still beating down upon them despite it being early evening. The patrons of the Red Lion were mostly standing outside, trying to catch a breeze on the bridge, and she noticed that the perfumer was open – which was odd, for it usually closed far earlier than they did.

A woman stepped daintily from the doorway then, her face hidden as she turned inwards to call a half-laughing farewell to someone inside. Her white-blonde hair was trussed into the most perfect curls, half pinned and half loose beneath an outlandish hat, with reams of cream and violet taffeta framing what looked like a pair of silk dahlias. Then she turned, and Evelyn realized with a sharpening nausea that surely only one woman in the whole of York could pull off a hat like that.

Lady Violet.

Her gaze latched onto Evelyn's like a hound sniffing out a fox, and she gave her a wide, surprised smile, opening her white lace parasol before crossing to speak to her.

'My, my!' she said, looking around. 'If it isn't Miss Seaton. What on earth are you doing here?'

Evelyn was painfully aware that, compared to the elegant radiance of Lady Violet, she no doubt looked like she'd spent half the day crouched over dusty books, lifting heavy piles before sunning her face by the water's edge. She was sure all of that was written in the oily slick of her skin, the grease-shine in her hair.

'Errands,' she said.

'Errands indeed.' Lady Violet gave her a catlike smile. 'I am sure I saw you walk out of that dank little bookshop. Is that where you have been spending your time, hmm?'

Evelyn kept her expression carefully blank. 'What business is it of yours how I spend my time?'

'Well,' Lady Violet said, leaning in beneath the parasol, so close Evelyn could smell the perfume upon her skin, 'your mother, in her *very interesting* letters to me, seems to think that *we* are engaged in some kind of charitable venture together.' Lady Violet lifted the parasol now, turning ever so slightly so that Evelyn could either meet her gaze or stare directly at the lowering sun. 'Now, where could she have got that idea, I wonder?'

Evelyn's heartbeat quickened. 'What did you tell her?'

'Oh, nothing yet,' Lady Violet said brightly. 'You see, I am under the impression that your mother doesn't have many people to write to, which means she sends me *reams*. It's very enlightening.'

Evelyn felt a twist of anger in her stomach, felt it flush her face. 'She believes you to be a kind-hearted woman – that is why. If she knew the truth, I am sure she would stop writing at once.'

'I cannot be so very cruel, Evelyn.' Lady Violet showed her two perfect rows of straight teeth. 'I haven't told her that you're lying. And nor will I tell her that I watched you coming out of the bookshop on Foss Bridge, which happens to sit near a very dirty-looking little public house.'

Evelyn gritted her teeth. 'And what do you want in return? Surely you are not doing this out of any friendly feeling towards me. You made your sentiments clear enough when you humiliated me in front of everyone we know.'

Lady Violet sniggered, as though Evelyn had told the most delightful little joke. 'That was a raucous night. You missed much of it, running out so early. Still, I must say I am glad your mother took a liking to Nathaniel.' Her expression grew serious then. 'That is what I want from you. In return for my silence.'

Evelyn was momentarily confused. 'You want . . . Nathaniel?'

'I want you to *distract* him,' she replied. 'He has been buzzing around me like a bee to a flower since the spring, and I am tiring of it. I thought he would leave once I'd made it quite clear that I would not accompany my family to Scotland, but he hasn't. He has been back and forth between York and London, York and Edinburgh, but always, *always* back to York. Back to me.'

'So then tell him you are not interested,' Evelyn said.

'It is not that simple,' Lady Violet replied. 'He is a close friend of the family, a beloved companion of my brother, and more than that, he—' She swallowed and then cleared her throat. 'I cannot entertain the man's affections of course – he is who he is, and I am who I am, and nothing in this world can change that. Nevertheless, I shouldn't like to hurt him, if I can avoid it.'

Evelyn's brow creased in a frown, for that sounded *very* unlike Lady Violet. 'So you believe the easiest solution is to push me in front of him?'

'Why not? It's what your mother wants. Now you simply have all the more reason to treat him well.'

'I treat all people well,' Evelyn snapped. 'Unlike you, I don't belittle people or use them.'

Lady Violet laughed then, the delicate, wind-chime laugh she used only when she thought something decisively ironic. 'My, my, but *you* have used *me*! You used my name as an excuse to your mother. Don't lie to yourself, Evelyn. You may not be as cunning as I am, but you are not innocent, either.'

Evelyn didn't know what to say to that. In fact, she couldn't seem to conjure a single word. It was as though she had frozen, despite the glaring sunshine, the bead of sweat sliding gently from her temple to her cheek. She stepped sideways, so as not to be facing the sun, and Lady Violet stepped with her, negating it.

'So? What do you say to our little bargain, hmm? You make Nathaniel fall in love with you, and I shall keep quiet about your little lie to your mother.'

Evelyn blinked. 'You never said you wished him to fall in love with me.'

'I had assumed that was clear?' Lady Violet rolled her eyes. 'Believe me, it is very easy. All you must do is act less like yourself and more like me.'

'I certainly shan't agree to *that*,' Evelyn said.

'Oh, for goodness' sake,' Lady Violet replied sharply. 'I don't care *how* you do it – just get it done. Or else your mother will know that you've not been passing your time with me at all, which will certainly beg the question of what you *have* been doing?' Her gaze was razor-sharp now, her plump lips pressed into a taut line. 'Tell me that you agree.'

Evelyn wanted very desperately to say no. She wanted to look Lady Violet in the eye and tell her that she wouldn't be blackmailed, that she'd sooner her nose fell off than act like her.

But then she thought of her mother – of how much it would hurt her to realize she had been lied to, not just by Evelyn but by Lady Violet, too. She thought of how happy those letters had made her, how they had given her a thread of hope that she was not an outcast after all. The honest thing would be to tell her mother it had all been a lie, but would it be kind to wrench that happiness away? Her mother had had so little happiness of late.

'Very well,' Evelyn said, through gritted teeth. 'But I do not like this one bit.'

Lady Violet shifted so that her parasol finally cast a shadow over Evelyn's face. Then she lifted a single gloved hand to signal to someone behind Evelyn's shoulder – whomever was manning her carriage, no doubt.

'You do not need to like it,' Lady Violet said, meeting Evelyn's eye one last time. 'You just need to do it.'

It was only later, as Evelyn stood in front of the bathroom mirror, blinking the soap from her eyes, her reflection blinking back at her, that she realized she had been set an impossible task.

She couldn't make the man fall in love with her. She knew what she was. She knew *who* she was. And she wasn't the kind to make pleasant small talk. She wasn't the kind to gloss over something that she disagreed with or the kind to laugh along with a man she found dull.

In short, she was nothing like Lady Violet. And she wasn't the kind of woman Nathaniel was likely to fall in love with.

But Nathaniel isn't like them.

As Lady Violet had all but said, he didn't have a title or a country estate – didn't have old money and the entitlement that seemed to come with it. He was who he was: an untitled American from Massachusetts. His parents had earned their fortune, had worked for it, so he no doubt knew the value of hard work, of trying to create something from nothing. Perhaps they would find common ground in that. Perhaps . . .

She scrubbed the towel over her face, pressing it to the stinging edges of her eyes. That didn't change the fact that she and Lady Violet were opposites. She was the moonless night to Lady Violet's summer day: with her dark eyes and her black-brown hair, curling as it fell to her shoulders. She'd even caught the sun a little on her walks to and from work, and her freckles were beginning to show for the first time in years: a faint wave across her nose that then fanned out into wide strokes over her cheekbones.

Whatever Nathaniel saw in Lady Violet, he would not find it in her.

But if the other option was for Lady Violet to tell her mother about the Emporium?

She sighed, flicking beads of water from her fingers, watching the ripples they made in the sink, silver in the moonlight.

Evelyn was lucky that her mother had returned to her habit of rising late, or else she would be subject to much more intense questioning about her daily outings. In truth, she wished she could simply be honest with her mother – but how could she, when her mother would equate Evelyn's having a job as a direct attack on their social standing? She didn't believe that her working forfeited their place in society, but then Evelyn had not clawed that place for herself like her mother had.

What she *did* understand was how it felt to be sneered at – how it felt to be snubbed. And her mother had suffered years of it. Decades, in fact. And if she discovered Evelyn had gone behind her back and was working, surely she'd feel that all those years of torment had been in vain: for here was her daughter, eschewing all she'd endured.

But what was the alternative – for her to leave the

bookshop? For all she had saved from her wages thus far to become the sum total of their fortune?

She pulled on her nightdress and padded back to her room. The moon shone through the high, crescent window, so full and bright that it bathed the room in threads of silver and swathes of dusted blue. She took the hidden jar from her sock drawer and counted out the coins.

Just seeing the money in her hand, knowing that she had earned it, filled her with a sense of pride. They didn't need her father. And they didn't need Nathaniel. She would keep adding pounds and shillings to this little collection, until she had enough to repay Aunt Clara *and* find her and mother a house to rent of their own.

That was worth any measure of discomfort with Nathaniel and any amount of her mother's anger.

And she wouldn't give it up now.

Chapter Twenty-Two

16th July 1899

When the day of the picnic came, Evelyn excused herself as quickly as she could after church. Luckily, her mother's attention was helpfully diverted by Mrs Quinn and her 'Proper Christian Ladies' Club'.

The park was busy; clusters of women strolled into town from their church services, while families sought shade under wide oak trees, for the sky was almost completely clear, the few clouds like white-grey brushstrokes against a brilliant, cerulean blue.

Naomi had found a spot just south of the library in the Deanery Gardens and was busy setting out the egg and bacon pie upon the glass cake stand in the centre.

'Gracious, that looks good,' said Evelyn, putting her basket down beside them as Naomi began to unpack stout little pork pies and triangles of cucumber sandwiches. In comparison, Evelyn thought the cream buns she'd bought from the baker's were a poor contribution, despite the elbowing she'd had to do in that crowded little shop to get them. Naomi didn't seem to agree though, for she beamed when she saw them and arranged them neatly on a plate.

'I know we have an agreement, you and I – the picnic in exchange for help with your dinner, but what if *I* make a run for it?' Naomi said. 'It feels like I've swallowed bees.'

'It's just a picnic,' replied Evelyn. 'And we're going to have a marvellous afternoon.'

'I wish my brain would listen to such reason,' Naomi said. 'I've been jittery all morning. The rector called upon me in the service earlier, and I almost leaped out of my skin.'

'It's excitement.' Evelyn gave her friend a smile. She could see the men approaching them from a distance. 'Just keep breathing, and all will be well.'

'This looks like quite the feast,' Jack said, sitting heavily down upon the blanket. He was red-faced, his hairline glistening with sweat. William was the same, his dark curls damp where they touched his forehead. Wherever they'd come from, they'd walked quickly under a hot sun to get here. 'And we only brought cheese and a new loaf.'

'Blue cheese,' William corrected. 'From the grocer's. The fancy, French kind. And apple cider. And green grapes.'

'We'll not go hungry, that's for sure,' Naomi said, taking two parasols and staking them into the ground to give them a modicum of shade.

William popped the cork on the cider, pouring them each a foaming glass. He gave Evelyn hers last, his gaze snagging on her dress and then flicking away rapidly.

'What is it?' she asked, instantly on edge. 'Have I got something on my clothes?'

William blinked, bewildered. 'What?'

'You're looking at me oddly,' said Evelyn.

'I am not looking at you oddly.'

'You are. You gave me the same look in the shop the other day – as though I had ink on my chin.'

'If you must know,' said William, lowering his voice

conspiratorially, 'I was thinking that your dress makes you look like some kind of sea creature.'

She looked down at the blue-teal of her dress and frowned. 'I don't know if that is better or worse than "peacock",' said Evelyn, taking the small china plate Naomi was offering her.

'Better,' said William.

'*Worse*,' said Jack.

William looked at her, tweaking an eyebrow in defeat. When the sunlight was on his face, his hazel eyes turned a glowing, golden-brown, bright compared to his rumpled black hair, and her mind wanted to say only one thing, which was: *beautiful*.

'This is my mother's recipe,' Naomi said, carving a wobbling slice of egg pie for each of them. 'You must let me know what you think.'

'It's odd,' William said, chewing thoughtfully. 'One would not think egg and cheese would make such a good pie, but it does.'

'That's also a compliment,' Evelyn explained. 'He tends to hand them out awkwardly.'

Jack chuckled. 'You're not wrong there.'

'I always wonder whether people who are bad at giving compliments are bad because they themselves never received many growing up,' Evelyn said, taking another bite. The quiche was heaven – buttery, creamy, cheesy, salty *heaven*. 'It would make sense, I think, if they are not used to them.'

If she had been looking at William when she said it, she would have seen his face fall, his eyebrows knit, but she didn't. Her attention was too readily focused on her plate.

'And what of people who are bad at receiving them?' asked William. 'What do you say of those people?'

Evelyn's mouth twisted into a line.

'Well,' said Jack, 'when you're a rich, famous author in London, I am sure you'll be able to live off egg pie every day if you so wished—'

'Quiche,' Naomi corrected.

'Nonsense,' said William. 'I'll live off caviar. And I'll have bacon and eggs each morning for breakfast. Or *truffles*. Isn't that what rich people eat?' His eyes slid to Evelyn's. 'Truffles?'

'How would Evelyn know?' scoffed Jack. 'She wouldn't be sitting with the likes of us if she did.'

William smiled. 'And yet she wouldn't be wearing a dress like that if she didn't.'

Evelyn put her plate down. 'So *that* is why you were looking at me funnily.'

William shrugged, popping a slice of cheese into his mouth. But the sparkle in his eyes said: *yes*.

'Don't pester Evelyn,' Naomi said quickly. 'This is a picnic, not the inquisition.'

'No, indeed, but *something* is missing.' William made a sweeping gesture with his hand. 'We have good food, good weather, time aplenty. Now all we need is a good story.'

'You're the author,' Naomi replied. 'Why don't you tell us part of your story?'

'Real stories are far better,' said William, shaking his head. 'And I am sure Evelyn has a few.'

She gave him a sharp look. 'I thought we were past your prying.'

'Really?' William looked at her. 'And here's me thinking we'd just begun to get to know one another. You never did tell me what happened at that ball.'

'I'd rather not,' Evelyn said.

Naomi sipped her cider. 'I would rather you two didn't argue.'

'I've a story about a ball,' said Jack, a crumb of cucumber flying from the corner of his mouth. 'Two, in fact.'

'Trust me,' said William, looking towards Naomi and Evelyn. 'You do *not* want to hear that one.'

'Rubbish.' Evelyn turned to Jack. 'We'd love to hear the story.'

'You'll regret it,' William said, waggling a finger.

'Not as much as I regret meeting you,' Evelyn snapped, earning herself a wide smile from William, which somewhat dampened her frustration, for it sent a fizzle all the way to the pit of her stomach.

Jack cleared his throat. 'Well, back when we had the farm in Pocklington, and I was going to be my pa's apprentice, before I realized how shit' – he looked hurriedly at Naomi – 'I mean, how *unsuited* I was to farmwork – it came time to retire the old bull.'

'Here we go,' said William.

'Pa had bought a new stud from the market, you see, and we didn't need two bulls running around, least of all because they'd try and gore each other. So Pa decided the old bull needed to be retired to the kitchen table. We could've butchered him straight away, but gelding them makes for better meat, and better meat sells for more. So Pa set out one morning with his ropes and his men and his pincers.'

Evelyn quickly put down the piece of cheese she had been nibbling.

'Anyway, the old boy saw it coming and thought "sod this". He led them on a merry chase for half the morning, and when they finally wrangled him down, he landed a kick so squarely between my father's legs that I reckon he was trying to give Pa a taste of his own medicine.'

William flinched visibly.

Naomi gave a little gasp. 'I don't think this story is particularly suitable for ladies, Jack. Was your father . . .' She swallowed. 'Was he well, afterwards? Did he suffer?'

'Ah, he was fine eventually.' Jack cut another slice of bread and pressed a thick wedge of marbled blue cheese into it before popping it into his mouth. 'But there's an important lesson to be learned there.'

Evelyn frowned. 'Don't be on the kicking end of a bull?'

'Don't geld what don't want gelding,' Jack said loftily.

'Thus proving my point that this story is *not* suitable for ladies,' said Naomi.

'Surely it's a motto *everyone* can live by,' William muttered.

Naomi cleared her throat, clearly quite desperate for a more seemly topic of conversation. 'I didn't know your family owned a farm, Jack?'

'Rented,' he corrected. 'Until the earl swapped us out for another lot. Said we weren't being *efficient* enough for the land, or some nonsense. But I've been back up through Pocklington since, and the new farmer isn't doing any more nor any better than we were.'

'Evelyn probably knows him,' William said.

Jack frowned. 'Why would Evelyn know the new farmer?'

'Not the farmer, the—'

'Let's discuss something else, shall we?' Evelyn said. 'The weather's fine, isn't it?'

William's eyes narrowed. 'Why is it that whenever the conversation turns to you, you steer it away? You're happy to listen to all our problems and make your assertions about the whats and the whys, and yet you won't tell us why a fine lady like yourself is working in a shop?'

'What are you talking about?' said Jack.

Naomi leaned in, whispering something in his ear, and Evelyn watched his eyes go wide.

She bristled. 'It is one thing for me to volunteer my stories, William – it is another thing entirely for you to go digging for them.'

'Because I have a feeling if I do not *dig*, you'd never offer them!' He turned to Naomi. 'Come on! Surely you must have noticed!'

'Everyone's entitled to privacy,' Naomi said firmly.

'Oh, really?' said William, a challenge in his eyes now. 'Very well. What do you know about Evelyn, Naomi? What do you *truly* know, that's not something frivolous?'

Naomi rolled her eyes. 'She's an only child,' she said, ticking it off her fingers. 'She lives with her mother and her aunt. She likes to sew in her spare time. She predicted the summer would be a hot one. She enjoys quiche, and she is a good friend.'

'See what I mean?' His voice became a fraction louder. 'Frivolous! Why don't you permit people to know you, Evelyn? What awful thing do you think will happen?'

Evelyn felt the pressure that had wrapped itself around her chest begin to squeeze tighter. 'I think that when I let people in, they have a tendency to disappoint me,' she said quietly. 'So how about you leave me to my secrets, William, and I'll leave you to yours.'

William raised an eyebrow. 'What secrets do you think *I* have?'

'Christ, there's a question,' Jack scoffed, reaching for another pork pie and biting into the golden-brown crust.

The humour dropped from William's face. 'What are you talking about?'

'London!' Jack said, slapping his friend on the back. 'You kept *that* a secret. I'd no idea you were so serious about being a writer, and then all of a sudden you announced you were bloody moving!'

'But that's not what *you* meant, is it?' William asked, turning back to Evelyn. 'You weren't talking about London.'

'No,' Evelyn agreed.

'Enough now.' Naomi rolled her eyes. 'You're as bad as each other.'

'No.' William put his plate down. 'Evelyn has accused me of being deceptive, and I should like to know why.'

'Calm yourself,' Jack said, placing a hand on William's shoulder. 'I'm sure she was joking.'

'It didn't sound like a joke.'

'Jack is right – I didn't accuse you of anything,' said Evelyn.

'You might as well have!'

'Jack?' Naomi said, putting her plate down. 'I think I should like to go and walk around that lovely tree. Will you chaperone me?'

'Chaperone you . . . to the tree?'

'Yes,' said Naomi pointedly. 'So that these two can settle their disagreement in peace.'

'There's no need to do that,' said Evelyn. 'William and I can put this aside for now. Can't we, William?'

'Not until you tell me this great secret you think I'm keeping.'

'I will tell you tomorrow,' Evelyn said firmly.

'You will tell me now!' His voice was loud enough for an elderly couple sitting together on a nearby bench to look over.

'Come on, Jack,' said Naomi. 'Let's leave these two to hiss at one another.'

Evelyn hurried to her feet, but Naomi was faster. She linked her arm through Jack's and gave Evelyn a wide-eyed look and then a wink.

'You're *infuriating*.' Evelyn sat back down with a sigh. She felt very small all of a sudden, rather like her governess had just scolded her for her poor French.

'Just *tell me*,' said William.

She looked past him and his stony glare, towards the buildings that sat around the edge of the park. Great, sandstone houses painted white now in the sunshine.

'Your family,' she said at last. 'I asked why you lived with your uncle, and you avoided it. But you see, I think Naomi is right. If you don't wish to tell me, then I shan't push you. I am sorry I pried.'

William pushed his hair back from his face and let out a long breath. 'Well, that's no secret,' he said, his voice weary all of a sudden. 'Just a half-sad story I don't tend to go telling everyone the moment I meet them.'

'Because you think they'll pity you?' Evelyn said. 'Treat you differently?'

He looked at her then, a crease between his eyebrows. 'Yes, actually.' He sounded surprised. 'How did you know?'

'Because that's what you said at the Blue Bell.'

'Ah.' William blew a breath through his lips. 'And here was me thinking you were psychic.'

'No. I just listen.'

It was quiet between them for a moment. And then he put his plate down. 'I'm sorry for prying, too. Jack would say something kind, like it was my imagination getting the better of me, but I was just being nosy. After all, it's not every day some fine lady comes to work in your uncle's shop. You're not from our world, you know? People like me or Jack or Naomi don't attend balls. Or talk like you do. Or wear church dresses worth twice my yearly wage.'

Her instinct was to cover it, to hide it, to change the subject or to stand up, brush the crumbs from her lap and walk away. She could feel it in the hiccupped beating of her heart, in the tight feeling that had drawn into her chest.

But instead she found herself saying: 'My father is a baron, but . . . we lost our fortune.'

'And that's why you have to work in the bookshop?'

'I have to work in the bookshop because I won't wait for someone else to fix the mess my father has created.' The words came out like a sizzle, her face suddenly hot. 'I won't sit there wondering or waiting when I can do something about it.'

She plucked a strand of grass from beneath the edge of the blanket, twisting it around her gloved finger. It would stain the silk, but she found she didn't care.

'I know what it's like to feel at the mercy of others,' William said softly.

'Do you?' Her gaze tracked to where Jack and Naomi were making their second circuit of the oak tree, disturbing a clutch of sleeping ducks, who quacked angrily and waddled from their path. 'I find most men don't understand it at all.'

'My mother couldn't cope with me, you see. My father was a navy man' – his top lip curled just slightly – '*is* a navy man. He's not dead. Anyway, he was away too much, and my mother had to work, and I was . . .' He looked at Evelyn and then looked away. He shrugged. 'That's when I came to live with Uncle Howard. It was only meant to be for a year at first. And then one year became three, and three became seventeen. I was lucky, really. I wasn't an orphan; I wasn't sent to the workhouse. Just sent to be a burden to my uncle.'

'And your mother didn't come back for you?'

William shook his head. 'But there you have it. My not-very-secret secret.'

Evelyn didn't know what to say. 'I don't think you're a burden to Mr Morton. Anyone can see how much he dotes on you.'

'He's a good man,' William replied. 'And a collector of lost things, it seems.'

Evelyn's gaze locked upon his. 'You think I am a lost thing?'

'I think we both are,' William said quietly, not looking away. There was a freckle she had not noticed before, just at the edge of his eye, and it was matched by another at the corner of his mouth, brushing the edge of his bottom lip.

'And I think, on Monday, we should make this competition between us a fair one.'

Evelyn tweaked an eyebrow at him. 'You mean you'll teach me all your secrets?'

'Not *all*,' said William.

They looked at one another and smiled.

'Silence at last!' Jack called loudly from the other side of the bandstand. 'I think they might have called a truce, Naomi.'

Evelyn tore her gaze from him and turned it to her cider cup instead, to the gentle sound of the fizzing liquid.

'I think they might have.' Naomi was speaking in the same overly loud voice. 'Which I suppose means it's time for cream buns!'

'I am sorry, too,' she said, 'for prying.'

'You're forgiven,' William replied, with a lopsided grin. 'If I ever get cross with you again, I'll just remember the image of you listening to Jack's gelding story while trying to eat a piece of blue cheese.'

She laughed then, the kind of laugh that shook the cider cup in her hand and caused her to slosh the liquid over her wrist. 'I was hoping no one had seen that.'

'I see everything you do, Evelyn,' said William, and Evelyn felt her cheeks flush as Jack and Naomi returned to sit between them.

Chapter Twenty-Three

William was true to his word, for come Monday, once they had dusted and opened the door and the regulars had collected their periodicals, he announced that he would take on the role of a customer.

'And then *you* will try and sell me something,' he said, dropping the book in his hand back into the box.

Evelyn felt a twitch of nerves sizzle through her. 'Very well.'

William stepped out of the shop, and there was a pause that stretched just a moment too long. And then he walked back inside.

Evelyn stepped forwards. 'Good day, sir—'

'No,' William said abruptly, and then turned and walked straight back out again.

Evelyn pursed her lips. True, perhaps she was too quick to greet customers. Perhaps that was off-putting?

When he stepped inside next, she waited. When he was near her, she said: 'Let me know if I can help you.'

He gave her a half-smile in approval, and then turned to the shelf and began studying a book intensely. He picked it up, turning a few pages.

'Would you like me to take that to the register for you?'

William snapped the book shut. 'No,' he said, sliding it back into place and striding once more towards the door.

She didn't see what she had done wrong that time. He'd shown interest in a book, and so she'd offered to help him purchase it. Wasn't that quite literally her job?

When William entered the shop for the third time, Evelyn met him at the front door, her arms crossed over her chest. 'You know,' she said, 'this will be a lot quicker if you actually *tell me* what I am doing wrong, rather than trying to train me like one might train a lapdog. Use your words please, William. You are a writer, after all.'

Something flickered across William's face then, amusement, perhaps, or abashment, and he said: 'I wasn't ready to buy the book. You needed to give me an extra push. Something like—' He cleared his throat, his voice sinking deeper: 'You know, I read that book last summer, and I wish I could go back and read it all over again. It's marvellous. A masterpiece.' He raised an eyebrow at her. 'See what I did there?'

'But I haven't read it,' Evelyn said flatly.

'Well, in that case you might try something like: I have heard wonderful things about that novel. I am sure it will win a prize for its prose – the author truly is a magician when it comes to words.'

She scrunched her face into a frown. 'But I don't know any of those things.'

'Well, you must act as though you do,' William said. 'Being a great bookseller walks a fine line between genuine anecdotes and telling people what they want to hear, and unfortunately you are incredibly bad at *both* of those things. Now go and pick up a book, bring it here, and tell me a story about it – something truthful, something about you.'

Evelyn felt her neck grow hot. 'What?'

'You know, an anecdote, a chapter you liked in it – *anything*. We'll practise.'

Evelyn frowned. 'Practise?'

'Yes. Fetch a book, bring it here, and tell me a story about it.'

'But—' She swallowed. She didn't like the idea of telling complete strangers stories about herself. She hated the idea, in fact – almost as much as she hated the idea of telling William the very same things. 'I don't want to.'

'Oh, come on,' William said dismissively. 'It's not so hard.'

'For you perhaps!' This came out louder than she'd intended – and sharper, too. Her heart was thumping; her face was red, her whole body tense as though she was preparing to run for the door. William must have noticed it, too, for his expression softened.

'Is this about what you said at the picnic?' he said. 'That you fear you'll tell someone something about yourself, and they'll disappoint you?'

She thought of her first nights at boarding school: of awakening to a bed full of flour, of the screeching laughter of the other girls and the roar of the house matron as she discovered it. She thought of how the teachers had made her sit at the front, how the other girls had left a gap around her, leaning away as though she were a noxious miasma. She thought of the ball, how grown women had done much the same.

It wasn't merely disappointment that she was worried about. Disappointment she had grown somewhat immune to, thanks to her father.

'Scorn,' she said quietly. 'I do not wish to invite scorn.'

William reached out and gripped her hand. She thought he would pull away when he noticed how warm she was, how flustered, but he didn't. He kept it there, his cool hand, his calmness, and her focus drew to a point at the place where their hands touched, the place where warmth and cold met. It was soothing.

'I won't scorn you, Evelyn. I promise.'

'Don't promise,' she said, her voice low. 'Please.'

He blinked, confused, and slid his hand from hers, pressing it to his own chest. 'Then shall I swear it? On my own heart, as though we were players from Shakespeare's stage? I, William Albert Morton, swear to you—'

'No,' she said, though the edge of her lip had now twitched up towards a smile. 'Just show me that you mean it. That's all.'

'Very well,' William said sincerely. 'But telling someone something about yourself doesn't mean you're giving away any of who you are. It just means you'll . . .' He reached for the word and missed, flailing for a moment. 'Gosh, I don't know – find common ground with people?'

'What if I don't want to find common ground with people?' Evelyn said, half in jest and half seriously. 'What if I would far rather they all left me well alone?'

'Then perhaps you should have enquired for work at the mortuary,' William said with a cheerful grin. 'Here, our business is *words*. And you will learn how to use them. Now, *choose a book*.'

Evelyn turned to the shelves. A sea of stories, an ocean of them, and she had to choose one that meant something to her. And not just that: one that came with a story she felt comfortable telling William.

She swallowed, her skin still feverish as she moved towards the novels, tracing a warm finger down the spines. She had lots of stories about books, but most of them involved her father, for he was the one who had read to her most often when she was a child. *Black Beauty* had been her favourite, while her father had preferred adventure novels: books with great whales come to swallow you whole, or dark corners of the world with thick vines and lurking dangers. He would blow all the candles out but one and read in the growing darkness, his voice as soft and soothing as the lapping of waves against the shore, and she would find herself drifting off and dreaming of dark waters, of hidden caves, of pirate treasure and distant lands.

She turned abruptly from the children's books, from the weight that had been pressing against her chest, and marched instead towards the adult fiction, plucking *The Mystery of Cloomber* from the shelves.

William looked at her, his dark eyes warm for once. Encouraging. 'Well?'

'My mother and I read this in the *Pall Mall Gazette*,' she said, looking down at the book's bright, silver lettering. 'Mama found it so unsettling that we could read it only first thing, during breakfast, or she complained she did not sleep soundly.'

'And you? You did not have trouble sleeping?'

Evelyn looked up at him, at his dark eyes framed by darker lashes, at the gentleness in his gaze, and found herself saying: 'My father always read me dramatic books when I was little, so I grew up less sensitive to them. Although *The Mystery of Cloomber* did give me the urge to order books about Buddhists from the subscription library, just to check what their powers truly were.' Her lip twitched at the memory. 'Turns out Mr Conan Doyle had rather exaggerated the power of enlightenment. Not to mention that Buddhists are not typically the kind of fellows who would chase you halfway across the world for revenge.'

William gave her one of his curling half-smiles. 'Writers do have an awful tendency to make things up.' He turned from her then, plucking another book at random. 'Now let us say you dislike this book—' He flapped a copy of *The Adventures of Huckleberry Finn* at her. 'Pretend you detest it, with every fibre of your being. Can you imagine that?'

She looked at the book. It was the sort of book her father might have read her. 'I find that I can.'

'Now, sell it to me.'

Evelyn cleared her throat. 'That book is excellent, and I believe you should buy it.'

William rolled his eyes. 'Sell it *better*. Tell me what I want to hear!'

Evelyn gritted her teeth. 'That book will take you on the most incredible adventure you've ever been on.'

'Now make it personal. Tell me an anecdote.'

'But I don't have an anecdote about that book,' Evelyn said.

'So make one up.'

'I can't just *invent* a story, William.'

'Of course you can!' he said, a fire in his eyes now. 'How about: I read that one recently and fell in love with it. I would buy it again if I could.'

'Very well,' Evelyn said. 'I read that one recently and fell in love with it.'

'Well, if you fell in love with it, then I'll have to buy it,' William said, giving her a wide smile. 'See? That wasn't so hard, was it?'

She ignored the flutter in her stomach. 'It wasn't easy.'

'And now it'll be a fair fight,' William said cheerfully. 'So when I win, I'll be able to lord it over you with no guilt whatsoever.'

'Oh, I should imagine there would be a little guilt,' Evelyn said. 'After all, if it weren't for you, there would be no competition.'

'If it weren't for me, I bet you'd have got all the way to Christmas without making a single sale.'

Evelyn was going to say something sharp in return, but she stopped herself. 'William?'

He blinked. 'Yes?'

'Thank you,' she said.

For a moment, she thought he would give her some witticism back, but instead he only said: 'You're welcome,' a small smile upon his face.

Chapter Twenty-Four

By the time Evelyn left that Friday – two hours earlier than usual – she had sold nine novels, two periodicals, and a trilogy to old Mr Baker, which was very impressive considering the typesetting was *far* too small for a man of his age. And despite the fact that they were rivals, William found himself feeling quite proud of her as he pulled the heavy curtains closed, locked the door, and took the takings upstairs to Howie, who was sitting at his desk by the window, scribbling something furiously.

'Just leave it there, lad,' he said, without looking up. 'And I'll see you Sunday for lunch. I'm making lamb surprise.'

William smiled. When he was a boy, 'lamb surprise' had meant Howie was cooking with whatever the butcher had on offer, usually offal or some kind of game. But William and Howie called it lamb so that it sounded fancy, and they drank their small ale from fancy glasses, too.

'I'll see you then,' William said fondly. 'So long as you're sure you don't need me this Saturday?'

Howie shook his head. 'Spend your Saturdays with that book of yours, like we agreed. William?'

He turned back to his uncle, who had put down his pen and was now looking at him over the rims of his glasses.

'I just . . . I'm so proud of you, Will. I know you struggled for a while there, but you found your way in the end. You persevered until it paid off, and for that I am proud.'

William gave his uncle a half-smile. 'Thank you,' he said, trying not to hear the voice in his mind say: *No. You are still struggling. You are still failing. The only difference now is that you're lying about it, too.*

It was half past six by the time William stepped out into the street, closing and locking the heavy door behind him. He hesitated and then reached to rub the snout of the nearest gargoyle. He'd seen Evelyn doing it, and he wasn't sure why, but now it seemed odd *not* to do it. And then, because he wanted to be fair, he rubbed the snout of the second one, too.

'Oh, thank God.'

William turned at Jack's voice, and his eyes widened. His friend was wearing full livery: long, smart black tails with a white collar and a gold-buttoned vest. There was an emblem stitched in gold on his lapel pocket reading *RSH*, and a handkerchief with matching initials was tucked into it. His red-brown hair was slicked back with so much oil it looked as though Jack had simply dunked his head into a vat of it. But the overall effect was . . . smart. Proper-looking, in fact.

'Is there a wedding I don't know about?' Will said, as Jack grabbed his arm and pulled him to one side.

'I need yer help,' said Jack. 'And I need yer to say yes straight away and not ask a ton of questions, 'cos I've only a half-hour for my tea break, and it took me fifteen minutes to walk here.'

'I dislike the sound of this already,' Will replied. 'But go on.'

'I need you to go to the Royal in an hour and a half, find Evelyn, and tell her the bookshop is burning down or something like that. Just get her out of there.'

Will's eyes widened further. 'What? Why?'

'Because Naomi got me to promise bloody weeks ago that I'd help, and I obviously said yes, and then what with the new job, I completely forgot. But then I saw Evelyn's name on the dinner reservations for tonight and remembered that Naomi's expecting me to come up with some excuse, but my boss watches me like a bloody hawk, Will, and I've already muddled up two orders today, and they've put me down in the basement, polishing cutlery. If I'm not on my best behaviour, I'll be out on my arse – or worse, begging for my old job as a night porter back from the Black Swan.' Jack gripped his hands, squeezing his fingers so tightly together that it hurt. '*Please*, Will. *Please help me.* Say you'll do it.'

'But . . .' Will shook his head. 'Why is Evelyn at the Royal? And why do I need to lie about the bookshop?'

'Evelyn's going to dinner with some man or other who she doesn't like. Or who she does like? I can't remember, but she asked Naomi for a good excuse to scarper out of there early, and Naomi volunteered me, and now I'm volunteering you.' Jack prodded at William's chest with his finger.

So *that* was why she'd left early today. Was it why she'd been acting so strangely all day, too? She had barely said a word to him, and when she did give him an answer, it was usually to a question he'd asked an hour ago and not the one he was asking there and then. She'd been distracted. She'd been flustered.

Had she been *nervous*?

Will shrugged, despite the curl in his stomach. 'Evelyn is a grown woman. If she wants to leave a dinner, she'll manage it on her own.'

'But I promised!'

'But *I didn't*.' Will started to walk down the street. 'Besides, I'm sure if you explained that it would cost you your job, Naomi would understand.'

'Sure,' Jack said, giving chase. 'She'd understand that

a promise from me is worth nothing! I want her thinking I'm *reliable* – that I mean what I say! Please, Will.' Jack was clutching at his hands now. 'Besides, I *know* you. For all yer spiked words, you'd not want to watch her suffer.'

'Whoever said that?'

'*Please*,' Jack repeated, gripping his hands all the tighter.

William sighed. 'Very well,' he said, extracting himself from his friend's grip. 'I shall do it.'

'I owe you for this,' Jack said, already starting to half skip, half jog away from him, back towards the hotel. 'I really owe you!'

'You owe me already,' William called after him. 'Remember the Blue Bell!'

'I'll pay yer back!'

William waved it away and watched his friend's black clothes merge into the clatter of people and carriages pushing towards the city.

'Well, this should be interesting,' he muttered.

Evelyn walked up the stairs of the Royal Station Hotel alone, her hem held in one clammy hand, her mother's dainty purse in the other.

Her mother was meant to be accompanying her, but around five p.m. she had begun to complain of a tight forehead, and by the time Evelyn was dressed and her hair was neatly pinned, her mother was quite sure it would deteriorate into a full-blown attack.

'There is nothing else for it,' Cecilia had said, tucking a loose curl behind Evelyn's ear. 'The Royal is a very respectable place, so I am sure we need not fear impropriety. I shall simply have to stay here and lie in the dark, and you will have to go to dinner alone.'

'Which is precisely how Cecilia and your father first dined,' Aunt Clara had interjected, earning herself a scalding look from Cecilia. 'Some draughty public house on the outskirts of the city, was it not?'

'You are misremembering,' Cecilia had said sharply.

'My memory is impeccable,' Aunt Clara had retorted. 'Although perhaps your motto was not that one needed to *bend* rules to one's needs but break them entirely? You were a lot more enterprising back then, Cecilia—'

'Ah,' Evelyn had said, turning to meet her mother's gaze. 'Is *that* what brought your migraine on? All your plotting?'

Her mother had flushed red. 'Ignore your dear great-aunt. She is going senile.'

Evelyn stifled a chuckle at the memory of Aunt Clara's furious retort as she gave her name to the man at the door. He ushered her inside, into the grand, candlelit dining room and eventually to a table framed by two elaborate balcony doors, open wide to the cooling night air and the city beyond.

'Sorry I am late,' came a voice behind her, and she turned to find Nathaniel, dressed dazzlingly in a black silk waistcoat, a perfectly starched white shirt, and a matching bow tie. He removed his top hat, revealing slick blond hair as he gave her a dignified bow. 'It is a pleasure to see you again, Miss Seaton. You look wonderful.'

Evelyn could only hope that Nathaniel's first thought when he saw her had been something kinder than: *by God, does the poor woman have only one evening dress?* His second thought no doubt mirrored her own: that it was rather a bold statement to dine just the two of them, even *if* the Royal was a respectable establishment. The upside of this, Evelyn supposed, was that Lady Violet would no doubt hear of it, and know she had taken their deal seriously.

'Please, call me Evelyn,' she said, holding out her hand. 'My mother sends her apologies, but she has been taken ill. One of her headache attacks.'

'Ah, my father gets those,' he said, taking the seat opposite her. 'He begins to see auras – colours all around him. I would rather like to see that, though I wouldn't like the headache that follows.'

'No, indeed,' said Evelyn. 'They rather incapacitate my mother.' *And always at the most convenient of times.*

'You look beautiful, Evelyn,' said Nathaniel. 'That colour suits you.'

She had been absent-mindedly fiddling with the gold-threaded napkin in her lap, but now she looked up, into his eyes. They were startlingly blue, the colour of cornflowers, and now in the flickering candlelight, his gaze felt warm upon her skin. 'Thank you,' she said.

He chuckled. 'And that's why I prefer British women. In New York, the society ladies always seem to want to trade my compliments in for better ones. They're never happy with "beautiful" – it has to be "the most beautiful" or "even more beautiful". I am forever forced to come up with another, better form of praise.'

Evelyn raised her eyebrows. 'I think people who seek out such praise from others do so because they never hear it from themselves. They don't tell themselves they are kind or good: they rely on others to do it for them. The irony is that until they can tell it to themselves, until they can listen to it and accept it, they won't believe it from the mouths of others. They won't hold it as a truth. That's why they seek more compliments from you, Nathaniel – and why you feel uncomfortable giving them.'

He looked at her, his pale eyebrows all but touching his hairline. 'What an odd thing to say,' he breathed.

'I have heard that once or twice before,' Evelyn replied, an amused smile tugging at her lips as she turned her attention to the delicate menu card on her right. 'The truffle beef sounds delicious.'

Nathaniel clicked his fingers as a waiter walked past. 'We

shall take the *poulet à la Marengo* and a matched red wine. Then the lobster, with your finest champagne.' He flashed her a guilty smile. 'Trust me – the Queen herself has eaten it. They bring the spices all the way from India.'

Evelyn set her menu down. There was little point in reading it if the man was going to order the entire meal for her – and little point in explaining now that she didn't like lobster. If she wasn't being blackmailed to be polite, she might have said something. As it was, she did what she imagined Lady Violet would do.

She smiled the sweetest smile she could muster. 'Do you memorize the menu in every establishment you dine in or just the Royal?'

'Just the Royal,' Nathaniel said amicably. 'Between my own business in London and the Duke's business here in York, I am up and down so much that I often find myself crawling through those doors half-starved.'

'And do you always order for your female companions without asking?'

Nathaniel had the grace to blush. 'I don't make a habit of taking women out for dinner, you know.'

'What of Lady Violet?'

His attention became rather transfixed by the white silk tablecloth. 'What of Lady Violet?'

'Don't you ever think of taking her out for dinner? Surely it would be more amusing than spending the day waiting for her in that lobby.'

His ears began to redden. 'Lady Violet doesn't think of me as a suitor.'

'And what of you?' she asked, her voice a little quieter. His ears were becoming *very* red, almost as red as the glasses of wine the waiter now placed carefully upon the table. 'Do you think of yourself as her suitor?'

'I think that is none of your business,' Nathaniel said

with vicious speed, and then he blinked. 'Please don't be offended – I didn't mean for that to come out so . . . so crassly.'

'*That* didn't offend me,' Evelyn said honestly. 'But in general, I like to be able to order my food for myself. I don't happen to like lobster.'

He fiddled with his collar. 'I thought it would impress you that I knew the menu, but you are right. Let me—'

He stood, dropping his napkin hurriedly on his plate, and Evelyn watched him go. The tables in here were occupied mostly by men, in clumps of threes and fours. There were a handful of women scattered amongst them, but they were the only couple, the only pair here alone – an impropriety her mother must have anticipated. And yet Cecilia was the one who had refused to cancel! So then it was acceptable to break the rules and dine with men alone, *in public*, and yet not acceptable to get a job? To work for a living? It all seemed rather senseless to Evelyn.

'Done,' Nathaniel said, sitting down rather less gracefully. 'You will have the veal instead.'

She was too exhausted to explain that he had once again chosen without asking her. Instead, she smiled and let the hum of the restaurant settle between them.

He was less nervous when Lady Violet wasn't around but less . . . sparkling, somehow. It was as though he'd been putting on a show before, and now the curtains were closed and the theatre was being swept, and whatever had energized him had dissipated, leaving the pair of them on either side of a stretching silence.

Nathaniel did not clink his glass of wine to hers; he simply picked it up and took a long gulp, and so Evelyn did the same. It was delicious, sweet and dry all at once, and it fizzed in her veins, flushing her cheeks.

Nathaniel cleared his throat. 'Listen, I must confess something, Evelyn. I asked you here tonight because . . . well,

I have something particular to say to you.' He swallowed then. 'I even asked your mother if she might find an excuse to stay away. I rather thought she'd ask more questions, but she agreed quite readily. I think perhaps she assumed it concerned . . .' He swallowed. 'Matters of the heart.'

So *that* was why Cecilia had seemed so satisfied as Evelyn had been getting ready. Because she *knew*. Then Aunt Clara was right: Cecilia wasn't bending her own rules, she was breaking them entirely. But what on earth did Nathaniel have to say to her that he could not say in front of her mother? If it *was* concerning matters of the heart, then perhaps it was about Lady Violet?

'I have been doing some digging,' said Nathaniel. 'In London.'

Now Evelyn frowned. 'Digging?'

'Into your father.' He finally looked up at her, his mouth twisted into a line. 'I know why you had to leave the ball so quickly that evening. Lady Violet told me about your father – about what she'd said, and how you got so mad at her for lying that you stormed out—'

'*That's* what she said?' Evelyn didn't know whether it was the wine or the last of the day's heat against the glass balcony doors, but she felt clammy all of a sudden.

'—but listen, Evelyn. Lady Violet can be cattish when she is backed into a corner, but she is not a liar, and I couldn't stand for you to ruin your friendship over such a thing. Lady Violet couldn't stand the thought of it, either. When she heard of my plan, she was so relieved that I might be able to find out the truth and help you both patch things up most amicably.'

'The truth?'

'Yes,' Nathaniel said. 'The truth about your father. About the money – about how he lost it.'

Chapter Twenty-Five

William sneaked up the red-velvet stairs, hidden between a trail of overly perfumed women.

He disliked the Royal. It was snobbish in a way that seemed unearned, given that the building was younger than he was. Nevertheless, they'd dressed the interior like a castle, all gold-plated ironwork and glittering chandeliers. Even the men who worked here seemed to think themselves gilded, for the footman on the door had turned Will away as though he were some peasant, forcing him to take a rather uncomfortable detour through the gardens, behind a set of blackberry bushes and eventually in through one of the lower floor windows. Which was why there was now a scratch on his cheek the length of his index finger, and another on his forearm.

He blamed Jack for it, with his ridiculous promise. Blamed Naomi, for making him swear to it. But mostly he blamed Evelyn. Of course she would choose a place like the Royal to have dinner.

At the top of the stairs, he left the ladies, trailing a group of men as they wound their way inside the restaurant instead, his eyes searching.

And then he saw her.

She was wearing the same rich emerald dress she'd

worn the very first time they'd met. Her hair – darker in the candlelight – was spilling in loose curls around her shoulders, and the frustration that had been knotted in his stomach dissolved, all his thoughts replaced with only one: Evelyn was *beautiful*.

He'd thought it when he first saw her, silhouetted in the carriage doorway, her face aglow with soft lamplight, and he thought it still. But now he saw it in the way she held herself. In the way her head tilted, in the curve of her neck, the flick of her wrist as she gestured, talking animatedly to the man opposite her.

Here, now, she looked perfect. She belonged in a room like this, wearing a dress like that. She suited it in a way she didn't suit a dark and dusty bookshop, kneeling on the floor or lugging boxes back and forth. The thought should have made him happy, should have felt like a victory of sorts, a validation, but instead he felt a curl of something in his stomach.

Because this Evelyn, this version of her, didn't look like she needed rescuing. She looked like she was enjoying herself. She was leaning forwards, her gloved hands reaching across the tablecloth, hanging onto the man's every word as though he were the most interesting person in the world.

This Evelyn felt distant to him, a million miles away from the woman who'd snapped at him two days ago for leaving books on the cellar stairs.

A waiter stepped past him with a frown, and Will took an empty seat, his gaze not leaving their table.

The man reached forwards, clutching at Evelyn's hand, and she didn't pull away. William felt the tug in his stomach become a sharp ache. Was he . . . jealous? Of the man sat opposite her, with his ridiculously oiled hair and his smart dinner suit? Or perhaps he was simply jealous of how she was looking at him. Like she was enthralled. Enchanted.

Don't be silly, he told himself gruffly. He was just frustrated –

that was all. After everything he'd done to get here, they were sat in splendour, enjoying their dinner. He wasn't going to ruin that – wasn't going to storm over there like some fool and lay waste to it.

And then she drew her hand back sharply and brought it to her mouth. He felt his stomach twist.

Was she . . . crying?

It looked like she was, like that man, whatever he had said, had made her cry. And the man seemed to know it, for now he was casting furtive looks over his shoulder, uncomfortable, worried someone would see them or hear them, and he leaned forwards, panic in his eyes as he reached for her hand once more.

But now she recoiled from him, and William felt his legs moving, felt himself bump shoulders with a waiter, heard the apology slide from his lips as he moved towards them, as he avoided chairs being pushed out and platters being carried and a trolley of cakes being wheeled past, until suddenly he was at their table.

He could feel the breeze from the balcony upon his face, could say: 'Evelyn! Thank goodness I found you. I need you to come back with me to the shop right away.'

Evelyn could hear only the thud of her own heartbeat in her ears; everything else had been drowned, replaced with a shattering roar. She couldn't even hear Nathaniel, whose hands were stretched across the table, reaching for her. She felt him clasp her fingers, felt him squeeze them tightly, and she pulled back sharply, pulled away, and then someone was calling her name, and the bubble that had formed around her popped like a soapsud.

Suddenly it was loud again: the clatter of forks upon plates, deep, tenor laughter, the glug of pouring wine, the sudden pop of champagne corks.

'Evelyn,' repeated a familiar voice. 'I need you to come back to the shop. Please. There's an emergency.'

Her mind felt slow, as though each thought were being pulled through honey. She turned. 'William?'

His black hair was messier than usual, and a long, thin scratch had collected a blood drop across his left cheek. There was a wild look in his eyes, a tremor to his limbs, as though he'd run the whole way here and still had energy to burn. But his voice . . .

'Excuse me?' Nathaniel said crisply.

'There is an emergency,' William repeated, giving her a pointed look.

And then suddenly she remembered. Her comment to Naomi. Naomi's idea. The promise. But she hadn't thought she really meant it. And that had been before she'd spoken to Lady Violet, before she'd agreed . . .

'Really! We are in the middle of dinner.' Nathaniel swatted at the air near William as though he were some buzzing fly. Then Nathaniel leaned in, a bashful expression crumpling his face. 'Evelyn, I am so sorry – I thought you must have had an inkling that . . . Your father was so notorious for it in London that I assumed—' He sucked in a breath, chewing at his bottom lip. 'But of course you had no idea. I can see that now. And I am sorry that I was the one to tell you.'

Evelyn's gaze flicked back to his blue eyes, to the sincerity behind them. She felt dazed and overwhelmed all at once, both sluggish and jittery, as though she had spun in too-quick circles and now she was staggering, trying to catch her balance while someone shouted for her to run.

She sipped her wine, her fingers trembling around the stem as a thousand thoughts struggled forth at once, and the same, few words circled in her mind: *It is a compulsion, for men like your father. A sickness.*

'*You* have said quite enough,' William huffed, holding a

hand out to Evelyn. 'And you needn't listen to it a moment longer, Evelyn.'

'Now, hold on a minute here,' said Nathaniel, turning. 'Who are you, exactly?'

'A friend,' said William, clearing his throat. 'A colleague. Who needs you back at the bookshop right away, Evelyn.'

Nathaniel turned to Evelyn. 'You cannot go. You must allow me to explain. To make this up to you—'

'Please—' Evelyn reached her fingers to her temples, which were pounding now, whether from the heat or the alcohol or Nathaniel's story, she didn't know.

Once they lose, they are so fixated on making the money back that they bet more and more . . .

Nathaniel turned to William. 'This emergency of yours – is anyone dead?'

'Nothing like that.'

'Anything on fire?'

'No, but—'

'Well then.' Nathaniel waved a hand. 'I am sure it can wait until tomorrow. I shouldn't like for us to leave it like this, Evelyn. Can't we just have a nice dinner? Pretend I never said anything?'

And your father made the biggest bet of them all.

Evelyn pressed her fingers to the sides of her head all the more forcefully. She wanted nothing more than to go with William, to step into the night and gulp in the cooling air, the quiet, as though she were a woman drowning.

But she had made a deal with Lady Violet. And if she broke it . . .

'Indeed, William,' Evelyn said, giving him a look that said: *I know what you are doing.* 'Perhaps it can wait until tomorrow.'

'No. It can't,' William said firmly.

Nathaniel lifted his chin a little higher. 'Come now. The lady has made her choice. You had better leave before I call someone over here and have you forcibly removed. You are ruining our dinner.'

William planted himself most firmly in the chair intended for her mother. 'Oh, am I?' he said. 'Because from the other side of the room, it looked like *you* were ruining it. Or do you always make women cry over their meals?'

The colour drained from Nathaniel's face. 'I was only trying to—'

'Stop it, the both of you.' Evelyn said, as the pain behind her eyelids stabbed once more. 'Nathaniel hasn't done anything wrong.' He had simply told her the truth – which was more than her father had ever done. 'And nor have you, William.'

She looked at him, into his dark eyes, and was surprised to find his concern was not fabricated, as she'd imagined, but sincere. He looked worried. He looked *angry*.

'Well then,' chirped Nathaniel, 'let us call that the end of it. I cannot imagine *what* could be such an emergency that some lowly clerk needs to drag a fine lady from her dinner.'

'I'm not a fine lady,' Evelyn said, her tone firmer now. 'And William is actually an author. Soon to be a very famous one.'

Now Nathaniel's eyebrows tweaked upwards. 'Oh?'

'Yes,' Evelyn said, enjoying the surprise in his expression. 'He has secured quite the deal.'

Nathaniel's blue eyes fixed upon William. 'With whom?'

William huffed a sharp breath through his teeth. 'What?'

'Who did you sign with? My father's company has deals with many of the big houses here to buy the rights to print their best works in the States. So, who was it? Routledge? Macmillan? Pickering & Chatto? John Murray?'

'It's none of your damn business,' William growled. 'Now, Evelyn, please—'

He pushed his chair back to stand up, but Nathaniel

leaned forwards, gripping William's forearm so tightly that she could see his knuckles streak with white. 'Then perhaps Longman? Chapman & Hall?'

William didn't struggle. He didn't try and twist from his grip. Instead, he looked Nathaniel straight in the eye and said, his voice low, 'Take your hand off me.'

Nathaniel didn't move. 'I am quickly running out of publishers to list. Unless it's Colburn? Bentley? Heinemann? No? My, my. If they are going to make you famous, then it must be one of the big houses. A smaller imprint will just peddle your work straight to yellowback, those throwaway novels one reads on the train. Unless that is what they sold you? Is that what you think fame is?

'Evelyn is exaggerating. I don't *want* fame,' William said, though his voice was stiff now, stilted. 'And nor do I want your nose in my business.'

'Ah, but you see, it's my business, too.' Nathaniel picked up his red wine, taking a long sip. 'And so I feel I am very well placed to give you a piece of advice: learn the name of your publisher. It will make for fewer awkward conversations in the future.'

William bunched his hand into a fist. 'This is why I don't like you people – why I avoid places like this.' His dark eyes fixed upon Evelyn, and now there was a fire within them. 'Do you know what? If you wish to sit here with a man who makes you cry, then do it. Sit here. Enjoy yourselves. You seem well suited.'

'William, wait.'

But he didn't wait. He yanked his arm from beneath Nathaniel's grip so forcefully that it rocked the whole table. It made the plates chatter and crumpled the cloth from beneath the glasses, the candles, sending Evelyn's red wine tumbling forwards and casting a great wave of it across her front.

She sat there for a moment, dazed, and then looked down at the purpling stain that was spreading, soaking through the silk of her dress.

'Oh, for goodness' sake,' muttered Nathaniel. 'You clumsy fool.'

William's mouth opened and closed, and then he stepped back, knocking the chair over with him with a resounding crash, and stormed out.

A hush fell over the room, and Evelyn, her cheeks burning now, stood up, her dress dripping. Ruined.

'Nathaniel, you will have to excuse me,' she said, with as much dignity as she could muster. 'I believe we shall have to suspend our dinner.'

'I believe so,' Nathaniel said, dashing his napkin to his plate. 'Listen, Evelyn, I'm sorry – this isn't at all how I thought the night would turn out. Perhaps I shouldn't have told you. I shouldn't have pried. I thought I was being helpful, truly I did. I thought—'

'I know what you thought,' she said, feeling the room's eyes upon her like coals against her skin. 'And I think eventually I will thank you for having told me. But tonight—'

'I understand,' he said, standing with her. 'Shall I call my carriage?'

'No.' She sucked in a shaky breath, giving him the best smile she could muster. 'I believe I am in need of a walk. Now, if you will excuse me.'

Chapter Twenty-Six

It took a great deal of effort to leave that room with her chin held high. It took even more effort to keep the blank expression fixed upon her face as she descended the stairs, as she stepped out into the cool night air.

It was still early, the clouds only just beginning to darken like a bruise over the rooftops. She could hear the whistle of a steam train pulling in at the station behind her, could hear the rattle-slam of the doors being swung open. Soon, there would not just be handfuls of people on this street but dozens of them, and they would all see her. With her skittering gaze and her ruined dress.

Your father was so notorious for it in London that I assumed ... She pinched at the bridge of her nose, willing the words away, pushing them down, into that dark place, the recess of her mind where she kept all the things she did not wish to look upon, did not wish to see.

But today, it would not work. Today, it simply made the words louder, made the twisting feeling in her stomach wrench all the harder.

How could he? How could he! They had lost everything. The house. Their belongings. Family portraits. Heirlooms. They had lost it all because of him. And all because of ...

She bit down on her inner cheek hard, trying to quell the ache in her throat, tasting the metallic tang of blood. She could not think about it now, not here, not in public, not with a train pulling in, not with so many people on the streets. She could not crumble yet. Could not cry.

And then a man stepped towards her.

A man with curling hair and long lashes and hazel eyes.

And he said: 'Evelyn, I'm sorry. Your dress . . .'

And for a moment, she wanted to reach for him, to wrap her arms around him and feel his arms around her and let it all out. All the fear she had been harbouring. All the worry. The guilt from lying to her mother. The frustration of having to keep it all a secret. The dread that Lady Violet would reveal everything. But most of all, the pain. Because the truth of why they had lost everything, the truth of what her father had done was worse than she'd imagined, and it cut like a knife into her stomach.

And then William said: 'Although, if you'd not made me sit there and listen to that man, then it'd not be ruined. You should've come with me straight away.'

And the moment broke, dissipating in the air like a curl of smoke, replaced with something far easier to manage. *Fury.*

Evelyn huffed out a sharp breath, blinking rapidly to clear the tears from her eyes. '*That* was a poor apology.'

'You're the one who should apologize,' he said. 'Do you know what I had to do to get into—' He shook his head. 'No, I'm not going to embarrass myself further. But needless to say, you could say sorry, too, for what you made me do tonight.'

'I didn't *make* you do anything!'

'No, but you made Naomi! *Three people* had to get involved just because you didn't want to sit through a dinner!'

Evelyn blinked. 'I didn't think she was serious,' she said. 'I didn't think she meant it!'

'People mean what they say, Evelyn.'

'Really? Because that's never been my experience.' Evelyn turned away from him so that he would not see the tears prick back into her eyes. 'I am not used to people actually keeping their word.'

William hesitated, and Evelyn pressed her fingers gently against her eyes, trying to dab away the wetness. People were spilling from the station now, into the dusky light of the street.

William came around to face her, his expression crumpled with a surprising softness that was written into the slant of his eyebrows, the downwards pull of his lips. 'That is a pessimistic world to live in, Evelyn. A world where people say one thing and do another.'

'Yes, well,' she said hurriedly, for there was a tremor to her voice now and she didn't want him to hear it. 'I can no more change it than I can unwind time and have you knock the wine over the tablecloth, instead of over my only evening dress.'

'I am sorry for that.' His voice was quieter now, sincere. 'Truly, I am. I was going to walk away, when I first saw you two sitting there. I was going to leave you in peace. Perhaps I should have.'

Evelyn sighed, looking away. 'No, you came at the right moment.'

He reached forwards then, placing his hand upon her forearm. His palm was warm against her skin, comforting. 'What did he say to you to upset you?'

She looked up into his eyes. But it was too shameful to tell him what her father had done.

'Nothing,' she lied – hating herself for lying and hating her father for making her. 'It was nothing.'

His frown deepened. 'It didn't look like nothing.'

'Well, it was.'

For a moment, he looked as though he wanted to say something. His mouth opened; a frown creased his brow. But then he shook his head. 'Very well,' he said. 'If you don't want to tell me, then don't. But let me walk you home. It's the least I can do after ruining your dress.'

She didn't look down at the silk. She already knew it was ruined, and she already knew no amount of cornflour could fix it. Her mother was going to be furious.

'Then let's walk slowly,' she said. 'My mother isn't expecting me home until late.'

William tilted his head to one side. 'I have an idea,' he said. 'Come on.'

Chapter Twenty-Seven

They tracked the curve of the river back towards the town centre, past the market square, the sky a patchwork of pink and red as the sun finally dipped below the horizon.

She knew it was improper to walk like this, the two of them alone at this time of the evening, but it had been improper to share a carriage with William that very first night, improper to sit at dinner with Nathaniel, goodness – even her *job* was improper according to Cecilia, and for once, Evelyn found she didn't care. There were still people out, men huddling in clusters playing dice, groups spilling out of bars and public houses, but none of them paid the pair of them any mind, and Evelyn and William paid them none, either. As they crossed the Foss Bridge, she saw the looming structure of the bookshop.

'You're wrong, you know,' he said, his voice as quiet as the gurgling river below them. 'About the world. Most people mean what they say.'

'For you, perhaps.'

'For you, too. Look at what Naomi did for you today. What Jack did. If actions speak louder than words, then I'd say those were some pretty loud actions.'

He walked closely enough that if she moved her hand just an inch to her right, she would meet his.

'And you. You did something, too.'

He gave her a rueful smile. 'I did. I climbed through a blackberry bush for you today, Evelyn. I've never done that for anyone before.'

Her eyes widened. 'What? Why on earth—'

William gave a half-laugh. 'Because they wouldn't let me in! Can you imagine?' He gestured down to his worn brown suit, to his rumpled hair. 'I'm the picture of elegance.'

'Aren't we both?' Evelyn looked down at the stain, which had darkened from a blood-red to the colour of ripe, summer plums.

'Can I ask you something?' William said, his gaze flicking to hers and then away. 'That man, tonight. Why were you with him? It's not—' He cleared his throat, pausing to lean over the bridge's edge. 'It's not often that women are alone with men at dinner, and you were on first-name terms, and . . . you see, Jack didn't tell me much, and so I didn't know if you were together, you and him . . . if you were . . . courting.'

William looked not at her but down at his hands. There was an ink stain between his index finger and the one beside it, and Evelyn felt something flicker in her stomach.

'No, we are not courting.'

'Ah. Well, that's good,' said William with a lopsided smile.

'Is it?'

'Of course,' he said quickly. 'Or else what I did tonight would be even worse, and I'd no doubt have an American knocking at my door and challenging me to pistols at dawn for my impropriety.'

'I don't think America is like that anymore,' Evelyn said. 'All guns and lawlessness.'

'Maybe,' said William. 'But all the same, I'm sorry he upset you.'

Evelyn blew a breath through her teeth. There was something about William that made her . . . *want* to tell him the truth. She had noticed it more and more, how she would collect little stories of her morning walks or quotes from Aunt Clara and keep them for when she saw him. She told herself it was because she wanted to make him laugh, to soften the tension that ran between them like wire, but more and more she had found the words readied at the tip of her tongue to be not just stories but secrets – the things she kept in that dark place in her mind, all clamouring to be brought forth, to be seen.

'It wasn't Nathaniel,' she admitted. 'It was my father. Nathaniel told me how he lost the money. It's been the talk of London, apparently, and . . .' She sighed, feeling her throat constrict anew. 'And I am so disappointed in him. So *angry*. I thought he was a better man than that. I thought—'

She bit down on the inside of her cheek, for the tears had sprung to her eyes again, and she wouldn't cry in front of him – she didn't want to cry in front of him. But now she was holding onto the stone bridge, feeling the coolness of it beneath her fingertips, watching the river smoothing into a blur of silver as the tears dripped down her cheeks, and William's hand was on her back.

She leaned into him, dampening his shirt, soaking the creased linen of his collar. She was just so tired of it all, so tired of pulling energy from a place that had long been empty. For once, she wished the world could curl around her, quiet and still, so that she could rest.

William said nothing; he just held her, and she felt his cheek come to rest upon the top of her head.

'I am sorry,' she said after a time, standing straighter and wiping at her eyes.

'Don't be,' William said, his arms still around her. 'I wish I could tell you that this sort of pain goes away, but I think it just becomes more distant.'

She wondered if he was speaking of his mother, of how

he'd come to live in York, with Mr Morton, of how the years had stretched, as he'd told her in the park.

'But it lessens?'

'It lessens,' William said, nodding. 'The longer you go without seeing someone, the harder it is to remember why you were so angry with them, I suppose.'

Evelyn rubbed the wetness from her cheeks. She wondered whether she would feel that way after seventeen years, too – but for now, the pain was too hot to grip.

Instead, she gave William a weak smile. 'Are you saying that if I left the shop for a week, you'd be less frosty towards me?'

'I am not *frosty* towards you,' said William. He was leaning beside her instead now, so that their shadows merged upon the water.

'Oh, I should say you are,' said Evelyn. 'You tried to steal my job, after all.'

'And then I climbed through a blackberry bush for you.'

'*Reluctantly.*'

He pressed his shoulder against hers. 'And offered to walk you home?'

'Out of guilt.'

He glanced at her then, his dark eyes gold in the lamplight, and there was something in his gaze that made her heart skitter.

'No,' said William softly. 'That is not the only reason why I am doing it.'

Her heart thudded even louder. 'Then it's because you know you cost me a carriage ride home.'

'You should be thanking me for that,' he said. reaching to tuck a curl that had come loose behind her ear. 'You shouldn't share a carriage with a man like that. You shouldn't *be* with a man like that.'

Evelyn swallowed. She had thought William might kiss her in the cab, all those weeks ago, but now she *wanted* him to. Here, upon this bridge, outside of the bookshop, she wanted him to close the gap between them, so that the lamplight cast only one shadow, but for once she had no words for it, only a tugging sensation deep in the pit of her stomach, willing him to sidle closer and extinguish the sliver of air between them.

'Nathaniel is not so awful—' she began, but the rest of her sentence was silenced as William leaned towards her and kissed her.

It was a gentle kiss, a questioning kiss, and she felt her body answer instantaneously, the heat pooling in her stomach and fizzing through her limbs as she gave him her answer, opening her mouth against his and kissing him back. His fingertips traced a line down the side of her neck, coming to rest in the dip at the base of her throat where her heart pounded a rhythm that stretched through her veins and down into the very pit of her stomach.

A whistle pierced the air, bouncing off the brick, and someone shouted: 'It's a bit early!'

William pulled back first, a flush upon his cheeks, casting a glance over Evelyn's shoulder. 'Come on,' he said, proffering his elbow. 'Let me walk you home, lest the Red Lion's patrons think we are the night's entertainment.'

And Evelyn nodded dazedly and walked alongside him, her heart still thundering in her chest.

A different kind of silence followed them as they walked. This was not the taut wire that Evelyn was used to; this was something else entirely – something low and rumbling that thrummed between them, that made the evening feel warmer, the moonlight brighter as dusk drew in above them.

When they reached the corner of Long Close Lane,

Evelyn stopped, and William stopped with her, his dark hair like spun gold beneath the lamplight.

'You may leave me here,' she said. 'I can walk the rest of the way alone.'

William's brow creased, and he turned to look along the empty street. 'I promised to walk you home,' he said, 'not leave you at the corner.'

'My mother will be watching for me,' Evelyn said, unlinking her arm from his. 'It is bad enough that I did not come with Mr Morris's carriage—'

'Ah,' said William, nodding now. 'I see. You don't wish her to know that a ruffian walked you home?'

'You are no ruffian,' she said, a smile twitching at her lips. 'Ruffians don't live on St. Leonard's Place and write with such a view. Nor do they tend to have large publishing deals with fine London imprints.'

William's gaze flicked to his feet. 'No, they do not,' he said. 'And yet all of that wouldn't be enough for me to walk you to your doorway?'

He said it casually enough, but there was a jagged thread beneath his voice now, and his eyes were firmly on the floor.

'My mother is expecting Mr Morris,' Evelyn explained. 'And you are not him. It will only encourage more questions.'

'I am not him,' agreed William, looking up at her now and giving her a resigned smile. 'But if that's what you want, then I shall leave you here, Evelyn. And I shall watch until you're at your doorway.'

'Good night, William,' she said, wondering whether to press a kiss to his cheek or to duck a curtsey, and settling upon neither.

'Good night, Evelyn,' he said, his dark eyes meeting hers. 'And sorry again about the dress.'

But as she walked towards Aunt Clara's house, she found

she didn't care anymore about the dress, nor about what her mother would say when she saw her. That was all distant now, sunk beneath a handful of beautiful words, hidden beneath the wonder of kissing William.

There was a lightness in her limbs, a soaring feeling in her chest that she had not felt before, and she all but ran the last few yards to Aunt Clara's doorway, William's words echoing as if he were stood beside her still, whispering them anew into her ear: *I climbed through a blackberry bush for you today, Evelyn. I've never done that for anyone before.*

And then the door swung open, and Aunt Clara's face appeared in the doorway, pinched and pale.

'What is it?' Evelyn said. 'What's wrong?'

Aunt Clara stepped back to let her through, and Evelyn saw the hat on the coatstand, the travelling cloak beneath it.

And then she heard it: male laughter from the morning room, footsteps upon the wooden floor.

And then there he was, standing before her, saying: 'My dear daughter, how I have missed you.'

He pulled her into a hug that smelled of dust and whisky, of horses and heat, and William's words slipped from her grasp and dashed upon the floor.

Chapter Twenty-Eight

'Where is Mama?' Evelyn said, wrenching away from him.

'In the morning room,' replied her father. 'But—'

She didn't wait to hear the rest of his sentence. She half walked, half ran for the door, closing it behind her and pressing her back to the wood. Inside, the curtains had been flung open, and there were so many candles lit around the room that it looked like a scene from a play. No wonder, then, that while her mother stood quietly at the fireplace, Aunt Clara was hunched by the door, her mouth twisted in fury.

'Evelyn!' Cecilia's voice was a mixture of reprimand and concern. '*Your dress!* What happened?'

'Tell me this is a dream,' Evelyn said, squeezing her eyes shut. 'Tell me he isn't here.' Her heart was racing, her teeth chattering in her skull as though she had plunged through ice and now floated in the black water beneath it.

'If this were a dream, I'd be taking the air at Whitby, not stuck in this mess,' muttered Aunt Clara.

'He wants to make things right,' Cecilia said softly, coming to stand beside Evelyn, pushing a stray curl behind her ear. 'He says he has found a way to get everything back. Isn't that wonderful?'

She felt the force with which her father knocked upon the door.

'Evelyn, I promise, there is an explanation for all of it.'

'*How?*' breathed Evelyn. 'I thought he was in prison?'

'A sponging-house is not a prison,' her mother said. 'One can leave as soon as one's debts are paid.'

'And are they? Paid?'

'Nearly all of them,' came the voice through the door. 'Please let me in, Evelyn. To be treated thus by my own daughter cuts me very deeply.'

Her eyes narrowed in fury. 'Whose fault is that? Yours – for making ludicrous bets with the men in your London club.'

Cecilia huffed a sharp breath through her teeth. 'What on earth are you talking about?'

Evelyn raised her voice. 'I know *everything*, Father. So do not come here and play-act as though your conscience is spotless, for I know it is not!'

'I could have told you that years ago, dear,' Aunt Clara said sardonically.

'*Evelyn.*' Her mother's voice was a warning. 'Come away from the door. Let your father in – let him speak.'

She looked at her mother, and for a moment she thought she would not move, that she would stand with her back to this door forever and bar him from the room. He'd left. He'd disappeared. And now *he* decided when he would come back? And once again, their lives would somersault around him, the sky swapping places with the ground, leaving her paddling upon tracts of air.

But then she saw the expression upon her mother's face. If her father was the sun, then her mother was the flower, tracking his every move, and now he was here, now he was close, it was as though nothing else mattered, as though she hadn't spent the best part of two years in a catatonic daze, mumbling her way about the house.

And that angered Evelyn more than anything else put together.

Cecilia placed a hand upon her daughter's forearm. 'Please, Evelyn. Give him a chance. If not for him, then for me.'

Evelyn saw the tears that pricked in her mother's eyes, and she sighed, stepping away so that her father could come through the door.

He was thinner than he'd been two years ago – paler, too – and the crumple of his shirt suggested he had ridden hard to get here. Their hair was the same colour, so dark it could almost be black, and it was from him she got her curls, though her father's own waves were slicked back so diligently with Macassar Oil that not a single hair had fallen out of place. Unlike her, his ears stuck out a little at the top where they met his heavy brow, and his wider nose had a bump in the bridge, the result of a riding accident when he was a boy. Unlike her, when he frowned it seemed his whole face changed, the smudges beneath his eyes darkening as he said: 'I had thought you would be a little happier to see me.'

Evelyn took a seat on the other grandmother chair, and Aunt Clara reached over to grip her hand, giving it a tight squeeze.

'Tell her, John,' Cecilia said, going to him and placing a gloved hand upon his shoulder. 'Tell her what you told me.'

'I am here to get us the house back,' her father said, flashing his perfect smile. 'If all goes well, we shall be back at Riccall Hall by the end of the autumn.'

'How?' There was no inflection to Evelyn's voice, no curiosity – just flat defiance.

'I have made arrangements to pay the debt each month, over a longer period of time,' her father said, twitching the material on his trousers and sitting on the faded settee, 'which would allow us to reclaim the house.'

Evelyn's eyes flicked to her mother. 'Have you told Mama how you lost the money?'

'Of course,' her father said. 'I made a bad investment. That is why I had rushed to London – to try to save the business, to stop it from floundering. Unfortunately, I was too late. The damage to its reputation had already been done, and though I did my best for two long years, I could not save it.'

Evelyn pulled her gloves from her hands, placing them in her lap. 'What kind of investment was it?'

'Really, Evelyn,' said Cecilia, with a nervous titter.

'To build a new railway line in Kent, just outside of London.'

'Then why didn't you write to us?' Evelyn asked, holding his gaze. 'Why did you not tell us any of this?'

'I received some letters, dear,' Cecilia said. 'Remember? In the spring.'

'When it had already gone to hell,' Evelyn said flatly, ignoring her mother's widening eyes at the curse. She turned back to her father. 'You did not visit us. For two long years, Father, we saw nothing of you.'

'I could not bear to come back with bad news. I wanted to have something good to tell you both.' He reached out then and gripped her mother's hand, and she saw her mother squeeze it back.

Evelyn narrowed her eyes. 'Tell me you don't believe this, Mama?'

'Of course I do,' Cecilia said, a sharp edge to her voice. 'And you should, too.'

Evelyn met her father's eye, saw his pleading expression, and there was a part of her that wanted to believe him – the child he had read stories to, the teenager who had ridden with him to York, the young woman who had sat with him in his study, listening to the scratch of his pen upon the page, the fire crackling in the grate. That part of her wanted to sit beside him, to say that she forgave him, that she was glad to have him back.

But there was another part of her, a louder part, that wanted to scream, to pull her mother up by the hand and march her from the room. How could they believe a word from his mouth? How could they know what he said was the truth, after all Nathaniel had told her? About his *ridiculous* gambling, betting time and again on more and more ludicrous things.

It is a compulsion, for men like your father. A sickness. Once they lose, they are so fixated on making the money back that they bet more and more; they take bigger and bigger risks, all with the hopes of regaining their fortunes. And your father bet the biggest of them all. He bet your home. He bet everything on it. And he lost.

'You gambled it away,' Evelyn said. 'I know you did.'

Her father nodded. 'In a way, yes. An investment is a gamble – a dangerous one. If I had been better informed, I would have invested less. But what's done is done.'

'No.' Evelyn shook her head. 'This isn't some fun wordplay. I heard, first hand, that you gambled money and then trinkets, and then when you had run out of the two of those, you bet our very home. To some seedy London businessman named Mr Clavell!'

Her father's eyes hardened. 'Whoever said these things is a liar – an inflator of the truth. A wager such as that would never be ratifiable, it'd never stand up in court. And besides – the only betting I have done is on the future; the only gamble I made was on this damned railway.'

'Nathaniel has no reason to lie,' Evelyn said. 'And *you* have every reason.'

'Who is this man?' her father repeated. 'You must know him well if you are using his Christian name.'

'Nathaniel Morris – they met at the Duke of Pembury's

ball,' Cecilia said quickly, and she gave Evelyn a meaningful look that said, in the space of a blink, *he must not know the extent of it.* 'They were at dinner tonight, at the Royal.'

Her father's eyebrows shot up. 'You were at dinner with a man *alone*?'

'I had a migraine,' said Cecilia, her voice more jagged now. 'A ghastly one, and I *know* I should have been there to chaperone, but they were in view of everyone, dear, and the Royal is a very respectable place. It is not as though anything untoward could happen in public.'

'Well, you are wrong there! Something untoward *did* happen, for apparently this man spent the entire dinner thinking he could say whatever he wished! I do not know what is worse: the idea that this man sat there disparaging me all night, or that you sat there, Evelyn, and listened to it! Who is this fellow, anyway? Morris, you said – one of the Suffolk Morrises?'

'He is an American,' Cecilia said quietly.

'Even worse! My God, Cecilia, what were you thinking?'

'Oh, John, do take a breath,' Aunt Clara muttered, 'or else I shall employ you as a set of bellows.'

John whirled on Aunt Clara. 'You will stay out of this, Mrs Huxley, or else—'

'Or else what?' said Aunt Clara, standing to her full height, which was a little above John's. 'Or else you will throw me out of my own home? You dare threaten *me*, after all I have done for you and yours? Well hear this: if *you* do not stop this shouting, then *I* shall call the police, and I am sure they would be more than happy to take you back to a cell to sleep in!'

'Enough!' Cecilia's voice rose above them all. 'Let us all calm ourselves. We are *family*, first and foremost.'

'No, we're not,' said Evelyn, coming to stand beside Aunt Clara. 'He left. He chose London over us. He chose gambling over keeping our house. Every decision he has made has left us in a worse position than the one before it.' Her eyes flicked to her father's. 'And you dare to question Mama's choices?'

'Evelyn,' he said, 'whatever you have heard has painted me as a villain, and I am not a villain. I am just a man who has made a mistake, and now I have come here to ask for your forgiveness. For another chance.'

She turned from him, tucking Aunt Clara's hand into her elbow. 'Come,' she said. 'I shall help you up the stairs.'

'You know I don't need help,' Aunt Clara muttered once they were out of the room, her voice so low that only Evelyn could hear it.

'I know,' Evelyn said, feeling her bottom lip trembling. 'But today, I do.'

Aunt Clara's hand tightened around hers.

Evelyn sat in her room, still dressed in ruined silk, looking dazedly at the thin light from the moon outside the small window. She had wished for this for so many nights when he had first left. When she had heard her mother crying through the walls, she had prayed that he would come back. But as the weeks had stretched to months, and the months to years, she had stopped. The hope had curdled into something harder, something sharper, and the hurt had been replaced with anger.

And now he was back: the part of her that had prayed for him to return was soothed, and the part of her that had prayed for him to never return was riled. Both of them sat within her now, each chafing the other, and her thoughts were so jumbled she could not seem to pick out a single one.

So she closed her eyes and tried to remember Will's face. How he had looked when he had said it: *I've never done that for anyone before.* How his voice had softened. She tried to picture the freckles upon his skin, the constellation they would make if she drew a line between them, from the corner of his eye to the corner of his lip, to the dip in his nose, to the edge of his jaw.

And it was this she fell asleep to, the thought of tracing a shape between his freckles, imagining each of them as a star, a galaxy of freckles, and Will's voice in her ear.

Chapter Twenty-Nine

24ᵗʰ July 1899

When William arrived at the Emporium on Monday morning, it was locked.

He checked his pocket watch. It was a quarter to eight, and Evelyn was usually here by now. In fact, Evelyn was always so painfully early that *he* had begun to feel like the late one for showing up on time.

He sat on the step, pulling his knees into his chest. He wouldn't bother knocking or shouting, because Howie wouldn't hear him. Even when the bell had worked, he wouldn't have been able to hear him, and he'd certainly not hear the metallic *clank* of it now.

He shifted, uncomfortable against the warm stone as the clock ticked from eight o'clock to eight-thirty and then towards nine.

Was this because of what had happened on Friday? Because he'd said *you shouldn't be with a man like that*, and then he'd kissed her on that bridge as though they were equals, as though there wasn't an abyss between them.

And then he'd stood and watched her walk the last steps home without him, proving that there was.

He'd known in that moment that he'd overstepped the mark.

Perhaps that was why she was late. He had made her feel uncomfortable, and now she couldn't bear the thought of seeing him? *Oh God.* If that were true, he wanted the ground to open now and swallow him whole. He couldn't bear a day of tiptoeing around her, couldn't bear her gaze sliding from his every time he asked her a question or answered one of hers. He put his head in his hands, twisting his fingers into the roots of his dark hair. He was a fool. A complete fool. And—

'Do you really not have a key?'

Evelyn stepped past him in a breeze of lilac soap and lemons, slotting the key into the door and opening it in a movement so swift that he still had his back pressed to it when it opened and had to scramble so as not to tip backwards into darkness.

'Good morning to you, too,' he said, rattled, and stood to brush the dust from his trousers.

Evelyn didn't return his greeting; she simply began snapping open the curtains with a ferocity he had not seen before.

'Are you well?' he called, trying not to hover too close to her, because she seemed more than irritated: she seemed *angry*.

'I would be better if you would help me, rather than standing there with your mouth agape,' she said, lifting a box from where it had been left half unpacked on Friday and carrying it behind the register to hide it. 'We are due to open in fifteen minutes, and this place looks a shambles. Is this what happens when I leave early? You do nothing?'

'I dusted, actually,' William said quietly, turning from her to survey the shelves in front of him for anything out of place. He wondered whether he should apologize. Get it over with. Just walk up to her and say: *I'm sorry for what I said.*

For the kiss. Only, that would be a lie, because he wasn't sorry. He had meant what he said, and he had meant to kiss her.

Which was what made this all the worse.

And then Evelyn snapped: 'William! *Help me* for goodness' sake.'

And he thought that perhaps now was not the time. Perhaps he would try later instead.

Evelyn leaned against the counter and took what felt like her first breath all morning. William had stepped outside for lunch, and now she was alone in the shop and could finally allow her knotted thoughts to unspool before her.

Her father had been home for less than two days, and already he had begun ordering her about. This very morning, as she'd come down the stairs, he'd stopped her in the kitchen and announced he would be going to the Royal Station Hotel for luncheon and that she was to come with him.

'I'm busy,' she'd said, plucking her hat from the coatstand. 'Our lives didn't stop just because you left, Papa. And nor will they stop just because you have come back.'

'But I'll be away on business from tomorrow, and—'

She'd let the front door swing shut upon his comments about *respect* and *being a family* again, though her fury had followed her all the way to the bookshop and had only begun to dissipate now, as she watched the flickering patterns created by the sunlight on the floor.

To make matters worse, William had been acting oddly all morning. On the handful of occasions when he'd spoken to her, he'd been so searingly polite that she wondered if he regretted what had happened on Friday. Perhaps that was the tension that now hung between them: he wanted to take back his words, his actions, but couldn't find a way to do it?

She sighed. Beside her was a stack of books to be shelved, and she fixed her attention on them instead. noting the quality of the binding and then tucking a little slip of paper with the appropriate price between their covers. It was calming work, and it required just enough focus for her mind to still. All the anxious chatter about William, about her father, about the dress – it all quietened, leaving just one thought, which she clasped now, as she opened the next cover and slid the next price-sheet between its delicate pages: she would not give up this job.

She would not give away the independence it promised, the future it ushered in. She would not fall so readily back into their old life, as her mother was wont to do, for Cecilia had come back from the city on Saturday sun-drunk and laughing with two fine new hats.

'Isn't it marvellous?' she'd said. 'Life will be as it was again.'

Evelyn opened a thin volume of French poetry and tucked the price between the pages. She did not think it was marvellous. She did not think a single word that had come from her father's mouth had been true. And she had gone to bed with more grit in her belly than ever before.

'Excuse me?'

She snapped the cover shut, looking up.

'Oh,' said the woman. 'It's you.'

It took Evelyn a moment to realize where she recognized the customer from. And then, with a heavy feeling inside her stomach, she said: 'Mrs Quinn! From . . . church?'

The woman's sharp little eyes roamed her face, her outfit, then settled upon the stack of books beside her. 'Your mother did not mention that you worked.'

'I don't,' Evelyn said quickly, knowing that if Mrs Quinn told her mother, it would not matter what Lady Violet said or did – a thought that filled her with more dread than relief. 'I volunteer.'

'I see . . .' she replied, her tone carefully balanced between curious and disbelieving. 'Well, I am looking for something for my ladies' club. Nothing racy or progressive, but something with a soupçon of lesser sins: disorganization, perhaps, or vanity.'

William walked in then, calling a greeting, and Mrs Quinn's gaze snapped to him, giving him a disapproving look.

'*The Picture of Dorian Gray* is about vanity,' Evelyn said. 'That could be an excellent fit.'

'And written by an utter scoundrel, if the papers are to be believed,' the woman said, shaking her head. 'I shall not subject the ladies to such things. What else do you have?'

Evelyn pursed her lips. '*Pride and Prejudice* has quite a vain character in Lydia. And it is quite gentle in subject matter otherwise.'

The woman's eyes narrowed. 'Do you have fifteen copies of it?'

'*Fifteen*?' Evelyn had not realized Mrs Quinn's ladies' club was quite so large. 'How often does your club meet?'

'Weekly,' said Mrs Quinn. 'We usually buy from Sampson's, but I saw the sandwich board on the street and thought I could haggle a better price.'

Evelyn resisted the urge to glance at William with her *I told you so* face. 'I could give you a bulk discount. Say, fifteen books for the price of fourteen?'

Mrs Quinn's eyes narrowed. 'No. Now I know *you* work here, I want something else. I should like your mother's name attached to the club. "By approval of Baroness Seaton" sounds grand, does it not? And they needn't know she's been disgraced. It's the title of honour that's important.'

Evelyn licked her lips, wondering how much to say. 'As charming as that sounds, it might be somewhat difficult.' *Because then Mama may wonder where I bumped into you, and I might have to explain that I have not been with Lady Violet all these weeks, but that I went against her wishes and got a job instead.*

'Then my buying these books might be somewhat difficult,' she said, giving Evelyn a half-shrug. 'I can always go back to Sampson's . . .'

'Wait! Wait,' said Evelyn, her mouth twisted into a grimace. 'Perhaps if you were to agree to keep my being here a secret, I could arrange something?'

Mrs Quinn's gaze sharpened. 'You wish me to *lie* to your mother?'

'Not exactly,' Evelyn said quickly, her throat suddenly dry. 'Just . . . refrain from mentioning it.'

'Do you know what the good Lord says about lies by omission, my dear girl?'

'That they are sins,' Evelyn said sincerely. 'But surely an action that helps the ladies of your club is not so very sinful? Was that not why you began your club in the first place?'

The woman's mouth pressed into a thin line, and she scooted her purse a little further up her arm. 'I can buy from Sampson's without having to lie to anyone, Miss Seaton.'

Evelyn moved around her, standing between her and the door. 'Will Sampson's give you fifteen books for the price of twelve? *And* my mother's endorsement?'

Mrs Quinn looked behind her, towards the door, and then down to her purse. 'If you have fifteen copies of what I want, then I believe we have a deal.'

Evelyn gave William the *watch the shop* eyebrow raise she had perfected, before darting towards the cellar.

She put the candle to one side and began to pull boxes from the shelves. Half of them seemed to contain *The War of the Worlds*, and she wondered whether Mrs Quinn could ever be talked into buying that when something flopped onto the floor beside her, and her heart jumped into her throat.

It was William's manuscript.

Ever since the first day she'd discovered it, she had kept finding excuses to check the cellar in case he had left it once more upon the table, but he never had. She knew she should slide it back into its hiding place, but instead she flicked to the last page, noting how much heavier it was. He'd added quite a few new chapters since she was last down here, but the most recent line looked like it had been written in a hurry, the ink blotting all over the page.

The regret was sour, like bile, and it sat in his throat. He shouldn't have done it. He shouldn't have said those things. But he had, and now he couldn't take it back.

It might not have anything to do with what had happened the other night. He wrote fiction, she rationalized. It might be completely unrelated, completely made up.

Or it could have *everything* to do with what had happened. Which would explain why he had been acting so oddly . . .

'If you're looking for the Austen overspill, it's on the mezzanine,' William called down the stairs. 'I can fetch it if you come back up.'

'Coming!' Evelyn said, stuffing the manuscript back into its hiding place.

Once Mrs Quinn had walked away, with one book tucked into her basket and a delivery date of Wednesday for the remaining fourteen, William gave her a shrewd look.

'Evelyn? Is something wrong?'

She blinked, looking up at him. 'What? No. Why?'

'Because you look like you wish to say something.'

'Not at all,' she said, flushing, busying herself in straightening the papers on the desk. 'What would I have to say?'

Something flickered across William's face that she couldn't read, and then in a quiet voice, he said: 'Nothing, of course.'

Chapter Thirty

That Friday, Aunt Clara made a steak and kidney pudding, served with split yellow peas that had been mashed into a kind of sauce. Her father served them each a slice, despite Aunt Clara's scowling, and then announced rather cheerily that he had booked them all tickets to the theatre for a performance of *The Importance of Being Earnest* on the first Saturday of September.

'Oh,' Cecilia said, her face falling. 'I thought you might have news as to when we can return to Riccall Hall.'

'The *theatre*?' Aunt Clara scrunched her nose as though the word was a foul smell. 'I hate the theatre.'

John sighed. 'Evelyn, I suppose you are disappointed, too? Do you despise art?'

'No,' said Evelyn. 'I do not despise art.'

'My darling,' Cecilia said, leaning forwards to place her hand upon John's forearm. 'You promised we would take a carriage soon—'

'And we will,' John said, spooning more of the rich, brown gravy over his plate. 'But everyone who is anyone shall be attending this performance. I have it on very good authority that the Duke of Wrexham is in York for the fortnight, and has purchased most of the theatre's tickets for the night.

Which means it shall be filled with the type of men with long names and deep pockets. The type of men who know a good investment when they see it.'

'*Now* it all makes sense,' said Evelyn. 'This isn't a family theatre trip. It's a *business* event.'

'I hope I am not expected to attend this,' said Aunt Clara. 'I'd rather spend the day at York Prison.'

'You are not expected to attend, no,' said John. 'And Evelyn, *some* business might be conducted, but the point is to spend time as a family. With or without Mrs Huxley.'

'*Charming*,' replied Aunt Clara.

'You *just said* you did not wish to come!' Cecilia whispered, earning a *humph* of displeasure from Aunt Clara.

'And,' her father continued loudly. 'Of course we can all take a carriage up to Riccall and visit. I have some business to tie up there, regardless.'

'How about next week?' Cecilia's eyes widened hopefully.

'Or the week after,' said John, nodding.

'Or never,' muttered Evelyn.

John let out a huff and dropped his cutlery with a clatter upon his plate. Evelyn watched a spot of gravy fly across the table and land close to her napkin, soaking quickly into the white lace.

'For goodness' sake,' he said, his fingers massaging his temples. 'I am simply trying to do something nice for the three of you. Mrs Huxley, you are welcome if you'd like. Cecilia, darling, we shall go to Riccall when it is convenient. And Evelyn. *Dear Evelyn*. How long are you going to punish me, hmm?' He looked up then, his dark eyes pleading. 'You've barely said two words to me since I arrived.'

'I have been busy,' said Evelyn.

'Busy?' Her father's eyebrows tweaked upwards then. 'Where *do* you sneak off all day?'

'I told you, darling, she volunteers,' Cecilia said, 'with

Lady Violet. You know, the Duke of Pembury's youngest girl. Perhaps they will be in attendance?'

'The duke detests York in the summer,' John said, shaking his head. 'I doubt very much that he would be there, which is surely a good thing.'

'Is it?' Evelyn chewed her split peas, her mouth curled at the edge. 'Why?'

Her father tutted, pulling a curl of paper from his vest pocket and flattening it out against the white lace tablecloth. 'Because the man dislikes me,' he said, passing it to Cecilia, who frowned.

'I didn't think the Duke disliked you?'

'Well, he does now,' said John. 'Forget our old friends, Cecilia. They are not the future.' He tapped the paper. 'This is.'

'But I thought—' Cecilia clutched the paper, crumpling the edge of it as her hand balled into a fist. 'I thought this would be our triumphant return, darling. I thought this would be—'

To Evelyn's horror, she saw that tears were welling in her mother's eyes, plopping onto her plate.

'Oh, Mama,' she said, pushing her chair back to go to her. She wrapped her arms around her mother's shoulders, cradling her. 'I know,' she said.

John huffed a breath through his teeth. 'Oh, for pity's sake. What have I done now?'

'Perhaps she hates the theatre as much as me,' Aunt Clara said, and John shot her a venomous look.

Cecilia patted Evelyn's arm in a way that suggested she wanted her to let go and then dabbed at her eyes. 'You said that life for us would start returning to normal. You said that was what you wanted. And that is what I want, too.'

'I do want that,' said John, pushing his peas around his plate. 'But it is not as simple as all that. Why don't I buy you a new dress for the theatre, hmm? Would that cheer you?'

'That depends,' said Evelyn, before her mother could reply. 'Would Mama need to pawn it, like all the jewellery?'

'Evelyn, *please*.' Cecilia shook her head quickly.

'She had all the gems replaced with paste. Did you know that? And all her gold chains replaced with brass.'

'Then we shall replace them, too,' said her father. 'Good God, I try to do *one* nice thing—'

'And I appreciate it,' Cecilia said. She was using the same gentle, plodding tone she used with Evelyn when teaching her a new stitch. 'But why do you not wish us to reunite with our friends, the people we have known for years?'

'I just told you why!' John said.

'Mama,' Evelyn gripped her hand. 'Why should you wish to speak with the very same people who have been ignoring you? Hmm? You yourself said they were poor friends not to have written.'

'Which is exactly why I think we should have new friends,' John said. 'Start completely afresh.'

Evelyn's eyes slid to her father. She doubted very much that this was *his* true reason and suspected more that it was the perfect excuse.

'I should like to show them that we may have stumbled but we did not fall,' Cecilia said, drawing herself up in her chair. 'I should like to show them that they made a mistake by not keeping in touch with me and that we Seatons will always refind our footing.'

'And what better way to do that, my dear, than by snubbing them now? In a new dress, no less?' John sat back, dabbing at his mouth with the napkin. 'To new friends,' he said, picking up his wine and holding it out into the centre of the table.

Evelyn watched Cecilia look at her glass and then at John, and then, for the briefest of moments, her eyes flicked to Evelyn's, her expression like a door creaking shut.

'To new friends,' Cecilia said quietly, clinking her glass against his.

Evelyn headed for the door. 'Thank you for dinner, Aunt Clara.'

'You're welcome, dear.'

'You are coming to the theatre with us, Evelyn,' her father called after her retreating back, 'so get all of your sulking out of the way now, by all means.'

She hesitated at the bottom of the stairs, half tempted to march back in there and tell him that she wasn't sulking, because she wasn't the young girl that he'd left behind. She was a grown woman now.

There was something . . . off about the whole thing. Why didn't he wish to see any of the people they knew here in York? Why was he avoiding Lady Violet's father in particular? And what exactly did he need to 'tie up' before going back to Riccall? Evelyn didn't know, but she knew who might.

Lady Violet.

Whom she had been rather successfully avoiding since her catastrophic dinner with Nathaniel, and whom she would now have to face.

Evelyn sighed and clumped her way up the stairs.

Chapter Thirty-One

This time, when Evelyn stepped through the door to the club chambers and asked for Lady Violet, she said very firmly: 'She is expecting me this time – I sent word ahead – so I do not wish to be kept waiting.'

The footman gave her a sleepy smile. 'Lady Violet was indeed expecting you. She said to tell any visitors that she and Lady Seaton went to visit a bookshop. I believe the name was the Lamplighter's Bookshop?'

'It's called Morton's Emporium,' Evelyn said automatically, before his words truly hit her, and a chill began to spread across her skin. She thought her mother had gone hat shopping. But if she was with Lady Violet, and Lady Violet had taken her mother to the bookshop . . .

Then she needed to hurry.

The Emporium was closed on Sundays, though Evelyn knew that sometimes Mr Morton would open the shop if the fancy struck him, because she'd find the receipts next to the till come Monday morning.

All she could do was pray that this was not one of those Sundays and that she would not arrive to find Mr Morton happily telling her mother that yes, Evelyn had been working there since June, and yes, that meant she had been lying to her, because no, how could she be volunteering with Lady Violet and working at Morton's Emporium all at once? And then her mother would turn to her, and either she would be angry and loud, or angry and quiet – the latter being much, much worse.

When Evelyn arrived at the bridge, red-faced and clammy, the bookshop looked asleep. The door was closed, the lights inside dimmer than the bright daylight, which was making sweat drip in beads down the back of her neck. For a moment, she wondered if the footman had been wrong, if Lady Violet hadn't come at all.

But then she saw the parked carriage.

Evelyn stepped into the shade of the Emporium's door, her hand flat upon the wood. She could feel the thrum of her own heartbeat in her palm, and she hoped beyond hope that when she pushed against the paint-flecked wood, she'd find the door locked and know that Lady Violet's trip had been in vain. But then she heard the clank of the bell, the squeal of the hinges as the door sighed open into darkness, and her stomach plummeted to meet her feet.

'Mr Morton?'

He hadn't opened all of the curtains, and for a moment she was light-blind, struggling to pick out the shelves from the shadows as her eyes adjusted from the sun's bright glare.

'Evelyn? What are you doing here?'

William stepped from between the shelves, wiping ink from his fingers, and she felt something in her chest quiver. He'd rolled his shirtsleeves up to his elbows, exposing the sinewy muscle of his arms, and his black hair fell in messy curls around his face. There was a sheen of sweat upon his forehead, his neck, that caught the dim light and turned his skin a beautiful, pearlescent silver.

William's surprise melted into a wide smile. 'Evelyn?'

She blinked, her gaze darting from his jaw to the off-white colour of his shirt. 'You've not had any customers in today, have you?'

William frowned. 'You know we're closed on Sundays. Have you taken a tumble? Hit your head?'

'Well, I walked straight in.'

'I propped the door open for some air earlier – must have forgotten to lock it. It's like an oven in here.' William flapped his shirt in emphasis, and she had to work very hard to keep her gaze on his face.

'You're sure no one has been? Two women, perhaps?'

'No,' he said, rubbing at the spot of ink purpling his index finger. 'Just you.'

'Good,' she breathed. 'That is very good news.'

Perhaps Lady Violet had taken her mother to the perfumer instead. Perhaps she'd never intended to bring her into the bookshop at all. Perhaps that was simply something she had told the footman to say, to make Evelyn panic? Evelyn heartily regretted sending Lady Violet word of her visit. She'd only given the woman more time to plot and scheme.

'Is that why you came?' William asked. He wasn't looking at her; his attention was fixed on his hand, where the skin was beginning to turn pink. 'To see if we'd had any customers? On a day when we're meant to be closed?'

She almost said yes, but there was something in the way he'd said it – a tremble to his voice – that stopped her. 'Why else would I come?'

'Perhaps you missed me.' He smiled at her, but there was none of his usual bullish humour in his expression; it had been replaced with something softer. 'Evelyn, about what happened—'

The bell clanked then, and Evelyn turned, but William's hand shot out, clasping hers, holding her there.

'Evelyn?' another voice echoed.

Evelyn felt a stab of something cold in her chest as she wrenched her hand free from his.

'Goodness me, you must know each other very well to be using Christian names.'

Lady Violet was silhouetted against the door, the feathers in her hat and the bright light from the bridge casting a shadow long enough to reach Evelyn's toes. She sashayed towards them, the iridescent blue of her dress dazzling even in the gloom.

'What, no greeting? Are you not happy to see me?'

Evelyn gritted her teeth. 'Where is Mama?'

'Oh, I've left her in the perfumer,' Lady Violet said, tracing a gloved finger along the nearest shelf. 'I thought you and I should have a little heart to heart first.'

Evelyn could feel William bristle behind her, though when he spoke his voice was low and pleasant. 'Aren't you going to introduce me?'

'Yes, Evelyn, aren't you?' Lady Violet batted white-blonde lashes at her. 'I should like to meet this mystery man of yours.'

'First, you will tell me what you are doing,' Evelyn said, holding an arm out to stop William from walking forwards, 'and why you have brought Mama.'

Lady Violet gave her a fawn-like look, all wide eyes and innocence. 'As a reminder, of course. Of our deal. Or had you forgotten about that?'

'Of course I hadn't forgotten.'

'Really?' Lady Violet took a step towards her. 'So then why did I learn everything about that night in a letter from Nathaniel and not from you?'

Evelyn swallowed. If Nathaniel had written, then Lady Violet knew how poorly it had gone, how she'd broken their deal.

Evelyn steadied herself. 'Before you do anything, you must know that what happened that night—'

'Was beyond belief,' said Lady Violet mildly, plucking a copy of *Insectivorous Plants* from the shelf and scrutinizing the green-gold binding. 'Nathaniel called you *charming*, and I cannot imagine a world in which *you* are considered charming.' She snapped the book shut. 'Was he drinking heavily? He does that sometimes.'

William took a step forwards. 'I'm going to have to ask you to leave.'

Lady Violet's eyes sparkled. 'Who are you? Evelyn's little guard dog? Go and bark somewhere else, will you? We're talking.' She turned her gaze back to Evelyn. 'I admit I was perplexed, but then I remembered the advice I had given you – for you to act less like yourself and more like me – and it made a little more sense.'

She reached for Evelyn's arm, her fingers curling around her wrist in a way that might have looked friendly to an onlooker but felt constricting. 'But there is something about that night he is not telling me. And so you will.' Her eyes flicked behind Evelyn's shoulder, her expression flattening. 'Are you going to stand there gormlessly and listen to us the whole time?'

Evelyn turned to look at William, whose expression was cool and blank.

'Please,' Evelyn said. 'Just give us a moment.'

He pushed a sharp breath through his teeth. 'Five minutes,' he agreed, disappearing once more between the shelves.

Evelyn turned to Lady Violet. Another version of her – perhaps one who still lived in Riccall – might have cowered from her forcefulness. But not this Evelyn. She leaned forwards and said: 'If you wish to know, then you must tell me something, too.'

Lady Violet screwed her lips into a thin line, though she tilted her head as if to say *go on*.

'My father is avoiding yours,' said Evelyn, dropping her voice so that even if William were close, he would not hear. 'In fact, he is avoiding most of those we used to socialize with here in York, but he is very specifically avoiding yours. Why?'

Lady Violet's brow creased. 'I should imagine your father would want to see mine given he is trying to sell us Riccall Hall. Imagine it: my father becoming your family's saving grace – and simultaneously the thorn in my side, for that is what has brought him down from Edinburgh to York, and now my life is a misery.'

Evelyn's skin felt cold all of a sudden, despite the oppressive warmth of the shop. 'Your father wishes to buy Riccall Hall?'

'He says he will gift it to my youngest brother when he marries.'

Evelyn dug her fingernails into her palm. So her father *was* lying. He had lied when he said they would be back there come autumn. And her mother would be heartbroken, all over again.

'Now, tell me exactly what happened at dinner. Nathaniel said you ate not a morsel,' she pressed. 'There must be a story there. What did you do to him between walking in the door and leaving to make him want to see you again?'

There was an edge to Lady Violet's voice that Evelyn hadn't heard before, a breathlessness that made Evelyn study her more intently. She was flushed, and she was twiddling the beads on her delicately embroidered gown with such ferociousness Evelyn was surprised it hadn't pulled any of them off.

This was not Lady Violet's usual impatience. This was something more. Was she . . . jealous?

'Well! Spit it out!' Lady Violet huffed.

'How he thought the dinner went splendidly I've no idea,'

Evelyn said. 'Nathaniel ordered lobster for me, which I hate, and I told him so. Then he revealed he had been digging into my family, which I also hated, and I showed him so, because I left before the entrees arrived.'

She didn't mention William. William was her secret, and she did not want to put him even further into Lady Violet's sights.

'So you dislike him then?' Lady Violet asked, her tone casual enough but her gaze intense, watchful. 'Nathaniel?'

'I don't dislike him,' Evelyn said honestly. 'I think he means well. But he executes it poorly.'

Lady Violet surveyed her, as though trying to sniff out the lie. Behind them, the mezzanine door banged shut. Perhaps William had had enough of their bickering and had retreated to his uncle's flat.

Lady Violet sighed, one hand resting against the boning of her corset. 'And yet if his letters are to be believed, he is fascinated by you,' she said. 'Regardless, the deal is off. I don't want you to see him anymore.'

'The deal is not off,' said Evelyn. 'It wasn't just you who decided the terms, remember? And just because you now find yourself lacking Nathaniel's attention, his affection—'

'Don't be preposterous,' said Lady Violet, her face flushing a delicate shade of pink. 'That has nothing to do with anything.'

'—doesn't mean we break our agreement,' Evelyn said. 'You at the very least need to keep up your side of the bargain. Especially after your little stunt today.'

Lady Violet huffed a breath through her teeth. 'I didn't really bring your mother,' she said. 'I just told Kemper to say that. I wished to rile you.'

'Well, consider me riled,' said Evelyn. 'Consider me sufficiently riled that I could walk up to Nathaniel this very day and tell him that you tasked me to divert him.'

Lady Violet's eyes darkened. 'You wouldn't dare.'

'I would dare,' Evelyn said, taking a step towards her. 'And when he asks to see me again – which he will – I shall agree to go. And if you have said anything to my mother, even in passing, even indirectly, about my working at the bookshop, I shall tell Nathaniel not only what you asked me to do, but why you asked me to do it. Because I am quite sure you are in love with the man and are simply trying to push him away because of your difference in rank.'

Lady Violet's mouth became a twitching line. 'That is a lie.'

'Is it?' Evelyn raised her chin. 'Let us find out, shall we? You tell my mother, and I shall tell Nathaniel everything.'

She thought Lady Violet might step forwards, too, might meet her in her anger, but she simply smiled. 'You know, they used to call this place the Lamplighter's Bookshop, but I had no idea it was because they still had lamplighters working here. That man you tried to hide from me – the one who called you Evelyn? – why, he looked like he's worn the same filthy pair of trousers for half a decade!'

Evelyn felt her face flush, felt something inside her begin to burn, hot and sharp. 'You leave him out of this.'

'Oh, I believe all the cards are on the table now,' said Lady Violet. 'I warn you, Evelyn. I am a dangerous woman to cross. Especially when I hold so many good cards and you so few.'

'Even one ace can trump the pack when played at the right time,' Evelyn said. 'Now, please leave.'

Lady Violet gave her a long, hard look and swept from the shop, the bell clanking behind her. Evelyn stood there for a moment, a hand at her throat. Her heart was pounding just as hard as it had been when she'd arrived, although now it was accompanied with a nauseating roiling in her stomach and a tremor in her hands.

'William?' she called into the gloom. 'Are you still down here?'

She waited in the silence, but there was no reply. *He must be upstairs,* she thought, stepping outside in time to watch Lady Violet's carriage rattle away, the dust from the horses' hooves kicking up a small cloud upon the bridge.

Lady Violet had lied and tried to manipulate her. Well, this time it hadn't worked. This time, she had fought back.

And this time, she would win.

Chapter Thirty-Two

At seven o'clock sharp, William stepped into the Red Lion, ordered himself a pint of beer and chose a seat by the window.

Nathaniel called you charming.

That was what the woman had said. And Evelyn had looked . . . surprised. Not a bad sort of surprised, either. And he'd felt something curl in his stomach so violently and so suddenly that all he'd wanted was for the pale woman to stop talking.

It all made sense now.

The reason why Evelyn had asked him to stand at the street corner and watch as she walked home. Why she had acted so oddly when that woman had come in to buy books for her club, why she'd asked her to lie to her mother, and why she'd said she 'volunteered' at the Emporium.

She was embarrassed of him. She had been embarrassed when he'd kissed her upon the bridge and embarrassed at the thought that he would walk her to her doorway, that her mother would open the door and see the kind of man who stood before her. William did not know which thought chafed at him the most: the idea that he had kissed her and she regretted it, or the idea that even his faux-life was not good enough. Even as an author, as a man who could afford to live in one of the houses upon St. Leonard's Place, even as the man he pretended to be, he was not enough.

Another pint thudded onto the table. 'Sorry I'm late,' said Jack. 'They had me polishing again. Yer know how many forks a place that big has?'

Will looked up. 'A lot?'

'Too many.' Jack took an enormous swig of beer, the foam clinging to his top lip. 'Did someone die?'

'What?' Will's forehead creased. 'Why would you say that?'

'Because you look maudlin,' said Jack. 'Unless yer sad 'cos you had to wait so long for me?'

Will scratched at the condensation on his pint glass. 'Can I ask you something? Do my trousers look . . . old?'

'Old?' Jack said, frowning. 'They just look like trousers.'

'Hmm,' said Will, bringing his glass to his lips.

'Forget your sad trousers,' Jack chuckled. 'I have news.'

'Good news?'

Jack leaned forwards a little, his hands splayed upon the table. 'It's about Naomi.'

'Oh.' Will had been expecting something like this. There was *always* a catch. 'What happened?'

'It's *good* news.' He wasn't looking at Will; he was looking at the liquid in his pint glass. '*Very* good news, in fact, because . . . I'm going to propose to her. I want to ask her to marry me.'

Will was silent for a long moment. And then he said: 'Have you lost your mind?'

'Hang on – before you say I barely know the woman—'

'You barely know the woman!'

'No, I've known her for years, really. Her mam's company sorted the laundry when I was working at the Black Swan, and we would talk a little here and there. I've always liked her, Will, but now I've got to know her, now I can see how kind she is, how considerate, how . . . ambitious and clever and brilliant she is . . . well, now I think I don't just like her – I love her. And I'd be a fool not to ask her. Don't you think?'

Will signalled to the bartender that they would have another round, despite the fact that Jack had barely touched his beer. He waited until the drinks had been set down before he spoke again. 'Not everyone will be cheering the pair of you on. You know that?'

'Of course I do. I'm not blind, Will. I see the looks we get. But we're not in America – there's no law against it – and for all the reproachful looks, there are plenty who don't bat an eyelid.'

'And you don't think it's too soon? I mean, it was only a month ago that we were all sat in the Blue Bell.'

'Nearly two months,' said Jack. 'It was the very beginning of June, and July's almost over now.'

'And you think two months is enough time to decide you wish to spend the rest of your life with someone?'

'For me it is,' Jack said, putting his drink down. 'When she held my hand at that picnic, I realized I never wanted her to let go. I think that's what love is, Will – realizing that whatever happens in life, you want this person to be by yer side.'

Will finished his drink in one gulp and slid the second tankard closer. The glass was cold, and it felt good to wrap his sweating palms around it. 'And you're not worried?'

'About what?'

'All of it,' said Will. 'She'll know you, Jack, better than anyone. She'll see all of you, on the good days and the bad.'

Jack shrugged. 'That's what I want.'

'But don't you worry that she'll see something she doesn't like?'

Jack tilted his head to one side. 'No, actually. I think that'll be one of the good things. Learning more about each other. And I don't think she's going to dislike what she finds out

THE LAMPLIGHTER'S BOOKSHOP 221

about me, just the same as I don't think I'm going to dislike what I find out about her.'

Will looked at his friend. There was a brightness in his eyes, as if he truly believed you could lay out all that you were on a platter – all of it: the good, the bad, the bits you were proud of alongside all that you tried to hide – and allow someone else to look over it. To judge it. To judge you, based on it. As if he expected, after all that, for them to be able to look you in the eyes and say: *I want this. I want you.*

Will shook his head. 'You're a braver man than I am,' he said, stitching a smile to his face. 'And if you love her, if you want to marry her, then I'll support you. Of course I will.'

'Really?'

'Really.' Will leaned forwards, clinking his glass to his friend's. 'I'm happy for you.'

Jack let out a long breath. 'That's a relief,' he said. 'Otherwise, this next part would've been so much harder.' Will raised an eyebrow in question, and Jack continued: 'You know that I've swapped jobs—'

'Obviously,' Will said. 'The forks made you late.'

'And I'm getting a much better pay packet, too, now that I'm not just some night porter.'

'Good,' Will said. 'The Black Swan never paid you enough.'

'Yes, yes,' said Jack. He was squirming now. Uncomfortable. 'But you see, when I propose to Naomi, I want to give her something. A necklace, perhaps. Or a bracelet. Alongside the wedding band, of course. Something to match.'

'I see,' William said. Though he didn't, not truly.

'So, I was wondering if I could borrow some money.' Now Jack looked at him, pleading. 'Then I can repay you from my pay packet every month. What d'you think?'

Will could hear his heartbeat all of a sudden, thudding in his chest. 'You want to . . . take out a loan? From me?'

'From your publishing money,' Jack said quickly. ''Cos you said they'd given you a lump sum, didn't you? So I thought it would be better to borrow from you than to try to borrow from some shady back alley dealer and then pay him double the amount in interest. Don't you think that makes more sense?'

Will took a long swig of his beer. It made complete sense. It was actually one of the most fiscally responsible ideas Jack had ever had. Of course, the only fly in the ointment was that Will didn't have money from his publishers. He didn't have a lump sum, and he certainly didn't have enough to buy the sort of trinket Jack was after.

'How much?'

'A few pounds,' Jack said. 'Perhaps . . . ten?'

Ten pounds. Will whistled. 'That's a lot to spend on a gift.'

'But I've done the sums, and I can repay you a pound a month, for ten months. I'll have to live frugally, but I can do it. And I figured that might help you, too.'

'Help me?' William could not possibly see how this would help him.

Jack stumbled then. 'Didn't you say you were worried you'd squander it all? That's why you took up the job with your uncle again, isn't it? So you didn't just bleed money? Well, think of this as another way of keeping some of it safe.'

Will blinked. That also made sense. Jack had thought this through a lot more diligently than he'd have imagined. 'And the wedding itself?'

Jack waved a hand. 'We'll do something small. She's only got her mam here, and while my sisters might come to the city, I doubt my parents will. I want to spend the most on the gift.'

'I see.'

'So? Will you do it? Will you help me?'

William looked at his friend, at the hope written into the

tilt of his eyebrows, at the way his fingers scratched at the pint glass in his hands almost rhythmically. He needed to tell him the truth. He needed to shake his head and say: *I'm sorry Jack, but I lied to you. I don't have that sort of money.* He needed to admit that he'd been lying this whole time. He needed to say absolutely anything other than what came out of his mouth, which was: 'Of course I'll lend you the money.'

Jack grinned, standing up. 'Another round here!' he called. 'And it's on me. Because I'm going to propose to the woman I love!'

Chapter Thirty-Three

Two days later, William stood in front of a dark door in the pouring rain, the gas lamp behind him flickering, his hair wet and curling at his shoulders, and he knocked.

The heat had burst over them like a bubble, and now the storm clouds had come to wash it all away. He was glad of it, really; the bookshop had been frightfully hot these past few days, and his bedroom in the boarding house even more so. Opening the windows hadn't helped; it had just felt like opening an oven door. Now, though, the heat was dissolving, and the alleyway he stood in was filled with the acrid smell of cold rain upon hot flagstones. He breathed it in deeply, trying to settle the pounding of his heart as the peephole slid back and a pair of eyes watched him from the gloom.

'Yes?'

'I was told there was a loan broker here,' William said, his mouth suddenly dry. It was a half-truth, for he'd overheard it at the Red Lion, as the men on the table next to him had sat counting pennies between them, trying to work out how to turn a shilling into a pound.

'How much are yer looking to borrow?'

'Ten pounds.'

There was a cough from behind the door, and the peephole

slammed shut. William stood there a moment longer and was about to turn away and slosh back through the alley when he heard the click-slide of bolts being released.

'Come in.'

He wrung his hair out on the doorstep before crossing the threshold. The house had seemed uninhabited from the outside, the windows dark, but now he was inside, he could hear people within its walls. There was a man speaking on the floor above, his booming tenor a hum that filled the entire hallway. Behind one of the closed doors on the left, someone was laughing, and below them came a rhythmic sound, a *clink-clink*, as though someone were working machinery.

'This way.'

William followed the man through the door at the end of the hallway, which was painted rust-red. Inside, there was a small desk pushed against the far wall, and six men dotted in various positions around it. William kept his chin up, forced himself to meet each of their eyes in turn. They looked like the kind of men one more readily found in London.

The kind of men you didn't want to cross.

'He wants a loan,' said the doorman. 'Ten pounds.'

The largest man stood and stepped from behind the desk. He was enormous, almost as tall as he was wide, with a shock of grey running though his brown hair. When he smiled at William, there was no humour in it, just a glint of gold from one of his tooth caps.

'How long for?'

'How long can you lend it me?' William asked. He was still stood awkwardly, and now he didn't know what to do with his hands. He settled for stuffing them into his pockets.

'Standard term is a month,' the man said. 'Past that, what you owe goes up. This is a business, you know.'

'A month?' There was no way he'd scramble ten pounds

together in a month. It would take Jack ten months to repay him. 'I'd need more than that.'

'How much more?'

The man's eyes were like hot coals upon him, and it made William want to look away, to study the papers on the desk or pick the dirt from beneath his own fingernails. But he didn't. He kept his chin raised, too.

'Six months,' he said.

The man raised his eyebrows. Around him, the other men began to chuckle.

'Three months,' the man said.

'Four,' said William.

The chuckling grew louder.

'No, see, you don't get it.' The man leaned over the desk. 'You don't get to decide these things, boy. *I do*. When you're the one doling out your hard-earned cash, you can choose when to get it back. But last I checked, I was the one with the money in my pocket, and you were the one standing in front of me with a begging bowl.'

William wanted to say that he doubted very much that the cash was hard-earned. He wanted to turn around and march straight back out the door. Most of all, he wanted the skinny man to the left of him to stop laughing.

'I'll give you three months. If you can repay in the first month, there's no interest. After that, it's twenty-five per cent, with a payment taken every month. If you haven't repaid us in three months, the interest doubles.'

William felt something curl in his stomach. 'So I would borrow ten pounds and repay you fifteen?'

The man to his left began to wheeze all the louder.

'Yes,' said the big man behind the desk. 'That is how numbers work.'

'It's extortionate,' said William.

'It's extortion,' the man corrected him. 'But if you ain't

desperate for the money, then go to a bank. I'm sure they'll take one look at you and come to the same conclusion I have: that you don't have two pennies to rub together. For them, o'course, that's a bad thing. For me? It works.' He leaned forwards then, his grin widening. 'You'd be amazed how good a motivator desperation is, how much a man can get done when he's running on it. A clever lad like you? I'm sure you won't have to worry about the interest. I'm sure you'll have it back to us in a month.'

William doubted that. His mouth felt dry all of a sudden, his palms clammy despite the shiver that had settled upon him from his wet clothes, his wet hair. He had no choice. Uncle Howard couldn't lend him the money – he'd already asked in a sort of roundabout way that afternoon, as his uncle was flicking through the post. He'd given Will an incredulous look and said: 'My boy, we're finally breaking even. You want me to undo all your and Evelyn's hard work? And for what?'

William had shrugged and made up some lie about sending for section signs to be painted, and Howie hadn't pressed him any further.

'Well?' said the man now. 'What do you think?'

'It's a deal,' William said, nodding. He could sell more books to afford the interest. He could do *something*. 'Where do I sign?'

'Sign?' The man snorted. 'No. We just need your name, and an address.' He turned to the man with the hissing laugh. 'Sort it out, will you?'

'My pleasure,' he said, unfolding himself from his chair.

Ten minutes later, William was back in the alleyway, now with ten pounds in his pocket, feeling more afraid than before he'd stepped inside.

Chapter Thirty-Four

Two weeks had passed. Evelyn's father was away on business, allowing her to breathe a little more easily, and the book sales both at the Emporium and at the station bookstand were doing well. Better than well, in fact, for Mrs Quinn's ladies' club was quickly helping Evelyn catch up with William's sales figures – much to his chagrin. Evelyn could not resist needling him though, for the bookshop sales seemed the one thing William was happy to talk to her about. Most other subjects seemed to result in him finding some errand to finish upon the mezzanine, or down in the cellar, or outside, and each time it happened she felt something inside her wilt.

There'd been something between them, that night on the bridge. She knew it. She'd felt it. But now it seemed as though whatever that moment had been made of was lost – and each passing day made her less and less sure it'd ever come back.

That is, until the letter arrived.

The ink upon the front was purple-black, almost the colour of plums; her name written in curling calligraphy.

'If that's postmarked from Calcutta, you can take it straight up,' said Will, thudding a box upon the table. He had declared rather suddenly that morning that they needed to sell more books at the bookstand, though now when she looked at the pile he was arranging for Gregory, she worried the boy would not be able to haul it all in his small cart.

'It's not for Mr Morton. It's for me. From Nathaniel.'

William put the book down, turning to look at her. His hair was even more dishevelled than usual, and there were bags as dark as bruises beneath his eyes.

'The man from the Royal? Why would he write to you?'

She knew why he was writing to her. Why he was writing to her *here* was another matter entirely. Was it a reminder, from Lady Violet? She dug her fingernail under the wax, unfolding the small square of paper.

Evelyn,

I hope you can forgive me for the mess I made of our last meeting. I have thought of nothing else since. I see now that I approached the whole thing incorrectly and that what I perceived as being helpful might merely have been harmful. I should like to make it up to you, if I can. What do you say to high tea? Or afternoon tea? Or simply a cup of tea? Anything so that I may stop this guilt from churning in my stomach. Write back as soon as you can, for I can be in York within the day.

Yours,
Nathaniel

'He has some nerve.' William's voice was low and appeared at her shoulder so suddenly she jolted.

'*As do you*,' said Evelyn, her pulse racing. 'One should not read another's post.'

'I am merely trying to share the burden with you,' William said, running a hand through his tangled black hair. 'After all, if he is going to berate you for that escapade, then he should also berate me.'

'Your chivalry shows itself at the most interesting of moments,' Evelyn muttered, leaning upon the desk.

William crossed to the other side of the register and leaned with her. 'You will not go, though? To see him?'

There was a trace of something in William's voice, like a string that had been tightened and then plucked, and it made Evelyn swallow.

If she didn't go, then she had nothing to hold Lady Violet in check. After all, she was quite sure the threat of her telling Nathaniel the truth was the only thing stopping Lady Violet from doing the same to her mother.

'Did I hear someone say a letter had arrived?'

They both started then, for Mr Morton was standing upon the mezzanine, his hat in his hand, his hair slicked back with pomade, and gave them both a cheerful wave before coming down to meet them.

'No,' William said. 'It is a note from Evelyn's . . .' He turned to her. 'What *is* he, Evelyn?'

'A friend,' she said. 'That is all.'

'A friend you met alone for dinner.'

'A friend that *you* insulted.'

'And yet,' William muttered, 'he still found you charming.'

Mr Morton stepped between them then, giving William's hair a ruffle as though he were a boy of seven and not a man of twenty-something. 'Don't pry,' he said fondly. 'Not when you have so much catching up to do. I tallied the sales last night and Evelyn is quite clearly winning, my boy.'

'It's the ladies' club,' William sighed. 'That's what's boosting her sales.'

'Well then, find a men's club,' Mr Morton quipped, a light

in his eyes Evelyn had not seen before. 'Now, I'm going to the station to catch the express post. Don't let the bookshop burn down while I'm gone.'

It was only when Mr Morton had left that William looked up at her, his dark eyes steady. 'I think you should refuse him.'

She turned her gaze to the desk, to the knots in the wood. 'And why is that?'

'Because,' William said, 'the man took you to a public place to give you awful news and made you cry! If those aren't two excellent reasons not to see him again—'

Evelyn shook her head. 'What happened at dinner wasn't truly his fault. I was upset at my father's actions, not at him.'

William huffed a sour half-laugh through his teeth. 'And what about what happened after dinner?' He leaned forwards on the desk then, and she noticed a loose thread in the weave of his shirt, just at the collarbone. 'What about what happened right here, upon the bridge?'

'What about it?' she said, ignoring the tautness in his voice, the twang in her own stomach.

'Oh, I see,' said William, his dark eyes bristling. 'So the kiss *did* mean nothing to you.'

'That's not true,' said Evelyn quickly. 'It meant something.'

'But not enough? Not enough for you to turn around and tell this man to . . . to . . . await the apocalypse before you deign to see him again?'

William bit down upon his lip, and Evelyn wished, in that moment, she could tell him all about her agreement with Lady Violet, about the promise that had been made and the consequences if she broke it: not least the fact that she would no longer be able to work here. No longer see him each and every day.

But telling him meant she would have to reveal the *terms* of their agreement, which involved her making a certain Mr Morris fall in love with her.

And suddenly, she did not wish for William to ever know that.

'It *did* mean something to me,' she said softly. 'But that doesn't change the fact—'

'That I cannot walk you home,' finished William bitterly. 'That your mother cannot catch sight of me.'

'No!' Evelyn felt her face flush now, felt the words come in one great rush. 'That would be the same for any man! My mother would ask a thousand question if . . . if an elderly bishop marched me to the door!'

'And yet if Nathaniel Morris had shown up in his carriage, I imagine you wouldn't have asked him to leave you at the corner?'

There was a challenge in William's eyes now, a ferocity she had not seen since that night at the Royal. 'And that is the true reason why you will not refuse him.'

Evelyn felt something crumple within her. 'I told you why I will not refuse him. I *cannot*.'

'I think you can,' said William. 'But you won't, and those are two very different things.'

And with that, he plucked his coat from the hatstand, and though the clock upon the wall read only a quarter past ten, he declared that he was going for lunch, slamming the door so forcefully that the bell's clank echoed in the quiet shop long after he had left, a hum beneath the din of Evelyn's thoughts, the loudest of which repeated the same thing, over and again: *He did not regret what passed between us then. But what if he regrets it now?*

Chapter Thirty-Five

An hour later, William had still not returned, and Evelyn sighed, stretching out the sore muscles in her back. She had spent the morning painting signage for Mr Morton, for it had been quiet and her mind had been too loud for her to stand and do nothing.

'William wanted to buy them all,' Mr Morton had explained, his face flushed from his walk. 'But I think we can manage making them ourselves, don't you?'

She had now almost finished the sign for fiction, having written it in smart, black lettering and then decorated the board with elements from her favourite novels: the white rabbit from *Alice's Adventures in Wonderland*, the emerald horse from *Sir Gawain and the Green Knight*. She even included a minuscule reference to *Felix's Unlucky Adventures in London* – William's own manuscript – adding the small, white marble that Felix wore around his neck. She had been reading it in fits and starts every time she went down to the cellar, and she had nearly finished the story. She was sure William would never notice the reference in the sign, for at a glance it could be a pearl just as easily as a marble, but it soothed some of the prickly thoughts in her mind to know she had painted it for him.

She straightened, splaying her fingers out upon the desk, trying to ease the cramp that had lodged between her index finger and her thumb.

The bell clanked then, and she looked up and smiled.

'Jack!' she said. 'This is a surprise.'

'S'my day off,' he said, taking off his jacket and slinging it over his arm. 'Is Will here? I've some news.'

'He's getting lunch,' Evelyn said, casting a glance at the clock. It was nearly half past twelve now.

'I'll wait,' Jack said, shuffling some books aside on the desk so that he could hop up onto it and sit there.

Evelyn grimaced. 'You might be waiting a while in that case. William has been "getting lunch" since ten this morning.'

Jack raised his eyebrows. 'Did something happen?'

She tilted her head, trying to find the words. Had William told him about the kiss? 'We . . . had a disagreement.'

'Ah,' Jack said knowingly. 'What's he done now?'

Evelyn pursed her lips. 'It's not what he's done so much as what I *will* do.'

Jack frowned, wiping a sheen of sweat from his brow and pushing back the hairs that had slickened beneath his hat. 'So he's cross with you for something you haven't done yet?'

The bell clanked again, and another familiar face walked through.

'Naomi!' She looked from Jack to Naomi and back again, then frowned. 'Wait, is it Thursday already?' That was the day they always took lunch together, sitting by the river when the weather was good; this week, it was Evelyn's turn to provide the food. For a moment she panicked, thinking she'd forgotten, but Naomi smiled.

'No, no, but Jack said to come by.' Naomi gave Jack a wide, delighted smile. 'Did I miss your good news?'

'Will's not here yet,' he replied, jumping down to greet her with a delicate kiss on the hand.

'He'd better be quick, because I'm starving,' said Naomi, placing her basket down on the desk.

'Eat, if you want,' said Evelyn. 'I'm sure Mr Morton wouldn't mind.'

'What's in there?' asked Jack, peering beneath the cloth. 'If there's a slice of that cheese pie, I wouldn't say no.'

Naomi smacked his hand back playfully, before pulling a corned beef and tomato sandwich from some wax paper. 'I've been at work since five. Huge order, not enough hands. Should make Mam and I a pretty penny though, so I shan't complain.'

'Evelyn was just about to tell me why William is being a donkey,' Jack said, returning to his seat at the edge of the desk.

Naomi took a bite of her sandwich. 'Oh, then please do go on, Evelyn.'

And so she told them how the letter had arrived and how William had made his opinions on her meeting the man again clear, how she'd told him she would see him, regardless, and William had stormed off.

The only part she left out was the kiss.

'Sounds like he's jealous,' said Naomi, through a mouthful of tomato.

'Jealous of Nathaniel?' Evelyn frowned. But she didn't feel anything for Nathaniel. When she was with Nathaniel, it felt rather like being sandwiched between two distant cousins at a four-hour dinner, speaking of utterly mundane things.

When she was with William, it felt as though the world began to sparkle.

Jack shrugged. 'He's rich, isn't he?'

'But William doesn't need to compete with a man like Nathaniel,' said Evelyn. 'Not when it comes to money.'

Jack raised his eyebrows a little. 'Money and success are

linked for William,' he said. 'If that man is rich, then it means he's successful.'

'I get the impression it's his father that has a successful business, rather than Nathaniel himself.'

'All the same,' said Jack, raising his eyebrows. 'Perhaps that's what Will's jealous of. His success.'

'But William is also successful,' said Evelyn. 'He has a job. He has his novel. He has a publisher. Why should he covet what Nathaniel has when he already has so much?'

Jack looked at her for a long moment. 'Because perhaps he thinks Nathaniel has something he doesn't have.'

Evelyn floundered, unsure of what to say to that.

'Listen,' said Jack, 'William always has something to prove. That's why he went to London, and that's why he didn't come back until he'd done what he'd set out to do. If you ask me, I think it's all a way of paying his uncle back.'

'For taking him in?'

Jack nodded. 'He was Will's last chance, you see. His mother was threatening to send him to the workhouse. Can you imagine? Being sent there by your own mother, when you have a home.' Jack sucked a breath between his teeth and shuddered. 'I think that's why success means so much to him – because he feels like he needs to earn his place, prove he's worth it.'

'Poor William,' said Naomi. 'What sort of a mother would do that?'

Evelyn bit her lip. 'I didn't know that,' she said. 'I mean, he said that his uncle had taken him in, but I didn't know his mother had threatened to send him to the workhouse.'

'Just . . . be patient with him, Evelyn,' Jack said. 'Underneath it all – Christ, *despite* it all – he's a good person, a loyal friend. He just . . . he gets jumbled sometimes in how he says things.'

The bell clanked then, and William walked through the

door, his black hair shiny with sweat, his white shirt damp at the collar. He looked at them, clustered around the register, and frowned. 'Was there a mother's meeting I'd forgotten about?'

'Jack has some news,' said Naomi.

'Just Jack?' William asked, coming to join them. He stood beside Evelyn, and she could smell the heat of the day on his skin.

Jack pulled four strips of paper from his breast pocket. 'How would the three of you like to join me at the theatre on 2nd September? I've four tickets to *The Importance of Being Earnest*. And it's in the evening, so perhaps we can all get dinner at the Blue Bell together beforehand?'

Evelyn felt her stomach drop into her feet. 'On 2nd September?'

'Where did you get those?' Naomi grabbed one of the tickets, inspecting it. 'These are good seats!'

'As a tip, if you'll believe it! I was looking after the Duke of Sutherland, and Sutherland—' Jack turned to Evelyn. 'He lets us call him that, doesn't like all the formalities of "Your Grace" and whatnot when he has his whisky – *anyway*, he has his drink, stands up and tucks them into my jacket pocket!' Jack turned a beaming smile to the four of them. 'Says they were tainted, because he'd heard some character or other was going to be there, and that had made him change his mind about the whole thing! And then he told me if I *do* go, to watch my purse and not take any bets offered. Odd, really, but as my Da always says: "Don't look a git horse in the mouth."'

'It's "gift horse",' said William.

'Clearly *you've* never tried to make a horse do what it doesn't want to,' said Jack loftily. 'It's "git".'

'I'd love to go,' William said. 'Evelyn?'

'I can't,' she said, not looking at him. 'I . . . I'm already going.'

'With Nathaniel?' asked William, his gaze flicking away to study his fingernails.

'No,' she said firmly, catching Naomi's eye. Perhaps she was right. Perhaps this *was* jealousy. 'Nathaniel isn't coming. I'm going with my family.'

'Ah, of course. You're just going for *tea* with Nathaniel.'

'Well, that's wonderful, regardless!' said Naomi.

'And we can come and find you once we arrive,' said Jack.

William made a face. 'I am sure we will only embarrass her if we do that,' he said, and Evelyn frowned.

'Of course you wouldn't embarrass me. I'd be delighted to come and find you. I just . . .' She cleared her throat. 'My mother doesn't know I work, that's all. And I should like to try to keep that secret.'

William's gaze flicked up. 'Are you so ashamed of it?'

'It's not that I'm ashamed, it's just—'

'Save it,' said William. 'You don't need to make any more empty excuses today.'

Evelyn felt his words like she'd been struck, the heat rising like a bruise upon her cheeks.

'Really, William!' said Naomi. 'You needn't be so ill-mannered.'

'It's fine,' said Evelyn, reaching out to touch Naomi's sleeve. 'Now, if you will all excuse me, Mr Morton said he wanted section signs, so I'm going to the cellar to paint some.'

As she retreated into the gloom, she heard Jack's voice say: 'You're a fool, William Morton. A prize fool.'

And yet she was the one who felt foolish.

Chapter Thirty-Six

Evelyn had been rehearsing her father's homecoming ever since Lady Violet told her he intended to sell Riccall Hall. In her mind, she would march up the thin wooden steps to the chamber he shared with her mother and scold him like he were the child and she the parent.

As it was, when she finally had her chance to confront him, he was the one waiting for her – peering out of the half-moon window in her own little attic room – and all of her lines about her mother's sadness, her frustration, and his deception floated from her grasp as he said:

'Do you know, I've always thought of attics as being for servants. Now you sleep here.' He shook his head. 'My grandfather George would be so ashamed.'

Evelyn thought of the strident painting they'd had in the breakfast room at Riccall Hall and pressed her mouth into a line. 'If you think you will get out of this by making me pity you, you are wrong,' she said, unpinning her hat with shaking fingers. 'I have spoken to Lady Violet, so I know you do not plan to win back Riccall Hall—'

'Riccall Hall was never *lost*,' her father said quickly. 'It was simply under question while the matter of my debt was being settled. And now it is settled.'

'I know you intend to sell it,' said Evelyn. 'So why don't you tell me why you are lying to Mama?'

For a moment, he said nothing, and she could hear only the thrum of her own heart in her ears from where she'd run up the stairs. And then he turned and sighed and sat heavily on the bed, the springs sagging so much that they looked as though they would touch the floor. 'You think little of me, Evelyn. I see that. And I understand why. I am sure in your eyes it looked as though I abandoned you—'

'You *did* abandon us,' Evelyn said, pacing the short distance from her dresser on one side of the room to her wash jug and bowl on the other. 'Stick whatever ribbon on that package you wish – it doesn't change what it is.'

'But I did not,' said her father. 'I went to London *for* this family, for our future, and I am working towards that same goal now.'

'By selling Riccall Hall.'

'By selling the land it stands on, yes. But the deal includes a tenancy agreement for you and your mother, for the rest of your natural lives.'

She stopped pacing and looked at him. 'And what about you? Would you live there, too? Or would you go back to London?'

He smiled a little, though he did not meet her eye. 'You think I really wanted to be down in London, trying to piece together a crumbling investment, and not at home with the pair of you?'

'Yes,' said Evelyn, pacing once more. 'Or else you would have visited. Or written more.'

'I wrote.'

'To Mother! You never wrote a single word to me.'

'Because you were angry at me, Evelyn, for a thousand things it seemed like—'

'Not a thousand things. A handful of things. But mostly

THE LAMPLIGHTER'S BOOKSHOP   **241**

because you moved to London, fired nearly all of the staff, and then never wrote to us again.'

'All of which I did for my family.'

She looked at him, at his crumpled shirt, at his brown hair that, unoiled, curled around his ears. tufted at his forehead. There were a million things she wanted to say, a million things she *had* wanted to say for the last two years, but now . . . Now, when she heaved a deep breath into her lungs, she found the weight that pressed there was too heavy.

'Does Mother know that is the deal?' she asked. 'That we would not own it? That we would rent it?'

She watched the lie form on his tongue, watched his eyebrows crease. And then he sighed and said: 'No, Evelyn. She doesn't know. And I would prefer if she didn't know.'

'She deserves the truth.'

'She deserves to be treated well,' John said, putting his head in his hands. 'She deserves better than I've given her, better than I can now give her. But I can at least spare her some of it. The shame of it. The duke would not reveal our agreement – that was part of the deal.' He gave a half-laugh then. 'Part of the reason for the criminally low price he would get is his silence.'

Evelyn pressed her mouth into a thin line, wondering whether that agreement included not telling Lady Violet, for that woman trafficked gossip like a grocer on market day. But she said: 'Do you know, Papa, I have a friend who thinks some lies are kind to tell. And I think that's what you're trying to tell me, that you choose the kinder lie. But from where I am standing, it is not kind. It is not kind to string Mother along. It is not kind to ask her to face the world, her peers, her friends without knowing the ground upon which she is facing them from. They all abandoned her, you know, when we moved here. They all stopped writing to her.

You brought so much shame upon this family that they could not bear to associate with her.'

John sat back, resting against the wall. 'I am aware,' he said. 'Why do you think I insisted you both be allowed to return to Riccall? I want to make it right, Evelyn. I want to undo what I have done.'

'Very well,' Evelyn said. 'But do not tell yourself that you did this kindly. You should have told us the truth from the beginning. The lies hurt more than everything else put together.' She felt a lump form in her throat then and turned away, so that he wouldn't see her crying.

'Evelyn,' he said, and she heard the squeak of the springs as he stood, and then felt his hand upon her arm. 'You must understand that sometimes . . . sometimes people lie because they are so ashamed of the truth that they cannot bear to face it, either. I needed you to believe that our life hadn't changed. I needed you both to believe that the future held bright things, for if you didn't believe it, then I couldn't either. I was ashamed of myself, ashamed of what I had done. And I'd hoped to fix it before you were involved. But I didn't manage it, Evelyn, and for that I am sorry.'

'And the theatre?' she said. 'What ploy is that?'

'No ploy,' he said. 'Just a chance for us to step out once more as a family. You must trust me on that.'

'I don't trust you,' she said, pulling away from him. 'How can I?'

'I will earn your trust back,' he said. 'I *will*. Just you wait and see.' And then he pressed a kiss to her temple and stepped from the room.

Chapter Thirty-Seven

The Friday before the theatre performance, just as Evelyn was locking up, William looked up from the register and said: 'Well, it's official. My winning streak has been broken.'

Things had been strained between them in the fortnight since the fight about Nathaniel, and the air in the shop felt heavy, thick with unspoken words. Now, though, William affixed her with the first genuine smile she'd seen all day, and Evelyn stood, brushing the lint from the hem of her dress. 'Really?'

'See for yourself,' he said, proffering the page.

She crossed to him and looked down at the sheet, at William's neat, curling handwriting. The only digit that seemed to break free of his otherwise constrained little lines was the number '5', repeated over and over.

'This can't be right,' she said quietly, tracing the figures etched in black ink.

'It's right,' said William. 'Howie reckons you might even deserve a bonus.'

'A bonus?' Evelyn looked up from the page. 'Why?'

'Because August was our highest ever month,' William said, warmth in his voice now. 'And because you've earned it. Here.' He reached under the desk and placed the bottle of whisky on top of the counter, alongside two glasses. 'While you drink it, you can have a think as to what you'll spend your extra pound and sixpence on.'

Evelyn looked at the bottle, at the honey-gold liquid inside it, and for a moment she was in their old parlour again, watching her father uncork his diamond-cut carafe, his low murmur lost to the crackle of the fire. That Evelyn would have thought a pound and sixpence was a tiny sum. *That* Evelyn wouldn't have known how much it would cost her to earn it.

'Evelyn?'

She blinked and shook her head just slightly, until the memory dissolved.

He poured an inch of whisky into both glasses. 'Any ideas?'

'You know, I saw a house for rent not so long ago, as I was walking home. Someone had scribbled an advert and stuck it in the window of the basket weaver's shop, and I thought it looked perfect for me and Mama, though I never even checked to see how much the rent would be. How much do you pay?'

'Seven shillings a week, and a shilling a month for waste removal,' William said, pushing the drink towards her.

Evelyn hesitated for a moment, for though she knew little, she knew enough to know that seven shillings was far too low a fee for one of the fine, sandstone houses on St. Leonard's Place. And then she looked at him and saw the odd expression on his face, and she laughed. 'Oh, I see. You're trying to trick me, aren't you? Prove how naive I am?'

'Indeed,' William said quickly, not meeting her eye as he clinked his glass against hers. 'Replace shillings with pounds and you have your answer.'

'Your publishers must be very generous then,' said Evelyn.

'By my count, that would put your yearly rent at almost six times your yearly wage!'

'Yes, well,' said William, swallowing a little. 'Perhaps it is a little less than that, actually. Now that I think of it.'

Evelyn looked down at the liquid in her cup. It would be a long time before she could afford a house like the grand old buildings on St. Leonard's Place, but each day was a step closer to *something*. Something of her own.

'To colleagues,' she said, clinking her glass against his. 'Even the ones who play tricks on you.'

His gaze was steady. 'To friends,' said William. 'Who don't understand the value of money but insist on making the bookshop lots of it.'

She laughed a little at that and drank. The whisky burned her mouth so fiercely and so immediately that she felt tears spring to her eyes, but she swallowed it determinedly and kept her mouth shut, refusing to cough.

'Well?' said William, his lopsided grin dimpling his cheek.

'Vile,' Evelyn croaked, though she took another sip anyway. 'Truly vile.'

'And yet, the only suitable drink when one has attained a pound and sixpence.' He poured another inch of liquid into each of their glasses. 'If you want, I can come with you. We can enquire about the rent.'

Evelyn took another sip. 'I imagine they have found tenants by now,' she muttered, as the alcohol stung her tongue. 'It was a while ago.'

'The next time, then,' said William. 'The next time you find something you think you and your mother would like, let me know. Then we can go and enquire together. I'll tell you if they're swindling you.'

'They might think we intend to move in together,' said Evelyn, 'and refuse to rent on the grounds of debauchery.'

William's dark eyebrow lifted. 'Debauchery?'

'Because we are unmarried,' said Evelyn, her mouth suddenly dry – no doubt from the amber liquid in her glass. 'And they would know it from looking at us.'

'Would they now?' He chuckled a little then, and a patch of red appeared upon his neck. 'And how would they know that?'

'I've no wedding ring, for a start,' Evelyn said, 'and besides, couples have a way about them.'

'Like Jack and Naomi, you mean?'

'Precisely,' Evelyn breathed, thankful for the diversion of topic. 'Now, they could pass for a married couple.'

'And we couldn't?'

He looked at her then, and she could feel the liquid fizzing in her veins, could feel it flushing her cheeks and sending a rush of warmth down her neck.

'I should go,' she said, though she didn't mean a word of it.

'We can't waste good whisky,' William said, pointing to his still-filled glass. 'And it's maudlin to drink it alone. Half an hour, that's all.'

She tilted her head in agreement, for the truth was she felt too content, too comfortable, to pluck up her things and step into the evening sunshine pressing against the door.

William leaned over the other side of the counter, his hands clutched around his glass. If she moved just a fraction to her left, she could brush his forearm with hers, could nigh on rest her shoulder against his, just like that night on the bridge. Instead, she lifted the glass to her mouth and took another sip, marvelling at how the stinging strength of it seemed to have reduced; now it tasted sweet and smoky all at once.

'You know,' she said quietly, 'I think you are right. I don't think I knew the value of money before, back when we had it. But I do now. And I think of how much we wasted, and it makes me . . .' She sighed through her teeth. 'It makes me *angry*.'

'You shouldn't be angry with yourself. You didn't know any better.'

Evelyn raised her eyebrows as if to say: *that does not make it any less bad*.

'Do you regret what happened?' William didn't look at her but down into his glass. 'With your family? Your father?'

'Of course I do. If I had had any choice in the matter, any control . . .'

He straightened, turning so that his back was resting against the desk. 'You wouldn't have chosen this, you mean? Working in a bookshop, with a man who wears trousers that look half a decade old?'

Evelyn wondered why the words scratched at a place in her mind, and then it struck her. 'You *were* still down here that Sunday! I thought you'd gone upstairs.'

William shrugged.

'*William*,' said Evelyn. 'Look at me.'

William didn't turn; he simply took another sip of his drink.

'*Look at me.*'

For a moment, she thought he would ignore her. But then he sighed, and he turned, and when he looked at her, there was something in his dark eyes that she could not read.

'I wouldn't choose what happened to my mother,' she said. 'But I like being here, William. I like working here. I like turning up each day and knowing that I have earned every penny of the money in my pocket at the end of the week.'

'And me?' he asked quietly. 'Would you choose me?'

She felt her heartbeat quicken in her chest. 'I meant what I said before, William. That it meant something to me.'

She looked at him, at the constellation of little freckles

that tracked from the corner of his eye down to his jaw. He was beautiful, even with his hair glistening from the heat outside, even with his crumpled shirt, and she watched him swallow, watched the skin at his throat flicker.

He leaned over the desk once more, his fingers clutching his glass. 'Evelyn . . . when I heard that man wanted to see you again, that same man who sat there and watched as you cried and did *nothing* but get embarrassed and look around—' He swallowed and looked away, and her heartbeat thudded in her ears. 'I wanted to kill him, Evelyn. I wanted to hurt him, for what he'd done. And that's not like me – I'm not like that. And then when you said you'd meet with him again, it was as if . . . It was as if there was something wrapped around my chest, as if I couldn't breathe.' He looked at her, his dark eyes searching. 'I don't think people feel that way about a colleague, Evelyn. Nor even about a friend. I think I feel that way because I care about you. I've come to care about you. And I don't want to see you get hurt.'

He reached his hand forwards just enough that he could lean it into hers, that she could feel the warmth of his skin, and for a moment there was no bookshop. There was just William and his trembling expression and her skittering pulse where their hands touched.

'It's the whisky,' he said loudly into the silence, shaking his head.

'No,' she said, curling her fingers around his wrist, anchoring him there. 'I would choose you, William. Not as a colleague, and not as a friend, as—' She swallowed, her heartbeat a roar in her ears now. 'As us.'

'Evelyn . . .' His voice was a breath, a caress, as he leaned towards her, turning the trickle of sunshine that lay between them to shadow, resting his forehead against hers so she could feel his black hair against her cheek, the coolness of his breath against her neck, and it pulled at something deep in the pit of her stomach. 'Don't say that.'

'Why not?' There was an ache inside her, and it would take so little for her to kiss him, to close the gap between them. 'I mean it.'

'You shouldn't.'

'Well, I do,' she said, and pressed her lips against his.

His eyes widened in surprise, and for a moment, she thought she had been wrong, that he would push her away, but then she felt his mouth open against hers, felt his arm snake around her waist, pulling her closer, and his eyes fluttered shut.

His lips were soft, one hand reaching to her neck, tracing a line against her jaw, and she was sure he could feel her soaring pulse, could feel how her heart slammed against her ribcage.

And then William pulled back.

'Evelyn, stop,' he said, and there was a thread of something that sounded like defeat in his voice. There was a tremor to his movements now, a jitter that had not been there before. 'You're drunk.'

'I am not *drunk*,' Evelyn said, feeling a flush rising in her cheeks.

'You say you would choose me,' he said quietly, 'but you don't know what you would be choosing.'

'That's not true.' She stood at the other side of the desk, her fingers gripping the edge of it until her knuckles turned white. 'I know you, William Morton.'

'No,' he said, still not looking at her. 'Besides, we've been drinking. We aren't thinking straight. *You* clearly aren't thinking straight.'

'But, William, *I* kissed *you*.' She had meant for it to come out firmly, strongly, but her voice was a whisper, her words catching, breaking. 'I told you—'

'Just go, will you?'

She opened her mouth and closed it again, all the words turning to ash upon her tongue as she stepped from behind the desk to fetch her hat, her jacket. She had half a mind to stalk from the shop without turning back, but she couldn't. She forced herself to look at him, for him to look at her.

'I've never kissed anyone like that before,' she said quietly. 'This is not how I thought it would be.'

The warmth in his eyes was gone, replaced with a coolness that was as thick as autumn fog and just as impenetrable, and she felt the humiliation wash over as he said: 'This is not how it should be. You're right about that.'

Chapter Thirty-Eight

You fool.

William put his head in his hands, his fingers twisting at the curls of dark hair on his head, pulling at the strands until it hurt, until it stung. He could still feel the press of her lips against his, could still feel the jumping rhythm of her pulse as he'd touched her neck. And then a voice in his head had said: *You're lying to her. You don't wish others to hurt her, but what are you doing? What will she say, when she discovers she has fallen for a lie? When she learns you're a failure?* And the fear of it, the panic had spread like a miasma in his veins, had turned the kiss from something beautiful, something soft and sweet and tender, to something awful.

The bell clanked then, and for a wild moment William thought it was Evelyn, returned, and that he would have a chance to apologize, to try to explain. But then Uncle Howie called: 'William, my boy, is that you whimpering like a shot rabbit?' And his heart sank.

'No,' replied William, rubbing his hand furiously against his cheeks.

He heard the soft pad of his uncle's footsteps against the worn rugs, heard the floorboards creak, until Howie came into view. He sat beside him on the floor, his back to the register's desk, and reached a hand to squeeze William's shoulder.

'Come now, my lad,' said Uncle Howie, his voice low. 'Whatever it is, it cannot be so bad as this. To sit alone in the dark on a Friday evening?' He gave his shoulder a squeeze. 'Is this because Evelyn sold more books than you?'

'No,' said William sullenly.

'Then what?' Uncle Howard said, leaning into his shoulder.

William wished he could tell him the truth. All of it. About his trip to London. About how small he had felt, how insignificant. How he had been too ashamed to admit that it had been such a failure, that *he* had been such a failure, so instead he'd concocted another lie, another life. He squeezed his eyes shut, pressing them so tightly that when he opened them again, spots swam in his vision and the bookshop had become a shade darker than before.

'I kissed her,' he said, his voice low. 'Evelyn. And tonight, she kissed me.'

Uncle Howard's hand, which had been patting William's shoulder rhythmically, stopped. 'I see,' he said. 'And . . . you think this . . . is a bad thing?'

'I *know* it is,' said William, pressing his thumbs into his eyebrows, to try to release some of the pressure there, or to hide his face, he didn't know which. 'She is who she is, and I am who I am.'

'You're a fine young man, William,' said Uncle Howard. 'You have a lot to offer to a young woman like Evelyn.'

William scoffed at that. 'Oh, I'm sure.'

He thought of his tiny bedroom in that cramped little house. Of how he had watched a patch of damp spread upon the ceiling and was counting down until it began dripping through. Of how he fell asleep and woke up to the sound of the baby screaming two floors above him.

Even with his calculations on their best month of sales, he did not have enough to repay those men. He'd have to move into that dank little basement room and shiver his way through the winter in order to have that kind of coin.

'Other people have so much more,' he said.

He thought of Nathaniel, of his smart suits and charming smile. He could give her a very different life – a much better life. And the thought of it hurt more than anything else ever had.

'People will always have more,' said Uncle Howard. 'But you're a good man, William. You must see that in yourself. I see it, and I think Evelyn sees it, too.'

William chewed on his lip. Perhaps. After all, she had kissed him. She had pressed her lips against his, and he'd felt his heart soar and melt, all at once.

'Jack says that if you care for someone, if you really care for them, then you should let them see all of who you are. He says that's what love is.' William turned his head to meet his uncle's eye. 'Do you think he's right?'

He thought his uncle might chuckle then, at Jack's sudden bout of wisdom. Instead, he looked straight at William and said with solemnity: 'Do you love her, Will?'

William opened his mouth and closed it again. The answer seared in his chest, hot as coals.

Yes.

He loved that when she sat between the shelves, she wouldn't notice she was humming until William hummed along with her. Then she'd snap at him to be quiet, please, because she was trying to concentrate. He loved that she spoke the first thing that came to her mind. That she thought he didn't notice that she rearranged all the books he restocked. And he loved that she'd kissed him as though it were the most natural thing in the world.

'Yes,' he said, and it was as though a weight had lifted from his chest, as though admitting it made it easier to breathe.

'Then you must tell her,' said Uncle Howard. 'You must.'

'I can't.'

'Of course you can! You walk up to her, and you say: "Evelyn, I love you."'

William shook his head, a half-laugh hissing through his teeth. 'As though it were so easy! By God, Howie, if her family hadn't lost all their money, we never would've met! Do you think a woman like that would've come in here? Would've even said two words to me? The fact we are colleagues is amazing enough, but for me to love her is lunacy. For her to love me back would be even more so, and only a fool would think otherwise.'

Uncle Howard looked at him for a long moment, and then said: 'Wait here. I'm going to show you something.'

William heard the creak of the stairs as Howie went up to the mezzanine, where they kept the philosophy books and the old travel vellums, and then the same creak as he came back down, a scroll beneath one arm and an unlit lantern in the other. He unfurled the parchment on the floor before them, pinning the curling edges down so that it would not spring back into a tight coil, and William saw that it was a map.

It looked like London, perhaps, for a thick river tracked through the heart of it, but there were too many other things he didn't recognize for it to be London: a star-shaped fort, for one, that looked like nothing he'd ever seen.

'I loved someone, too, once,' Uncle Howard said softly, tracing a finger along the wide river. 'They'd come to England for university. I must've been not much older than you are now. Twenty-five, perhaps. Twenty-six. We'd both run for the train to Edinburgh and both missed it, and we stood there on the platform, red-faced and panting, realizing our shared poor luck.' He smiled a little then, and there was a wistfulness to it that William had never seen upon his uncle's face. 'I had never fallen in love before. Never realized how accurate it was to say "fell", because that's what it felt like. Like I'd missed a step. It happened so quickly it was as though the ground was beneath my feet one moment and gone the next.'

William's brow creased. 'And then what happened?'

'They went back home, to Calcutta.'

'Calcutta . . .' said William. 'That's where you send all your letters, isn't it?'

Uncle Howard nodded. 'I was meant to leave with them. The thought of never seeing them again, of eight months being all the time we got together, was too painful. But I had to find a way to break it to my father first. He wanted me to take over the bookshop, for it to stay in the family, and I didn't know how to tell him that I couldn't take over, because I was leaving him alone here, in York. Your mother had already moved to Liverpool, you see, though you weren't yet born.' He gave William a small, sad smile. 'And then . . . my father died – suddenly and unexpectedly – and I postponed my trip for six months, thinking I could sell the shop and pull together some money to start a new life over in India. And then Christmas came and went and six months was up, and I wasn't ready. So I postponed once more, for a year this time. And then a year stretched to two. And then eventually you came along and offered me the excuse I had been looking for all along.'

William's frown deepened. 'Had you changed your mind? Decided you didn't want to go?'

'I *did* want to go,' Uncle Howard said, reaching to rub at his eyes beneath his glasses. He turned his face from him, though William could see that a tear had tracked down his cheek. 'I wanted so desperately to go.'

'So then why didn't you?'

'For the same reason you don't want to tell Evelyn that you love her,' he said quietly. 'I thought it was lunacy. That I was a fool. That the situation was too difficult. That I would travel halfway across the world only to be hurt or abandoned or rejected. I told myself that it was better to stay here. Better to stick to what I knew: York, the bookshop. Better to make my father happy and keep the shop in the family. My life here was small, perhaps, compared to the vastness of India, the newness of it all, but it was safe. And of course, I let myself hope a little, throughout the years. I told myself that when you grew up, that's when I would do it – when I would finally make the leap. I told myself that once you were a man grown, I would leave. I would write and tell the person I loved that finally, finally I would come. At least, that's what I told myself. And then you grew up, and I told myself something different. Too much time had passed. They would feel differently. I would feel differently. I couldn't make it across an ocean at my age. The crossing would take too long. I couldn't handle the heat.

'You've been a grown man for a while now, William, and I am growing old, and I am still finding excuses. Still making decisions based on fear.' He blew a breath through his teeth then. 'In fact, I've been making decisions based on fear for so long I don't know how to make them otherwise. And I don't want you to do the same, William. I don't want you to end up like me: a man in his fifties, with nothing but a stack of letters instead of a life he should've lived.' Uncle Howard sat back then, resting his head against the desk. 'Don't sit with your love in your stomach all your life until it sours. Go out and tell her. Because if all these years have taught me anything, it's that it is better to have tried and have failed than to have never tried at all. Do it, William. Before it is too late.'

William reached up, taking his uncle's hand in his own. 'But surely it's not too late for you either? You receive letters every week. Surely that means this person still loves you? That you still love them?'

His uncle let out a deep, deep sigh. 'I have given them a shadow of love, for years. Letters instead of embraces. Words instead of whispers. What kind of man does that? What kind of man hides, in fear?' He squeezed William's hand tight. 'For goodness' sake, Will. Tell the person you love that you love them. And let whatever will happen after that happen.'

Chapter Thirty-Nine

2nd September 1899

Evelyn's father had hired a carriage to take them to the York Theatre Royal, much to her mother's delight. As the sleek black horses trotted their way down Colliergate and past the gothic spires of the Minster, Evelyn felt as though she had stepped through a mirror. It looked so much like her old life that she should have felt at home, should have found comfort in the familiarity, but that was gone, and it had been replaced with an odd sense that she was now on the outside, watching it happen, observing how similar it looked and yet how different it felt.

Before, she would not have appreciated the speed at which they had gone down Walmgate, past the bookshop and over the little bridge, but now that she had spent so many mornings walking the length of it, watching the same woman bring her wicker baskets out in the morning and back in the evening, she marvelled at it. Now that she had spent so many days working in the quiet gloom of the Emporium, she wanted to twitch back the carriage curtains, allow some sunshine onto her face, though her mother's sharp glance in her direction told her it would be unwelcome.

Her father had made good on his promise and bought them both new dresses, and now Evelyn felt as though she were costumed as a peach; there was so much pale orange taffeta around her throat, bunching at her waist, that she could barely move. Having spent so many days in blouses and skirts, she found that wearing a full dress with a corset felt ridiculous. Constricting. It was an image of her old life, with all the knowledge of her new one, and it was like sitting on a pebbled beach – all she could feel were the sharp little reminders that this was not how it was anymore, and however it might have felt before, it didn't feel that way now.

'Goodness,' said Cecilia, as they stepped from the carriage into the mass of people milling outside the theatre – an imposing stone building that looked ancient, though in truth it had been built only a century and a half earlier – 'It looks like half of polite society is in attendance.'

'A perfect stage for our re-entry then,' said Evelyn's father. 'Look, there's Lord Asterley. Come, let me introduce you to him.'

Evelyn's eyes searched the crowd for William, for his shock of black hair, his crumpled shirt. His words had rung in her ears ever since she'd left the bookshop: *this is not how it should be*. There had been something broken in his expression, in the way his shoulders had curved inwards, as though to protect himself from her, and she'd felt embarrassed enough to leave. But now she wondered if she should have stayed, if she should have walked towards him, not away from him, and pressed a hand against his chest to see if his heart thudded in time with her own.

But William was not in the crush of people outside the theatre, though she saw the ghost of him reflected in other dark-haired men, other lithe shadows. This was a sea of strangers: the men in their high, starched collars and silk, patterned cravats; the women in reception dresses: longer sleeved than formal evening gowns and with slightly higher necklines. And then, finally, her eyes landed upon someone she did recognize, and her lips curled into a grimace. For there stood Lady Violet.

She was facing away from her, but Evelyn would know her fair hair anywhere. Lady Violet was resplendent in a gown made from rose-gold silk, one arm tucked into the crook of a tall, blond man's elbow.

She had had a long time to regret what she'd said in the bookshop. She had thought that perhaps if she gave Lady Violet a taste of her own medicine, she might feel better, more in control. As it was, she'd felt as much the bully she'd accused Lady Violet of being. She had threatened her because she'd felt scared, because she'd felt cornered.

Wasn't that why Nathaniel had said Lady Violet did it, too? Why she was so brackish with people, so ready to bite – because she herself felt backed into a corner? Evelyn wondered if she should apologize to her and try to calm the feud between them once and for all. A promise for a promise. One secret for another.

But then the man at Lady Violet's side pressed a kiss to her cheek, so swift, so discreet that almost no one saw.

Except Evelyn.

And she realized then that the man beside Lady Violet was Nathaniel – the very same man she had told William would *not* be here.

Lady Violet looked round, as though she'd sensed Evelyn's eyes upon her. She returned her gaze with a sharp little glare, then unhooked her arm from Nathaniel's and stalked off through the clusters of people with such strident purpose that Evelyn knew she was looking for one person in particular.

Cecilia.

Evelyn picked up her skirts and followed at pace, pushing

through the walls of dark suits and pastel dresses to try to reach her mother first, to pull her away. Distantly, she heard the first theatre bell ringing, calling the audience to their seats, and she wished her mother would turn, would go into the cool gloom promised behind the theatre's arched doorways, but she simply stood there, chatting to her father and another man, and Lady Violet was getting closer, though perhaps Evelyn would reach her first—

William had thought long and hard about what Uncle Howard had said. He'd sat up most of the night with it, his thoughts like a thousand scattered marbles.

He did not want to be like Uncle Howard, living with the regret of never having spoken, and as he rounded the corner to the theatre the following day, his hands shaking, his heart thudding in his throat, he knew he had to tell her. And though fearful thoughts clawed at him – what if he couldn't bring himself to speak? What if she refused? – one thought within him burned bright: what if he told her, and she felt the same way? She had kissed him, after all, had closed the gap between them by pressing her lips against his. It was this thought that had kept him awake as night once again became day, as the sky turned from indigo to orange to pink and then, finally, to a blue so crisp and clear he could drink it.

What if she loved him back?

Uncle Howard had lent William a very fine three-piece dinner suit, so it required very little lying on William's part to make it through the azure blue doors at the far end of the lobby and into the smoking lounge where the great folk awaited the show's bell.

He searched the crowd for Evelyn, his gaze snagging upon every dark-haired woman, his heart soaring and sinking like a swallow at dusk, but she was not here. Perhaps he was early? Or perhaps she was late. Either way, he had already made up his mind to wait for her upon the theatre's steps when he heard her name bubble up from the crowd of men clustered by the window.

They looked like the type of men who would dine at the Royal, the type who wouldn't give William a second glance. And so he took a seat within hearing distance, and he listened.

'You are newly partnered with Lord Seaton, too?' asked the first man, whose heavily lidded eyes made it look as though he were ready to sleep.

'On the American railway project,' agreed the second, his moustache wobbling with each nod. 'A relatively small initial investment, I should say, for the return.'

William tilted his head a little, his grip tightening around the stem of his champagne glass. Apparently 'relatively small' for these men was between £150 and £200 – three times his yearly wage – and William had to work very hard not to spit his drink back into the glass.

'Then you are all fools,' said the third, whose coal-black beard was impeccably trimmed. 'The man is a known charlatan. Do you know how much he lost on the rail project in Kent?'

'Ah, but that's England,' said the first man. 'This is America. There is far less red tape.'

The black-bearded man snorted. 'So claims Lord Seaton, the very same man who used to fritter away his weekends in York making deep-plays that cut his coffers almost in half. A sour laugh hissed from his lips. 'The man is a manipulator, and if you haven't handed the money to him yet, I recommend you keep it most firmly in your own pockets.'

'I have already paid him,' said the second man, whose moustache was wobbling even more now.

'And I,' said the first.

'Then you will have to hope he has turned over a new leaf,' said the black-bearded man. 'Otherwise, that money will be lost.'

William didn't realize how hard he'd been gritting his teeth until he felt the beginnings of a headache settle behind his eyes. Evelyn had said her father had come home with nothing but debts to pay, but here he was, pocketing several hundred pounds from two men alone.

Perhaps there was a fortuitous railway project in America. Perhaps Evelyn's father had put aside the sort of reckless behaviour that had caused him to gamble away their family home.

Or perhaps he hadn't.

Either way, he needed to tell Evelyn.

Chapter Forty

The deep voice behind her was so close that Evelyn started, a rush of impatience blooming in her chest.

'Nathaniel, I do not have time for this,' she said, barely breaking her stride.

'Evelyn, please.' He clutched her wrist, holding her in place. 'Just give me a chance to apologize. You never wrote me back.'

She watched Lady Violet reach Cecilia, watched her cast one final glance backwards, her eyebrows raised in warning: *look what I could do.*

'Evelyn?'

She turned her attention back to Nathaniel. There was a petulant look upon his face, like that of a child denied his toy. 'My letter?'

'Honestly, Nathaniel,' she huffed. 'Why are you doing this?'

He blinked at her. 'Why am I . . . apologizing?'

'No,' said Evelyn, dropping her voice as a footman with a tray full of champagne glasses walked past. 'Why are you pretending to care what I think about you, when you and I both know the only person in this room whose opinion matters to you is wearing a rose-gold gown.'

Nathaniel's gaze flicked to the floor. 'I don't know what you're talking about.'

'You are in love with her,' said Evelyn. 'I saw it that first day in the lobby of the club chambers, and I can see it still now.'

'Did Lady Violet put you up to this?' he asked, swallowing hard. 'Or is this another of your pretty assertions, like the New York society ladies?'

Here it was: her chance for revenge, for retribution. To strike, rather than being struck. She could say yes. She could tell him the truth, the whole of Lady Violet's plan, or she could concoct an even worse lie.

But then I shall be as bad as her.

Evelyn shook her head. 'No, Nathaniel. Lady Violet did not put me up to this. I can see it, as plainly as everyone else in this room.'

'Not everyone,' he said, his gaze lifting over her shoulder and holding there. 'But I decided long ago that I will not love what I cannot have. Which is why you must forgive me, Evelyn.' His blue eyes flicked to her now, pleading. 'For prying, and for making such a mess of our dinner. I do not want you to despise me for one mistake.'

Evelyn looked up at him then, into the deep, lapis blue of his eyes. She wasn't used to men like him speaking so forwardly. Still, she supposed he wasn't English, and so perhaps her expectations for him to be upright and enigmatic were misplaced. 'I don't despise you,' she said truthfully.

'But have you forgiven me? For prying?'

She looked away. The embarrassment of it was still there, the memory of an ache in her stomach, and though hindsight had taught her to be grateful for what she knew, she was not grateful that she had learned it in such a way, that she had been forced to manage her shock amongst an ocean of faces.

Nathaniel's expression softened. 'Please, Evelyn. What must a man do to earn your forgiveness? Do you want me to beg? To make a spectacle of myself? Because I'll do it. I'll get down on my knees and beg you.'

'You need not beg me,' said Evelyn, but to her horror he was already kneeling, two hands reaching up to clasp hers in his, and she felt the room's eyes swivel towards them, felt Lady Violet's scowl burning into the side of her face.

'Please, Nathaniel,' said Evelyn, a wave of embarrassment as strong as nausea crashing upon her. 'You do not need to do this. Stand up.'

'Not until you forgive me,' he said.

'I forgive you,' Evelyn said hurriedly. 'Now *stand up*.'

'And promise you will take tea with me.'

She gritted her teeth. The room had quietened around them, not to a hush, thank goodness, but to enough of a dull murmur that she knew people were straining to listen, and she felt the heat from her cheeks spreading down her neck.

'If I agree, then will you stand?'

'Oh, at once.'

'Very well then,' Evelyn said. 'I will go to tea with you.'

'Excellent,' said Nathaniel, rising gracefully to his feet.

The conversation around them started up again, though the flush on her face did not reduce as Nathaniel stepped closer, leaning so he could whisper into her ear.

'I shall send a note for you when I am next in York. And this time, I would like a reply.'

She caught Lady Violet's eye then over Nathaniel's shoulder, felt the weight of her boiling glare, and Evelyn realized that it didn't matter that she hadn't told Nathaniel. It mattered that Lady Violet *thought* she had told Nathaniel, because now Lady Violet was pulling her mother aside, and the second bell rang, louder than the first, telling everyone to take their seats for the performance.

And the crowd began to shuffle inwards, though one figure remained still, standing directly across from Evelyn.

It was William.

She had thought it a lie, the idea that a person could take your breath away, but she realized now as she looked at him, as her heart stuttered in her chest, that she'd never seen such a beautiful creature as him.

He stood between Jack and Naomi, his shirt starched and pressed until it was startlingly white against his black hair, which had been combed and oiled, his curls deftly positioned. Only a single unruly strand had escaped, curling down towards his eyebrows.

But then their eyes met, and the flicker of heat in her stomach turned to ice.

Had he seen that whole spectacle, seen her and Nathaniel? She needed to speak with him, needed to explain, but as she stepped forwards, he stepped backwards, gripping the top of Jack's arm and ushering him and Naomi into the tide of people.

'William!' Her voice was loud enough that he should have heard, and she saw Naomi spot her and wave.

But William did not stop; he merely shook his head and pressed them onwards, answering her question with his silence.

Of course he'd seen.

William couldn't have missed them.

The man had been kneeling before her, both hands pressed into hers, and the moment looked so intimate, so private that his instinct had been to look away.

But he hadn't.

He'd forced himself to watch as Nathaniel raised himself to his feet, as he smiled and bent to whisper something into

Evelyn's ear that made her cheeks flush red. William had closed his hands to fists and squeezed and squeezed until he'd felt his fingernails score the soft skin of his palms.

Because he hadn't considered this other possibility. What if he was too late? What if she had already made her choice? What if she had lied to him when she said she wasn't interested in a man such as Nathaniel? It was possible, seeing as she had lied about him being here. Why had he been kneeling before her? Was it a proposal? And if it hadn't been, then why had she been blushing as though they shared some secret?

Another voice in his mind spoke then, a softer one, trying to soothe the maelstrom of thoughts: *It's better this way*, it said. *If love is showing all you are, then you cannot do that, can you? You cannot love her if that is built upon a lie, but perhaps Nathaniel can. Doesn't she deserve that? Doesn't she deserve all of a person, rather than a shadow of one? Doesn't she deserve someone successful, rather than you?*

The bell rang then, and the crowds parted, and William had turned from Evelyn's gaze, from her pleading expression, had gripped Jack's arm and ushered him and Naomi inside.

Chapter Forty-One

The carriage ride home was less than pleasant, for Evelyn's fear was right.

Lady Violet had told her mother.

Cecilia had gripped Evelyn's elbow as the final bell shrieked through the theatre and whispered, her voice low and flat with anger: 'You know, Evelyn, for all you berate your father, I think you and he are more alike than you think. How could you lie to me like that?'

And the panic had seared in Evelyn's chest, as hot and sudden as steam.

Now, they all three sat in silence, her mother's gaze upon the window, Evelyn's upon her mother, her father's upon the floor.

Her mother was right; Evelyn was no different from her father. She had lied, just as he had lied, and she would try and excuse it just as he always did. She prided herself on being honest, on saying things how they were, and she had held onto that with one hand and held the lie in the other, and not considered the glaring hypocrisy of it all. And if she was not honest, if she was not the kind of person who spoke candidly, then who was she?

Who was she?

It was only once they'd stepped inside the cool gloom of Aunt Clara's house, only once the door had closed that her mother said: 'Now then – you will tell me *what on earth* has been going on.'

'I can explain—' said Evelyn, following her mother into the morning room and watching as she dragged the curtains shut with such force that the metal rings shrieked horribly.

Aunt Clara's voice called from the kitchen: 'If you're going to argue, can you wait until I've steeped my tea?'

'You were the one who said we needed to break the rules if we were to find our way back! I went to a ball unchaperoned. A *dinner* unchaperoned. And all the while *you* held fast to the hope it would lead to a proposal!'

'"Bend" the rules, I said. "Bend", not "break", and that did *not* include lying to me,' Cecilia said, as John stepped into the room and took a seat upon one of the grandmother chairs, an expectant look upon his face. 'Your daughter has been *working*,' she exclaimed. 'In a *shop*. Every day, Evelyn told me that she was volunteering with Lady Violet. And every day, instead, she has been going to some godforsaken bookshop in town and working there. For *months*. She has been lying to my face. For *months*. And I have been writing to Lady Violet and thanking her profusely for all her help, her kindness towards you, Evelyn. For *months*!' Her voice was climbing now, from a hoarse whisper to a veritable shout. 'And now she tells me that it was all a lie. And I must seem the biggest fool in all of York, for I was the only one who did not know – who did not see it! Lady Violet herself had to tell me, and the Lord only knows, Evelyn, if she hadn't, would I have ever found out? Would you have ever told me? Or would you have continued lying to my face, day in, day out, watching me write and send letters that made me out to be a complete fool!'

Evelyn shook her head. 'Mother, please. I didn't lie to

embarrass you or to make you a laughing stock. I lied because I knew you would not approve—'

'Cecilia,' said John, his voice low. 'If this has been going on for months, then how did you not notice?'

Her mother's mouth opened and closed again, and Evelyn watched the flush rise on her cheeks. 'Because—'

Evelyn knew the end of that sentence: because her mother had sunk back into her miseries, cloaking herself in the habit of sleeping little and rising late.

Aunt Clara stepped through the doorway then, a cup and saucer in her hand and an expression upon her face like a snarling lioness. 'Because she has had to deal with all your rubbish,' Aunt Clara spat. 'Don't you dare question *her* actions underneath my roof. Your wife has put up with more from you in twenty-five years than most wives do in a lifetime.'

'My wife has had things that a woman of her birth could only *dream of*,' countered John. 'And I shall not take orders from the likes of you.'

'Enough!' said Evelyn, placing herself between her father and her great-aunt, as though that would do anything to dampen the crackling tension in the air. 'Mama, I was trying to help you. I was trying to save up enough so that we could move out of here—'

'Because my house is what, a hovel?' Aunt Clara exclaimed. 'I take the pair of you in, and you repay me by wishing to leave me behind as quickly as possible!'

'I didn't mean it like that, Aunt,' Evelyn said, feeling suddenly like a rabbit caught between three wolves. 'I just know how reluctant you were to let us stay, and I wanted to do something good that would help us all. I was saving up for a deposit, Mother—'

'I told you,' Cecilia said, fixing her daughter with a trembling look. 'Getting a job was the one thing I expressly forbade—'

'Because you are under some notion that it will make us *less* than we are! But it didn't, Mother. *It can't.* Because we can only be who we are.'

Cecilia wiped hurriedly at her cheeks. 'What we are is *disgraced*.'

'Father did that,' Evelyn said. 'Not me. Not my job. You yourself said that rules are meant to be broken—'

'Bent,' said Cecilia. 'Rules are meant to be *bent*.'

'How much do you have?' It was her father who spoke then, his hands clasped over his stomach, one leg resting on the opposite knee. 'How much have you earned?'

'Fourteen pounds and eight shillings.' She'd spent only what she'd had to, and saved the rest.

Her father's eyebrows raised a fraction. 'Oh my child, that is nothing – worthless pennies. How much are you paid per week at this shop?'

'Does it matter?' Cecilia said, flopping down at the other end of the settee. 'You will never go back there, Evelyn. Do you hear me? Your time working at that shop is over. Done.'

'But, Mother—' The panic stripped her like lightning does a tree, peeling everything back until all that was left was fear. 'I cannot simply *not go back* to the Emporium – I am employed there.' *And William. I have so much to say to William.*

'Employed without my permission.'

'I am twenty-four years old!'

'Answer me,' said her father, his tone calm in comparison to theirs. 'How much do you earn a week?'

'A pound and two, providing we sell enough. And I have been selling enough, at least lately. Mrs Quinn came in, you see, and she has a book club, and—'

Her mother's face paled. 'Not Mrs Quinn from church?'

Evelyn belatedly realized the gravity of her mistake.

'Is *that* why you strong-armed me into lending her my name as a sponsor?'

'But, Mama, she did not say anything because—'

'Because you told the whole world to lie to me?' Now she saw the depth of the fury in her mother's eyes, read it in the tremble of her lips. 'You are a hypocrite, Evelyn. You told me that you sympathized with me when I complained that none of my friends would speak to me – and yet you go and do something that would ensure they not only never spoke to me again but spent the rest of their lives laughing at me!'

'Mama, please—'

'No.' Her mother shook her head, placing her hand upon her mouth. '*You* have not spent the last twenty years trying to fit yourself into a place that does not want you, that will not have you, that wants to put you back down into the hole you crawled out of and leave you there, in the darkness.' Cecilia's eyes were shining now; a tear rolled down her cheek, catching between her fingertips, and Evelyn could feel her heart hurting, could feel every excuse she had ever used to justify this to herself dissolving on the air, floating into mist.

'Do you know what they called me when I married your father, Evelyn? Awful things. And yet I didn't care. I was determined to make a place, not for me but for *you*. I wanted to give *you* every chance, Evelyn, and you . . .' She let her arms flop at her sides. 'You have thrown it in my face.'

'Mama, please—' There were tears trickling down Evelyn's own cheeks now. 'Forgive me. I did this for you. To *protect you*. All I've ever wanted was to make you happy.'

'No,' said her mother. 'How can I forgive you, when I do not know who you are anymore? My daughter is honest. She is kind. She would never have lied so . . . so *cruelly* to me, for so long. She would never sneak behind my back and shame me to the world. You cannot be her, for my daughter would never hurt me so.'

And with that, she stormed from the room.

Evelyn stood there for a moment, wanting desperately to follow, to grip her mother's hand and hold it and hug her and apologize over and over, until her mother pulled her into her arms and spoke softly into the top of her head and said *I forgive you*. But she knew from the rage she'd seen in her mother's eyes that that could not happen today.

It might not ever happen.

'Your mother is very upset,' her father said, standing slowly, picking invisible lint from his trousers. 'But I find myself quite proud of you, Evelyn. You did what you needed to do for this family, and for that . . .' He patted a hand to her shoulder, giving it a squeeze, and she flinched, drawing back from him. 'All the same, you will not be returning to that bookshop. Write a note, and I shall drop it off on my way back into the city.'

Evelyn blinked. 'You are going back into the city? To-night?'

'I have business to attend to,' her father said, leaving Evelyn to sink into the weathered velvet of the sofa, to put her head in her shaking hands, and to feel the panic draw over her like a cloak, thick and heavy, as she realized that all she had worked for had been unravelled.

And William.

All those days spent with him that she had taken for granted, and now . . .

Now it was gone.

And she had only herself to blame.

Chapter Forty-Two

While Evelyn sat in Aunt Clara's morning room, William found himself once more in the room behind the rust-red door, his heart thudding loudly in his ears.

He was sitting upon a wooden stool, his hands tied with rope behind his back, and instead of the scene he had come upon before, six or seven men dotted languidly about the room, he faced only two of them this time: the enormous man who had given him the loan and the skeletal one who had laughed too much. The rest of them were stood behind him; they were the ones who had jumped him on his walk home from the theatre and dragged him the full way here, ripping the collar of Uncle Howard's best dress shirt and splitting the skin of Will's cheek in the process.

'Your first payment's overdue, son,' said the beefy man, the one with the shock of grey running through his brown hair. He was leaning against the table and seemed to have gilded more teeth in the time they had been apart. William wondered whose debt had been called in for him to afford that. Would his money be spent the same way, buying golden molars for a loan shark?

'We said three months.' William wished his voice was steadier, but he found he had no control over it. His whole body was tense and trembling, as though he was already running out of the door.

'We said, if you repaid within the first month, there'd be no interest.' The man took a step towards him, leaning so that they were at eye level. 'Did you really think I'd sit there for three months with *no* repayment coming in whatsoever?'

William bit his lip; he suspected the man did not want to hear him answer *yes*, and nor did he wish to seem naive. 'I need a little more time,' he said.

'Empty his pockets.'

'Right you are, boss.'

William wished he was the kind of man who would lash out, struggle against them, kick, perhaps, or shout. As it was, he was numb, shame and fear alternating in waves as they dragged him roughly to his feet and tipped every coin from his pockets.

'There's no more than a pound and six here, boss,' said one of the men around him.

The scowl on the enormous man's face told William that this was not what he had been expecting. Which was understandable, William supposed, seeing as he was dressed in Uncle Howard's finest suit and had been grabbed coming out of a theatre performance, all of which suggested he had a lot more money than he truly did.

'You'll need to pay me more than that, son,' said the man. 'The agreement was the full amount back in my pocket in three months, plus interest owed. Now, I'm no mathematician, but I reckon interest owed for this month is two pounds and ten shillings. Is that right, Brone?'

The skinny man on the other side of the room nodded. 'That's right, boss.'

William felt his heart thud all the louder, felt his vision began to spot and speckle. Even with Jack's pound he'd have next to no money for coal. For food. For *rent*.

'I think we got off on the wrong foot here,' he said. 'I was under a false understanding, and clearly I've mis-communicated something to you. Perhaps we could start all this over again? I can repay you at a lower rate – say, a pound and a half a month? Across six months. You would have your money back by March.'

'By March, you'd owe me a lot more than ten pounds, boy. How much exactly, Brone?'

The skinny man looked at his boss and then plucked up a piece of paper and began to scribble. 'About thirty-three pounds, boss. After six months of repayments.'

'What?' The fear that pulsed through him was sharp and cold. 'But I only borrowed ten!'

'I'm beginning to think you don't understand how this business works,' growled the gold-toothed man, so close now that William could smell the whisky on his breath, the cigar smoke on his lapels. 'Each month you don't repay me, the interest gets added on top. What's the interest on ten pounds, Brone?'

'Two pounds ten shillings.'

'Which doubles after three months. And you want to pay me back a fraction of that. So you see the problem, don't you boy?'

William gritted his teeth. 'Yes.'

'Good.' The man gave him a pat on his cheek that was so hard it stung. 'Then you'll understand why it's in your best interest to pay me the right amount. And pay day was yesterday. So where's the rest of my money, boy?'

'At home,' said William sullenly. The money for his groceries, for his candles and coal was at home. He only had his rent and Jack's pound in his pocket.

'Go with him,' said the big man, 'and collect our first payment. If you keep it up at three pounds, all this nasty business will be behind you in a few months.'

'Or else you'll be seeing a lot more of me,' said Brone, giving him a wide smile that was all teeth.

Later, once the men had gone, and there were but three shillings left to his name, William trudged upstairs to where his landlord, Mr Lache lived, his face burning with shame as he said that he was very sorry but that he'd need to take the basement room from now on.

Mr Lache looked at Will's torn collar, his cut cheek, and narrowed his eyes. 'Payment in advance,' he said, holding out a thick hand. 'Or else it goes to someone not involved in whatever shit you've got yourself into.'

'I already paid you a deposit on the upstairs room,' William said, exhausted. 'Surely you can just transfer that over?'

'That deposit covered your first week's rent,' said Mr Lache. 'This is a new room. A new rental agreement, so if you want to take it, you'll need to pay the two shillings, plus a shilling for the month's waste disposal, and because I'm a kind man, I'll ignore the fact that your rent for the upstairs room was due yesterday.'

William curled his fingertips around the last three coins in his pocket. 'But then I'll have nothing left,' he said, and to his horror, he heard his voice crack a little.

Mr Lache's eyes hardened. 'It's a simple choice: be impoverished and homeless, or simply just impoverished. What are you going to do with only three shillings, anyway?'

William didn't know. He felt the panic of it grip his throat like a vice, wrap its cold fingers around his neck and squeeze and squeeze until he felt he couldn't breathe.

'Here,' he said, putting the coins into the man's clammy hands. 'I'll move my stuff.'

'I'll get the key.'

* * *

Half an hour later, William sat upon the single bed in the basement room, the springs digging into his thighs, his measly belongings scattered between the mould and the damp patches. He closed his eyes, trying to stop himself from shivering, from feeling the chill that seemed to seep from the walls and curl around his bones.

He could still see flashes of the day in the darkness behind his eyelids: the gaudy make-up of the stage actors; the sound of his leather boots scraping against dry flagstones down the alley; Nathaniel kneeling before Evelyn, clutching her fingers in his.

Only then did he feel a pain in his chest, as though they had struck him there, not on his face.

It is for the best, said the voice in his head. *Look at you now. You have nothing. You are no one. And she deserves better.*

Chapter Forty-Three

When William arrived at the bookshop early on Monday, there was a letter resting against the black varnish of the door.

It was addressed to his uncle, and before William had even stopped to consider whether he should open an envelope that wasn't for him, his finger had already slipped beneath the seal.

Dear Mr Morton,

I am sorry to inform you that I cannot work at the bookshop any longer. I only hope this makes your life easier come December, as you'll no longer have to choose between your nephew and me. That must be a silver lining, mustn't it? If not for you, then for William. Or perhaps that is just something I am holding onto in order to make myself feel better about leaving you both in the lurch like this.

I have enclosed the key. Please say hello for me whenever you can to Edgar and Allan (that is what I named the gargoyles).

With my very best wishes, and my most heartfelt apologies,
The Honourable Miss Evelyn Seaton

William stood there for a long moment, a slight tremor in his hands causing the paper to rustle ever so gently. There was nothing in her letter for him. No real mention of him, in fact, other than how she would make their competition null and void. Is that what he was to her – a footnote? And if this was a farewell – for surely it read like one – then where was his goodbye?

He stepped into the cool gloom of the bookshop and slammed the letter down upon the register, not bothering to put it back in the envelope. He didn't do what Evelyn did, opening each of the curtains carefully, pinning them back. He flung them open and watched as the dust bloomed into the room, as it filtered down in glittering mists against the cool, September sunshine.

She hadn't even said why she wasn't coming back, hadn't given a reason, and it made his thoughts spin wildly, spooling like thread from a ream. Perhaps it was him – perhaps she had finally deemed him insufferable? Or perhaps it had been something to do with her mother not approving of her work? In truth he didn't care what it was, so long as it wasn't the question that circled, over and again: *Had Nathaniel proposed?*

William had learned three things from his trip to the theatre. The first and most pressing was that watching the woman you love blush while another man knelt before her felt the same as slipping a knife between your ribs. The second was that nothing makes you feel more lonely than being in the presence of two people madly in love with one another. Jack and Naomi had been gushing, and it had taken all that William had not to be miserly and brackish with the pair of them.

The third thing he had learned was that Evelyn's father had made a pretty penny with his investments, for other than the three men in the blue lounge, there were at least six more who had given the baron money. He'd hoped to tell Evelyn that today, but it was clear from her letter that she wasn't coming back.

That they would not speak again.

He plucked the letter back up, as though there might suddenly be more writing upon it than before. Looking at the spindly loops of her handwriting now, he wondered if the smudges were because she was writing too quickly for the ink to dry or because she had been crying as she wrote. The ink had run thrice, a triangle of splotches around his name.

But he shook his head. *That is hope speaking, not reason,* he thought, pressing his fingers to his temples to try to massage away the tension that pressed there.

For the last two nights he'd lain awake, his mind flitting back and forth between thoughts of Evelyn, and attempts to calculate how he could afford to stay housed, warm, and fed on a miserly budget. For that was all he would have once those men had collected their share.

The answer had been even more depressing than he'd imagined.

It would be easier if you admitted your lie to Uncle Howard and asked to move back into your old room upstairs, the voice in his mind said. *Then at least rent would be cheaper.*

He'd considered it, too, as the frigid night had crested into a cool, golden dawn, as his head had begun to throb with worry, with tiredness. But the lie had spiralled now, unravelling into darkness, growing and growing until it was bigger than him, bigger than he'd ever imagined.

He heard the creak of the upstairs floorboards and turned to see Uncle Howard on the mezzanine.

'There's a letter here for you,' William called up.

He watched as Uncle Howard's lamplight paused and swung in his direction instead. 'A letter? So early?'

'From Evelyn,' William said. 'I opened it, I'm afraid, although it was addressed to you.'

Uncle Howard nodded. 'I shall be right down.'

A knock came at the door then, and William checked his pocket watch with a frown. They still had ten minutes before they opened. He handed Uncle Howard the letter, watching as he scanned the words.

'So she has resigned,' Uncle Howard said, looking at William as though he were something fragile, something that might break. 'Was this . . . was this after you spoke with her at the theatre? After you told her?'

'I didn't speak to her at the theatre,' said William. 'She was with someone else.' The image of Nathaniel kneeling before Evelyn had been scorched into his mind, and now it smouldered there in thick, black lines.

'So then why has she resigned?'

William shrugged. 'You know as much as I do.'

'And you don't want to ask?' said Uncle Howard. 'You don't want to know?'

'Of course I want to know. But her letter made it sound like she's saying goodbye. Like we won't speak again.'

'And that's what you want, is it?' His uncle looked at him pointedly. 'For you both to never speak again? That's something you want to happen?'

William opened his mouth and closed it again. *It's better this way,* said a voice in his mind, but for once he didn't listen. 'I don't want it to be goodbye,' he said, the words so quiet they were almost a whisper. 'I don't want that to be the last time we speak.'

'Well then,' said his uncle. 'Don't let it be.'

The knock came again, more tentative this time, as though the person on the other side was considering walking away. 'I'll get it,' William said. 'It's almost time to open anyway.'

'Promise me,' said Uncle Howard. 'Promise me you won't just let her fade into the distance. Don't make the same mistake I did.'

William paused then, for there was a roughness to his uncle's voice he had not heard before, a deep kind of regret that plucked at his own heart. 'I promise,' he said, and then hurried for the door.

When William swung it open, he saw it wasn't a customer at all. It was Jack, dressed in his work livery, and he was grinning from ear to ear.

'Two things,' he said. 'I asked Naomi, and we're getting married!'

William smiled widely and pulled his friend into a bear hug. 'You didn't have to make yourself late for work to tell me,' he said. 'But I am happy for you both.'

'I'm not on my way – I'm just coming home,' said Jack. 'Guess who my last guest was?'

William shook his head.

'Baron Seaton,' said Jack. 'Evelyn's father. And guess what he was up all night doing in the Royal's bar?'

William found he could guess this one more easily. 'Gambling?'

'Gambling,' said Jack. 'Discreetly, of course, but from the sounds of it he was losing. Losing *big*.'

William scrunched his hands into fists at his sides. He needed to tell Evelyn, to warn her. He turned back into the shop. 'Uncle Howard?' he called. 'Do you think you could manage without me for a few hours?'

'Of course,' Uncle Howard called back.

'Good,' said William, grabbing his jacket and stepping out into the cool, autumn breeze with Jack. 'Because I have something I need to do.'

Chapter Forty-Four

As William half walked, half jogged the length of Walmgate towards Porthaven House, Evelyn looked from the crumpled paper in her hands to the row of sandstone houses in front of her. The air was cooler, crisper, and while the trees in the park behind St. Leonard's Place were still green, soon the whole city would be painted in swathes of copper and bronze. For now, it was just a promise on the wind, written in the curls of morning mist slowly dissolving from the river.

Evelyn pulled her jacket closed at the neck, pushing open the little gate of the nearest house and climbing a short set of stairs to reach the door, which was painted in sleek black gloss. She knew William lived in one of these buildings – she simply did not know *which* – and she could only hope that she would have time to try the doors on each of them before her mother finished haggling down the price of mulberry silk and stepped out of the dress shop.

The further William walked down Walmgate, the more he realized he was placing a lot of trust in a memory of walking Evelyn home some weeks ago. Once the shops mostly disappeared, the street opened out into housing, and the roads on either side became more frequent, closes and smaller streets revealing row upon row of identical brick houses. He thought he'd missed the turning to her road and would have to backtrack – but then he saw the lamp-post that marked it and the small, half-hidden sign that read *Long Close Lane*.

He wanted to tell her about her father. He wanted to warn her that he was gambling again, that perhaps the investments he was taking from the men at the theatre were the same money he was spending so frivolously. But the further he'd walked, the more he'd wondered whether that was the only reason he was coming here. After all, he could have sent a note. He could have written a letter.

But he hadn't done that. He had grabbed his jacket and walked straight from the shop. And if he stood before her now and told her only that her father was a fool, then he was an even greater one. Because Uncle Howard was right. When you loved someone, the words wished to come out of you. He wanted to say it, wanted to tell her, wanted to see the look upon her face, to see whether she'd look him in the eye. And though his heart beat an irregular pattern in his chest when he thought of what she might reply, he knew that his uncle was right. He had to try.

But there were two sides to that coin. What use was it to try to protect Evelyn from her father's actions, if he himself proffered love and lies with the same hand? Jack had said that to love someone was to show them all of you, and the further William walked down the street, looking up at the dark brick, the small circle windows in the tops of the houses, the pigeons nesting lazily upon the roofs, the more he realized that the bubbling feeling in his stomach was the knowledge that if he loved her, if he truly loved her, then he was going to have to tell her.

He was going to have to admit that he had lied.

Because the alternative – deceiving her and being just as

bad as her father, lying to her and hurting her the same way she'd been hurt that night at the Royal – was too painful to think of, too awful to bear. And even if the thought of saying the words made his skin feel clammy and his forehead bead with sweat and his fists tighten at his sides, even if he told her everything and she turned from him, then at least he would have done the right thing. At least he'd have put all of himself out there for her to see. For her to accept or to reject, as she wished.

He had reached the middle of the street now. On the night he had walked her home, she'd left him at the corner, and he had watched until she stepped inside before leaving. He couldn't tell exactly which house she had gone into, so there was nothing else for it: he would have to knock until he found the right one.

But luck, for once, was on his side. A moment after he'd rapped his knuckles against the flaking red paint, he heard a woman's voice call from within: 'Whatever you're selling, I don't want it.'

'I am not selling anything,' William said, calling loudly through the wood. 'I am looking for Miss Evelyn Seaton. Does she live here?'

There was a pause on the other side of the door. And then he heard footsteps, before it opened just enough to reveal a security chain and a pair of inquisitive blue eyes. 'What do you want with Evelyn?'

'To give her a message,' said William. 'Is she home?'

'You've no letter in your hands.'

'I know,' said William, feeling his cheeks grow red. 'I thought to simply tell her.'

'Did you now?'

The woman's curious gaze disappeared as she closed the door in his face. Then he heard the click of the chain on the other side, and it opened once more to reveal an impressively tall woman of around seventy, with eyes like a stormy sea and hair as white as sun-bleached coral. The dress she wore was wide enough to fill the entryway, and she stretched one arm across the doorframe, too, making it quite clear that William was *not* being invited inside.

'You know, in my day, men wrote delightful long letters. Now do you all just turn up to your sweetheart's doorstep and bark at them? My, my. And people wonder why the world is spiralling so abysmally. This! This is how it begins. What next, I wonder – you start sending messages via telegram?'

It took William a moment to realize that he was meant to speak. 'Look, I'm from the bookshop. I . . .' He trailed off, unsure what to say, for in that moment he realized he didn't *know* why Evelyn had left. Perhaps her family still didn't know about her job? And if they didn't then he did not want to be the one to reveal it.

The woman's blue eyes narrowed. 'The bookshop?' she repeated. 'So you're not Nathaniel?'

'I'm not Nathaniel,' said William, though he felt a prickle of something sharp in his stomach now as he realized she'd said *your sweetheart*. Were they sweethearts, Nathaniel and Evelyn? Was that what he'd seen at the theatre? 'Was Evelyn expecting Nathaniel?'

'Evelyn is out with her mother,' said the woman, 'so I doubt she was expecting anyone. Another reason why one shouldn't gallivant around the city willy-nilly. How hard could it be to give a person a little foresight into your actions, hmm?'

'I'm sorry,' William said, taking a step back from the door. 'I can see I've interrupted you at a bad time.'

'It is always a bad time,' replied the woman, though her voice had softened a little now, and lost its edge. 'If you're not Nathaniel, then who are you?'

'William,' he said. 'William Morton.'

'I've not heard of a William Morton. What message did you wish me to give to my great-niece?'

William wetted his lips. 'I should really give the message to Evelyn herself,' he said. 'It's a little long-winded otherwise.'

He watched the woman's mouth pinch into a thin line. 'Once more, I am reminded of a marvellous invention called *the letter*,' she said. 'But very well. I shall tell her that a man came to give a message and it was private enough that I was not allowed to hear it.'

William wasn't sure if he imagined it or not, but he thought the edge of her mouth began to curl upwards, just a little, into the beginnings of a smile.

'Thank you,' he said. 'And I will write, next time.'

'You see to it that you do,' said the woman, and watched as he walked back down the street. She was still watching as he reached the corner, and it was only when he reached an arm up to wave that he saw her go back inside and close the door.

He would write a letter. He would write a thousand letters if he had to. But the buoyancy that had carried him from the bookshop, that had lifted him the whole way here had begun to hiss as air poured out, for each of the woman's words had been a needle:

Not heard of a William Morton.

Nathaniel.

Sweethearts.

Chapter Forty-Five

Despite the size of St. Leonards Place, there were only five residential townhouses, the rest of the sun-dappled crescent having been dedicated to the York Subscription Library, the Fine Art Institute, the De Grey Rooms, two schools, and a theatre. Five times Evelyn knocked, and five times she had to endure the raised eyebrows, the expressions that ranged from pity to concern to downright antipathy that a woman would show up on one's doorstep and attempt to deliver a letter by hand.

She took a seat at a nearby wrought-iron bench, looking down at the letter in her hand. The very reason she'd wanted to deliver it to his house and not to the bookshop was that she didn't want to see him take it – didn't want to watch him read the words that had taken her so long to write, to arrange. A hundred attempts lay black and charred in Aunt Clara's fireplace, the letter in her hands the last of many.

But now, she did not know where else to reach him. Had she been wrong, about the houses? She stood up and crossed the road, heading back towards the dress shop, so that if her mother looked outside, she would see that Evelyn was being obedient, and also so that she could gain a little perspective on the crescent of sandstone buildings. But no – they were the ones both William and Jack had mentioned. And then, later, when she'd pointed them out again, she was sure William had confirmed it.

Was she misremembering?

She didn't know. But what she did know was that her mother would not simply let her waltz back to Morton's Emporium. When she had finally calmed down and deigned to speak with Evelyn again, very late yesterday evening, it was the second thing she had said, after: 'I haven't forgiven you yet, Evelyn.'

They had both been standing in Evelyn's room, Evelyn staring at the darkness collecting behind the half-moon window, her mother at her writing desk, the newly mended evening dress in her hands, making tutting noises as she inspected the stitches. Evelyn had thought it had turned out quite splendidly, with a river of carefully stitched flowers spilling from the neckline down to the waist, curving like a vine, covering the stain but extending past it, too, so that they looked deliberate.

'Aunt Clara said your mother never quite forgave you, either,' said Evelyn. 'That's why you and Grandmother Ethel never spoke.'

'This was completely different,' said her mother, her gaze upon the stream of carefully stitched roses before her. 'She thought I had made a mistake.'

'And yet you surely thought what you did was for the betterment of the family?'

Cecilia had looked up then, her gaze flattening. 'It *was* for the betterment of the family. What *you* have done—'

'Is the same, Mama.' Evelyn had taken a step forwards, reaching out to clasp her mother's hand. 'I know you wished for a future in which you no longer had to work, but that's not what *I* want. I want to be the master of my own fate.

And for me, that means putting coins in my own pocket. It means being independent.'

'If you are working then you are dependent,' said her mother. 'By the very definition of it.'

'Are you not dependent, also? Upon Father – for your home, your clothes, your jewels? I think we learned the extent of our dependency when the carriages arrived at Riccall Hall and took everything away.'

'That is different,' said Cecilia sharply, her expression as taut as wire as she placed the gown upon the bed.

'No,' Evelyn replied. 'It is not. And just like you saw a way to fix it and broke every rule you came across on the way, I have done the same – because I am your daughter, Mama. What you have inside you, I have inside me, too.'

Her mother had looked at her then, her gaze softening in a way that Evelyn hadn't expected. 'Of course you do,' she said. 'I have always known that. I just hadn't expected it turned against me.'

'It wasn't against you, Mama,' said Evelyn. 'You *placed* yourself against me, when you decided to equate our social status to our actions.'

'Which was foolish of me,' said Cecilia quietly, sitting beside the dress on the bed. 'I thought if I acted a lady long enough, I would be accepted as one. But twenty-five years of trying has proved that unless you were born into it, they will not accept you, no matter how hard you try.'

'So let us stop trying,' said Evelyn. 'Let us carve our own place in this world, instead.'

'I did that once before,' Cecilia had said. 'I will not do it again.'

Now, a carriage clattered past at speed, dragging Evelyn roughly from her reverie and back to the cobbled street. She watched it rattle towards the bridge, no doubt in a rush to meet the lunchtime steam train down to London, and Evelyn looked up, back towards the dress shop, to find her mother walking towards her.

But this time, she was not alone.

'Lady Violet,' said Evelyn, standing to her full height so that she could meet Lady Violet's fluttering gaze without flinching. 'Mr Morris.'

'Miss Seaton,' said Nathaniel, flourishing a bow, which earned a scowl from Lady Violet. 'How lucky to stumble upon you.'

'Lady Violet and I met in the dress shop,' said Cecilia. 'Isn't that quite the coincidence?'

'And so *timely*, too,' said Lady Violet, a curving smile upon her lips. Today, she was clad head to toe in green, from the curling peacock feather in her hat all the way to the silk upon her satin shoes, and it made her skin look like marble in comparison. 'Why, Nathaniel and I were just talking about you, Evelyn.'

Nathaniel reached to scratch at an eyebrow. 'I am not sure we need to reveal our private conversations—'

Lady Violet placed a silencing hand upon his sleeve. 'Nathaniel has been trying to select a place to take tea with you, you see.' To Cecilia, she said: 'I don't condone drinking tea outside of one's parlour, personally, Lady Seaton, but . . .' She tilted her head disapprovingly. 'Regardless, I said to poor Nathaniel that the quality of the tearooms did not matter, for Evelyn's attention had already been quite thoroughly diverted. And *not* by the charming Mr Morris here.'

'What are you talking about?' Evelyn said, feeling her face grow hot.

Lady Violet gave her a faux-surprised look. 'Why, your man at the bookshop of course! I saw the way he came to your protection when I came in that Sunday. Such a *well-trained* little guard dog.'

Cecilia's eyebrows spiked. 'What man at the bookshop?'

'You know the one,' said Lady Violet, her gaze locked upon Evelyn as she took another step closer, a smile dancing upon her lips. 'Tall. Wild black hair. Manners as dastardly as his trousers.'

Nathaniel's gaze flicked to Evelyn and then away. 'You know the one, Evelyn,' he said, in his quiet drawl. 'It was the same man who joined us at dinner.'

Cecilia's eyes grew wide. 'You never mentioned *that* detail!'

'Because it doesn't matter,' said Evelyn, feeling a heat begin to flush her cheeks as another carriage rattled past them. 'It doesn't mean anything.'

'Oh, but I think it does,' said Lady Violet. 'Because although Nathaniel is a good sport, he is not going to tolerate losing you to the kind of man that has worn the same pair of trousers for a decade—'

'A *decade*?' interrupted Cecilia.

'—unless that man is worthy of you. And so that is what we set out to discover. As your friends, we were merely looking out for you.' Lady Violet's smile widened, until it was all teeth. 'And do you know what we discovered?'

'Let me guess,' said Evelyn, her heart thudding a rhythm in her throat that made it difficult to breathe, 'he was found wanting.'

'Oh, *much worse*,' said Lady Violet, lowering her voice. 'He has been lying to you.'

For a moment, it was as though all the sound had been sucked from the street and there were no jingling as the horses trotted past, no distant merchants, no pigeons cooing from the rooftops. There was only the *th-thump* of Evelyn's own heart, as she repeated Lady Violet's word back to her: 'Lying?'

Nathaniel nodded solemnly. 'He doesn't have a publishing deal, Evelyn. In fact, barely a single publisher in London knew his name, and those who did remembered him only because he was the rare breed of fool that chose to sit and wait while they read his work.' To Cecilia, he said: 'One tends to remember crushing someone else's dream when one does it face to face.'

'I am sure,' Cecilia breathed.

'So, there you have it,' said Lady Violet. 'I suppose now we know why he wears such monstrous trousers.'

'William wouldn't,' said Evelyn firmly. 'He wouldn't lie – not like that.'

'You speak as though you know this liar rather well,' said Cecilia sharply.

Nathaniel gave Evelyn a look so achingly condescending that she could have slapped it from his face. 'Unless of course he wanted to hide the fact that he had failed and that every publishing house in London had slammed their doors in his face? Unless he wanted to pretend to be someone he wasn't?'

Evelyn looked down at the cobbles beneath her feet. What was it Jack had said that day in the bookshop? *Success means so much to him because he feels like he needs to earn his place, prove he's worth it.* And when she'd knocked on the doors of St. Leonard's Place, not a single person had even heard of his name.

Was Nathaniel right? Had William been lying this whole time? But if he had, then he hadn't just been lying to her – he'd been lying to everyone: to his uncle, to Jack, to Naomi. He'd lied to them all.

'Excuse me,' Evelyn said, turning abruptly. 'I suddenly have quite a headache.'

'You may take my carriage home if you wish,' said Mr Morris. 'The both of you.'

'Oh, but I wished to look at the hats,' said Cecilia pleadingly.

'You stay, Mama,' said Evelyn. 'And I shall go.'

'I shall send word about our tea,' said Nathaniel, beckoning his carriage and helping her inside with all the gusto of a man who had taken his own measure, and come out on top. 'It will be nice to have no interruptions this time.'

And the tone of his voice was confident, as though he knew that this would be the end of it.

The end of her and William.

Chapter Forty-Six

Back at the bookshop, William stood at his position at the register, watching the hour hand slowly count towards closing time. Upstairs, it sounded as though Uncle Howard had invited a rugby team to help him run from one side of the building to the other, and it was only when his uncle appeared, red-faced and breathless on the mezzanine stairs, that William realized something truly odd was going on.

'How did it go?'

'She wasn't there,' William said, pushing aside the piece of blank paper that he'd been staring at for close to twenty minutes. 'But it got me thinking, Howie, about how if you love someone you should tell them everything. And I . . . I have something I should have told you a long time ago.'

'Hold it for just two seconds,' said Uncle Howard, his eyes sparkling as he flipped the sign to *closed*, 'for I have made a decision.'

William's brow creased. 'What decision?'

'I am going to do it,' he said. 'I am going to go to India. I have booked passage for January. And I am going to leave you in charge of the shop.'

Whatever reaction Uncle Howard had been expecting, it

was not the fearful '*What?*' that came from William's mouth. 'But you can't do that!'

'Of course I can,' he said, walking towards him. 'You've shown how well you can be trusted. Just look at the sales this place has had! Not only can I leave feeling confident that you are capable of managing it – I can leave knowing that you'll make a better job of it than I ever did. And don't go talking about your book, because I've thought of that—' Uncle Howard paused in case William wished to speak, but he merely shook his head, feeling his cheeks flush scarlet with shame. 'If Evelyn won't come back, then perhaps you could train an apprentice and have them work the days when you will be in London? You cannot live down there – you weren't happy in London; I could tell from your letters, from how short they became. And I don't blame you. It takes a certain kind of person to revel in a city so big it could swallow them whole, and you, my boy, are not that person. But this way, it would be perfect, don't you think? You would have a solid income, and I would have somewhere to come and visit! Not to mention we'd keep the bookshop in the family, which I shouldn't be proud of, but I am.' He gave William a warm smile. 'So, what do you say?'

William looked at his uncle, at the fierce pride in his eyes, the warmth he exuded, and in that moment, he crumbled. How could he have lied to him? The man who took him in, who only ever wanted the best for him, who gave and gave and never took anything in return? How could he have stood here all these months and lied to his very face? What kind of person does that?

An awful one, said the voice in his head, and William could only agree as the tears began to well in his eyes, tears of sadness and guilt and frustration and shame, as they rolled down his cheeks and soaked into the crumpled material of his collar.

'I lied to you,' he said, and his voice was low, his throat constricting around the words. 'I have been lying to you this whole time, Uncle.'

And he told him all of it.

How he had arrived in London and felt not only small but insignificant. How he had spent too much money renting a room in Soho where he could hear the rats scuttling through the pipes at night. How he had gone, time and again, to fancy publishing offices all across London, from the Strand to Carnaby Street, from Holborn to the Seven Dials, and how they had sent him away with nothing but sharp little words. How he had felt the bright flame he'd cradled in his chest begin to sputter and dim, and then eventually, it had died altogether. How he had sneaked onto a train at King's Cross and hidden in a cramped, foul-smelling toilet almost the entire journey up to York, for fear the ticket inspector would find him and cast him off before Doncaster. How he'd concocted a lie when he'd come home, and how it had worked well for a time – until it hadn't. Until Jack had asked to borrow money William didn't have. Until his pride had made him say yes.

'That is why I cannot take over the bookshop. I am indebted to a man who will no doubt break my kneecaps if I miss a payment, and I can't afford to pay the interest, let alone repay the ten pounds I borrowed. I live in a basement so damp I could no doubt place a cup at the base of the wall and collect washing water for the morning. I am a failure, Uncle. I am a fraud. And I do not deserve to take over your life's work, your father's life's work. I am not your son, not your responsibility, and this—' He wrapped his arms around his own body, as though if he squeezed hard enough, he might just disappear. 'I am not your problem to solve.'

Uncle Howard, whose face had been growing paler and paler as William spoke, was quiet. William didn't want to look up, didn't want to look at him, but he forced himself to, to see the hurt in his uncle's face, the hurt that *he'd* caused – and saw only sadness, saw his own tears mirrored upon his uncle's cheeks as he pulled him into a rough hug and held him there.

'My boy, why do you think this place is called Morton's Emporium, and not the Lamplighter's Bookshop? You are not the first man in this family who has wanted to be something other than he is, who wanted to tell the world a new story. But know this: you *are* my son, William. You always have been, and you always will be, and don't you ever think otherwise. Don't you dare ever think otherwise.'

He squeezed him so hard William felt the breath pushed from his lungs, and then he stepped back and said: 'Now, who do you owe this money to? And how much, total?'

William felt a flicker of panic in his stomach. 'This isn't your debt. You cannot pay it.'

'I can and I will,' said Uncle Howard. 'The bookshop will manage. How much do you owe?'

'I've paid a month's interest,' he said quietly. 'And I owe more. The original loan was ten pounds.'

The muscle in his uncle's jaw flickered. 'Very well. And where can we find him?'

'He has a counting house on North Street,' said William.

'Then we shall go now,' said his uncle, 'with the full sum, and you will put this behind you once and for all.'

William looked at his uncle, at the ferocity in his gaze. 'You don't have to do this.'

'Of course I do,' said Uncle Howard, resting a warm hand upon William's shoulder. 'We are family, you and I, and this is what family does. We are there for the hardships as well as the good times, and we help each other through them. Do you understand?'

William nodded. 'I understand,' he said.

'Good,' said Uncle Howard. 'Then show me where this man is.'

When Aunt Clara opened the door, she peered behind Evelyn for a moment, as though expecting to see someone with her, and then ushered her inside.

'Mother is still in town,' Evelyn said, hearing how hollow her own voice sounded, though now she was past the point of caring. 'She stayed on to look at hats.'

'I wasn't looking for your mother,' Aunt Clara replied, closing the door before helping Evelyn unpin her hat from her hair. 'A young man stopped by for you earlier, and I had half a feeling he would stay and wait for you.'

Evelyn's hands froze, halfway outstretched to the coat rack. 'What was his name?'

'William Morton.'

Evelyn threw her hat hurriedly onto the stand. 'What did he want? Did he leave a message? Was he disappointed that I hadn't written – is that why he came?'

The edge of Aunt Clara's mouth curled upwards. 'You know, your mother would hate him. Good looks and poor prospects are a mother's worst nightmare.'

'But William doesn't have poor prospects,' Evelyn rebutted. 'He's going to be a—' She was about to say *published author*, but then she stopped herself. Perhaps he wasn't. If what Nathaniel said was true, then William wasn't anywhere near published at all. But that didn't mean he was nothing. 'He's a bookseller,' she finished. 'And a good one, at that. Besides, his uncle owns one of the nicest bookshops in the whole of York. And even if he wasn't a bookseller, even if he was a vagrant on the streets, it wouldn't mean he wasn't all that he is: kind and loyal and patient when he wishes to be and . . . a good man. William is a good man.'

Aunt Clara's eyes shone with a mischievous kind of

humour. 'But a step or two down from a nobleman's son, my dear, and that is what your mother wants for you.'

'Yes, well,' Evelyn said, feeling the weight return to her chest, the pressure of expectation. 'Perhaps I am more alike her than she thinks. Perhaps I shall see what everyone expects me to do, and then walk in the opposite direction.'

'Towards a young man who didn't deign to write a letter?'

Evelyn felt her stomach drop just a little. 'He didn't leave a message?'

Aunt Clara shook her head. 'It sounded like it was too private for that.'

'Then I have to go to him,' said Evelyn. 'I have to see him.'

Now, Aunt Clara's lips pursed, a little of her usual strictness beginning to curl into her posture. 'Your mother expressly forbade you from going back to that bookshop.'

'Just as *her* mother forbade her from marrying my father?'

Aunt Clara twisted her mouth into a line. 'Ethel never forbade it exactly. But she made her feelings clear about it. Besides, whenever your mother was intent on breaking rules, she had the decency of concocting an exceptionally credible excuse.'

Evelyn looked at her great-aunt, at her eyes, the colour of a stormy sea, and watched as she pulled a scrap of paper from her pocket.

'What's that?'

'A very urgent grocery list,' said Aunt Clara. '*Very* urgent. You will have to go right this moment, because you know I am a beast without my sherry.'

Evelyn didn't need to look at the note to know that it was *not* a shopping list. Instead, she pressed a kiss to her aunt's cheek. 'Thank you,' she said, snatching her hat back from the stand.

Chapter Forty-Seven

As Evelyn half-walked, half-ran the familiar path down Walmgate towards the bookshop, something was different.

There was a fretful anxiety coursing through her, coupled with an excitement that rang like a bell from her stomach all the way to her fingertips, and despite the cool breeze that had settled with the dusk, she could feel a light, clammy sweat on her brow.

She had so much to ask William, and so much to tell him. She still hadn't explained what he'd seen at the theatre – for when he saw Nathaniel there, he must have felt betrayed. Felt lied to, and that was why he had turned away from her. But more than that, she wanted to tell him *why* she did not wish him to think she was with Nathaniel – and why that mattered. It was that thought that made her hands shake so violently she had to curl them into fists at her sides, had to force her feet to move across the flat, grey flagstones of the street, sidestepping empty crates for collection, the wicker baskets being unstacked and brought inside.

Because I love you.

Because I am in love with you.

Because . . .

She checked her pocket watch as she began to near the

bridge. It was a quarter to six, fifteen minutes until closing time, so hopefully the shop would be quiet and she would find William alone. As she stepped into the bookshop's porch, she rubbed little circles into the gargoyles' noses, before sucking in a deep breath and laying her hand upon the door handle.

And then she saw the sign.

Closed.

Closed? Already? She pushed the handle down, but the door was locked. All of the curtains had been pulled shut, too, and she could see nothing in the windows but her own reflection in the glass.

She frowned and crossed to the newsstand on the other end of the bridge, the man that had looked on at her pityingly all those months ago.

'Jerry?' she called. 'Have you seen Mr Morton this evening? Has anyone come out of the bookshop?'

'They both left together,' the man called over his shoulder, as he bent to give a man in a flat cap a cup of tea in a cracked mug. 'Sometime around five.'

'Did they say where they were going?'

Jerry turned to give her an incredulous look, and she shook her head.

'No, of course they didn't. Thank you anyway.'

She hovered on the bridge for a moment longer, wondering whether to wait. The sky was greying fast, with thick clouds that promised rain pulling in from the east of the city.

'I'll come back in the morning then,' she said, as much to herself as to anyone. She cast a final look at the familiar black door, the unmatched pair of gargoyles, before making her way back up the street, although this time her breath was slow, and the jittering feeling had sunk so deeply beneath her skin that she could no longer feel it at all.

* * *

As Evelyn neared Porthaven House, she heard someone shouting: the same word over and over, a bark that ricocheted against the brick walls of the houses and bounced its way down the street.

It was only as Evelyn drew close that she realized the voice was her mother's, and it was her father's name she was calling.

'*John. John!*'

Evelyn broke into a run. The front door was open, and her mother was halfway outside, her eyes wide with panic as they looked up and down the street.

'What is it? What's happened?'

Cecilia fixed Evelyn with a hollow expression. 'You were right,' she said. 'You were right. Your father, he's—'

'He's what?'

'He's gone back to London. He took his case. He's gone back to London, and I don't think he's coming back.'

Evelyn looked from her mother to Aunt Clara, who was standing behind her in the doorway, her usually severe expression replaced with something softer.

'But why?' Evelyn said. 'He said his plan was to get back Riccall Hall – for us to live there again! He said that was what he was working towards.'

'Well, he lied,' replied Aunt Clara. 'All he was working towards was getting enough money to pay off his debtors.'

Evelyn's brow creased, her thoughts suddenly so loud it was hard to pluck a single one from the maelstrom in her mind. 'How did he get the money to pay off his debtors?'

'He has been taking investments,' said her mother. 'I assume that is how he will pay it off.'

'But those people will be expecting a return on their money, will they not? If he is paying that money forwards to his debtors . . . how will he repay the investors?'

'By finding new investors,' said Aunt Clara. 'And beginning the cycle all over again.'

Evelyn shook her head. 'But if that's true then he'll never be out of debt. He'll always be owing something to someone.'

'He does not want to stop living his old life, even though he can no longer afford it – even if that means his wife and child have to rely on the charity of the same family he spent so long shunning.'

'Aunt Clara!' Cecilia said, clutching at her throat.

'No, enough of this.' Aunt Clara rounded on her. 'Evelyn dances around your feelings because she's too afraid you will sink into melancholy again, but as a woman who has spent most of her life in melancholy, I have no such qualms.' She placed one hand upon Cecilia's forearm. 'You have spent all this time thinking that you are not good enough for that man, that you married above your station. You have spent years telling yourself that you are lucky. Lucky to live in such a house as Riccall Hall. Lucky to be with a man who did not care about your humble beginnings. Lucky to have the fine things that you only dreamed of given the family you came from. Well, let me tell you something, my dear.

'Having money or high birth or a title does not make you a good man. Goodness is something you must earn, through your actions and your words. And, my darling, that husband of yours has only shown you time and time again that he is *not* a good man. In my opinion – and I'm sorry to say this in front of you, Evelyn, as he's your father – but, in my opinion, he has never been a good man.

'But of course you never listened to me, Cecilia. All you had to do was convince yourself that your family didn't like him because he was different from us. You did that. And you called yourself lucky.' Aunt Clara's eyes were bright now, fierce. 'But you never once stopped to ask yourself if you were happy. You never once stopped to ask yourself if *he* deserved *you*.

'I will not do you a disservice now by being polite, by telling you something placating, by saying that he will return or that he will apologize. You have heard those kinds of things for too long, my dear, from people who do not know you and who certainly do not know him. These are his true colours, Cecilia. This is who he is.'

Cecilia was quiet for a long moment, and then her head drooped, and she let out a low, slow sigh. 'I wish you were not right, Aunt Clara.'

'Now, tell Evelyn the rest of it. She deserves to know.'

'The rest of it?' Evelyn didn't think her stomach could sink any lower than it already had. 'There's more?'

'There's more,' her mother said, fixing Evelyn with a wobbling look. 'He took his case, as I said, but he took your money, too.'

'*My* money?' Evelyn blanched. 'He took my money? But he said it was pennies! That it was worthless!'

'I tried to stop him,' said Cecilia. 'But he said he needed it more than we did—'

'Absolute codswallop,' spat Aunt Clara.

'And he said he would repay you as soon as he could.'

Evelyn felt her face grow hot, felt the first wave of shock give way to something that pulled from a place far deeper. 'You said he was going to London?'

'Yes. He left in a carriage for the station.'

Evelyn grabbed her pocket watch. 'The next train doesn't leave for another hour,' she said. 'If I am quick, I can catch him.'

'Catch him? And do what?'

'Get my damned money back,' Evelyn replied. 'That money was for us! For our future! Not for him.'

'But you cannot run the whole way to York Station!'

'Yes, I can,' said Evelyn, turning from her. 'I can make it if I hurry.'

Chapter Forty-Eight

Back at the shop, William and Uncle Howard sat on either side of the register, sipping whisky. William's debt was paid, although the toothless man hadn't looked happy about it. He'd scowled as he said: 'But we were going to have so much fun together,' a sentence that had dripped cold water down William's spine and made Uncle Howard's grip on his forearm tighten.

'Thank God you told me, boy,' said Uncle Howard now, clinking his glass against William's. 'You got in with the wrong sort of people for a moment there.'

William bit down on his lip. 'For the wrong sorts of reasons, too.'

Uncle Howard shrugged. 'We all want to do well in this world, William. We all want our endeavours to succeed. But if they fail, it doesn't make *you* a failure. Refusing to pick yourself up and try again is what does that.'

William blinked, looking at his uncle. 'You think I should go back to London?'

'Not yet,' he said. 'I think you should work on the book again first. Let someone read it, perhaps. Ask for some help? Then try again.'

William finished the rest of his whisky in one stinging

gulp. Before tonight, that thought would have brought him out in a cold sweat. But now that everything was out in the open, now that he almost had a blank slate to work from again, he found the idea was just taxing, rather than terrible. 'Perhaps,' he conceded, 'although I imagine I'll be quite busy here for a time.'

He would have to work twice as hard now to recoup the loss. Jack would pay his share of it back of course, but that was in ten months' time, and he wanted the business to go back to doing well far, far sooner than that. Perhaps he would send more books down with Gregory. Perhaps he would try and entice more people in by hanging some of the signs Evelyn had painted. He would have to do something. The thought held extra weight now that he bore sole responsibility for it. Uncle Howard was going to sign the shop over to him when he left for India, and its success or its failure would be all William's responsibility, and while that curled a little in his stomach, it also filled his lungs with air.

Because now he had something to offer Evelyn. A future to give her. Something true. Something *real*.

And he had to tell her.

'You should start with that damned bell,' said Uncle Howard. 'I've been meaning to fix it for years and have never quite got around to it.'

'I never understood how it broke in the first place,' said William, standing up and striding towards the door. He opened it and considered leaving it so, for outside the air was cool, and there was a thread of lavender blowing in from the laundries, cutting through the smell of woodsmoke from the brick kilns to the north. He listened to the gentle *clunk* of the bell as he moved the door back and forth, trying to see why the clapper wasn't moving when he did it.

'You needn't do it now,' said Uncle Howard.

'I know. I'll just take a—' William broke off, his gaze

snatching on a familiar figure running across the bridge towards the bookshop, her hair flung loose of its pins, her face flushed pink.

For a wild moment, he thought Evelyn was running towards him, running *for* him, that she'd crash into his arms and he would hold her and tell her everything, that he loved her, that he was sorry to have lied to her, and she would reach up and trace a hand down the side of his cheek, and it would be like the night they had kissed, except this time he wouldn't pull away.

This image dissolved as she flew past him, past the bookshop, and for a moment he was speechless, and then he was shouting: 'Evelyn! What is it? What's wrong?'

She slowed, looking around bewilderedly until her gaze found him. She pressed one hand to her chest as she gasped: 'It's my father. He's taken my money and is bound for London on the last train. Help me, William – you might run faster than me.'

'He's *what*?' The anger was swift and sharp. 'He stole your money?'

'Please, William, we're running out of time—'

'We'll hail a cab,' he said, reaching for his hat before realizing he hadn't snatched it off the hatstand, and waving his hand madly in the air instead, trying to catch the attention of the nimble little carriages trotting down the road. 'Were you truly going to run the whole way there?'

'I was going to try.'

When a cab finally stopped, he helped Evelyn up into it, before remembering Uncle Howard and the bookshop, and darting back.

'I need to rush out!'

Uncle Howard's voice called from within: 'William, really, you don't need to fix the bell now.'

'Just watch the shop – I promise I'll explain this all later.'

Whatever Uncle Howard grumbled in return, he didn't hear; he was already racing back towards the carriage and hoisting himself up into the cracked leather seat.

'York Station please,' Evelyn said. 'As quick as you can.'

It wasn't like the carriage they'd taken the night they met; this one was one of the smaller, roofless day carriages. As the horse broke into a canter and the cart picked up speed, the wind was cold enough to cool some of the sweat that had beaded Evelyn's brow, that had slid from her hairline down past her cheeks.

She was shaking, her hands trembling so much that as she tried to push her hair back into the pins, she succeeded only in disarranging her hair all the more. She was desperately trying not to let her thoughts skitter ahead of her – to what happened if they were too late, if her father had already boarded the train; or to the other possibility: what happened if she found him? What would she say? How could she put the feeling that was boiling inside of her into words?

'What's the plan?' William's eyebrows were slanted in concern, his dark eyes fixed upon her. 'Get the money back, of course, and then what?'

And then what, indeed? Would she forgive him? Or was this it? Evelyn shook her head, feeling tears prick her eyes, which she tried to blink away, only causing them to roll down her cheeks. She was trying to marry the idea of who her father was as a person, based on his actions, against the father from her memory, the father of her childhood. And that was the hardest part of all.

'Honestly? I don't know.'

William reached for her hand, holding it. 'Whatever I can do,' he said. 'However I can help, I will.'

'We just need to find him,' Evelyn replied, wiping away the wetness from her cheeks. 'Before the train departs.

I just hope he hasn't boarded – I cannot bear the thought of running between the carriages.'

'If it comes to that, I'll do it,' said William. 'I can be catlike when I want to. Look at how I sneaked into the Royal that night.'

Despite it all, she felt the smallest of smiles twitch at her lips. 'Thank you,' she said.

'Of course,' he replied, and squeezed her hand.

Chapter Forty-Nine

York Station was busy. Evelyn dashed ahead, William close on her heels as he threw a shilling to the driver and followed her past the wooden ticket booths and out onto the platform. Evelyn had been to York Station only twice – but even now, she was struck by the sheer size of it. It was the biggest station in all of England, a fact she'd been proud of when making small talk with London aristocrats but which now filled her with panic.

'The first-class carriages are always at the front of the train,' said William, pointing up the platform, to where the silver stars had begun to stitch themselves between the station's arches. 'If your father's waiting, he'll no doubt be waiting up there.'

'Unless he's in the lounge,' Evelyn said, looking in the opposite direction, to where the Royal Station Hotel stood.

'Then we'll split up,' William said. 'You go the lounge – I'll run up the platform. If we can't find him, we'll meet back here.'

'Then what? We board the train and hunt the carriages?'

'One step at a time,' said William, giving her shoulder a squeeze. 'Now hurry.'

As Evelyn ran towards the lounge, she garnered a few odd looks from those waiting, but she paid no heed. She didn't care if the entire population of that platform turned and stared at her today. They could think whatever they wished, for surely nothing would be as bad as the truth.

'Ticket, madam?'

Evelyn pulled up at the doorway, looking past the uniformed man and through the half-frosted glass behind him. There were figures inside; she could see them moving, but it was like watching fish beneath ice, and there was no way to tell whether one of them was her father.

'I'm not travelling,' she said. 'But my father is going on the London train, and I really must see him before he departs.'

The man's mouth scrunched at the edge. 'This lounge is for first-class passengers only. If you're not travelling, then you are not a first-class passenger, madam.'

'Then call him to come out and see me. I shan't go anywhere until you do.'

The man's brow furrowed. 'The train is arriving in seven minutes. No doubt he'll come out of his own accord shortly.'

The door opened then, and another gentleman stepped past, taking off his smart black hat when he caught sight of Evelyn. She seized her chance. She slipped past him, ignoring the guard's angry shout, and ran into the lounge. The first room was filled with brown leather sofas and was almost empty. The second room, however, had seats and a tea stand, and it was here she found him, reading a newspaper and smoking a cigarette as though he hadn't a care in the world.

'You have superseded even my lowest expectations,' she said, snatching the paper from his hands, forcing him to look at her. 'How could you do it, Father! How could you do it to me? To Mama?'

She watched the colour drain from his face as he stood up. He pulled down his waistcoat and leaned in with a low, rough voice. 'Evelyn, darling, this is neither the time nor the place—'

'I don't care.' She raised her voice even louder, so that the men clustered in this room and the sparse few in the next could no doubt all hear her. 'How could you walk out on us like this again? And with *my money* no less!'

'I am so sorry, sir.' The man from the doorway had caught up with her and was now staring, stony-faced, at Evelyn. 'She sneaked in here. Shall I have her removed?'

'We shall both go,' said her father, taking Evelyn by the arm and pulling her away from the table. 'We shall not discuss this here.'

'Why?' Evelyn retorted. 'Are you embarrassed by me? All I am doing is holding a mirror to your actions, Papa. If you are feeling shame, you should direct it inwards.'

'I am not *embarrassed*,' her father grunted, though the tightening grip of his hand around her forearm said otherwise. 'But you must understand, my darling, I had no other choice.'

'Stop *lying to me*!' She snatched her arm away from him, following him to the platform and feeling the cooler air hit her face. 'For goodness' sake, *enough*. Tell me: did you ever intend to get Riccall Hall back? Or was that a lie, too?'

Her father looked away, as though willing the train to pull in. 'You must understand, I had the best intentions—'

'It is a simple yes or no,' Evelyn said.

He didn't look at her. 'No,' he said. 'I would never have mustered the money to be able to claim it back, my darling.'

'But *you said* we never lost it! You said it was merely "under question".'

'I lied,' he said quietly. 'And nor do I have the bargaining power to persuade the duke to rent it to you and your mother. Not now, anyway.'

Evelyn felt a lump form in her throat. She'd known that was the answer – deep down, she'd always known it – but it didn't remove the sting of hearing it. 'And your investments,' she said. 'Is there truly a business? Or are these men simply paying off your debtors?'

Now her father looked uncomfortable and shifted from one foot to the other. 'Listen, my dear, business works in ways you do not understand. You must put in money to get out money, and that is all these gentlemen are doing.'

'And you?' Evelyn said. 'Are you putting in money?'

'I am the brokering agent,' her father replied, picking up his suitcase and beginning to walk up the platform, for the announcer had called that the train would be pulling in shortly. 'My job is to connect inventors who need capital with the men who can provide it.'

'Convenient, seeing as you have no money of your own and had to resort to stealing from your own daughter.'

Her father pinched at his brows. 'My sweet, if I thought you would begrudge me it this much, I would not have taken it. I imagined you would want to help me.'

'Why should I want to help you gamble?'

'I do not do that anymore,' her father said, walking more quickly now, as they were amongst the thickest crush of people, all waiting for the third-class carriages to pull in. Evelyn looked back down the platform and saw the tell-tale puffs of smoke as the train began to draw closer. 'That was a mistake I made in the past, and now I am rectifying it.'

'You are breaking Mother's heart.'

Her father didn't pause. He simply kept walking. It was only when he'd reached the top of the platform that he put his bag down, turned back to her, and said: 'I broke your mother's heart long ago. We were miserable together, your mother and I, and we had been for years. My mistake was not in leaving; it was in coming back. My mistake was giving you a hope that we could piece our lives back together.'

He reached out then, as though to touch her cheek, and she stepped backwards, flinching from him.

'You left me, too, you know,' she said, and felt her bottom lip tremble. 'I thought you loved me.'

'I do love you, darling. I will always love you.'

'Then why did you leave?'

He gave her a piteous look. 'I had no choice.'

She shook her head, the tears flowing down her cheeks now. 'There is always a choice. *Always*. And you chose whatever life you had in London over me. You chose to drink and to gamble and to be seen about town with all sorts of women, but you didn't give us the same choice. You left us trying to piece together our old one, without you. And it was nearly impossible. And if it hadn't been for Aunt Clara's kindness, we might have ended up in the workhouse. Did that thought even *cross your mind* while you were spending all of our money, while you were taking beautiful women to the theatre and having your pictures drawn for the papers? You made a choice, Father, and that choice wasn't me, and it wasn't Mama, and I really, really wish I could hate you for it. It would be so much easier if I could hate you for it, Father. But I still love you, and that makes it so much worse.'

The train was pulling in; she could hear the great clank of it rolling across the tracks, the whistles as thick clouds of black steam rolled upwards.

Her father sighed a long sigh and reached into his jacket pocket. For a moment, she thought he would offer her a handkerchief, but instead he held out her purse.

'Here,' he said. 'Take it back.'

The train was alongside them now, and men were jumping down, opening all the carriage doors, while the train let out a piercing whistle.

'Take it, Evelyn! For goodness' sake.'

She held out her hand and let him thump the soft velvet into her palm.

'I am sorry I have not been a better father to you,' he said, his voice low. 'You do not deserve it, and neither does your mother. You deserve better, Evelyn. But I cannot give you better. I cannot be anyone other than who I am, and I have to go to London. I have to pay off my debts. I have to do this, Evelyn. Do you understand that? But it doesn't mean I don't love you. I do.'

The train whistled again, and he gave his brown leather suitcase to a young boy, before stepping into the carriage. The door slammed shut, and he leaned down from the small window, and Evelyn felt a wrenching ache in her throat as the train began to move, slowly at first, and then quicker. Away from her.

He didn't speak; he simply blew her a kiss and waved until the train was out of sight.

'Evelyn?'

She turned to see William standing behind her. 'I'm so sorry, Evelyn.'

He opened his arms then, and she stepped into them and cried as he hugged and squeezed her, and she said: 'I know.'

Chapter Fifty

They didn't speak in the cab back to the bookshop, for Evelyn could barely draw a breath between the sobs, and William did not know if anything he could say would comfort her. Instead, he just held her, feeling her shoulders shake, her breath heave in her chest. He knew the pain she was feeling. He had felt it himself, when he realized that his mother would not come back for him. It was a particular cruelty, to have one's parent turn their back on you, and it still sat like a rock in his stomach. Though time had smoothed some of the edges, it had not smoothed them all.

When they arrived at Morton's Emporium, William realized belatedly that perhaps Evelyn would not want to be here, that she might want to go home instead. It was getting late. But when he turned to ask, she was already stepping from the carriage, already moving for the front door. He paid the driver and followed her inside.

Howie stood at the hatstand, helping Evelyn off with her jacket.

'I see he told you then, my dear,' he said, his voice soft. 'Just know that it is all sorted, and William is in no danger anymore.'

William felt a bolt of panic run through him, as sharp and as shocking as though he'd been struck.

'What?' Evelyn turned, bewildered, her gaze upon him. 'What danger? Told me what?'

William looked at his uncle and shook his head, and Howie saw immediately the mistake he'd made. 'Ah,' he said, stepping backwards. 'Forgive me – I fear I have misunderstood.'

Evelyn turned back to William. 'What is he talking about, William? What danger?'

'We don't need to discuss this now,' William said. 'Not while you are so upset, not after your father—'

'Tell me.' She wiped the wetness roughly from her cheeks. 'Please, if you are in trouble, I should like to know. What is it, William?'

'I'm going upstairs to pack,' said Uncle Howard. 'I shall leave you two to talk.'

'Pack?' Evelyn's expression was quickly becoming one of panic. 'Where are you going?'

'To India.'

'To *India*?'

'And I am leaving the bookshop to William.'

'*What?*'

Howie gave a weak smile. 'I'll let him tell you everything.'

Once Howie had retreated upstairs, William took Evelyn's hand and drew her over to the register, pulling up one of the chairs for her. He poured them each a finger's width of whisky. Then he went to the door and swung the sign to *closed*.

'Listen, Evelyn, I haven't been telling you the truth.' He forced himself to keep looking at her, to watch her expression go from worried and open to guarded and closed. 'I am not going to be a published author. I don't have a publisher in London. I don't live on the square that borders the park, and I don't have a hefty advance to live off.'

She put down her glass. 'I know.'

William blinked, bewildered. 'You *know*? How?'

'Because I wrote you a letter, at the same time I wrote Mr Morton one. And I went to leave it at your house. Only, I didn't know the number, so I knocked on every single one of those doors – and no one had even heard of you.'

William felt his cheeks flush a deep scarlet. 'I am sorry you had to do that.'

'And I know you have no publisher. Nathaniel told me. He did some digging.'

William grimaced. 'I could have guessed I'd made an enemy there.'

'But tell me, William – why did you lie to me?'

He rubbed at the back of his neck. 'It wasn't just to you – it was to everyone. But most of all, it was to myself. I wanted more than anything to come back from London and for all of that to be true. That was my dream. And . . .'

'And if other people believed it was real, you could, too?'

He met her eye. She wasn't looking at him with disgust, as he'd thought, but instead with a gentleness that made his confession feel so much worse. 'Yes,' he said softly.

She nodded, swirling the amber liquid around in her cup. 'I understand why you wanted to come back from London with good news, rather than bad.' She glanced up at him now, her dark eyes unreadable. 'But success isn't what makes you lovable, William, just as failure doesn't make you unlovable. I hope you know that.'

He should have felt her words like balm against an open sore, but he didn't. Instead, it just caused the roiling feeling in his stomach to grow all the stronger.

'That's not all of it,' he said, picking up his own glass and drinking it in one. 'There is also the matter of the bookshop.'

Evelyn frowned. 'The bookshop?'

This time, it was much harder to look at her, much harder

to force himself to meet her gaze, as he said: 'You see, Jack asked to borrow some money. And I should have just told him, there and then – I should have said that I didn't have the money.'

'But you didn't.'

'I didn't,' William agreed, feeling his heartbeat start to thud in his ears. 'And then of course I had to get the money. And I couldn't go to Uncle Howard, because the bookshop was only just doing decently again, and so I went to some men who would lend me it instead. Except, these are not the kind of men you should borrow from, not even when you're desperate. They lure you in and trick you into paying much, much more than you'd ever borrowed.'

Evelyn's expression was growing taut, tense. 'Go on,' she said.

'And I couldn't repay them, neither quickly enough nor significantly enough. And I was in trouble. I'd already moved out of my small boarding room into an even smaller one, and I couldn't cut my costs back any further without starving myself.'

'So you gave the debt to your uncle, instead?' Evelyn's tone was brittle. 'And you threatened his business with it?'

'Uncle Howard offered,' William said quickly. 'He offered to help me, and I'll work hard to repay him in the meantime, for though Jack will repay me, that won't be for some time. The business can handle it – just – though we will need some very strong sales, and—'

Evelyn shook her head. 'Do you know who you sound like?'

William felt as though he were walking into a trap, and yet he said: 'No?'

'My father,' she said, standing abruptly, leaving her still-full glass on the desk. 'Neither of you think about how your stupid actions affect other people, affect their lives – their livelihoods!'

'Evelyn, I'm sorry. Wait, please—' William scrambled after her as she snatched her hat and jacket from the hatstand. 'It wasn't like that, I promise you. I didn't plan on dragging Uncle Howard into it – I didn't plan on that at all. I made a mistake, a horrible mistake, and—'

'And that is the problem, isn't it?' When she looked at him now, he saw that tears were shining in her eyes, and it hurt more than he could have ever imagined. 'All you care about is crafting the world the way you want it, lying and lying until it all looks right, even though you know it is wrong. You lived a lie on credit, and now someone else must pay!'

She stormed from the door, leaving William staring after her, wanting so badly to follow her, and yet his legs would not move.

Because in a way, she was right. He hadn't thought about how it might affect Uncle Howard, how his lies would ripple outwards and touch those around him.

And perhaps that meant he was like her father, after all.

Chapter Fifty-One

Evelyn half walked, half stumbled her way back down Walmgate. The street was a blur, her eyes so full of tears that it was like looking out through shards of broken glass, and it took all of her might not to let herself crumble then and there on the street. As it was, she hugged her arms tightly around her own body, kept her head down, and focused on putting one foot in front of the other until she saw the turning for Aunt Clara's street and then the tall house that she'd thought looked so odd when she arrived and now looked like home.

She didn't know which she was most hurt by; all she knew was that there was an ache inside of her, a hollowness, and it made her want to double over, to curl into a ball upon her bed and draw up the covers and lie there until she had no more tears left. Her father, William – were they the same? She had known her father was capable of it – she'd known from the day he'd gone to London and left her to try to pick up the shattered shards of her mother – but she hadn't expected it of William, hadn't expected him to sink just as far, to mire himself into the same problems just as deeply.

Perhaps that was what hurt the most: the jarring crash of reality against the warm little bubble she had cocooned herself with: one in which William was as he'd been before and she was in love with him.

She had trusted him.

And he had thrown it in her face, just as her father had done.

She knocked upon the door, and when Aunt Clara opened it, Evelyn stepped into her arms and buried her face in her shoulder and said: 'I hate him.' And she didn't know which of them she meant, only that it was true.

A month – or was it six weeks? – later, Evelyn's mother rapped her knuckles against the attic room door. Inside, Evelyn was still abed, and she groaned, rolling to face the wall and pulling up the covers so that her mother would not see the state of her hair.

'Darling?' Cecilia's voice, when it came through the wood, was light but threaded with caution. 'Might I come in?'

'If you must,' came Evelyn's reply.

Cecilia stepped inside, and walked immediately to the window, opening it up to let some of the frigid autumn chill into the room. 'The trees are looking splendid outside my darling. All the shades of red and yellow! Do you want to go for a walk today and see them? Perhaps we can even collect a few choice specimens and press them? Or paint them?'

Evelyn didn't remove the cover from her head. 'No, thank you, Mama. I am not six years old.'

'What about a nice trip to the market? Aunt Clara needs more bread, and Mrs Billingham has agreed to lend her the cart and donkey. You know, I think that creature is starting to like me. When I take my morning walks to the end of the street and back, he haws at me from her little fenced front garden.'

Another Evelyn might have smiled, but she could not muster the energy for it. 'I am glad,' is all she said.

She heard her mother's quiet sigh and listened to her

footsteps draw closer, until she felt her narrow truckle bed sink down at one side, and her mother's hand come to rest upon her shoulder.

'Come now, just because you hide your head under the covers does not mean your problems go away. That young man William has written again today. Do you want me to open it? To read it to you?'

Evelyn shook her head.

'And what of the note from Nathaniel? He wishes to see you. What should I reply to him?'

'Reply and tell him to stop writing letters,' Evelyn said firmly. 'I'll meet him for tea when I am good and ready.'

'But don't you think it might be nice to go out? To get dressed?'

'No. I absolutely do *not* think that.'

Her mother sighed. 'I cannot believe you haven't even *looked* at what I am wearing.'

Evelyn narrowed her eyes. 'Is this a trick to get me to sit up?'

'See for yourself,' said Cecilia.

Evelyn pulled the covers down just enough to see her mother. She was dressed in what must have been one of Aunt Clara's old gowns, an utterly ridiculous lace-and-frills concoction from much earlier in the century, but it was the hat that was the crowning glory. She wore a bonnet so deep and so wide that it was a wonder she could see anything of the sides of the room at all, and it was decorated with so much lace that it looked like the cap a child might wear to a baptism.

'What do you think?' Cecilia asked, turning her head left and right so that Evelyn could see how much care she had put into the neat rolls of her hair.

Evelyn, despite herself, smiled. 'I think it looks awful,' she said. 'Did Aunt Clara truly wear that?'

'No, but her mother would have – your great-grandmother.' Cecilia pushed a lock of lank, greasy hair from Evelyn's face. 'Please come downstairs, my darling. Eat something. I can draw a bath with heated water for you, and you can wash off some of this grime.'

'I don't wish to, Mother.'

'I know,' she said, stroking Evelyn's forehead. 'But you will feel better for it. I always did, once you had forced me up and out of bed.'

Evelyn looked at her mother. 'It is not only me that Father hurt, Mother. How are you faring so well with this?'

Cecilia sucked in a deep breath through her nose and reached to untie the silk bow that sagged beneath her chin. 'You want to know how I am feeling?' she asked. 'Honestly?'

'Honestly.'

'I feel . . .' She placed the bonnet between them on the bed. 'I feel sad, of course, and angry, for all that he has done, but I also feel as though a door I have always kept open in my heart has finally shut, and now I can move forwards. I can move past it.'

Evelyn sat up a little then, shuffling to give her mother some more space at the bed's side. 'Really?'

'Really. And more than that, Evelyn – I think . . . I think I owe you an apology. As well as my forgiveness. Because I think you are right. You did exactly what I did, and I treated you worse than my mother treated me, because I was just so . . . so *angry*.' She gave her daughter a trembling smile. 'But I wasn't angry at *you*, darling. I was angry at your father. And when you said I was dependent on him I realized *why* I was so angry.' She shuffled closer, squeezing Evelyn's hand tightly in her own. 'When John and I fell in love, I thought I would never have to spend another day afraid for my future. I thought that I would be safe with him, secure. And yet he put us in a position where all of those old feelings came rushing back, and I fear . . .' She swallowed, a tear sliding towards her jaw. 'I fear I took that out on you. And for that I have to ask for forgiveness.'

'You do not,' said Evelyn softly. 'I am not cross with you for that. You *should* be angry at him. He promised he would get the house back, and even that was a lie.'

Her mother drew her lips together. 'I loved that house,' she said. 'And I loved our time in it, but even if your father had somehow bought it back, I do not know whether I could have ever settled there quite so comfortably again. I would imagine every carriage coming down the driveway would be coming to rip the rug from beneath our feet once more.' She reached for Evelyn's hand and gave it a squeeze. 'Besides, Aunt Clara has rather taken a liking to us. She has invited us to stay for as long as we want. Forever, if we so wish it.'

'And you would want that, Mother?'

Cecilia tilted her head to one side, and then smiled a little smile. 'You know, having some company after all these years is really rather lovely. Not that you weren't an excellent companion, my darling, but I cannot expect you to be indoors all the time.' She hesitated, then said tentatively, 'Especially if you wish to take your job back.'

'I don't know about that,' Evelyn replied. 'There's going to be a new owner, and I am not sure if I should like to work with him.'

'Well, regardless,' said her mother, 'a wise person once told me that true friends stand by your side through trials as well as joys, and Aunt Clara is the only one who has done that. She is a good friend, and I am coming to quite enjoy living here.'

Evelyn matched her mother's small smile with her own. 'Ready a bath,' she said, 'and I shall come down when it is done.'

'Nonsense,' said Cecilia, whipping the covers back. 'You will come down now and have something to eat while I boil all the kettles. Come on.'

Evelyn looked at her mother. 'So long as it doesn't involve carrots,' she said.

Chapter Fifty-Two

Once the shop had closed, William sat at the small window table of the Red Lion, a pint of small ale making rings on the wood and a blank sheet of paper before him.

He had written to Evelyn every day since she'd stormed from the bookshop, and every day when the postman came, he'd felt his heart soar – and then sink as the man shook his head. Is this how Uncle Howard had felt, all of these years? If it was, then William did not know how he had lived in this limbo, this between-world where everything was waiting and time stretched and contracted in odd, senseless ways.

Jack pulled back the chair beside him and put his pint of bitter down carefully, so as not to drip liquid onto the page. 'You still writing to Evelyn?'

'I am,' said William, looking up at his friend.

When he had finally told him the truth about it all, Jack hadn't stormed out, like Evelyn, or looked worried, like Uncle Howard; he'd merely clapped William around the ear and called him a *bloody idiot*, and then spent a half-hour berating him for agreeing to lend him the money, before giving him a rough bear hug.

'And how is that working out for you?'

William put the pen down beside the empty page and

placed his face in his hands. 'Excellently, of course. She has replied to every single one.'

'Mmm,' said Jack, taking a long sip of his drink. 'You know what I reckon you should do?'

William peeked out at him through his fingers. 'If you say propose, I shall pour this beer onto your lap.'

Jack cracked a smile. 'I reckon you should show her that you are sorry, rather than telling her.'

William frowned. 'What?'

'She won't read your letters, will she? So then why not *show* her that you're sorry. Show her that she can trust you.'

'Show her how?'

Jack shrugged. 'I don't know. I can't do *everything* for you William. I just reckon if the problem is that you lied—'

'I think the problem was more that I put the bookshop in debt with my lies.'

'Yes, well,' said Jack. 'So then, why should she believe what you say? If you want the woman to trust you again, you have to show her that you're different.'

William took his hands from his face and began to tap a rhythm on the wooden table. What was it she'd said to him, all those months ago? *Don't promise. Show me.*

'Her father lied to her and then left. I have to show her that I won't – that I am different.'

'Exactly. And sitting here all "tortured writer" isn't going to help.'

'Do something,' William said, nodding. 'Do something . . . Jack, you're a genius.'

Jack's grin widened. 'I've heard that before, you know.'

'I think I know exactly what I need to do,' he said. 'Would Naomi help us?'

'If you ask her nicely enough,' Jack replied.

* * *

Evelyn was thankful she had taken her mother's advice and bathed, for the following day Naomi was at the door, her dark hair pinned beneath her laundry cap.

'You are a sight for sore eyes,' Evelyn exclaimed, pulling her into a tight hug.

'Yes, well, I've missed you. I figured I'd better start coming here for our lunches instead.' Naomi stepped back. 'I have a *lot* to tell you, and I imagine you have much to tell me, too.'

'You start,' Evelyn said. 'My news is maudlin.'

'Well.' Naomi puffed out her cheeks. 'Firstly, there's a man *very* interested in the business – Mam's and my business, I mean. He owns a chain of laundries between here and Argyle, and he's coming down next week to go through all the paperwork. If he likes what he sees, then perhaps Mam can go back to teaching again! So we shall have to cross our fingers and see. And secondly . . .'

She gave Evelyn a smile twice as radiant as the dappled autumn sunlight threading through the window. 'Jack proposed! Oh, in the most romantic fashion, too. He asked if he could take me out for dinner, just the two of us, and he'd brought this long velvet box with him, and when he opened it I was just astounded. I thought the dinner was just about the gift, but then he took up my hand and asked me to marry him, and it was . . .' She let out a little breath. 'It was magical, Evelyn. Truly.'

'I'm so happy for you,' she said, matching her friend's smile with one of her own. 'When is the wedding?'

'December, if we can manage it,' Naomi said. 'I've always wanted a Christmas wedding. I can picture it! Snow on the ground, a hot fire in the grate. All I need now is to mend my best dress.'

Evelyn paused for a moment, her eyes flicking from her friend's narrow shoulders to her feet. 'Come with me,' she said, taking Naomi's hand and pulling her through the door.

In the attic room, she gestured for Naomi to take a seat on

the newly made bed, and went to her closet, pulling out the emerald-green gown. She turned it, so that Naomi could see the flowers, how they were stitched the full way down the front, and her eyes widened.

'It's beautiful, Evelyn.'

'It's yours,' she said, holding it out to her. 'Please. It can be your something old and your something new, for I added these myself.' She ran her hands along her embroidery, feeling a little swell of pride. For all her mother disliked them, she thought it rather her best work. 'You didn't need to walk me all the way home that day that we met, but you did. Kindness begets kindness, I reckon.'

'Ah, you weren't as lost as you think,' Naomi said, taking the dress from her and admiring the sheen of the material. 'And this is too lavish a gift.'

'Nonsense,' said Evelyn, waving a hand dismissively. 'You've been a good friend to me, Naomi, and I should like to be a good friend back.'

Naomi stood then, putting the dress down on the bed reverently and giving Evelyn a tight hug. 'William told me what happened between you. And with your father. I'm sorry, Evelyn.'

'Thank you.' Evelyn felt her throat begin to ache anew. She wished she could think of it, could speak of it without feeling the sadness of it, but somehow she had not been able to push this down, tuck it away like she had everything else. This sat upon her chest, waiting for her. 'I expected it from my father, and though that does not lessen the hurt of it, it at least lessened the shock. But William . . . I *trusted* William. And he lied.'

Naomi reached over and clutched at her hand. 'But William is not your father,' she said quietly. 'He made a single mistake, for a good reason.'

'What "good reason" does anyone have for getting another into debt?'

Naomi blinked at her. 'Did William not tell you *why* Jack asked for the money?'

Evelyn shook her head, and Naomi swallowed, reaching beneath her collar to draw out a delicate gold pendant in the shape of a swan. 'It was for my wedding gift, Evelyn. Jack feels wretched of course, and has tried to promise all sorts to make it up to William – paying him back early, working his days off at the bookshop. He can't help but feel . . . *we* can't help but feel . . . well. Responsible. At least in part. And so I thought I would come and see whether perhaps . . . perhaps you're aiming some of the anger you feel towards your father at William?'

'No,' said Evelyn, although she could hear her mother's voice in her head, her quiet admission that she had done the very same thing – misplaced her anger. 'Perhaps,' she amended reluctantly. 'But how do I know this is a single mistake?'

Naomi seemed to consider this for a long moment. 'We never *know*, Evelyn. We just believe it. But I believe people deserve a second chance. If no one was ever given that, then how would we learn from our mistakes? How would we grow? If we had one shot at everything in life, we would all be utterly miserable. It would make each failure life-ending. And that's simply not the case.'

Evelyn gritted her teeth. William was not alone in making mistakes, either. She had made her fair share, in lying to her mother, in how she had dealt with Lady Violet.

Naomi gave Evelyn a flat, frank look. 'At least *read* his letters. He feels awful, Evelyn. He *looks* awful.'

'Does he?' A thread of concern welled inside her.

'Listen,' Naomi replied, reaching for Evelyn's hand and squeezing it. 'William is a good man, who made a mistake. A foolish mistake, granted, but only because he was trying to help his friend. And now he is paying for it. But William is not the same man as your father. And if even a part of your anger towards him is because of what your father did to you, then ask yourself: does he deserve that? Do *you* deserve that?'

Evelyn opened her mouth and closed it again, for she didn't know what to say to that. Her thoughts were a thousand needles all pressed into a roll, and whenever she reached for one, she got pricked by them all.

Naomi stood, brushing the lint from her skirt. 'I say this out of love, but if you feel lost now, Evelyn, it is not because you cannot find the path forwards. It is because you are deliberately turning away from it, because you'd rather dwell in righteous unhappiness, cocooning yourself away from future hurts, than do the scary thing and trust someone. Forgive someone.'

Evelyn shook her head. 'I know what you're doing,' she said.

'Then you know why I am doing it,' Naomi replied. 'May I come back to collect the gown? I can bring a protective case for it, for you know it'll rain as soon as I step outside with a bundle of silk in my arms.'

'Yes, yes, of course,' said Evelyn, not quite listening to her.

'Oh!' Naomi turned at the doorway. 'And I forgot to say: Mr Morton leaves for India the evening of Friday 1st December. We're going to do a tea for him in the shop that afternoon, and I know he's hoping you might stop by to see him off. Can I tell him you'll come?'

Evelyn looked up. 'Will William be there?'

'I should imagine so,' Naomi said. 'But I believe Mr Morton has earned a farewell, don't you think? After all he's done for you?'

Evelyn nodded. 'Tell him I shall be there.'

* * *

Jack and William stood inside the bookshop, both peering up at the impossibly high cobwebs that had clustered in the corners. The shop had long closed, and now the only light came from the gas lamps that William had lit, so that he could see the scope of what they were planning to do.

'How handy are you with a paintbrush?' he asked Jack.

Jack shrugged. 'I'll give it a go,' he said, as a sharp knock came at the door, and Naomi stepped through.

'She'll come,' she said. 'Friday 1st December.'

'That doesn't give us much time,' said William. 'Six weeks? Seven? But it should just be enough. I can work through the nights, so long as Uncle Howard wouldn't mind.'

'I'll help, too,' said Jack. 'Whenever I'm not on shifts.'

'And me,' said Naomi. 'For you can't work day and night with no rest.'

'If that's what it takes, I can,' said William, feeling his heart thudding arrhythmically in his throat.

'And Mr Morton has agreed to this? All of . . .' Jack waved vaguely in the air. 'All your ideas?'

William nodded. 'We'll begin tomorrow.'

Chapter Fifty-Three

1st December 1899

While the autumn gave way to the cold gusts of winter and the copper leaves dulled to a muddy brown, Evelyn had been thinking. She had been thinking of what her mother had said, of what Naomi had said, of what she had said to William – and of what she had then done.

She moved slightly, pushing a strand of hair back into place. She *had* directed some of the anger she'd felt towards her father at William, and he did not deserve that. He had made a mistake, and he had lied to her – but he had not abandoned her, had not stolen what little she had earned. Where her father had hidden his guilt, had waited until he was discovered, William had confessed. Where her father had deflected blame, William had taken ownership. Where her father had made excuses and expunged his guilt, William had apologized, had begged for her forgiveness.

'Evelyn?'

Her mother's voice called up the stairs, drawing her from her reverie and back into the room. She was sitting in her mother's bedroom before the small, clouded mirror, wearing her nicest day dress: reams of satin the colour of lake water, fastened neatly with a brown leather belt. Downstairs, her mother would help her pin the matching hat amongst her plaited hair.

'There is someone here to see you.'

Evelyn listened to the quick, shushing steps coming up the staircase, and then Lady Violet appeared in the mirror, her usually immaculate hair messy, her face flushed and red. Her dress was the same colour as the clouds gathering outside the windows, and it matched the expression upon her face as she crossed to Evelyn.

'Please do not go to see Nathaniel tomorrow,' she said urgently. 'Do not go for tea. He is going to propose to you, and I could not bear it if he did.'

Evelyn's mouth twitched into a line, and she turned back to the mirror, though now her fingers were trembling where they gripped the brush. '*Propose?* Surely this is some ploy of yours Lady Violet—'

'How I wish it was!' Lady Violet sat in a flurry of silk upon Cecilia's bed. 'He bought a ring from London. It's ugly, of course, but he is going to use it to propose.' She looked at Evelyn in the clouded glass, and for the first time, Evelyn could see everything written there: each emotion a ripple, pooling inwards.

'But why would he propose to me?'

'Because he *loves you*,' Lady Violet said, flopping backwards on the bed so that all Evelyn could see were mountains of grey silk. 'And because he thinks you will say yes.'

'He doesn't love me,' said Evelyn, turning in her chair. 'And nor will I say yes.'

There was a pause, and a rustle of silk as Lady Violet rotated herself so that she could see Evelyn's face, so that she could study it, her lips pursed into a thin, pink line. 'And you are not lying to me?'

'I am not lying,' said Evelyn curtly. 'He loves *you*, Lady Violet. I knew it from the moment I saw him in that lobby, waiting for you. Why else would a man sit there for three afternoons in a row?'

'Because Papa made him?'

Evelyn fixed Lady Violet with a flat look. 'Did your father make him kiss you on the cheek that night at the theatre?'

Lady Violet's eyes widened. 'I thought no one had seen that.'

'I saw it,' she said. 'And I see the way he looks at you. He loves you, but I think he believes that *you* do not love *him*.'

'Well, of course he believes that,' she said softly. 'I've made him believe it. I thought it was a bad fit, the daughter of a duke and an American with no birth, no title . . . It seemed so impossible, but now, the thought of losing him . . . I can't bear it. I don't care what Papa thinks.' Her voice cracked. 'I want to be with Nathaniel.'

'Then tell him so,' said Evelyn, crossing to her. 'Go and tell him the truth.'

Lady Violet looked at her through pale lashes. 'I know you didn't reveal our plot to him,' she said softly. 'I never thanked you for that.'

'No, you didn't,' said Evelyn, a wry smile upon her lips now. 'Though you did tell my mother I was working.'

Lady Violet grimaced. 'Yes, well. I thought you were doing the same to Nathaniel.'

Evelyn held her hand between them. 'Then how about we call a truce?'

'A truce?' Lady Violet eyed her hand warily.

'Indeed,' said Evelyn. 'On one condition.'

Lady Violet raised a single, perfectly plucked eyebrow.

'Go and tell Nathaniel that you love him. *Today*.'

Lady Violet hesitated for a moment, looking from Evelyn to her hand and back again.

And then she reached out and took it.

* * *

Evelyn was feeling quite buoyant until she arrived at the bookshop an hour later.

Sheets flapped in the chill winter wind: they were covering everything from the flaking sign that bore the shop's name to the broken lanterns, the yellowing windows. The only parts of the shop that weren't covered were the door, with the sign set to *closed*, and the two gargoyles hidden in the shadow of the porch.

Evelyn bade farewell to Mrs Billingham and her mother, who rattled onwards to the city, and then she stood there for a moment, taking it all in. Perhaps Mr Morton had changed his mind about leaving it to William? Or perhaps the bookshop hadn't been able to shoulder the debt, after all? Either way, the shop looked as though it was closing, and she felt the sadness well within her at the thought of all her memories of this place, all the times she had heard the broken bell clank. And what would happen to all the books?

She rapped her knuckles against the door, listening as footsteps drew closer. Would it be William? The thought of seeing him again made her stomach churn, both from excitement and trepidation, but as the door opened, the bell rang – a beautiful, chiming sound – and Naomi's face appeared in the gloom.

'Evelyn,' she said, her voice oddly low, oddly soft. 'Would you mind stepping outside with me? And I will need to put something over your eyes, if you don't mind.'

Evelyn frowned. 'What are you doing here? Where is Mr Morton?'

Naomi's smile widened. 'I know it's cold, but I promise we won't be stood outside for very long. Will you come with me?'

Naomi squeezed herself out of the shop so that Evelyn could not catch a glimpse of the inside, which seemed dark and empty. 'Very well,' Evelyn said, frowning. 'We can stand outside for a moment.'

'And I can blindfold you? You'll have to trust me.'

Evelyn looked down at the silk tie in Naomi's hand and then up at her friend. 'I trust you,' she said. 'I have no idea what is going on, but I trust you.' And she meant it. She truly meant it, and it filled her with a gentle kind of happiness as Naomi wrapped the silk around her head, tight enough that she genuinely could not see.

'Ready?' William's voice came from somewhere to her left, and she felt her heart rate increase, felt it thudding in the base of her throat.

'Ready!' came another voice, and then beside her Naomi joined in: 'Ready!'

In one smooth motion, the blindfold slid from her face, revealing Jack and William and Mr Morton, stood on both sides of the doorway, each holding a rope.

'And . . . go!' William called, and they pulled the ropes as one, and all of the sheets that had been covering the shop came down, from the sign, from the windows, and Evelyn just stood there.

She was frozen, staring, because for a moment it didn't make sense.

The bookshop looked brand-new. The sign was freshly painted in swirls of gold, and the paint that had once flaked between the white stucco walls now gleamed a dark, oily black. The lanterns above the sign had been fixed, too, and glowed a deep, honey-yellow, spilling warm, flickering light onto the street. Even the windows looked new, although perhaps they had simply been viciously scrubbed, for each tiny glass pane reflected the pale-blue sky like a mirror, a patchwork of clear glass.

'What do you think?' William asked, as he came to stand

before her, so close that she could smell the sweet wax in his hair, the lemon soap on his skin.

'It looks wonderful.'

'It's for you, Evelyn.' He fiddled with his collar with shaking fingers, his voice cracking a little as he said: 'I so desperately wanted to be the man who came back from London a success that I forgot how to be the man I am.'

William's gaze didn't leave hers, but he picked up her hand and ran the pad of his finger across her palm, his bare skin warm through the thin material of her gloves. It made her heart skitter. 'And the man I am loves you, Evelyn. Utterly. Completely. I have tried to think of a thousand ways to say it – I have written and burned dozens of letters, for words are not enough. Just like words were not enough for me to tell you how sorry I was. Sorry that I lied. Sorry that that lie spiralled. I wanted . . . I wanted to show you how much I love you. How sorry I am.' There were tears beading in his eyes now, sliding down his pale cheeks, like pearls in the slanting sunshine, and she wanted to reach up to catch one, to wipe it from his cheek. 'Just tell me I'm not too late,' he said, 'that you and Nathaniel . . .'

'There is nothing between me and Nathaniel, William,' Evelyn said, her smile softening. 'Just an awkward ball and then a dinner – and you were there for half of that.'

William swallowed. 'But the theatre, I saw him kneeling before you, and . . .'

'Will thought he was proposing,' Jack piped up.

'Jack, for God's sake—' William said, his cheeks flushing a deep crimson.

Evelyn was still holding his hand, and now she interlaced her fingers with his, drawing him closer.

'You are not the only one who must ask forgiveness, William,' she said softly. 'I was angry at my father, and I took it out on you, and you didn't deserve that. You deserve someone who will tell you each day that they love you, that we are only human, all of us, and that we will make mistakes, and that you will be loved regardless. That is what you deserve, and I'm sorry.' She looked at him then, cupping his chin with the palm of her hand, feeling the tremor in his throat, the trembling that matched her own. 'I love you, William,' she said, her voice a whisper. 'And I will love you through the good times and the bad times, through success and failure. I will love you through it all. If you will have me. If you can forgive me.'

He smiled at her then, a slow grin as warm as the lamplight above them. 'Have you not read the sign? Of course I forgive you.'

She looked past him to their friends, red-faced in the chill December air, at Mr Morton's wide grin as he stood in the doorway, and then her gaze travelled upwards, to the shop. To the new sign above it, painted in curling, golden paint, lit with the soft glow of roaring gas lamps. Instead of *Morton's Emporium*, it now read: *The Lamplighter's Bookshop*, and then in small, white text below it: *Est. 1899 by W. Morton and E. Seaton.*

'My great-grandfather didn't want people to know who he was,' said William softly. 'He wanted to hide it. And for a long time, I thought that was the sensible thing to do. But I don't believe that anymore, Evelyn. And that's because of you.'

'And because "Morton and Seaton's Book Emporium" was too many words for a sign that size,' said Jack.

'Shh!' said Naomi.

'I do not know what to say.' Evelyn's voice came out thin, cracking as she took it all in.

'Say you'll take your job back,' said William, reaching to push a stray strand of hair from where it clung to her eyelashes. 'I know it'll be hard work and that we'll have a lot to do to ensure business is steady, but we can do it. I know we can.'

Evelyn knew it, too. She knew that they would be happy here, that they would be successful. And they would have to sweat for it and toil for it, and they would have good days and bad days, but she would take them all and be glad for them all, for she would be with him.

'Of course I will.'

William's smile was like a sunbeam, radiant and beautiful, and as he bent his head to hers, he whispered: 'Thank the Lord for that, because it took me almost a full week to paint that sign.'

'I love it,' she said.

'I love you,' he breathed. And then he kissed her, and it was as though the winter had melted away, for his lips were hot against hers and soft as a summer's breeze, and she felt the warmth spread across every inch of her skin, from the flush that had risen on her cheeks to the tightening feeling in the pit of her stomach. Behind them, she heard Jack let out a great, echoing *whoop*, before shouting: 'Well now, you'll have to take my advice, William, after that display.'

William pulled back, his face split in a wide grin, and Evelyn realized belatedly that they were still stood outside the bookshop and that a street full of people had turned to watch them. And she did not care. She even waved to Jerry at the newsstand, who put two fingers to his lips and let out a whistle so loud and ringing it bounced off all the buildings and reverberated in her ears.

'Come on,' said William. 'Let us show you what we've all been working on.'

The bell sang when they stepped through the door, and it had been buffed and polished until it gleamed as though it were gold, not brass. The walls had been revarnished, and signs hung over each of the sections so that anyone walking into the shop would know what they could find and where. Even the register's desk had been oiled, and upon it sat a bottle of red wine and five glasses, which they now clustered around.

'Well?' William asked, the wine glugging merrily as he poured it.

'I think it looks marvellous,' she breathed, and then turned to Jack, Naomi, and Mr Morton, who were congregated a pace or two away. 'You all did this?'

'William did the lion's share,' said Mr Morton, giving his nephew a hearty pat upon the back, and causing William to slosh red wine over the cup's rim. 'He's barely slept for the past month.'

'You should've heard him swearing as he painted all those signs,' said Naomi with a chuckle.

'They're not as creative as yours,' William said, giving Evelyn a sheepish grin. 'Besides, I wasn't sure people would want a picture of Plato's head on the philosophy section sign.'

'Not the way he painted it, anyway,' said Jack. 'Looked like a bloody sausage, except the kind that'd give you night-mares.'

'It wasn't *so* bad,' said William, though Naomi's raised eyebrows and sliding glance told Evelyn that it most definitely was.

Mr Morton looked from William to Evelyn and back again. 'I think my great-grandfather would be proud to see the bookshop looking so loved. It's a pleasure to know I'm leaving it in safe hands.'

Evelyn turned then, her smile faltering. 'Mr Morton, are you really leaving? I'd begun to hope that was a ruse!'

'No, that's real,' he replied, pushing away a strand of hair that had pulled free of his ponytail. 'But not today. The boat sets sail at the end of January, so I told a little white lie.'

'And might this trip have something to do with all the letters from Calcutta?' Evelyn asked, the inflection in her tone showing she knew she was being nosier than was proper. 'The ones we were always to bring straight upstairs to you?'

'Yes, actually,' he said, his cheeks reddening just slightly. 'Because the person on the other end of those letters is someone I love very dearly and someone I miss very much. And I should have done this years ago.'

'Well now,' said Naomi, 'then I think this is cause for a celebration! Evelyn and William taking on the shop, Mr Morton starting a new future in India—'

'And you and Jack getting engaged,' said Evelyn. 'We have a lot to celebrate, it seems!'

'And the flat,' said Jack, lifting his glass to clink against the rest of theirs.

'The flat?' Evelyn said.

William gave Jack a sharp look. 'One thing at a time,' he said.

'Oh, come now.' Jack took a gulp of wine. 'At least *tell her.*'

Evelyn looked at the smiling faces around them and then at William, who put down his glass.

'We also gave the flat upstairs a lick of paint,' he said.

'That's an understatement,' muttered Jack. 'We gutted the thing.'

'In the hope—' William said loudly, cutting across him. 'In the hope that one day, you might want to live here with me. Above the bookshop.'

'It's a large flat,' said Mr Morton. 'And there would be a guest room for me, when I visit from India, or for your mother, if she wanted to stay with you.'

'And you would have a much shorter walk to work,' said William, his fingers working at the tablecloth, bunching the linen and then releasing it.

'Surely if we were to live together, a certain question should be asked first,' Evelyn said, looking at him now, feeling her heartbeat thudding so loudly in her ears that it was like a drum beat, like the march of an army.

A smile curled at the edge of William's lips. 'I'm sure that could be arranged,' he said, taking Evelyn's fidgeting hand in his own and holding until it stilled.

Chapter Fifty-Four

12th June 1900
York

Mrs Billingham's cart was parked just outside the bookshop, much to the dismay of the carriages trying to get past on the narrow bridge. From it, Evelyn drew her final hatbox, clasping it in one hand and reaching for Mrs Billingham's bony fingers with the other.

'Thank you,' she said, 'for all of your help.'

The woman gave her a kindly smile. 'Tell your mother I will collect her on my way back.'

Evelyn nodded and stepped back, waving as the cart trotted merrily away across the bridge. Then she turned and stepped back into the bookshop, where her mother and William were stood together at the register.

'Is that the last of them?' William called.

'That's the last of them,' she confirmed, looking down at the little hatbox in her hand, the cluster of worn, leather suitcases piled at the desk.

The last time she moved, she had been struck with how little she had, how meagre her life had seemed. Now, she had the same number of suitcases, the same number of hatboxes, and yet, as she looked from her mother to her husband and then at their shop, she was struck with how much richer she felt now, how lucky she was.

'It's a lovely little bookshop,' her mother said, reaching for her daughter's hand. 'I do not know what I pictured, but it certainly was not this. I was just telling William that Aunt Clara and I are going to start our own little reading club.'

Evelyn's eyebrows piqued. 'You're not tempted to join Mrs Quinn's?'

'Goodness no,' said Cecilia. 'Aunt Clara was very adamant that she would read only riotous books, and I am tempted to agree with her. They give one *much* more to discuss, and you know Aunt Clara. She is a woman of a thousand and one opinions.'

'And all of them right,' said Evelyn, her mouth curling into a smile.

The bell chimed then, and the postman stepped through, taking off his hat and ducking a short bow to them all. 'Post for you this morning, Mr Morton, Mrs Morton.'

'Ah! Perhaps there'll be another note from Uncle Howie,' William said, striding forwards to collect them. He passed two envelopes to Evelyn, one of which was heavy and large, then opened the third himself.

'Oh, yes! Look,' he said, showing her a postcard of a building as grand as the Houses of Parliament, with tall, arched windows and elaborate Grecian columns. The street in front of it was filled with single-horse carts and carriages, people dressed all in white crossing beneath white parasols, and there was even a tram, following curving tramlines. Underneath it, the neat print read: *View of Writers Buildings, Calcutta.*

'It's beautiful,' Evelyn said. 'How is he?'

'I hear India is stunning,' said Cecilia. 'Although hot.'

'Yes, Uncle Howard says it's devilishly hot,' William confirmed, skimming the back of the card. 'But that he is very happy.'

'And that is what matters,' Evelyn said, opening the smaller of the two of her letters and smiling. 'It is a wedding invitation.'

Her mother glanced over and nodded. 'I received one, too. I thought Lady Violet's father might be furious, but it seems he has become quite taken with the man.'

'What man?' William said, placing his chin on Evelyn's shoulder to read it. '*Nathaniel Morris?* He's invited us to his *wedding*?'

'And I think we should go,' Evelyn said, reaching to brush her finger against his cheek, 'seeing as I am the one who made the match.'

'I must say I was a little surprised,' said Cecilia. 'I hadn't imagined the two of them together.'

Evelyn tilted her head to one side. 'I think they are rather perfect for one another. And I think they knew that, too. I simply reminded them of it.'

William reached past her and picked up the third package, which was heavy as sin. 'Now, what on earth could this be?' he said. 'It feels like legal papers. You're not trying to divorce me already, are you, darling?'

'Ah! That is my cue,' said Cecilia, giving Evelyn a knowing look and pressing a kiss to her cheek. 'I want to pop to the perfumer next door before Mrs Billingham gets back.'

William's humorous look began to wilt. 'Why is your mother leaving? Oh God. Is it bad? Surely something this heavy can only be bad?'

'Open it,' said Evelyn, turning back to William once they'd seen her mother from the door, feeling her stomach begin to flicker. 'And you will see.'

William's eyes narrowed as he untied the brown parcel twine, and then carefully unwrapped the paper. Inside was a letter, and beneath it was . . .

'But Evelyn . . .' He brushed his fingers over the stack of paper. 'This is my novel. This is . . .' His frown deepened. 'How did you even . . . ?'

She merely smiled at him. 'What does the letter say?'

William swallowed. When he picked it up, his hand was trembling slightly, causing the paper to shake. '"Dear Mr Morton,"' he read, his voice cracking a little. '"I am afraid that, while your story has a fair enough premise and while the character's"—' He put the letter down immediately. 'Evelyn, please, why make me read this aloud?'

'Keep reading,' she said, stepping forwards to hold his other hand. 'It is *good* news.'

'Good news?' The colour seemed to drain from his face. '*Good* news?'

She laughed. '*Keep reading.*'

William cleared his throat. '"While the character's plight is interesting, I do believe the manuscript requires much additional work – see my attached notes. Nonetheless, I would be delighted to" . . .' William looked at her. ' . . . "to publish it once this work is completed." Evelyn! What have you done?'

'Nothing,' she said, her smile widening. 'I just sent it out to some more people. And Nathaniel might have helped me a little, in finding the right fellows to contact. And my mother might have facilitated some of the to-and-fro with the letters.'

'So you lied to me,' William said, putting the letter back atop the stack of paper. 'When I asked you what you've been doing down in the basement all these weeks—'

'I told a little white lie,' she said, pressing a kiss to his nose, 'because if I had told you the truth, that I was copying out your manuscript, you would have stopped me.'

'You're right – I would have stopped you,' said William, pushing his hair from his face. 'You wonderful, infuriating woman.'

She felt his arms snake around her waist. 'I believe in you,' she said.

'I believe in us,' he said, his voice a whisper against her neck. 'It's us, Evelyn. Now, and forever.'

'Now and forever,' she agreed, kissing him softly, tasting the morning's honey bread upon his lips. 'Now and forever.'

Acknowledgements

Writing is a solitary art, but I've been incredibly lucky to never once feel alone in it. Thank you to my family, to my Mum and Phoebe, who didn't say I was mad to leave London and follow my love of writing, and instead supported me every step along the way. To my Nan, who shares my love of historical fiction (we can, and do, talk for hours about it). To my friends: Emily and Ruby, Becky and Rachel, and everyone that has asked when the book is coming out, when they can finally read it. To my Dad and brothers Elijah and Caleb, to Lorna and Richard, Amy and Dan, to Kenneth's family, and everyone that sent my story about grief and a goldfish around the family chat until I believed perhaps I *can* do this writing thing.

Thank you to all the writers around me. To my incredible, creative, supportive colleagues at Mojang. To the writers on my Master's degree at Stockholm University, to Anna-Karin, Dan, Clairellen, Sofia and Ting, and all the ways we support each other through our shared love of this mercurial craft. To the Stockholm Writers Festival, and Catherine Pettersson, and all the support that stems from that wonderful community of writers she has cultivated around her. Without Catherine and Sofia Fransson, I would never have plucked up the courage to pitch to my agent Caroline Hardman, who alongside Jo, Hana, and Thérèse, believed in my writing and encouraged me to keep going until we found the perfect home that was HarperFiction. Thank you to Kate Bradley and her wonderful team that fell in love with *The Lamplighter's Bookshop* just like I did, and shared my excitement in sending it out into the world. Thank you to Katie Lumsden who edited this novel with such care and meticulous attention, and helped me figure out the sums (why did I include so many sums? I'm so terrible at them!) of Will's debt, alongside a myriad of other things.

And finally, from the bottom of my heart, thank you to Kenneth, who prepares the pot of coffee, and wakes me up when my writing alarm goes off (even when I desperately try to sleep through it). Who asks me every day how the book is going, and answers my odd, writerly questions with thoughtful consideration, and without whom none of this would have been written. You are my spark, my bright moment even when the world feels dark, and I love you.

If you enjoyed *The Lamplighter's Bookshop*, turn the page
for an extract from Sophie Austin's new novel,
The Memory Binder . . .

COMING 2026

Chapter One

Ava's face was still puffy when she arrived at the theatre that afternoon, her eyes red, and for a moment she wondered whether tears still blurred her vision: for already there seemed to be a great snake of people outside the Penny-Farthing, a restless coil of hats and coats pushing towards the box office, and Bertie – who stood, red-faced, and shouting: 'Last tickets! Get the last tickets for tonight's show!'

Ava's gaze tracked upwards then, to the name that hung above the theatre in great, white letters. Her name.

The sight of it alone should have filled her with happiness – for this wasn't just months of toil, but years of it. Years of struggling to fill the hole that her mother had left behind.

But instead she felt nothing.

She'd felt nothing since Jem had come to her door that morning, and shattered everything with but a handful of words.

He'd looked dishevelled, for the heat that'd hung low over the city for days showed no signs of bursting. An Indian summer, the *Liverpool Mercury* called it – and it spun threads of gold into his copper hair, darkening the pale splash of freckles across his cheeks.

But it was the smudge on his face that drew a smile from

her – for she could imagine him at the apothecary, pinching powdered charcoal into delicate, glass bottles, and then rubbing it straight across the crooked bridge of his nose. Her first instinct had been to reach up and clean it away, but he'd recoiled from her touch, stumbling backwards on the porch steps.

'Don't. Please.'

She'd faltered a little at that, but she'd kept her smile in place. For Jem was often like this – warm as the summer's sun one moment, and clouded the next. She'd learned as a child to take his sullen moods in her stride, and now that she was a woman grown – and they would spend their lives together – she tried to treat them as one might treat a shower of rain.

Safe in the knowledge that even the heaviest deluge would not last forever.

'Well,' she said, trying to inject as much warmth into her voice as she could. 'It's good you are here early. Oliver still hasn't risen. Between his late nights and my father's . . .' She trailed off, unsure of how best to describe Pa's latest regression – the boarded windows, the ruined settee – and settled on an exhausted shrug instead. 'I'm glad to see you.'

Jem kept his gaze upon the floor, his brow knotting.

'I'm not here for your brother. It's you I wanted to see. You I needed to see.'

His voice was low, urgent, and her heart began to slow. 'Goodness, Jeremy Foster,' she said, leaning upon the doorjamb. 'And here I thought you immune to such tenderness.'

'What?' Panic speared his voice. 'No, Ava. Listen—' He removed his hat, pinching fretfully at the brim. 'I came to tell you that I . . . I can't do this.'

Stupidly – foolishly, she'd assumed he was talking about

the show, and she'd laughed. 'But you needn't do anything! You only need to sit in the audience. It's me who needs to command them.'

For that was the hard part. Her mother had always said it was like casting a spell, but Ava knew well enough that mesmerism was not magic. Mesmerism was suggestion. It was stepping onto a tightrope before an audience, and fighting to keep them enthralled so she did not fall. So she did not fail.

But Jem hadn't returned her wide smile. And she'd felt some of the warmth that had pooled in her stomach begin to sour as she saw how his hands trembled, how his throat bobbed each time he swallowed.

'Not the show, Ava. This. Us. I can't . . .' His frown deepened, and finally he looked up, his hazel eyes meeting her clear, grey ones. 'I can't marry you.'

And just like that – he'd ripped the air from her lungs, and replaced the solid ground beneath her feet with endless tracts of sky.

'I'm sorry. I know my timing is rotten, I know you have the show tonight, but I just . . . I didn't want to embarrass you. I didn't want you to have to explain why the man at your side on opening night had suddenly disappeared.'

Ava opened her mouth to speak, for a thousand words had readied themselves on her tongue, a thousand questions – and then she'd looked up at him, with that beautiful, pitiful smile, and his dirt-smudged, crooked nose – and they'd all dissolved like ash on the wind.

'It's not that I don't think we'd be good together,' he said quickly, his words a torrent now, one that she could drown in. 'I think we'd find a way, you and I. We'd have managed. But . . . that's not all there is to life, is it? "Managing"? You'd want more than that, Ava. I'd want more than that.'

She could do nothing more than nod, as though she

agreed with him. As though his words made sense – when the truth was, none of them did. For she'd never thought they were 'managing' together.

She'd thought he loved her.

'So . . . that is what I came to say. And I am so sorry, Ava. I am so very sorry.'

She hated how his voice cracked as he said it. Hated that even now she wished she could reach out and comfort him, when in fact his words had built a wall between them.

One she knew she could not breach.

'Please do not hate me,' he said, his voice small.

'I could never hate you,' she said softly, forcing herself to look at him, to meet his trembling gaze with her own. And then she forced herself to smile, as though her heart was not aching inside her chest, and say: 'I really must be getting ready. The show—'

'Of course.' His face flushed a little at that, the redness creeping in splotches down his neck. 'I hope it goes well for you tonight. It's a big night, after all.'

'It is,' she'd echoed, fighting with everything she had to keep her voice steady, her expression clear. 'I'll let Oliver know you will not make it to the theatre.'

'Yes,' said Jem, turning slowly to leave. 'And I really am sorry, Ava.'

She'd waited until she'd closed the door behind her to let herself dissolve. To let her body sag, until she was sat in a pool of her own skirts, her breath coming in ragged gasps. She had been clattering around the house all morning hoping to awaken her brother, hoping she could see him before she had to leave for rehearsal, but now she wished with all that same might that he would stay abed. That he would not walk down their creaking staircase now and find her slumped against the door.

She'd awoken with the prospect of so much come to

fruition at once. Her name upon the theatre, just like her mother. Her mother's ring upon her finger.

And now?

Now the grandfather clock in the living room announced dolefully that the hour had come for her to leave for rehearsal, and she still could not bear to move. And yet she did – pushing herself up, hovering her face before the cracked mirror in the hallway, and seeing nothing but a blur of pale blonde hair, the smudge of red beneath it bright against her light blue dress.

There was a part of her – the largest part – that wanted to walk up those creaking stairs into her room, and let her tears seep into her pillow. But she knew she couldn't. She couldn't let them down. Miss Lillian, Miss Fairchild, Mr and Mrs Green, Stanley – goodness, even Tommy. They were all relying on her.

And she couldn't crumble. She couldn't crack. At least not yet.

And so she'd plucked her coat from the rickety stand, and walked to the theatre – and now she stood upon the uneven cobbles of Williamson Square, the heat faltering with each sullen raindrop, staring at the name that hung above it.

The Memory Binder.

Her mother's act – finally her own. Years of work distilled into a handful of white letters.

And she felt . . . nothing.